Ghoster HEIGHTS

WONDERBOUND

WRITTEN BY
KELLY Mellings & Corey Lansdell

ILLUSTRATED BY
Lisa LaRose

LETTERED BY
Becca Carey

EDITED BY Rebecca Taylor
DESIGNED BY Sonja Synak

PUBLISHER, Damian A. Wassel
EDITOR-IN-CHIEF, Adrian F. Wassel
SENIOR ARTIST, Nathan C. Gooden
EVP BRANDING & PRODUCTION, Tim Daniel
VP SALES & MARKETING, David Dissanayake
PRODUCTION MANAGER, Ian Baldessari
MANAGING EDITOR, WONDERBOUND, Rebecca Taylor
DIRECTOR, SALES & MARKETING, BOOK TRADE, Syndee Barwick
ART DIRECTOR, Sonja Synak
SOCIAL MEDIA STRATEGY, Alex Scola
DIRECTOR, EVENTS & SOCIAL COMMERCE, Dan Crary
MANAGING EDITOR, VAULT, Der-shing Helmer

WONDERBOUND
Missoula, Montana
readwonderbound.com
@readwonderbound

ISBN:978-1-63849-073-9
LCCN:2022907312
First Edition, First Printing, September, 2022
1 2 3 4 5 6 7 8 9 10

For information about foreign or multimedia rights, contact: rights@vaultcomics.com.
Printed in USA

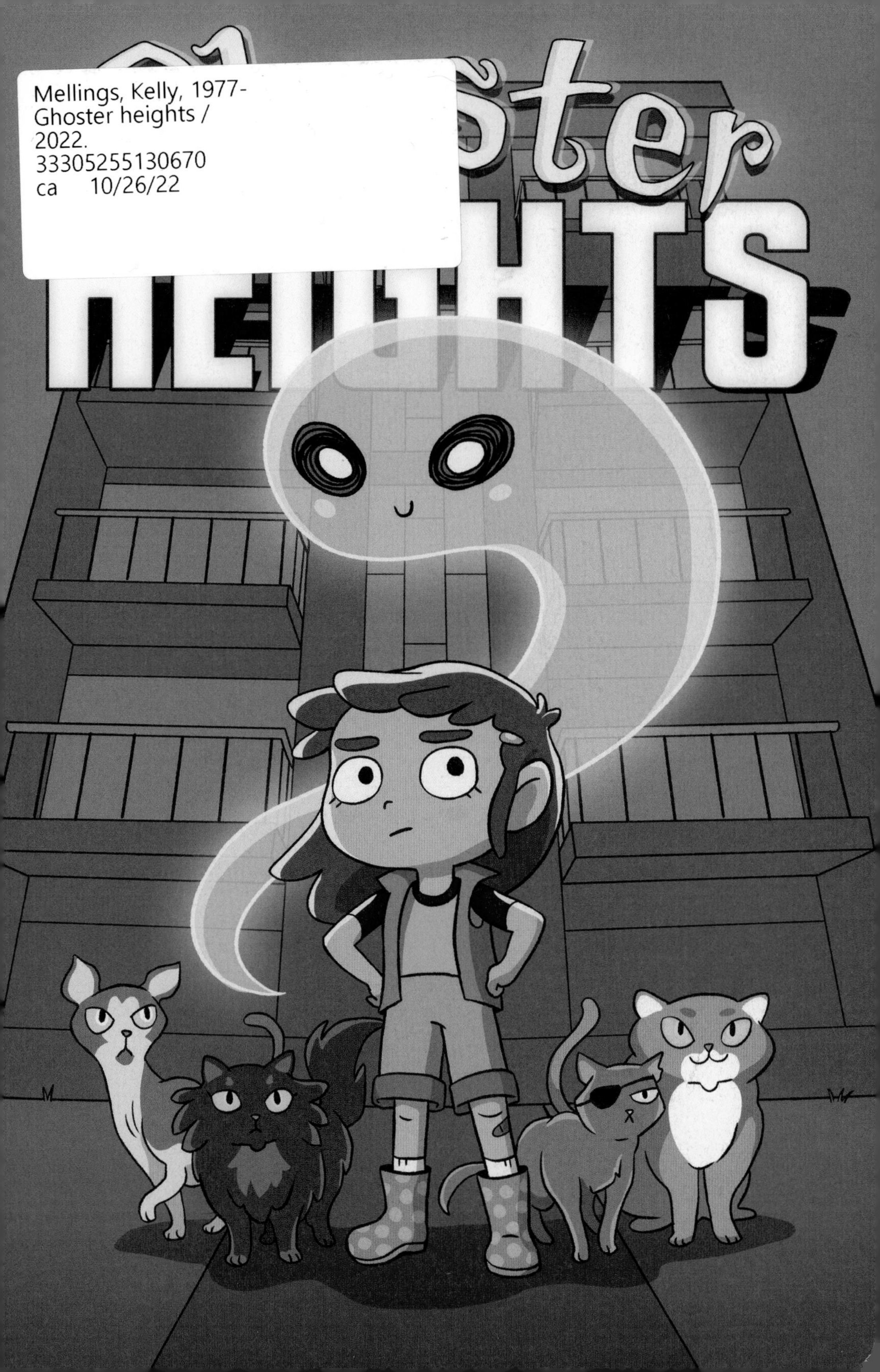

DEDICATIONS

To my strong Ukrainian Baba and her 18 children (including my mom, Noreen), thank you for keeping our family's traditions alive and for keeping our hearts and stomachs full.

And to my little monkeys, Vérité and Mina, especially Mina, who thought up the idea of a cute girl with attitude holding a ghost on a string like a balloon.
—Kelly

Kim, Emmeline, James, Mom, Dad, Gerald, Curtis, GHOSTER HEIGHTS wouldn't exist without you.
Thank God for you.
All my love.
—Corey

Thanks to Matthew, my husband, and the biggest supporter of my work. And thanks to Sophie, who is a dog. (I hope at least one of you reads this comic.) :3
—Lisa

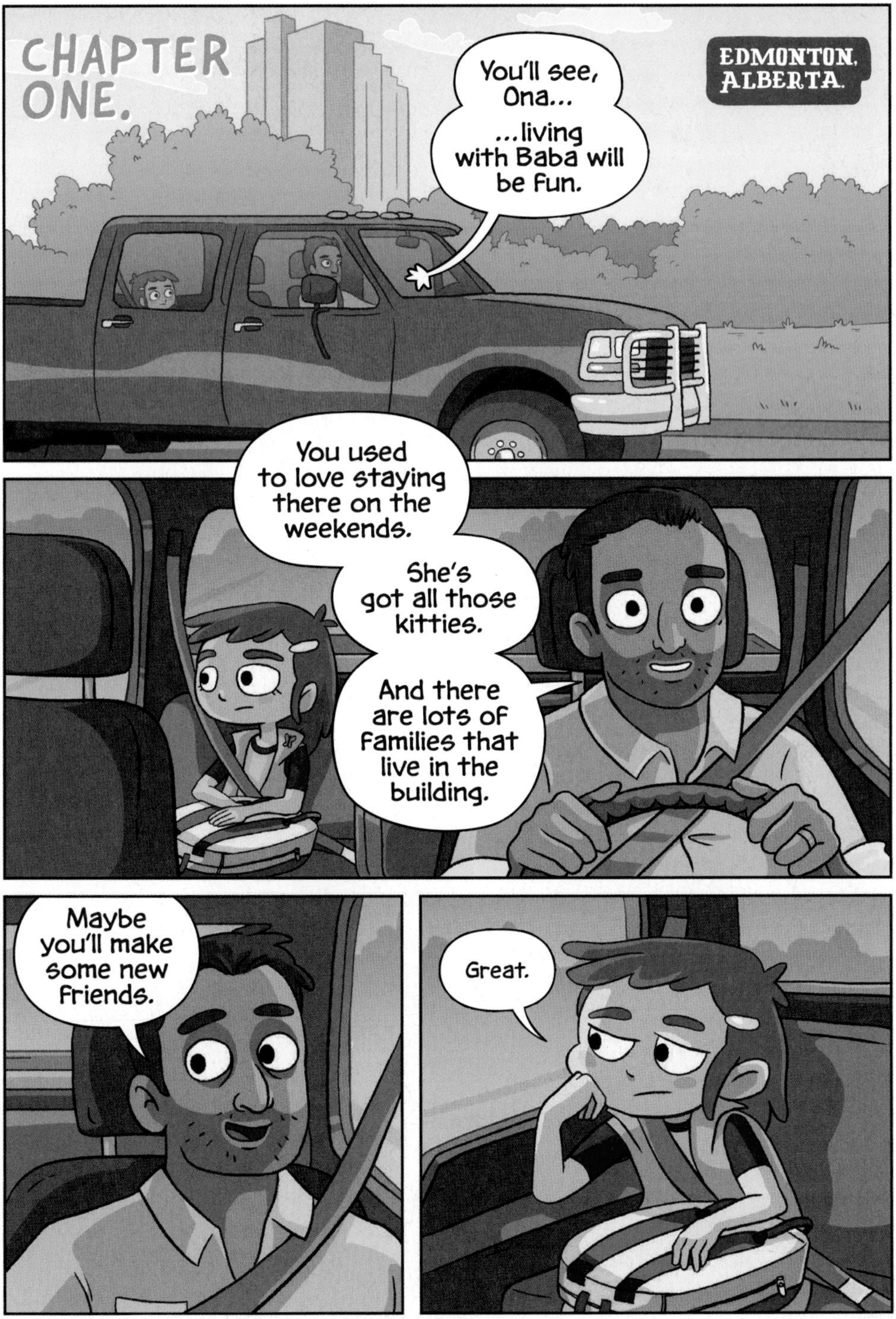
CHAPTER ONE.
EDMONTON, ALBERTA.
You'll see, Ona...
...living with Baba will be fun.
You used to love staying there on the weekends.
She's got all those kitties.
And there are lots of families that live in the building.
Maybe you'll make some new friends.
Great.

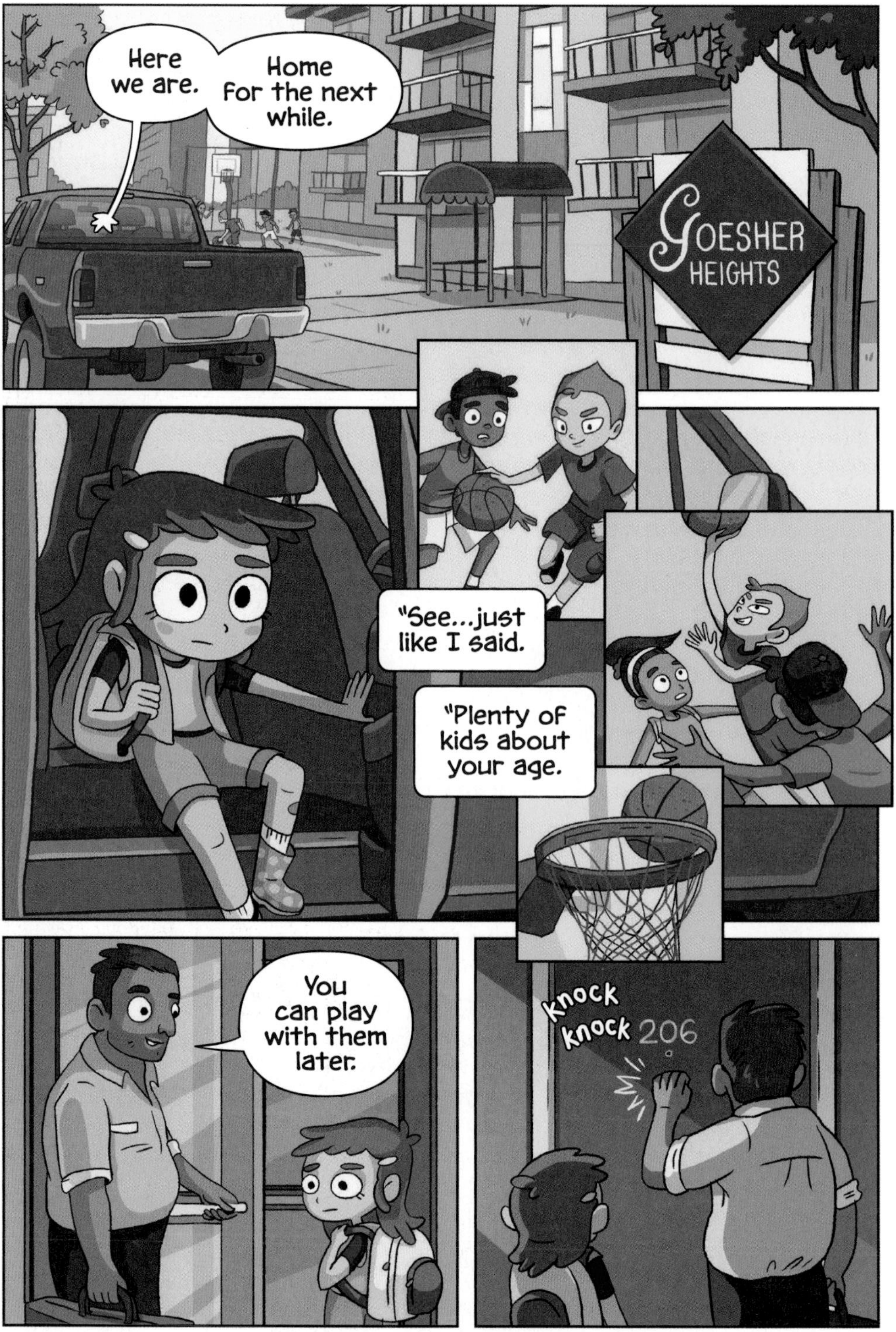
Here we are.
Home for the next while.
GOESHER HEIGHTS
"See...just like I said.
"Plenty of kids about your age.
You can play with them later.
knock knock
206

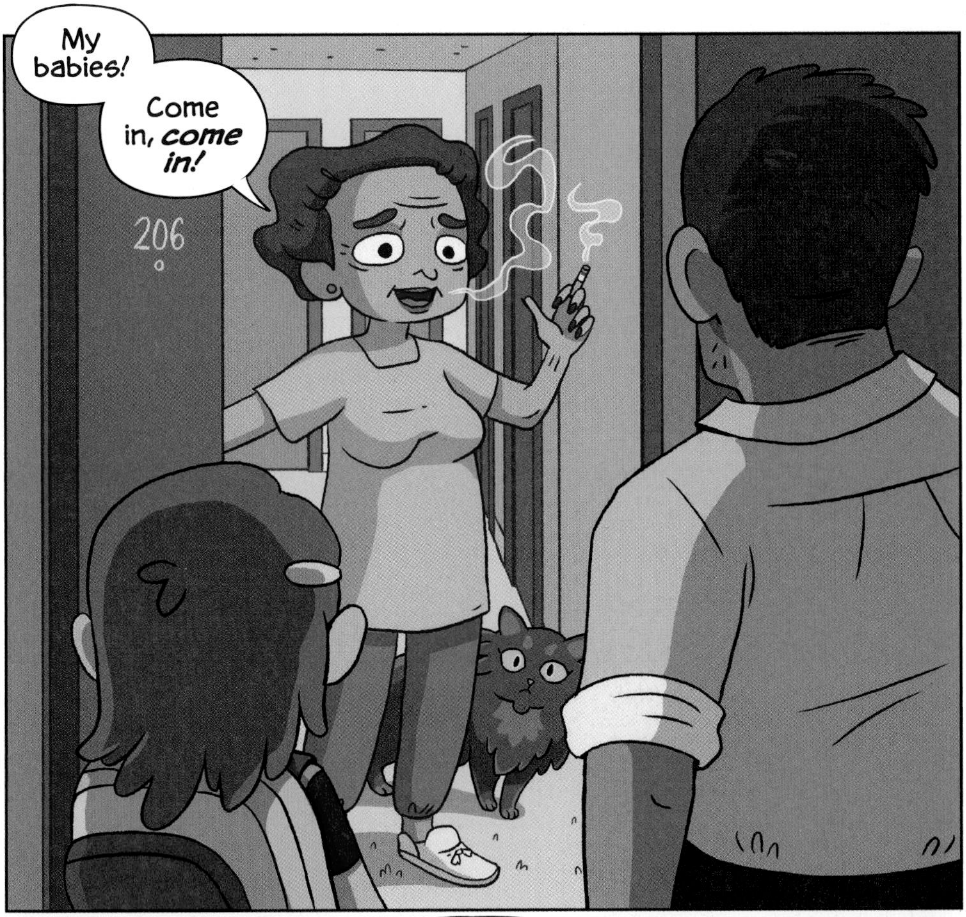
My babies!
Come in, *come in!*
206

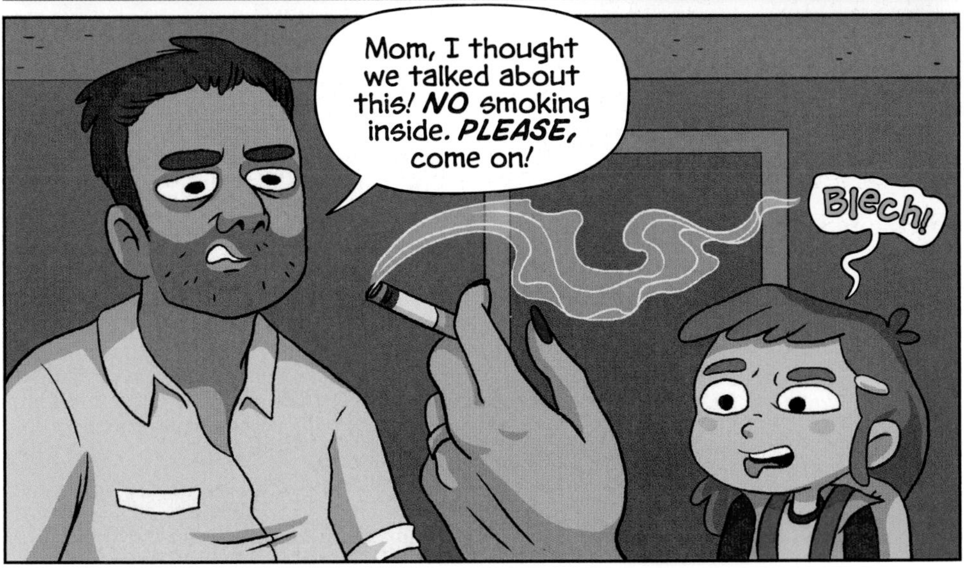
Mom, I thought we talked about this! ***NO*** smoking inside. ***PLEASE,*** come on!
Blech!

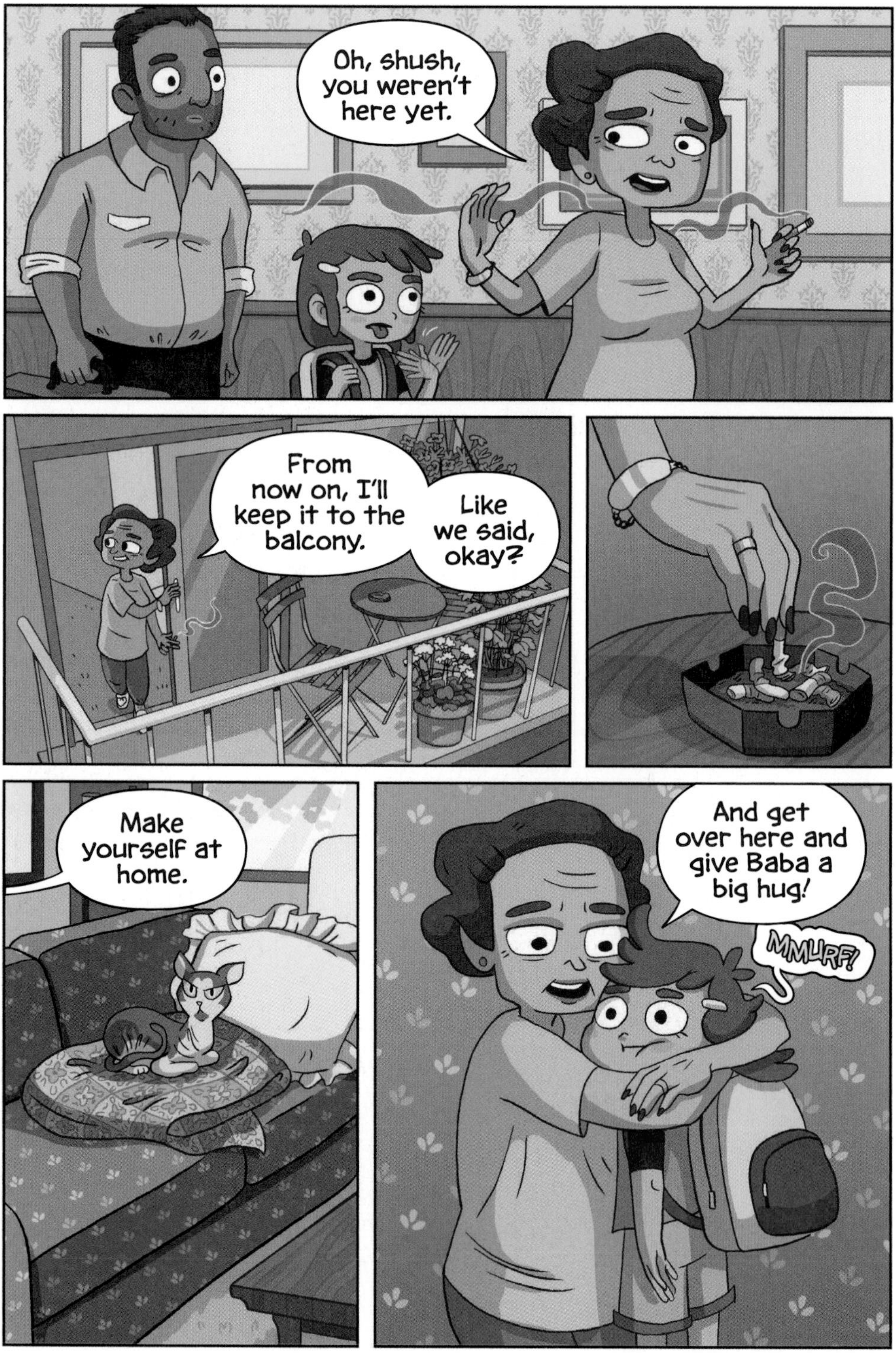
Oh, shush, you weren't here yet.
From now on, I'll keep it to the balcony.
Like we said, okay?
Make yourself at home.
And get over here and give Baba a big hug!
MMURF!

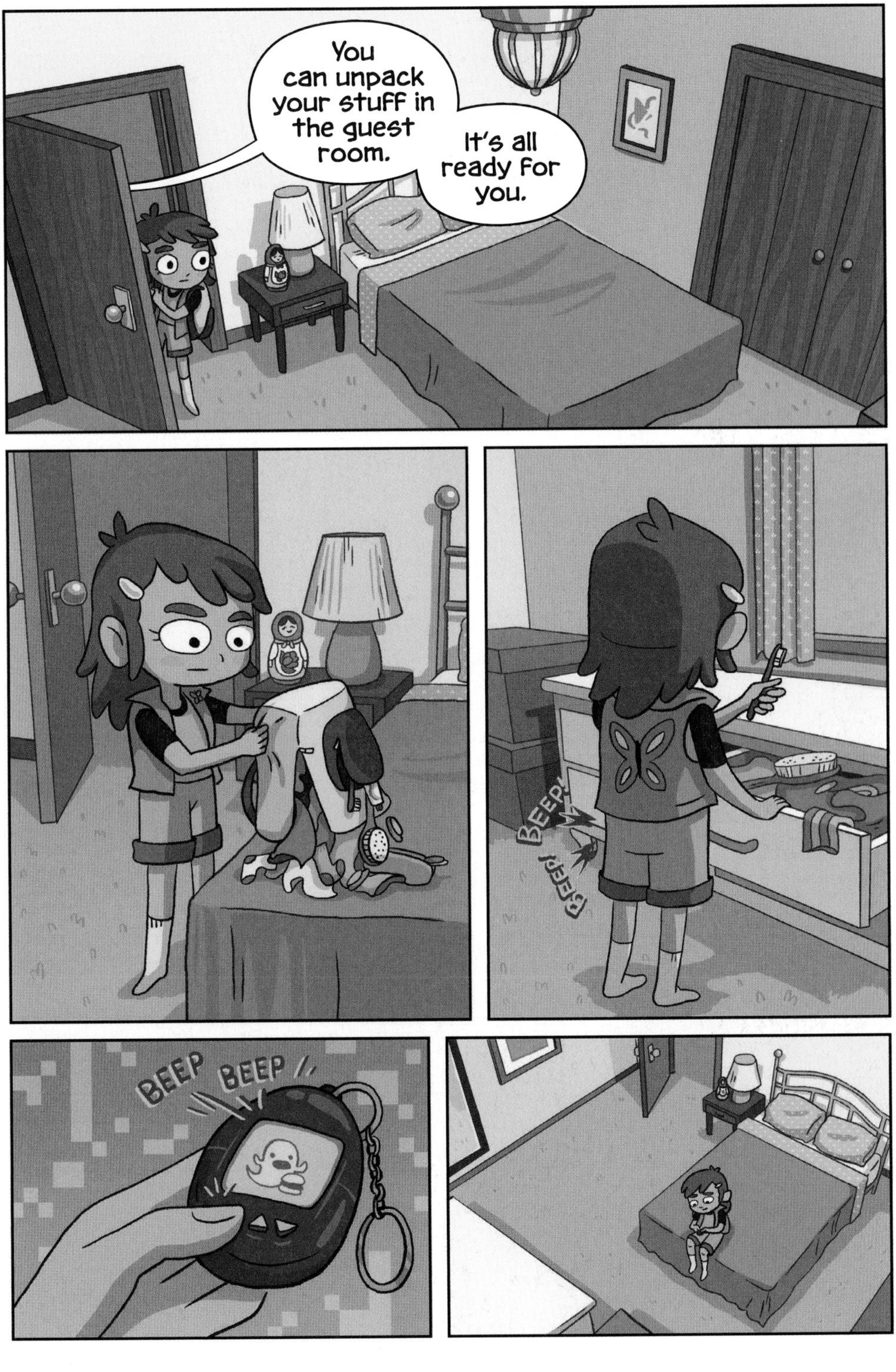
You can unpack your stuff in the guest room.
It's all ready for you.
BEEP!
BEEP!
BEEP BEEP

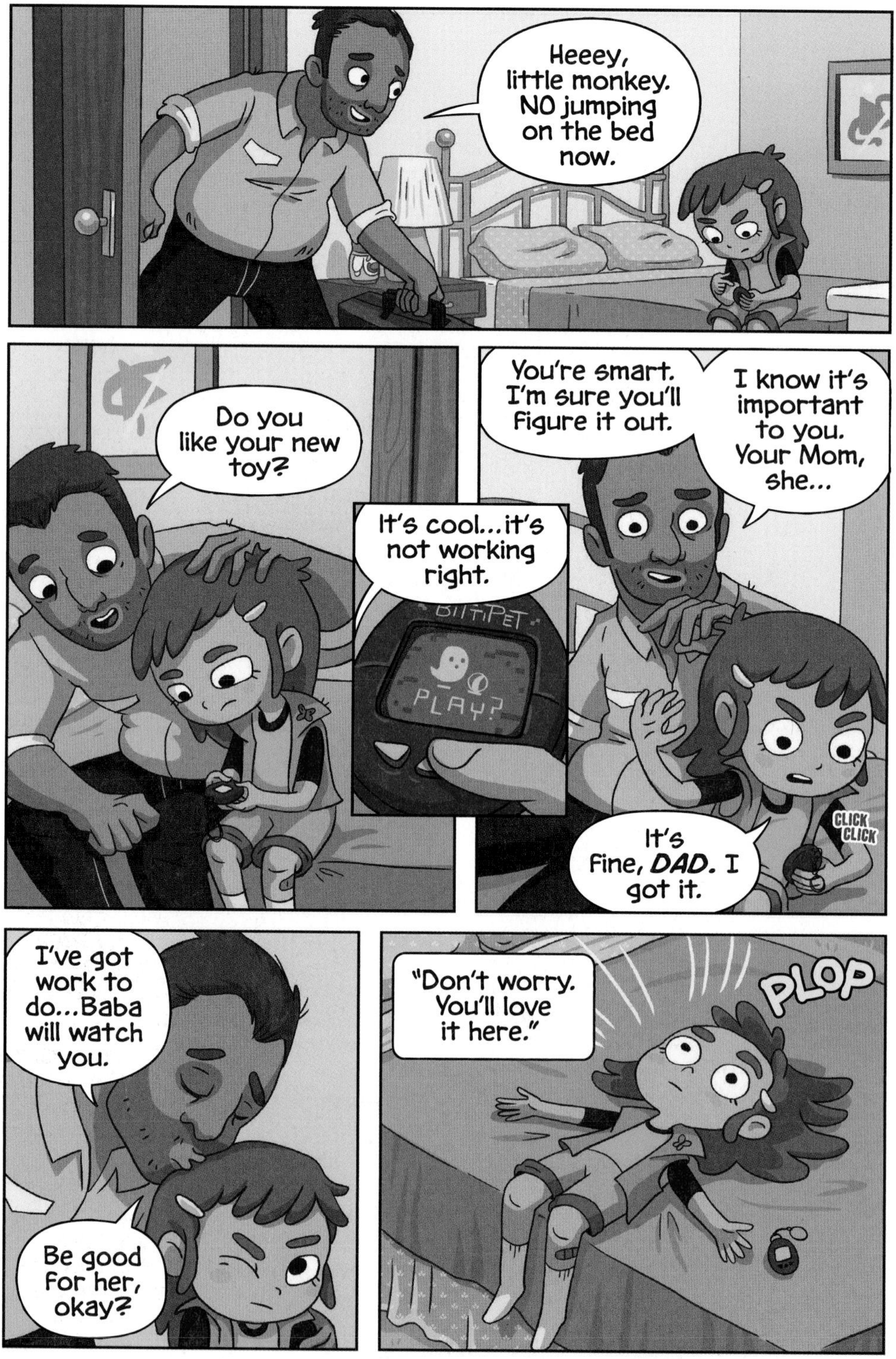
Heeey, little monkey. NO jumping on the bed now.
Do you like your new toy?
It's cool...it's not working right.
PLAY?
You're smart. I'm sure you'll figure it out.
I know it's important to you. Your Mom, she...
CLICK CLICK
It's fine, DAD. I got it.
I've got work to do...Baba will watch you.
Be good for her, okay?
"Don't worry. You'll love it here."
PLOP

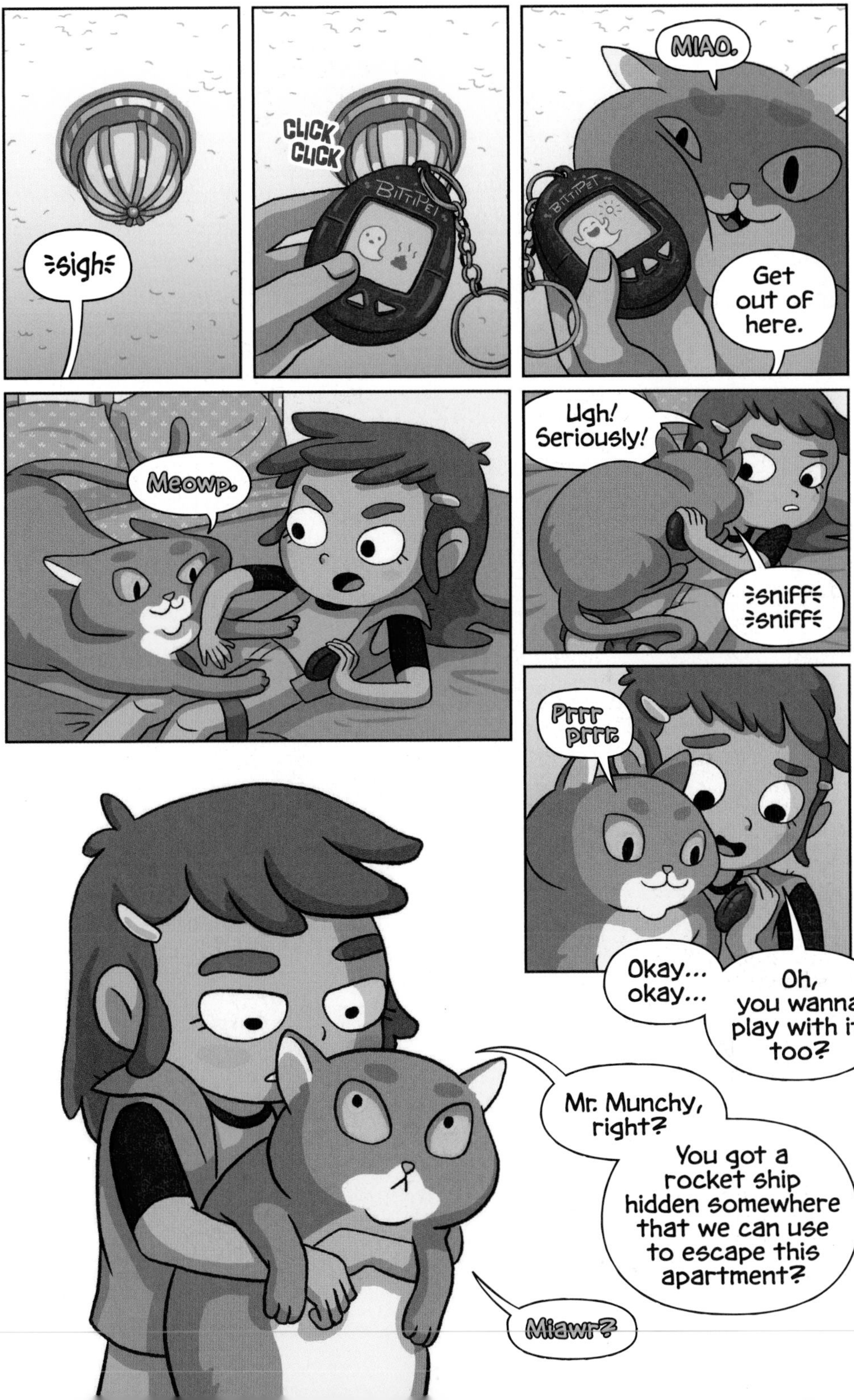

sigh
CLICK CLICK
BITTIPET
MIAO.
BITTIPET
Get out of here.
Meowp.
Ugh! Seriously!
sniff sniff
Prrr prrr.
Okay... okay...
Oh, you wanna play with it, too?
Mr. Munchy, right?
You got a rocket ship hidden somewhere that we can use to escape this apartment?
Miawr?

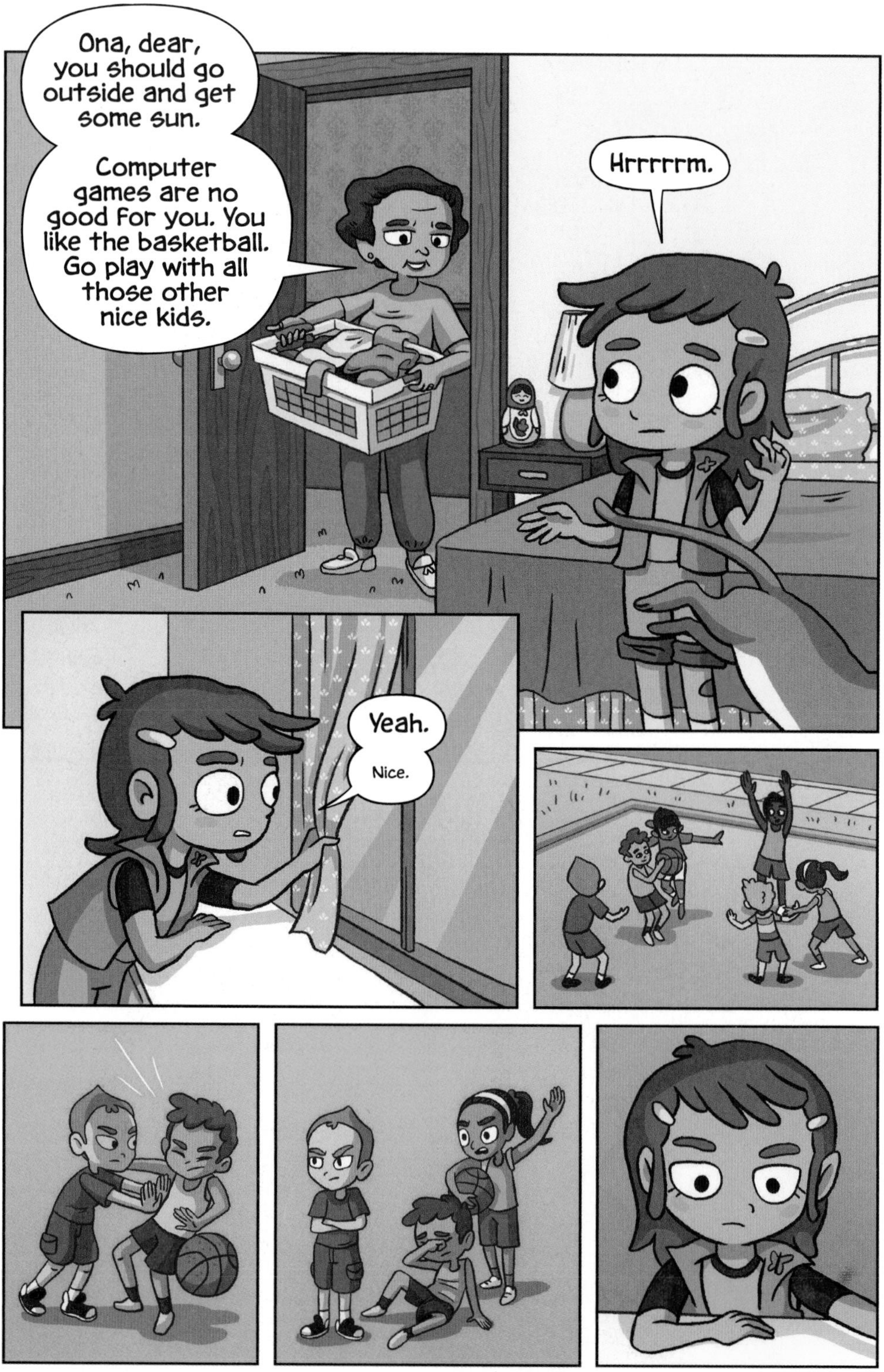
Ona, dear, you should go outside and get some sun.
Computer games are no good for you. You like the basketball. Go play with all those other nice kids.
Hrrrrrm.
Yeah.
Nice.

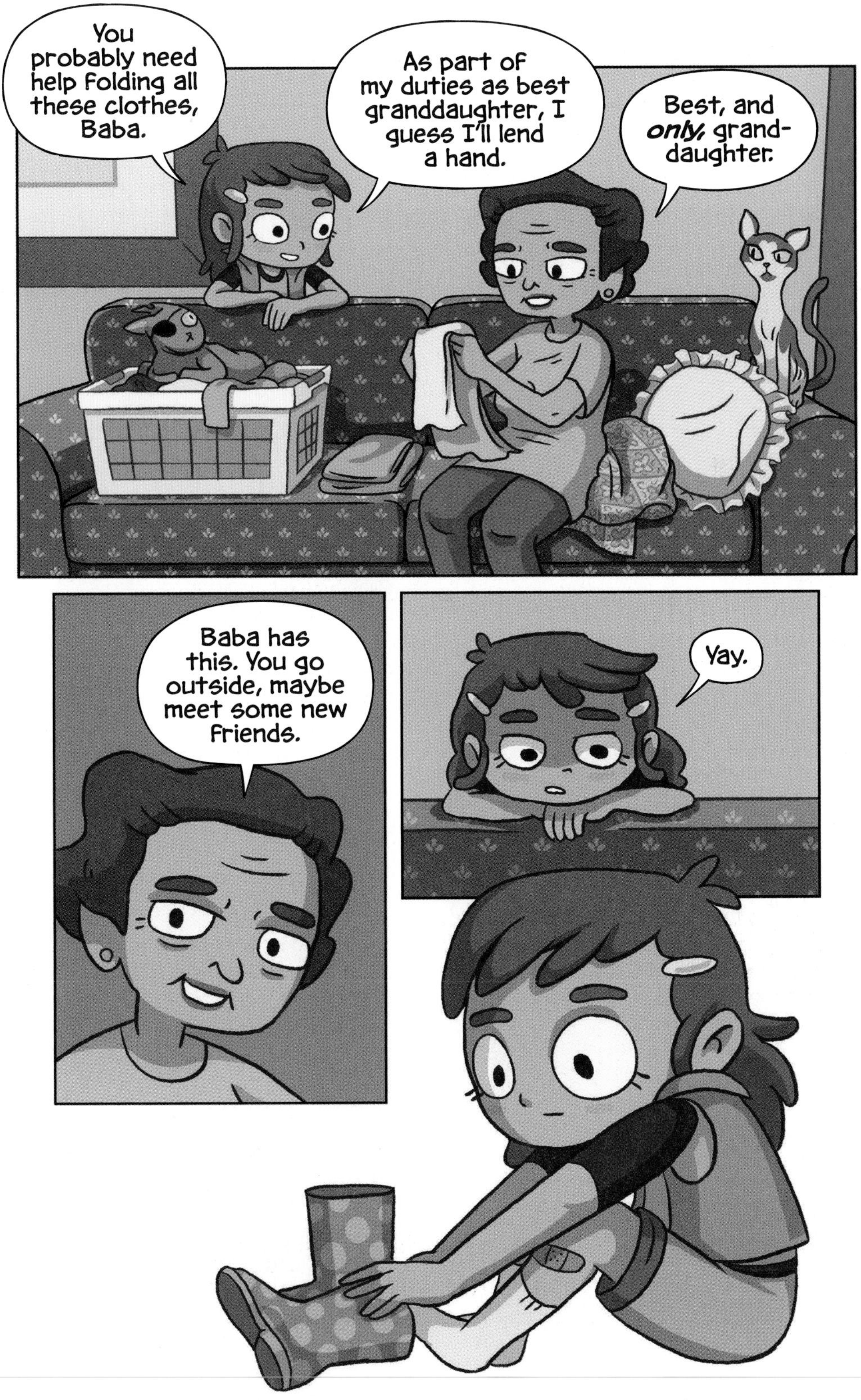
You probably need help folding all these clothes, Baba.
As part of my duties as best granddaughter, I guess I'll lend a hand.
Best, and *only,* grand-daughter.
Baba has this. You go outside, maybe meet some new friends.
Yay.

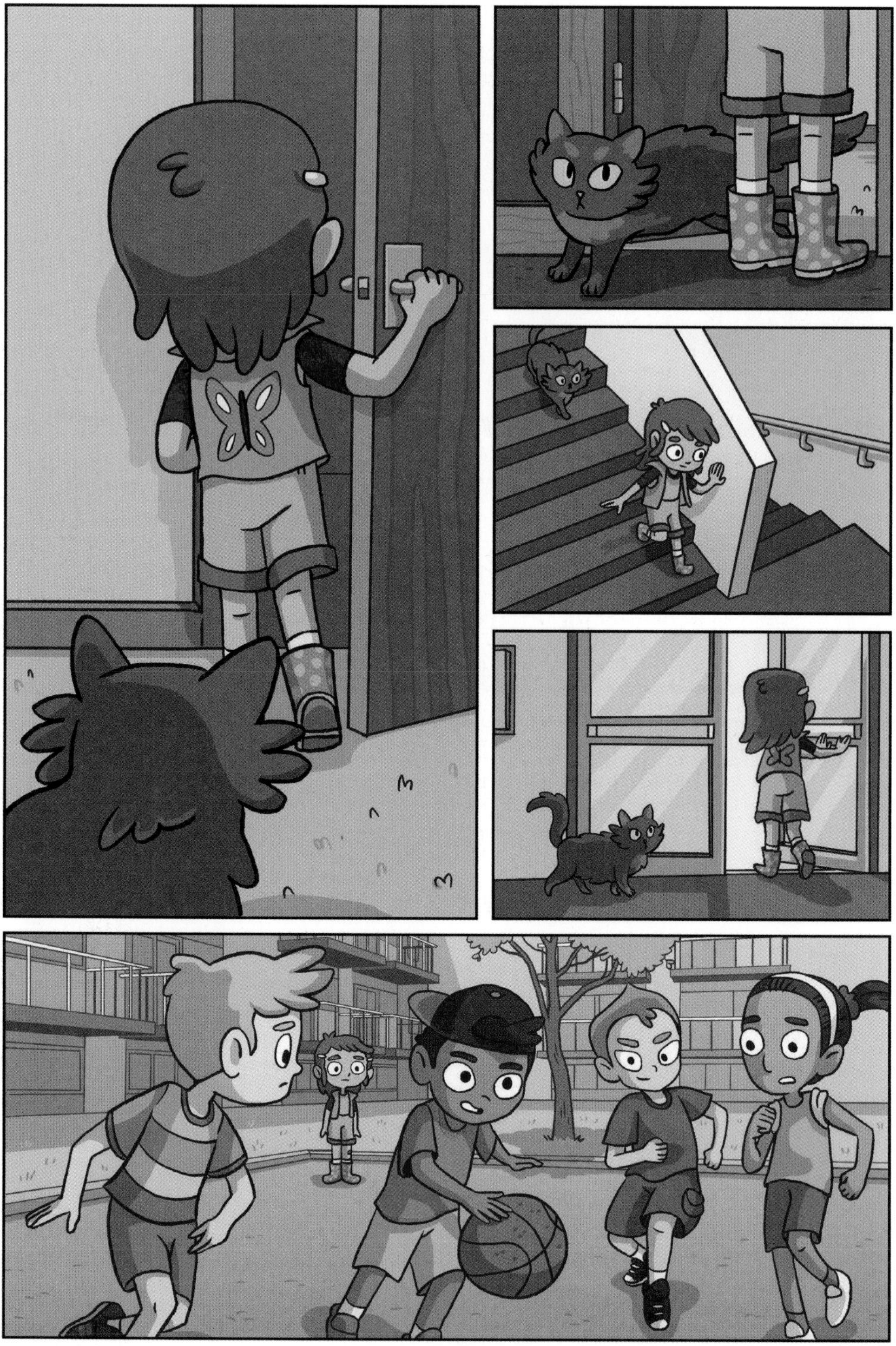

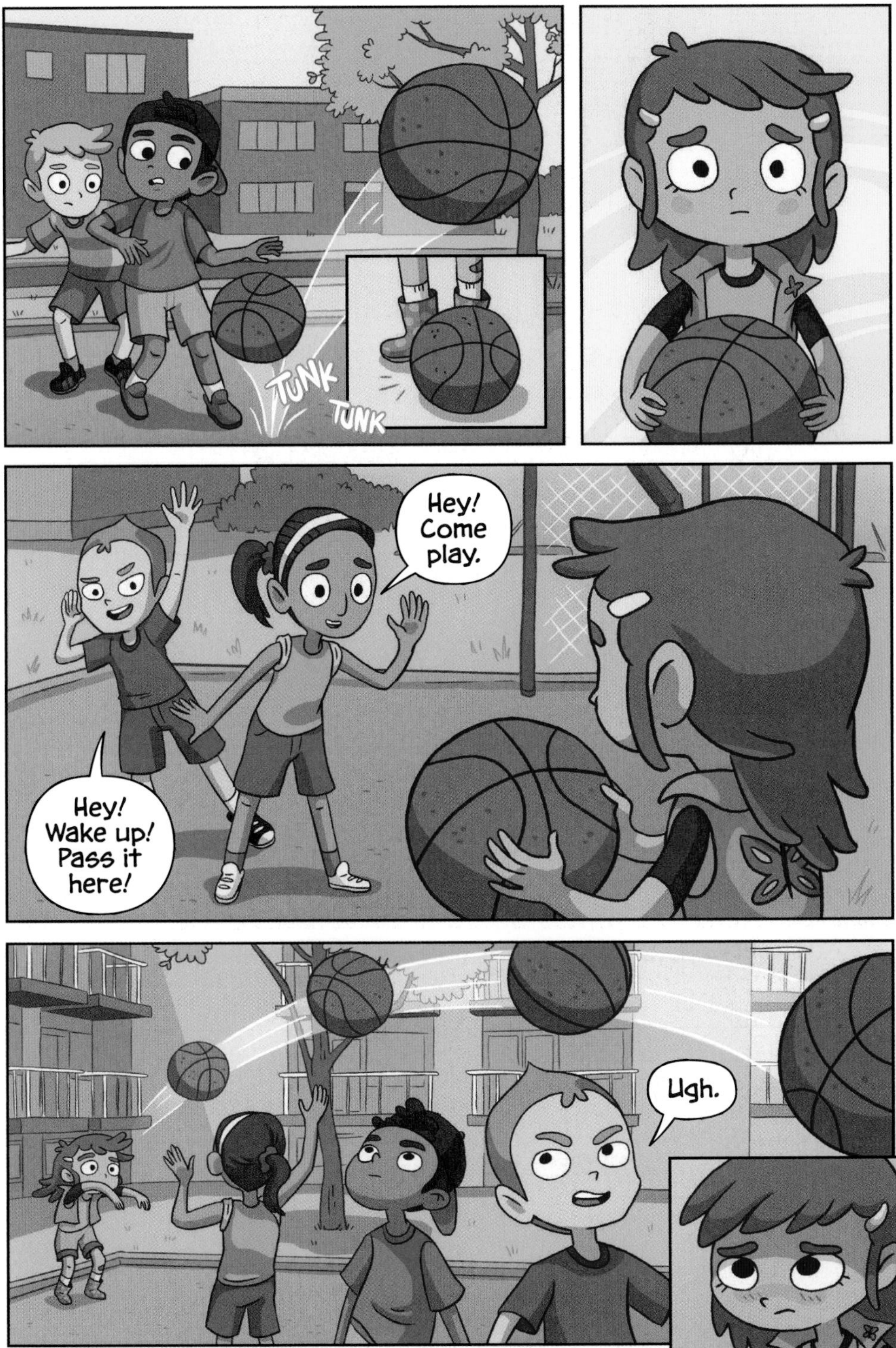
TUNK
TUNK
Hey! Come play.
Hey! Wake up! Pass it here!
Ugh.

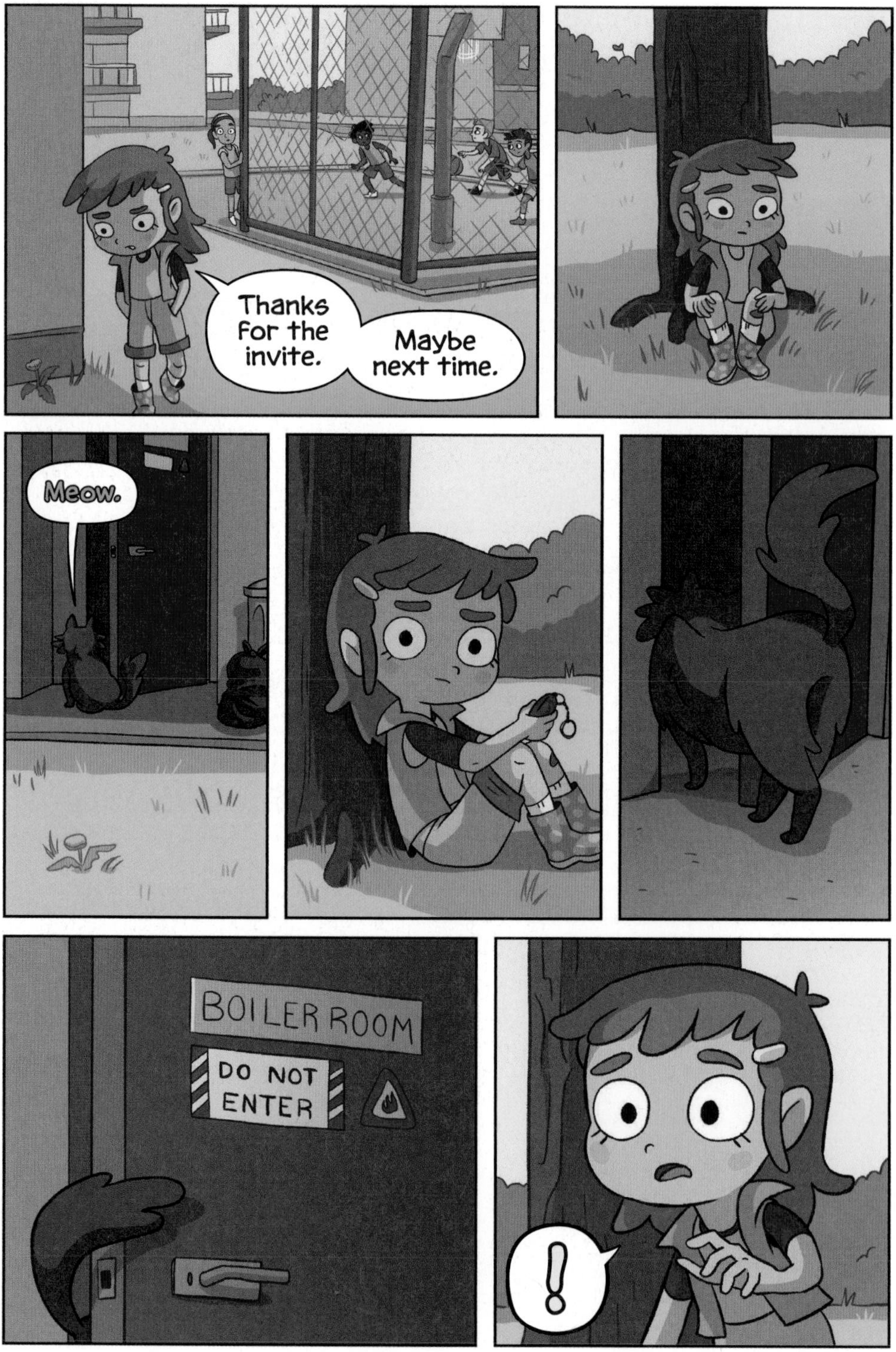
Thanks for the invite.
Maybe next time.
Meow.
BOILER ROOM
DO NOT ENTER
!

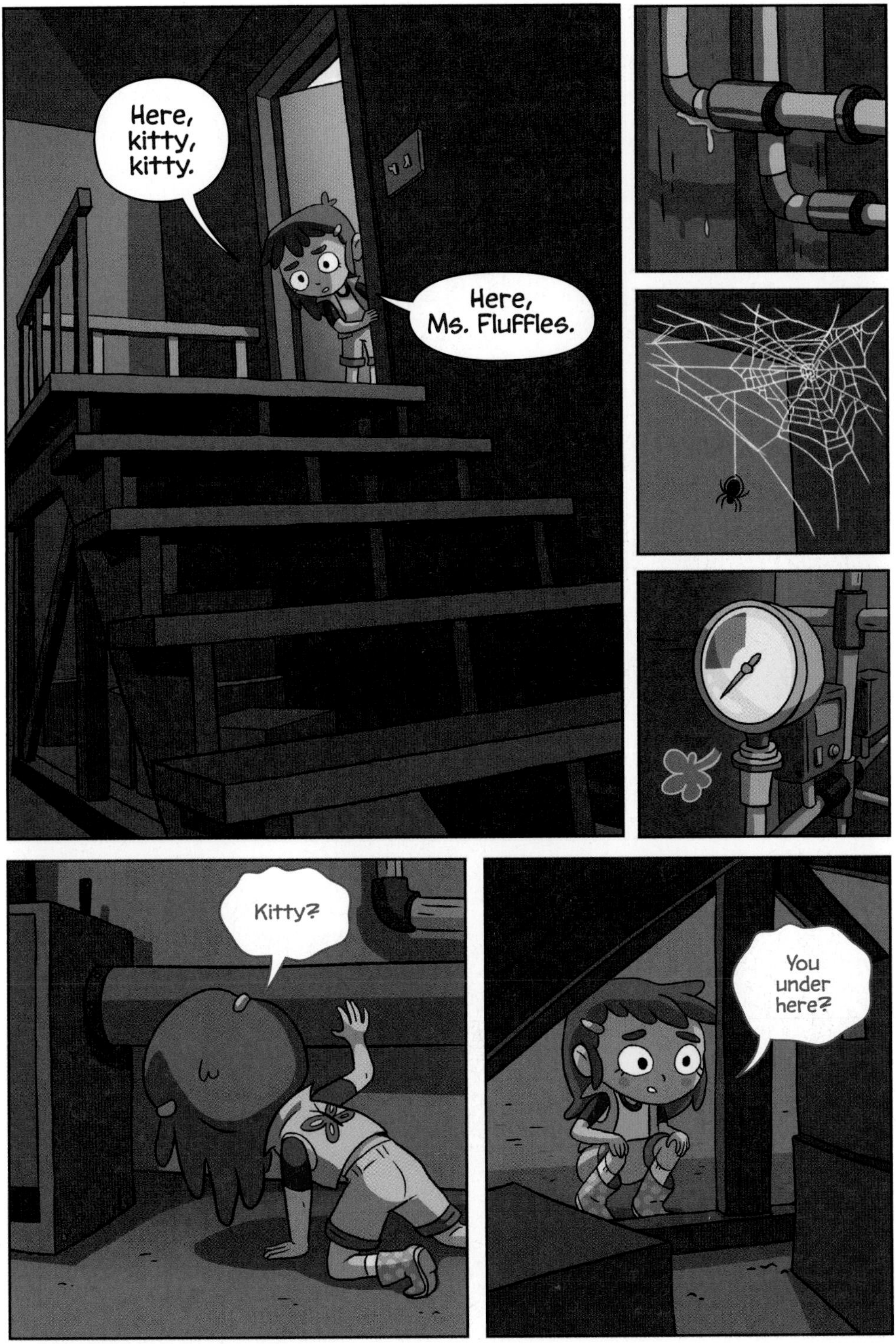
Here, kitty, kitty.
Here, Ms. Fluffles.
Kitty?
You under here?

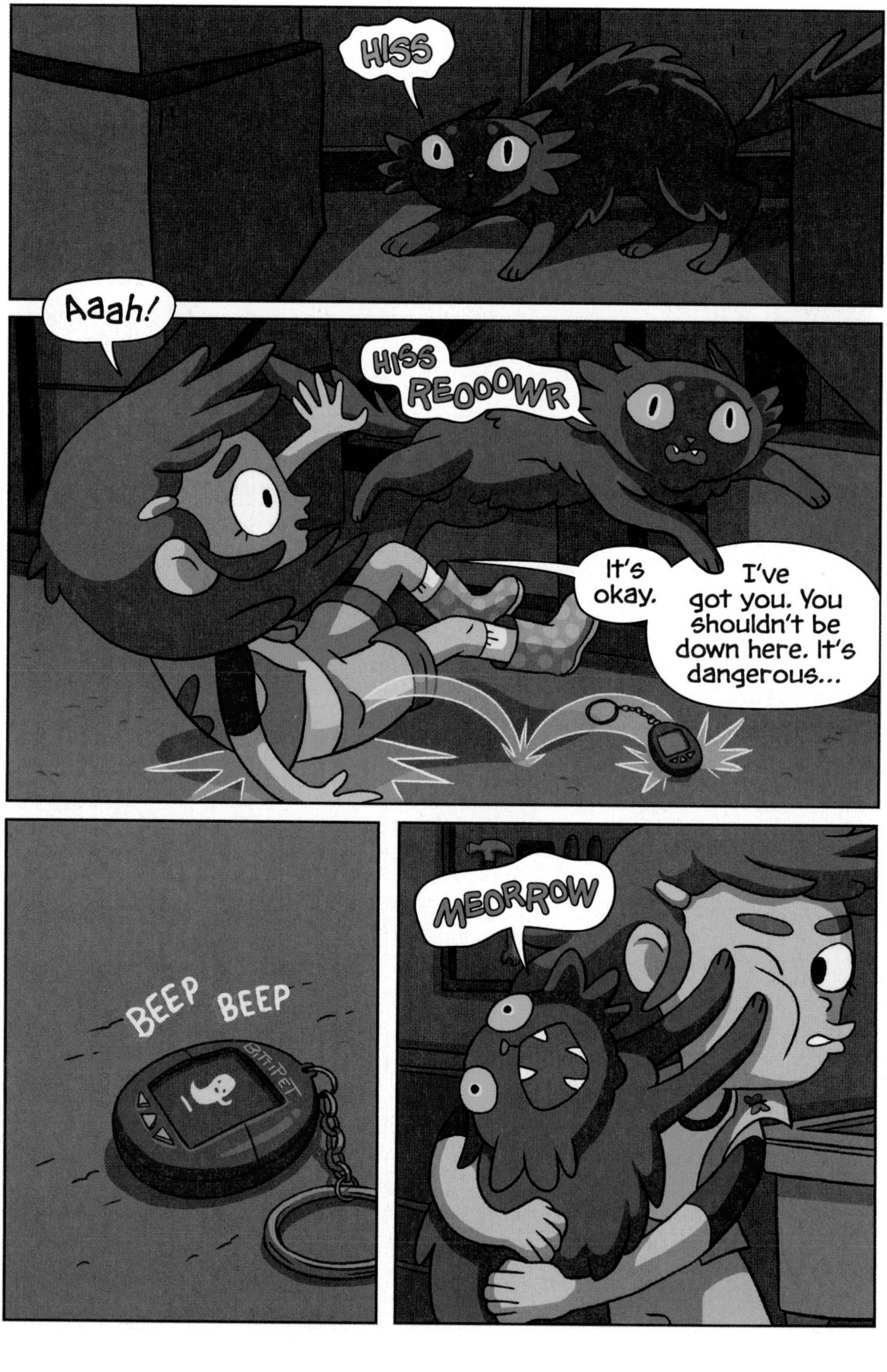
HISS
Aaah!
HISS
REOOOWR
It's okay.
I've got you. You shouldn't be down here. It's dangerous...
BEEP BEEP
BITTPET
MEORROW

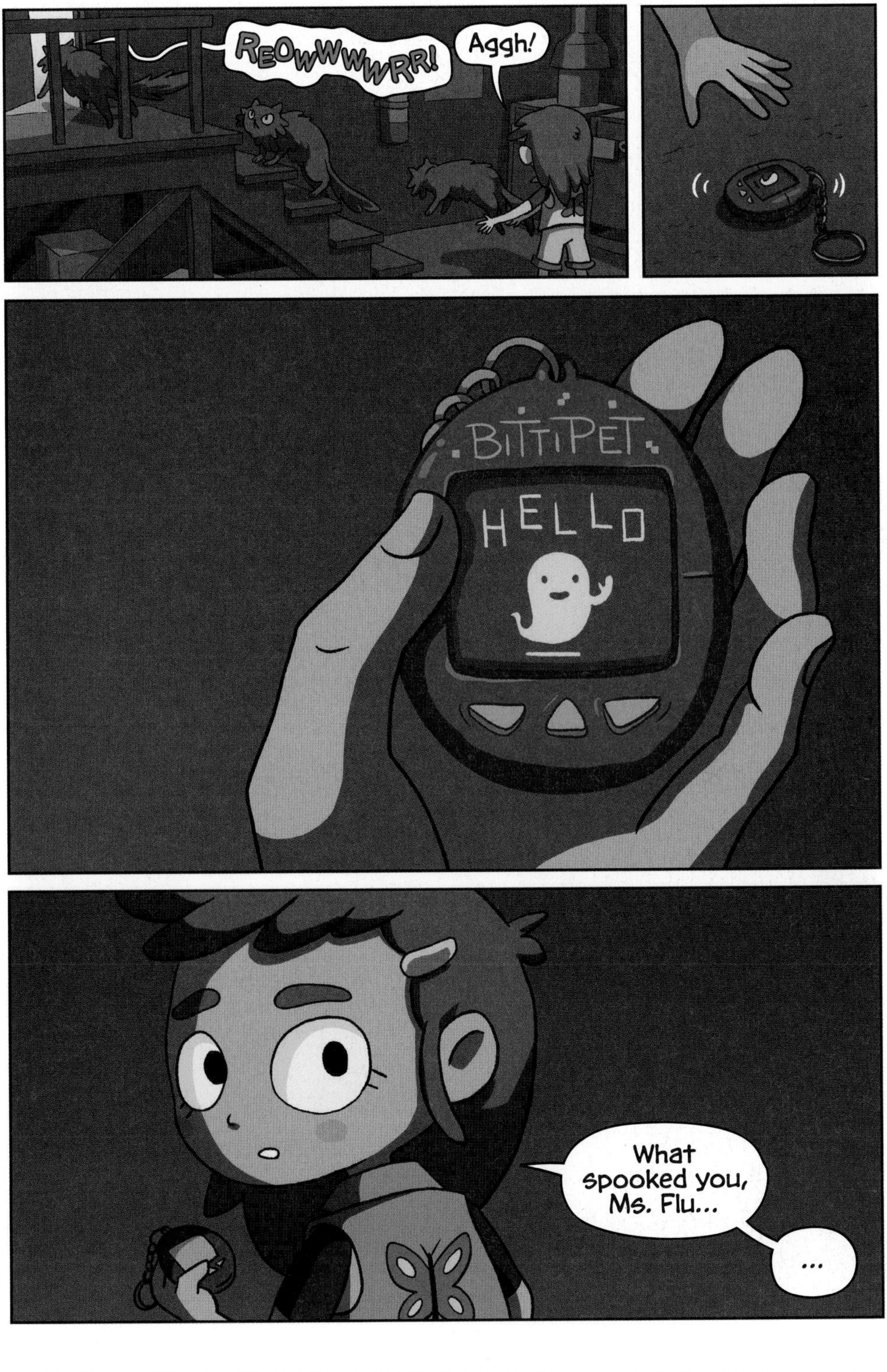
REOWWWWWRR!
Aggh!
BITTIPET
HELLO
What spooked you, Ms. Flu...
...

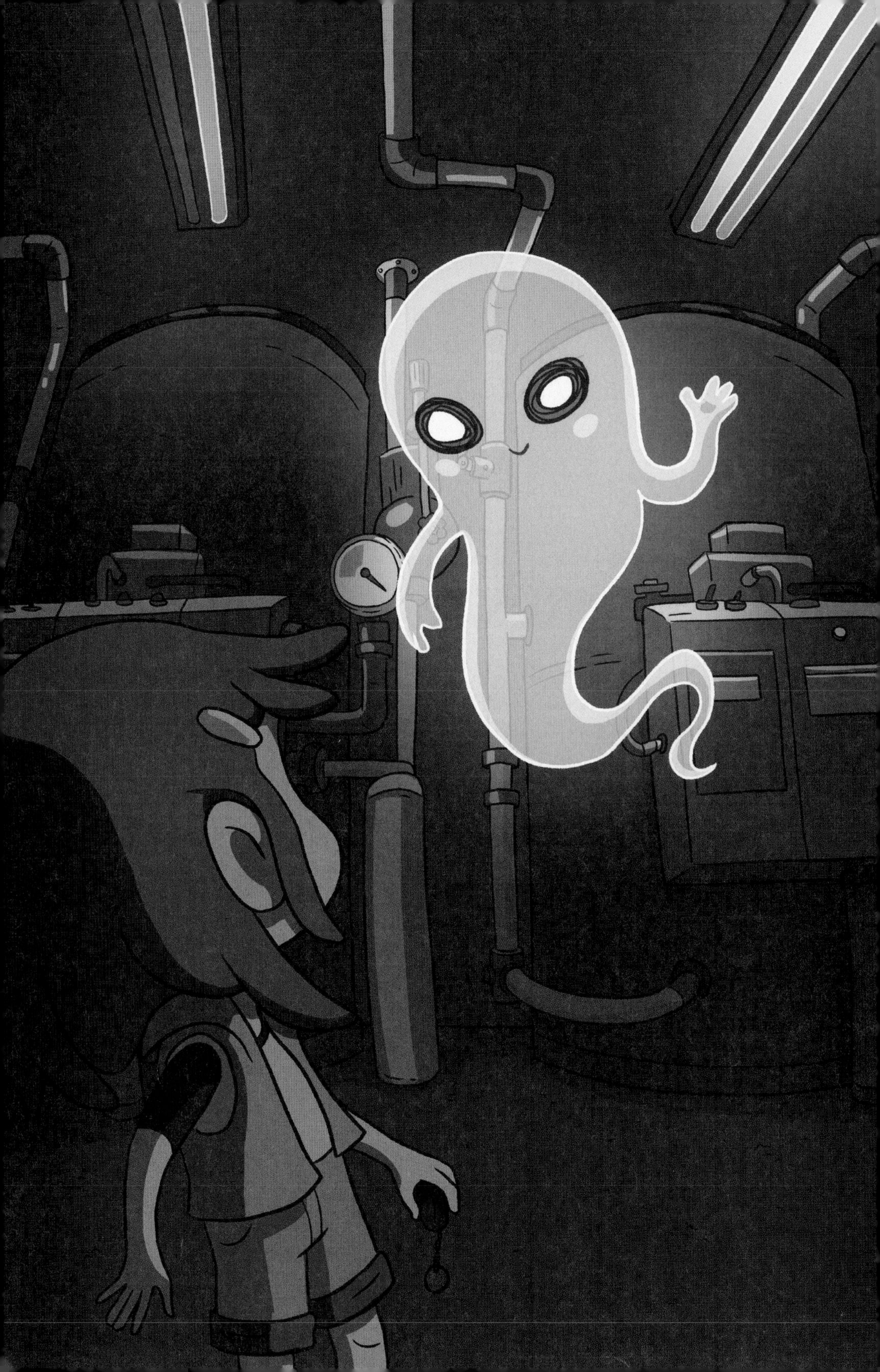

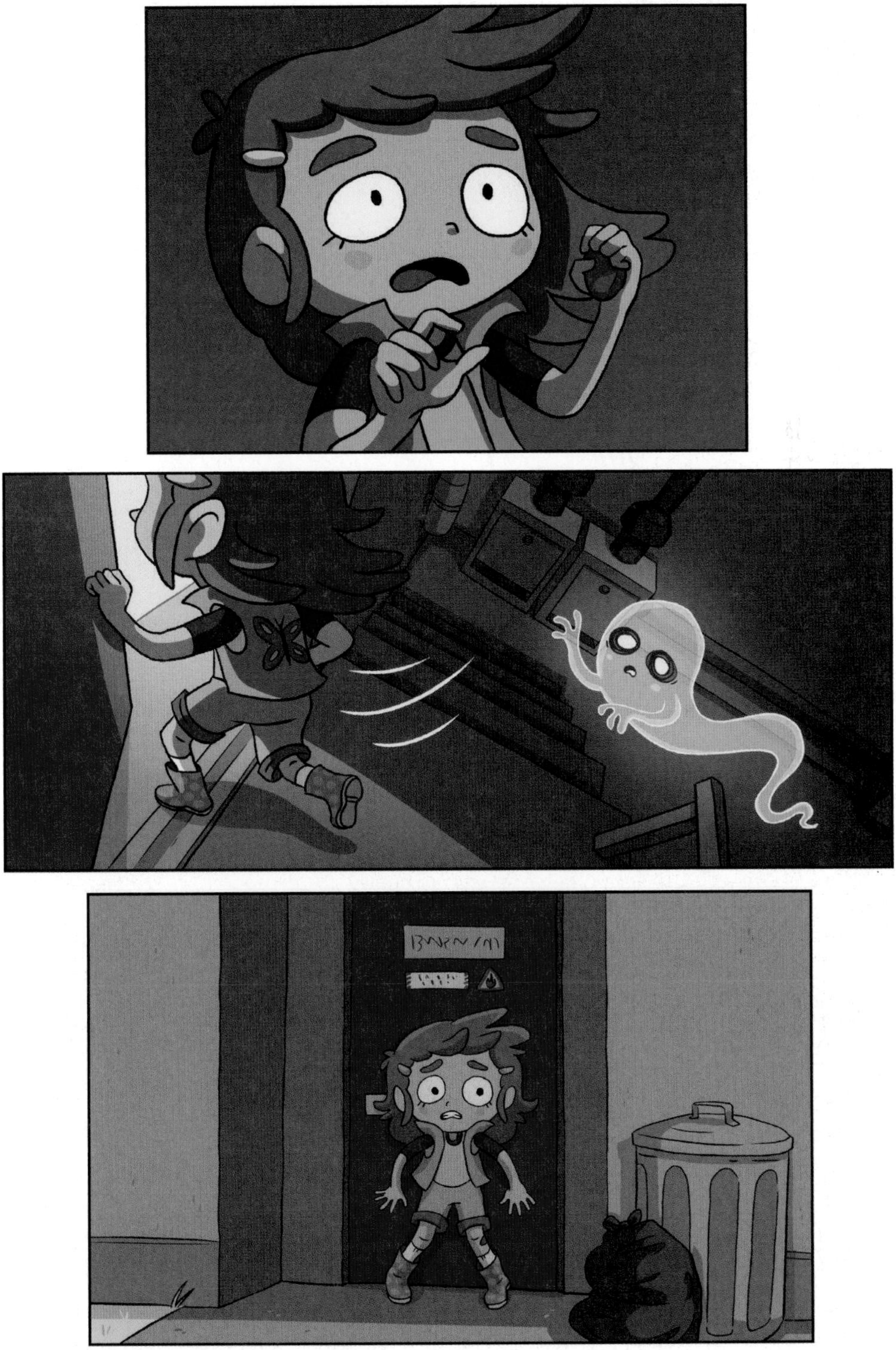

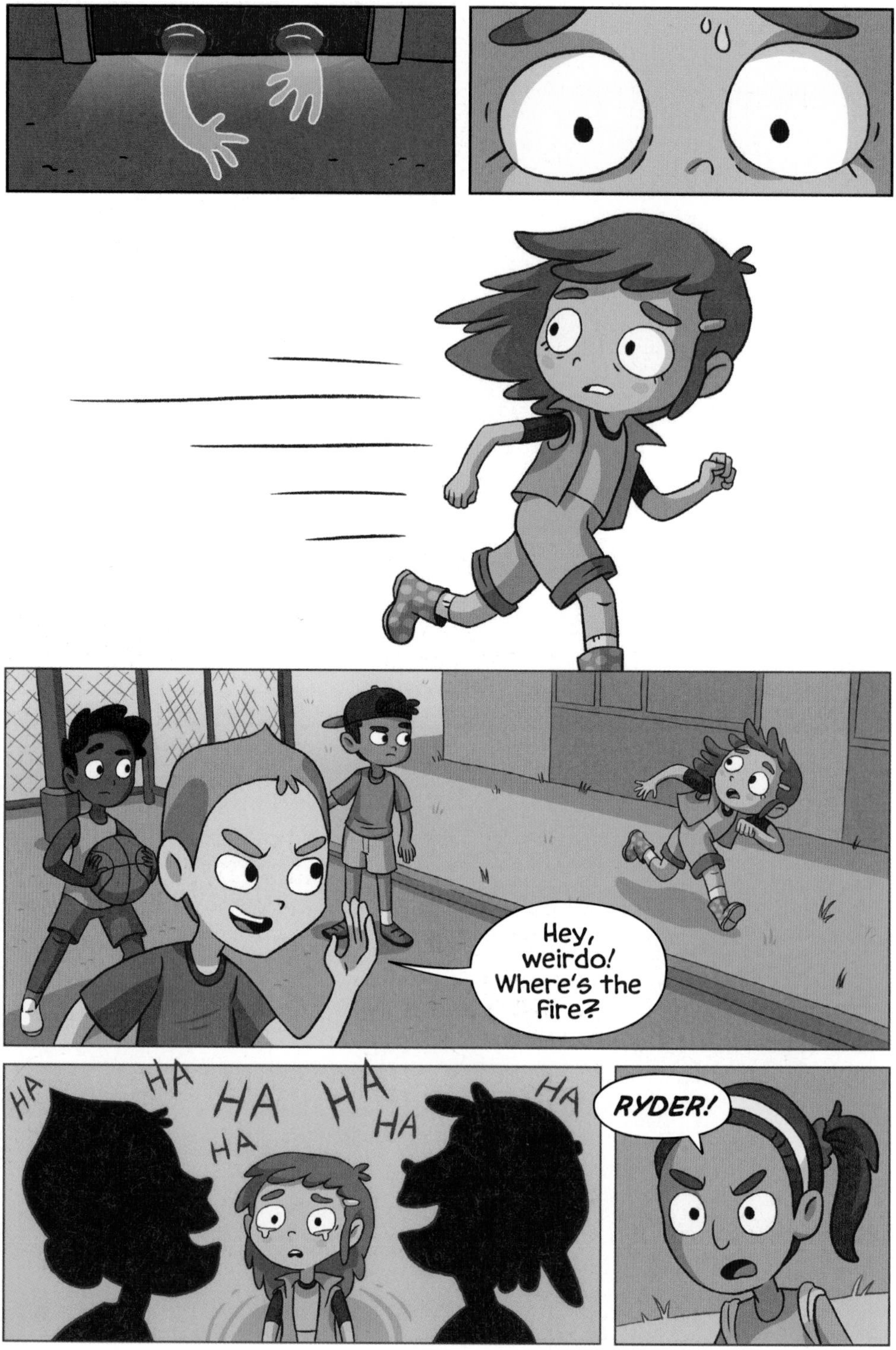
Hey, weirdo! Where's the fire?
HA HA HA HA HA HA HA
RYDER!

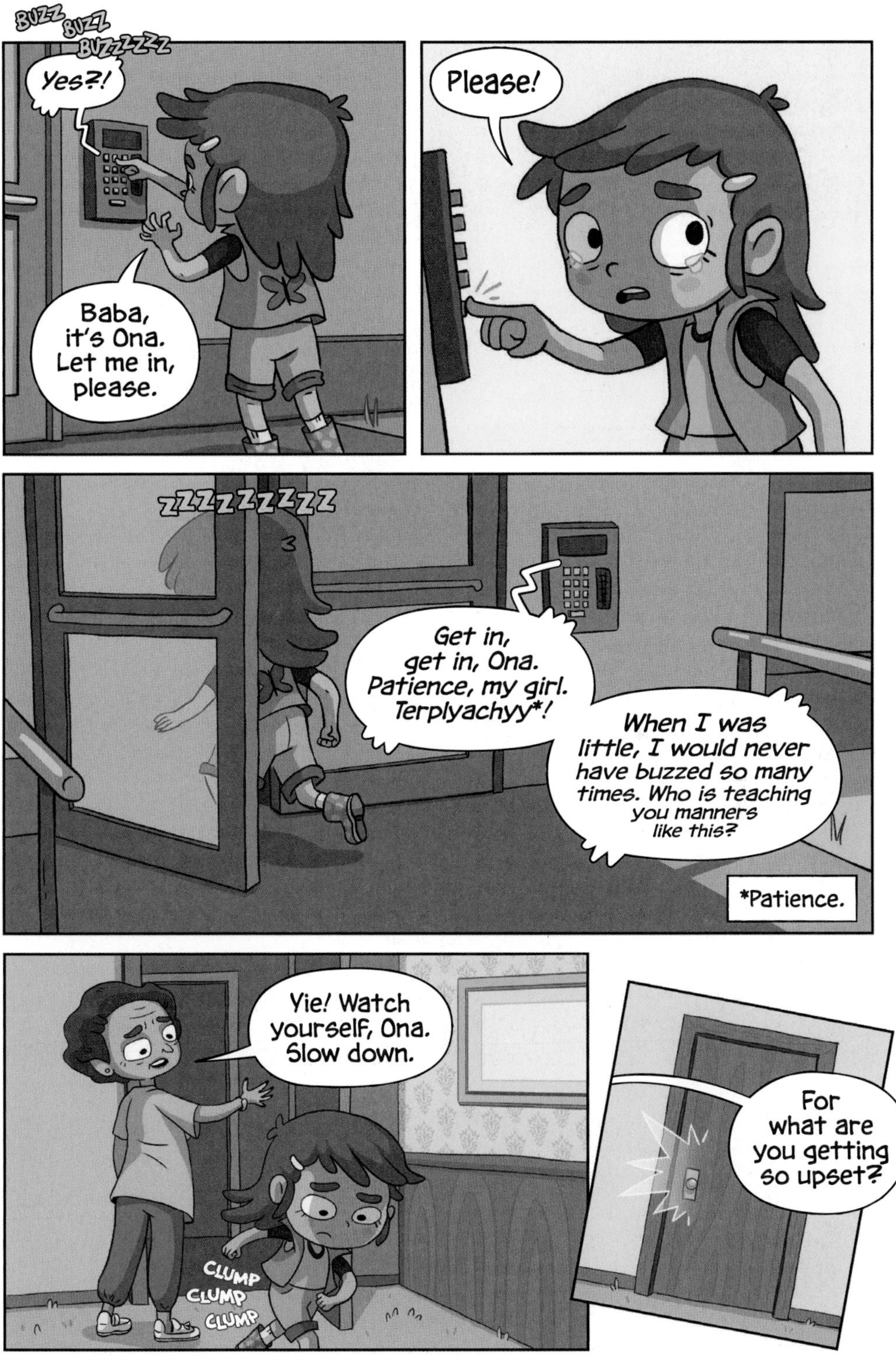
BUZZ BUZZ BUZZZZZZ
Yes?!
Baba, it's Ona. Let me in, please.
Please!
ZZZZZZZZZ
Get in, get in, Ona. Patience, my girl. Terplyachyy*!
When I was little, I would never have buzzed so many times. Who is teaching you manners like this?
*Patience.
Yie! Watch yourself, Ona. Slow down.
CLUMP CLUMP CLUMP
For what are you getting so upset?

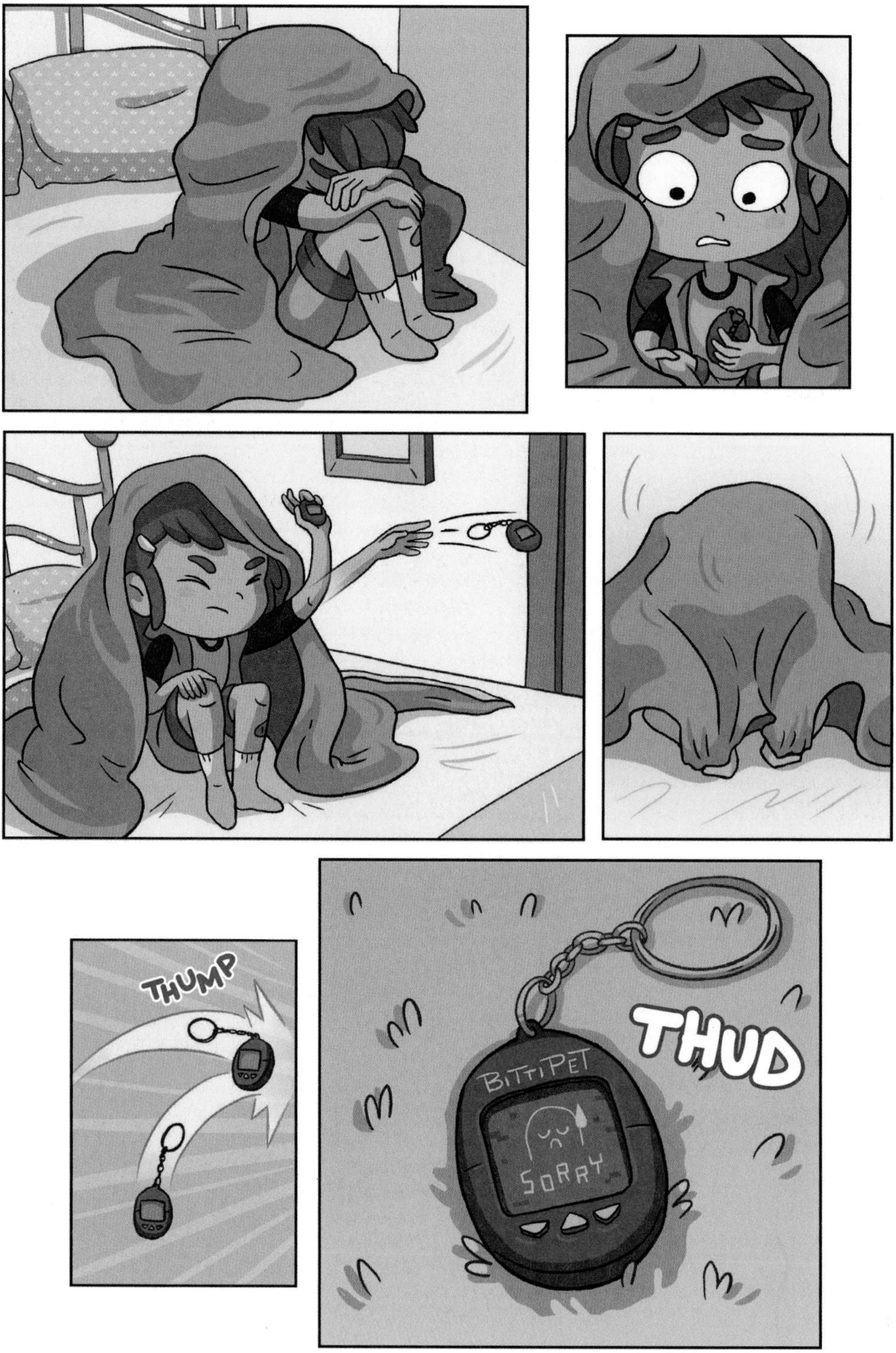
THUMP
THUD
BITTIPET
SORRY

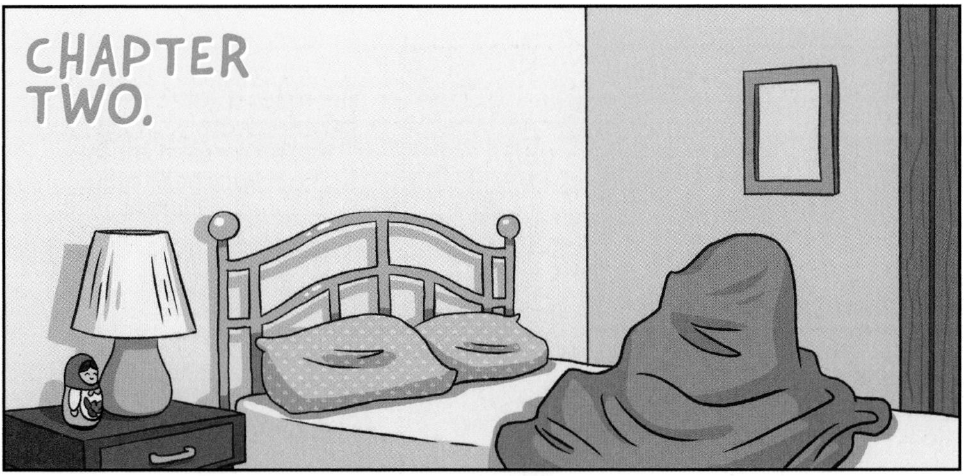
CHAPTER TWO.

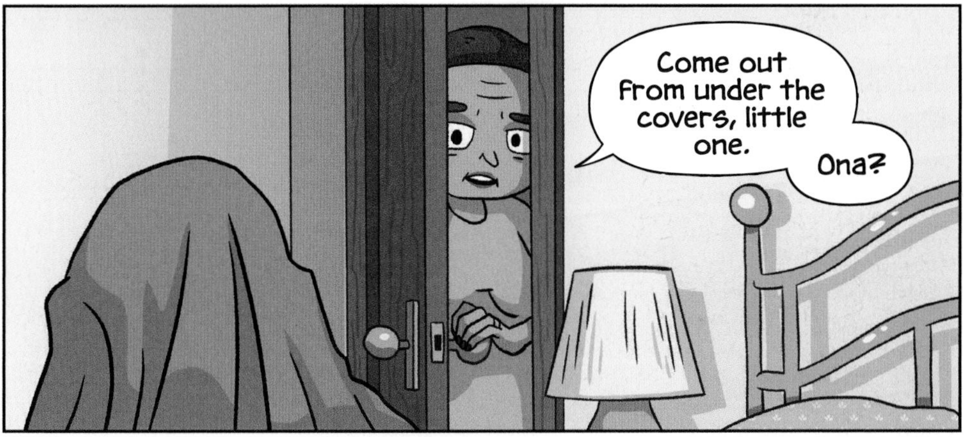
Come out from under the covers, little one.
Ona?

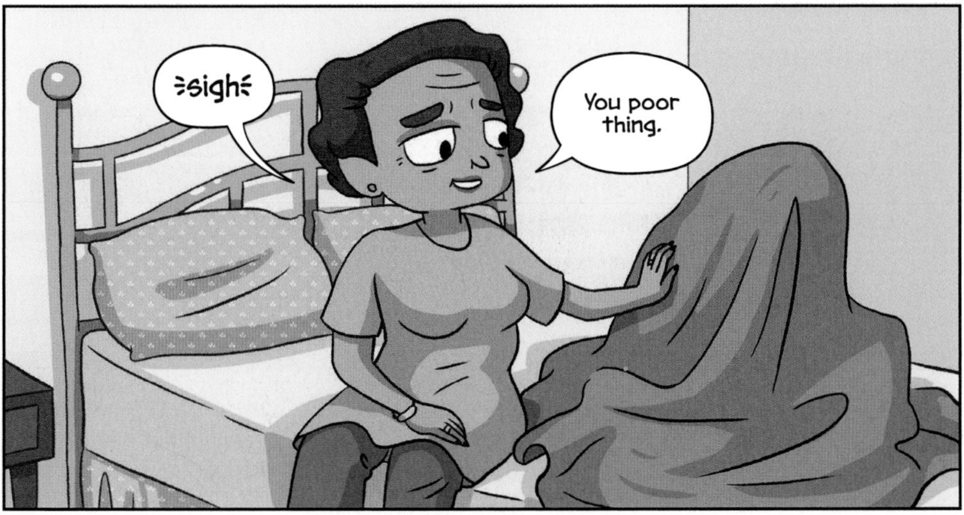
sigh
You poor thing.

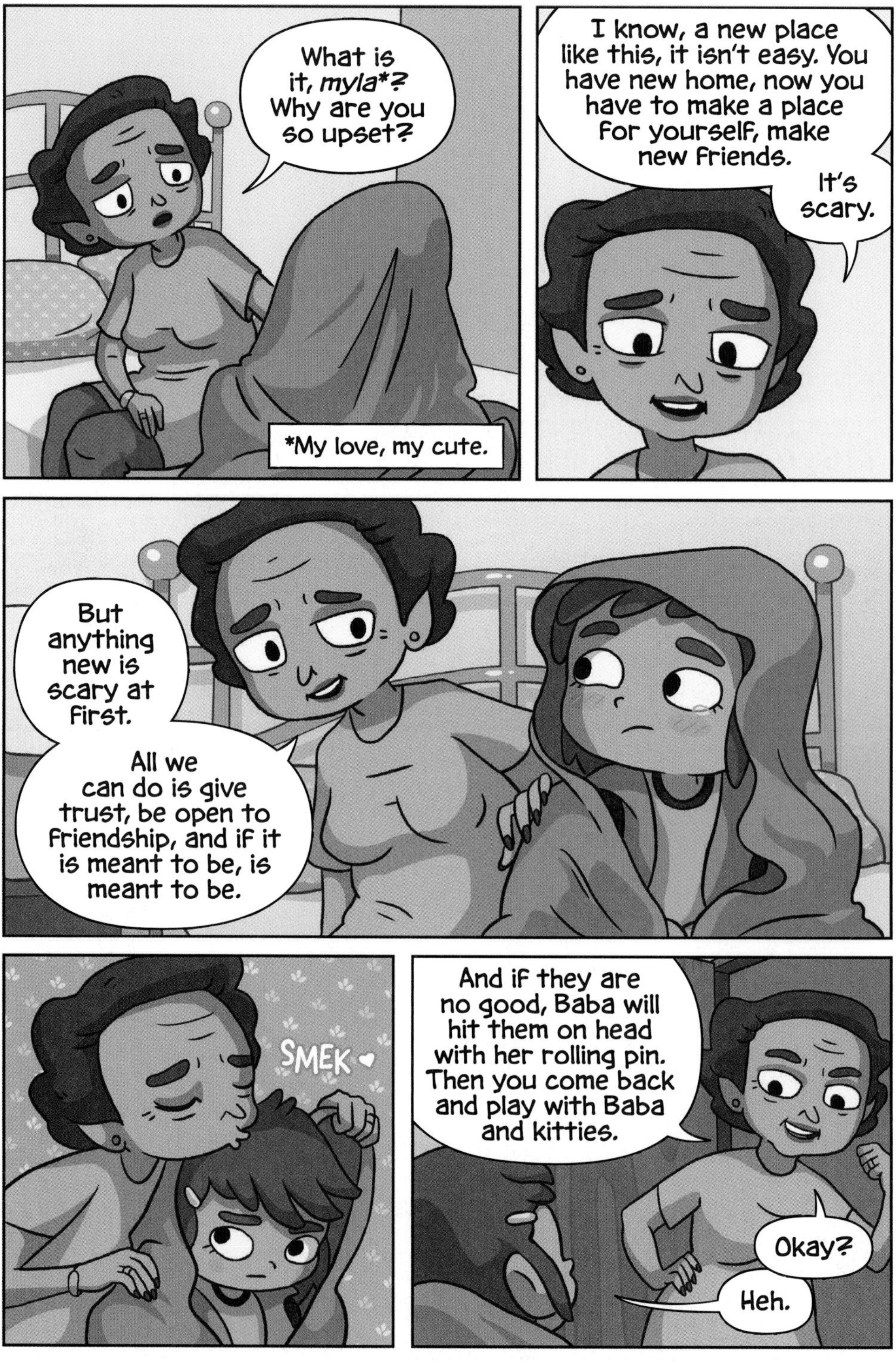
What is it, *myla**? Why are you so upset?
*My love, my cute.
I know, a new place like this, it isn't easy. You have new home, now you have to make a place for yourself, make new friends.
It's scary.
But anything new is scary at first.
All we can do is give trust, be open to friendship, and if it is meant to be, is meant to be.
SMEK
And if they are no good, Baba will hit them on head with her rolling pin. Then you come back and play with Baba and kitties.
Okay?
Heh.

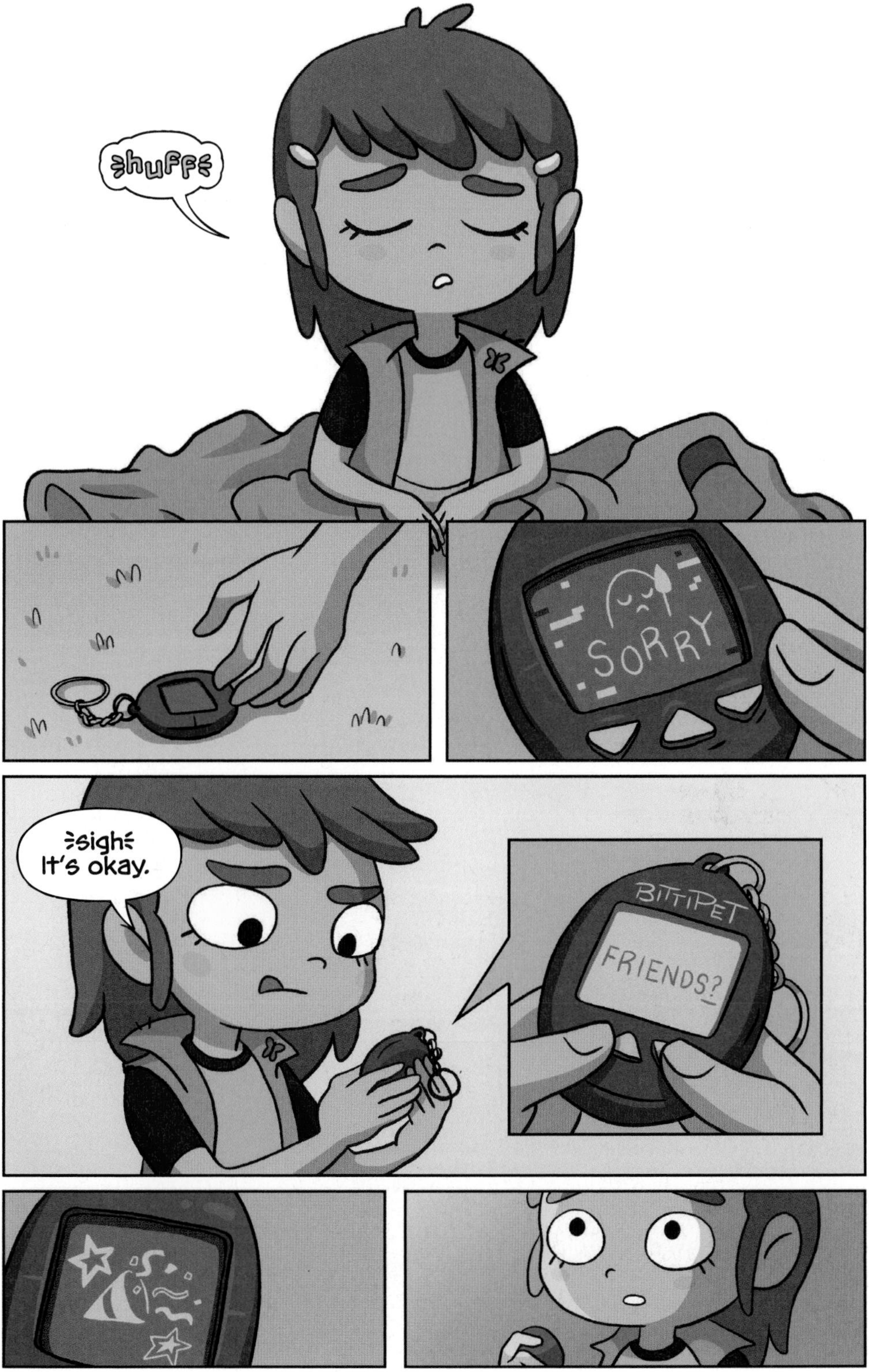
huff
SORRY
sigh
It's okay.
BITTIPET
FRIENDS?

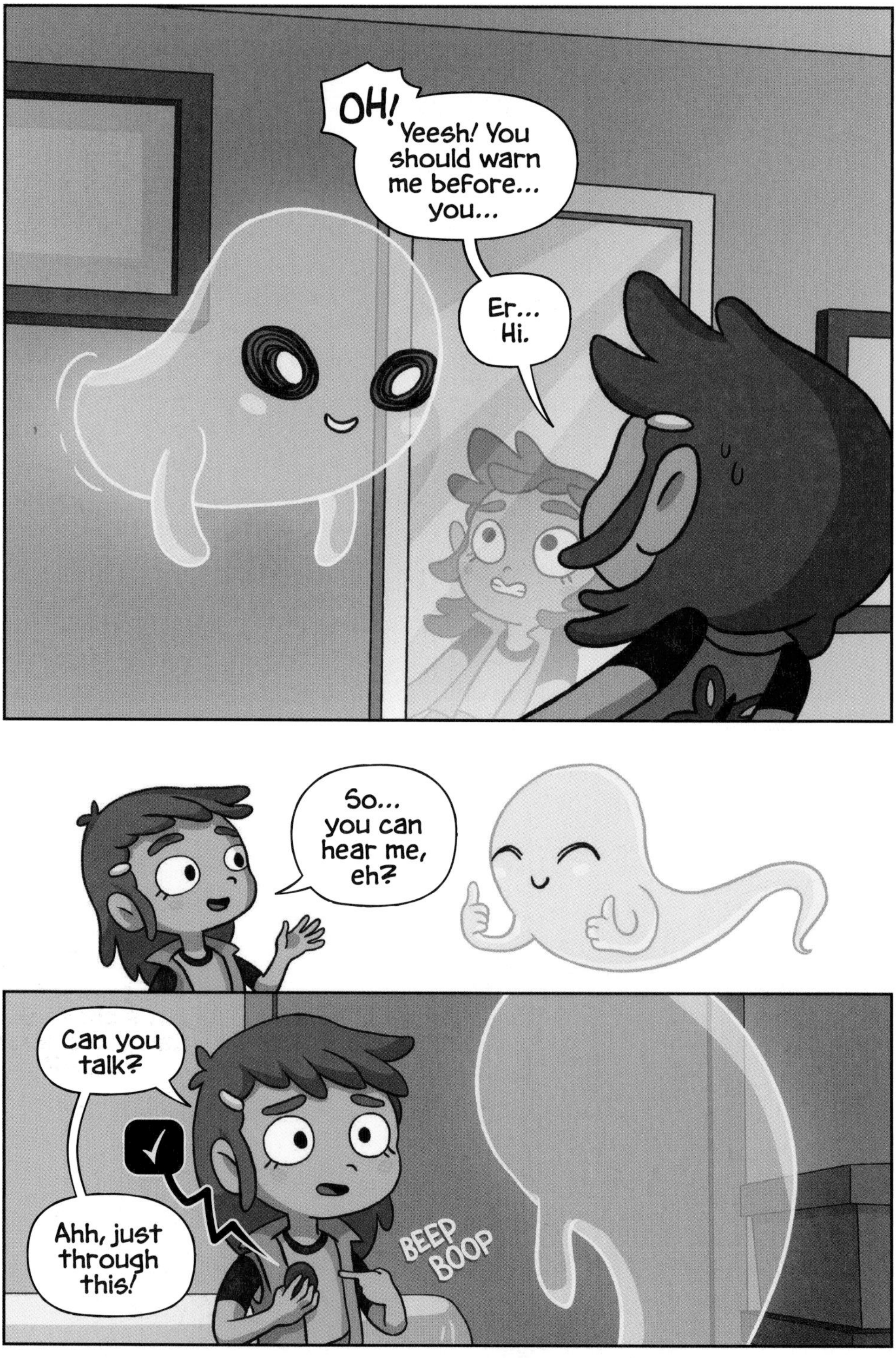
OH!
Yeesh! You should warn me before... you...
Er... Hi.
So... you can hear me, eh?
Can you talk?
Ahh, just through this!
BEEP BOOP

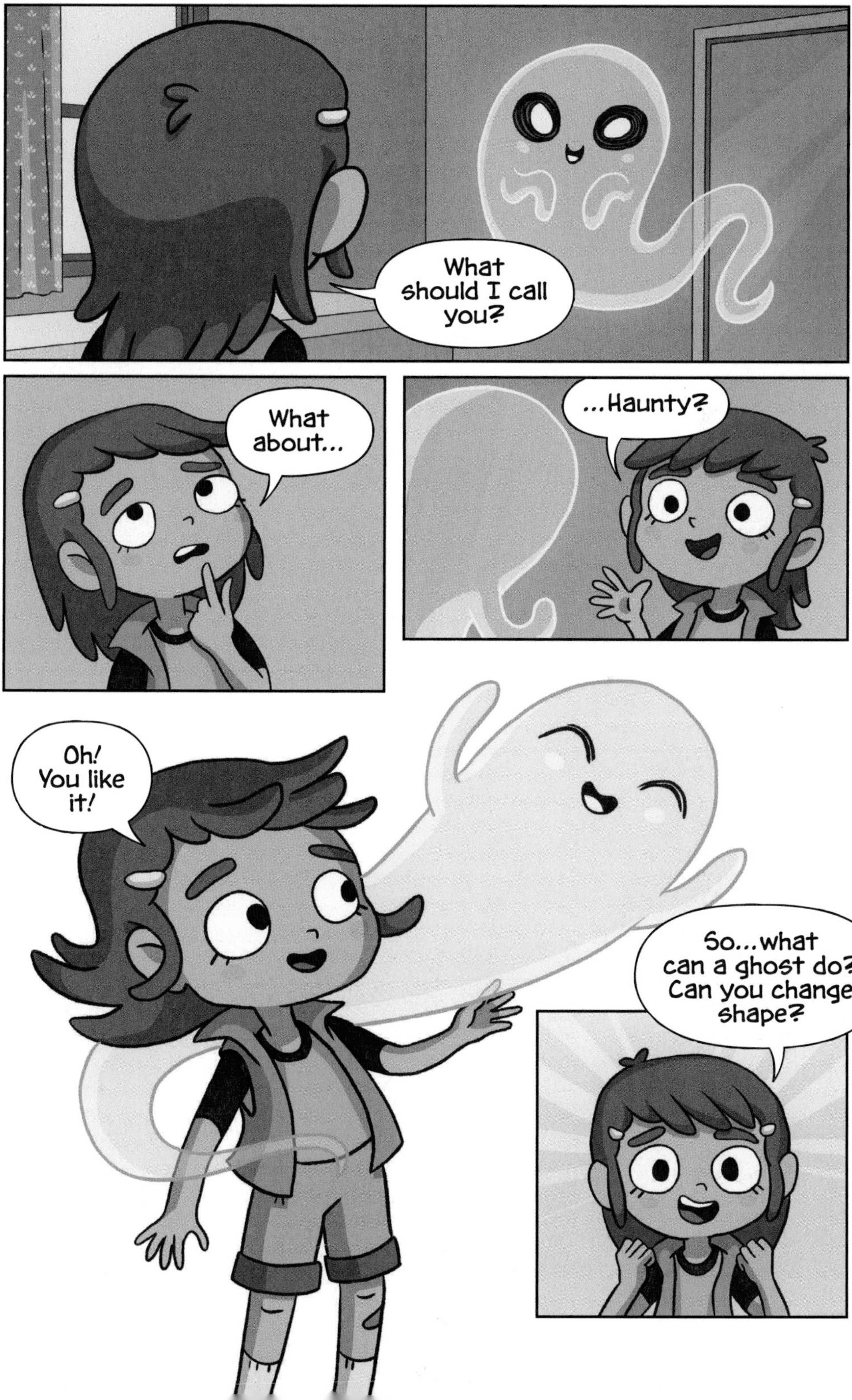
What should I call you?
What about...
...Haunty?
Oh! You like it!
So...what can a ghost do? Can you change shape?

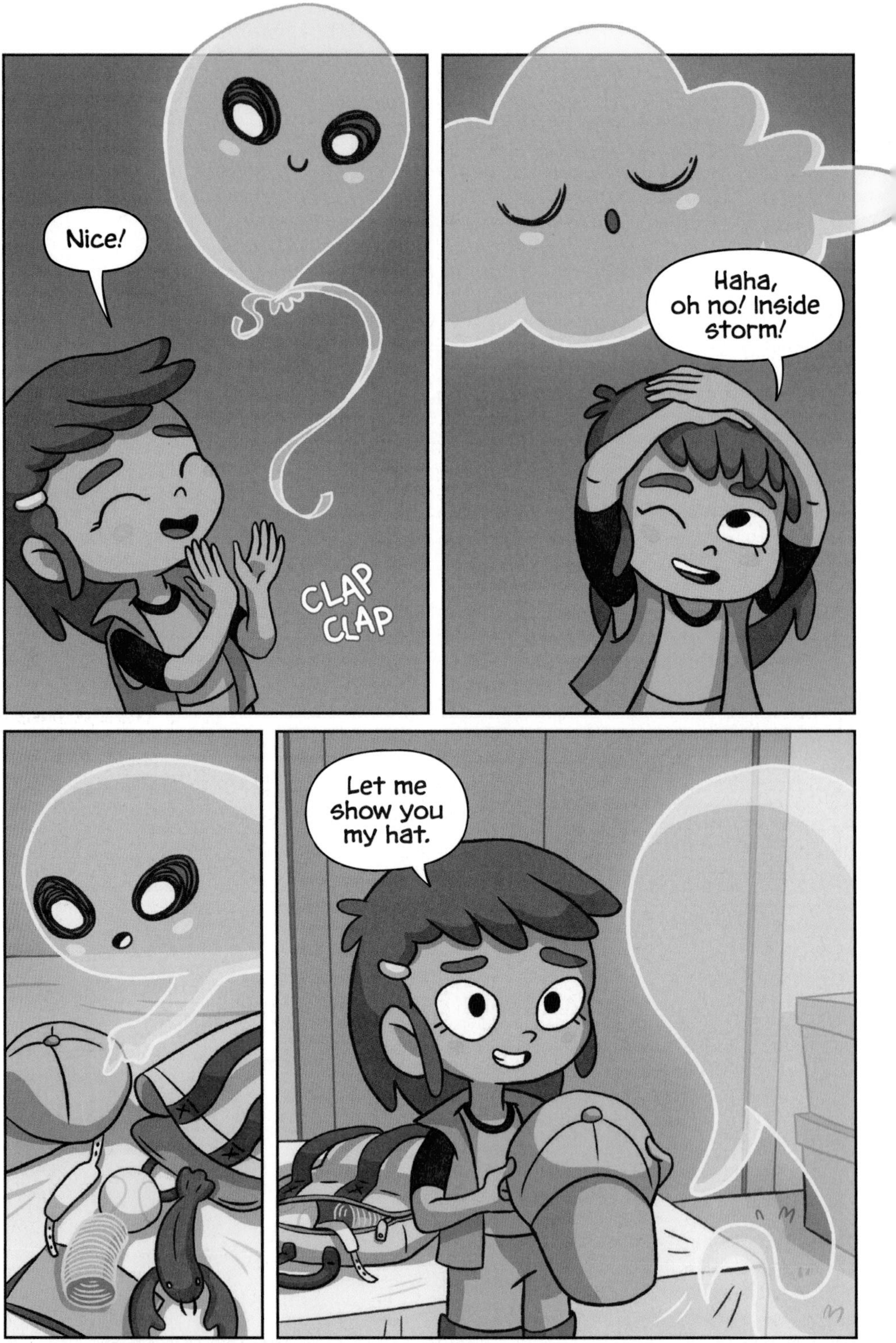
Nice!
CLAP CLAP
Haha, oh no! Inside storm!
Let me show you my hat.

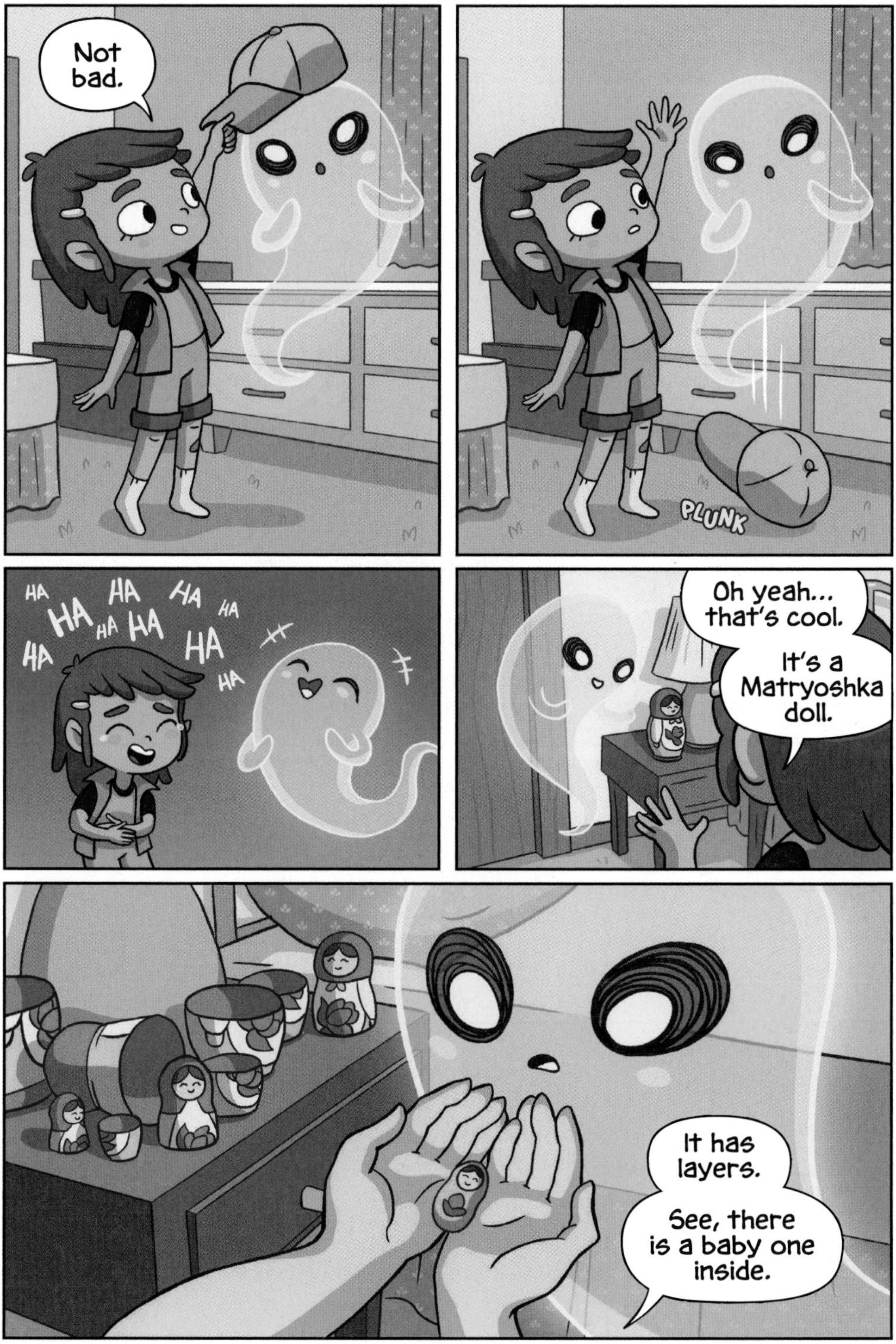
Not bad.
PLUNK
HA HA HA HA HA HA HA HA HA HA
Oh yeah... that's cool.
It's a Matryoshka doll.
It has layers.
See, there is a baby one inside.

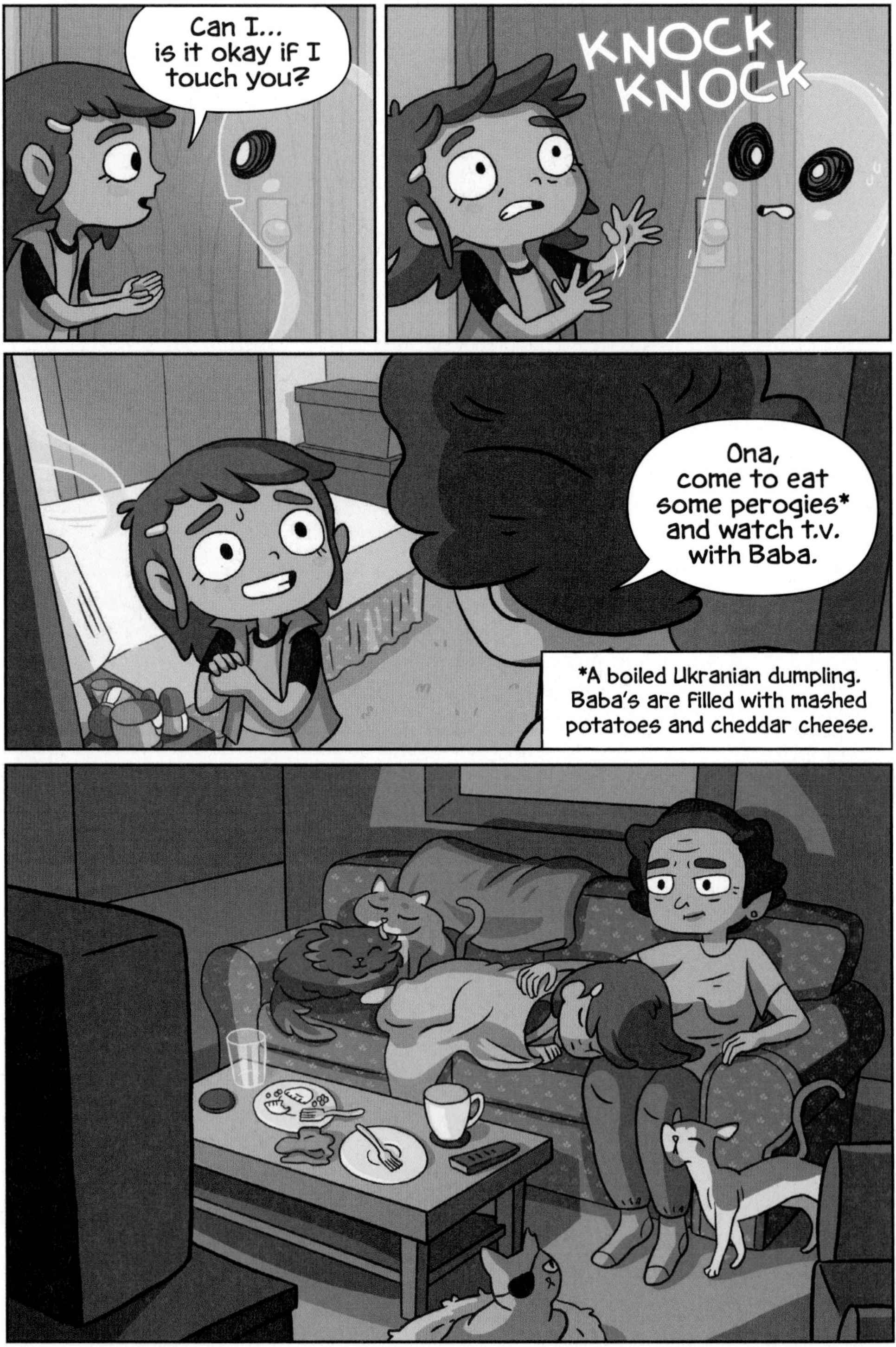
Can I... is it okay if I touch you?
KNOCK KNOCK
Ona, come to eat some perogies* and watch t.v. with Baba.
*A boiled Ukranian dumpling. Baba's are filled with mashed potatoes and cheddar cheese.

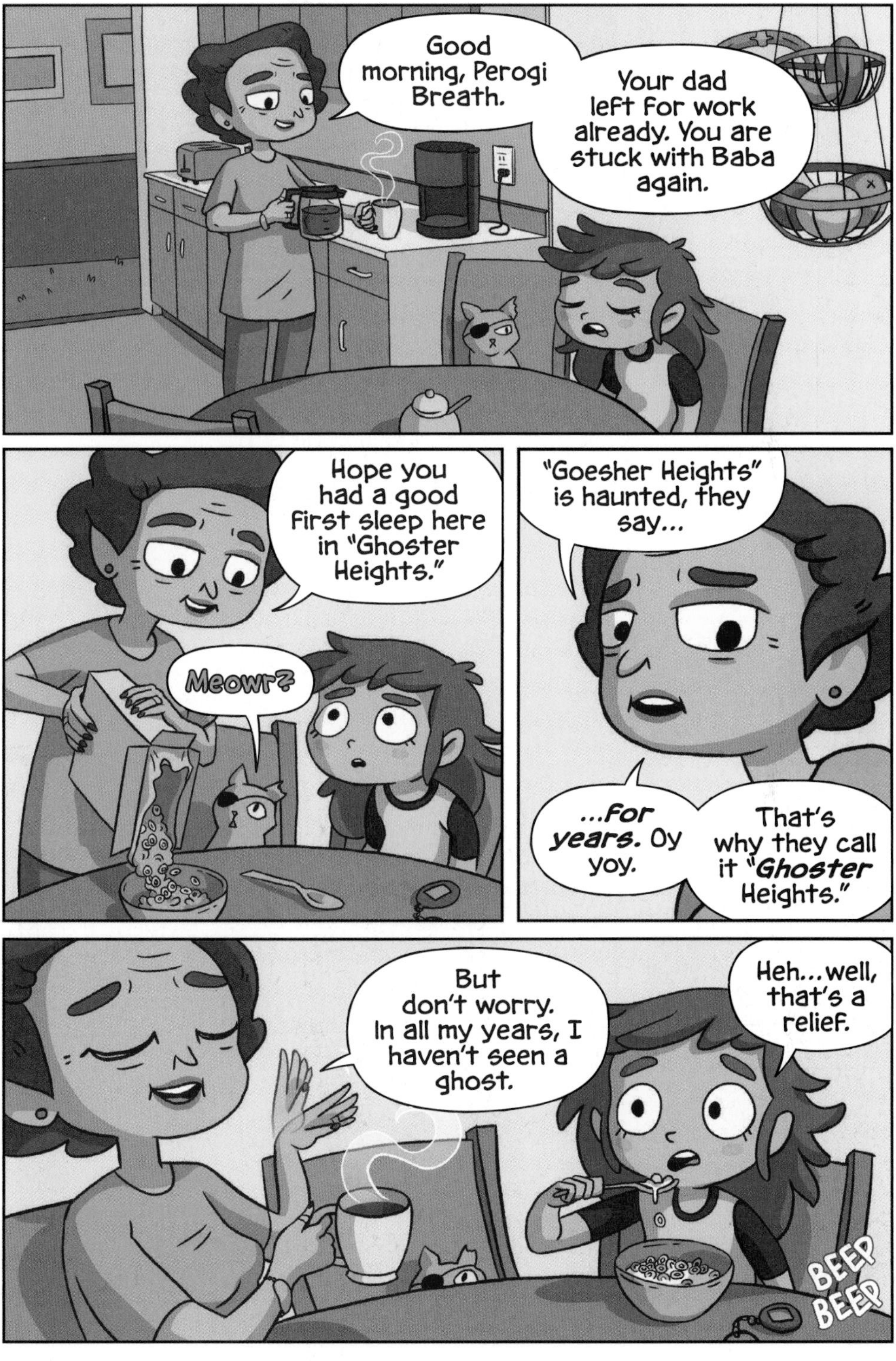
Good morning, Perogi Breath.
Your dad left for work already. You are stuck with Baba again.
Hope you had a good first sleep here in "Ghoster Heights."
Meowr?
"Goesher Heights" is haunted, they say...
...*for years.* Oy yoy.
That's why they call it "*Ghoster* Heights."
But don't worry. In all my years, I haven't seen a ghost.
Heh...well, that's a relief.
BEEP BEEP

I'm going to a meeting about the upcoming community rummage sale in a bit.

People around here need something to do to keep them together.

Okay, I'm going to go outside.

"That's my girl. I knew you'd get back out there and make some friends.

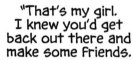

"Plus fresh air is always good.

"Remember to take the key in case I'm not here.

And don't worry about the cats going outside. They always come back home.

Where else would they get so much food?

34

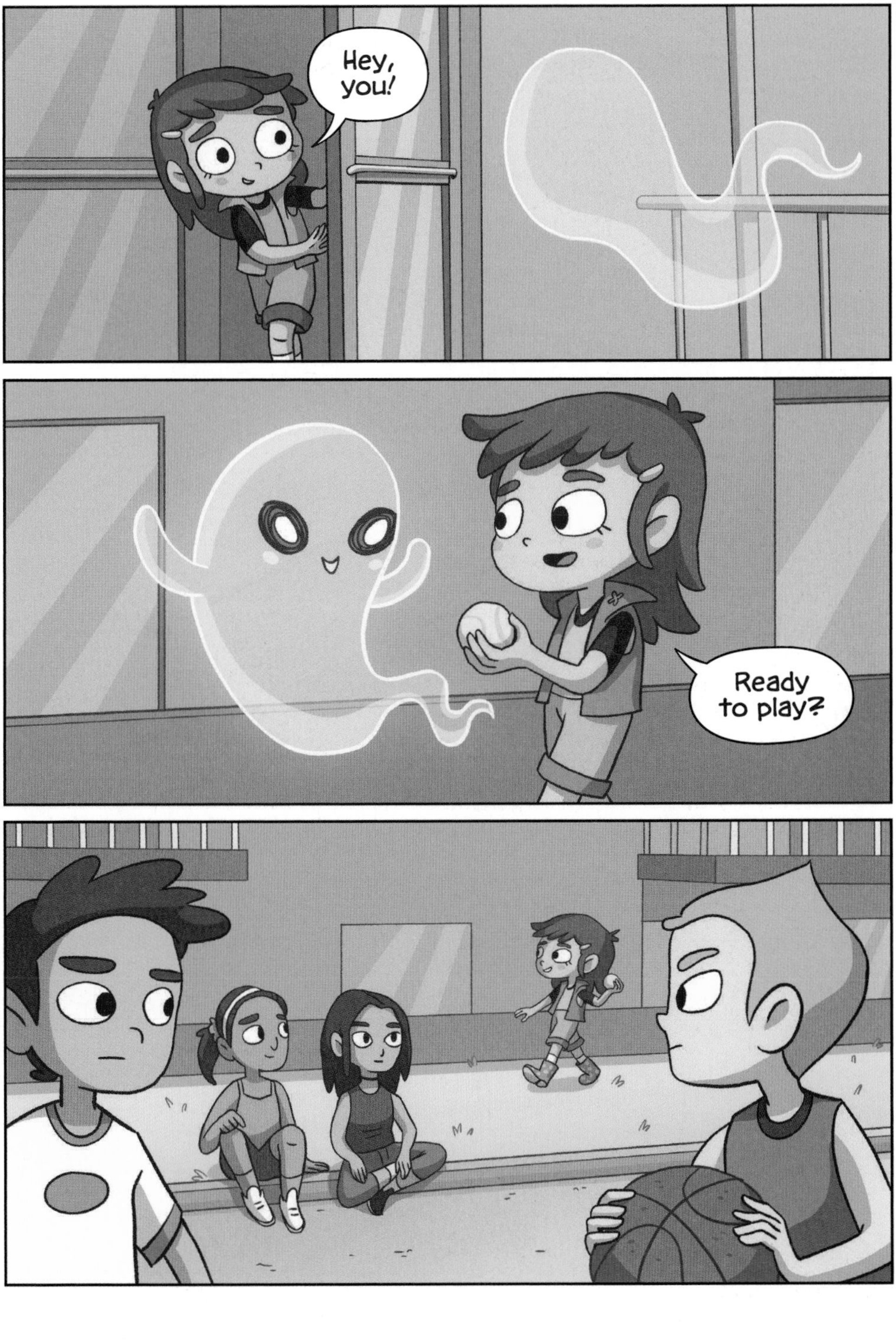
Hey, you!
Ready to play?

PING

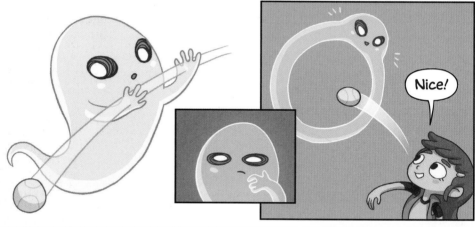

Nice!

Mwrrrrrr.

PING

No fair, I need a bigger target, Haunty.

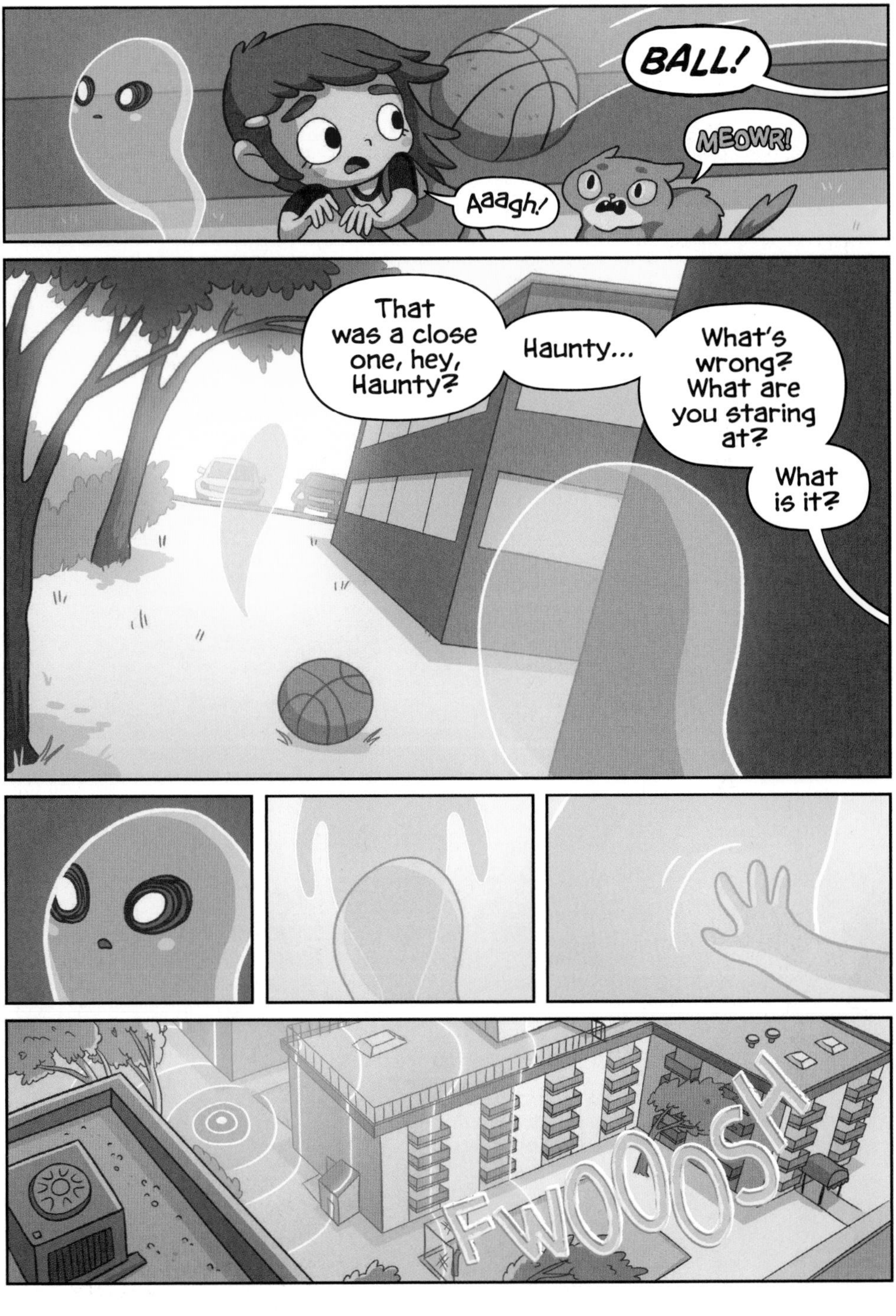

BALL!
MEOWR!
Aaagh!
That was a close one, hey, Haunty?
Haunty...
What's wrong? What are you staring at?
What is it?
FWOOOSH

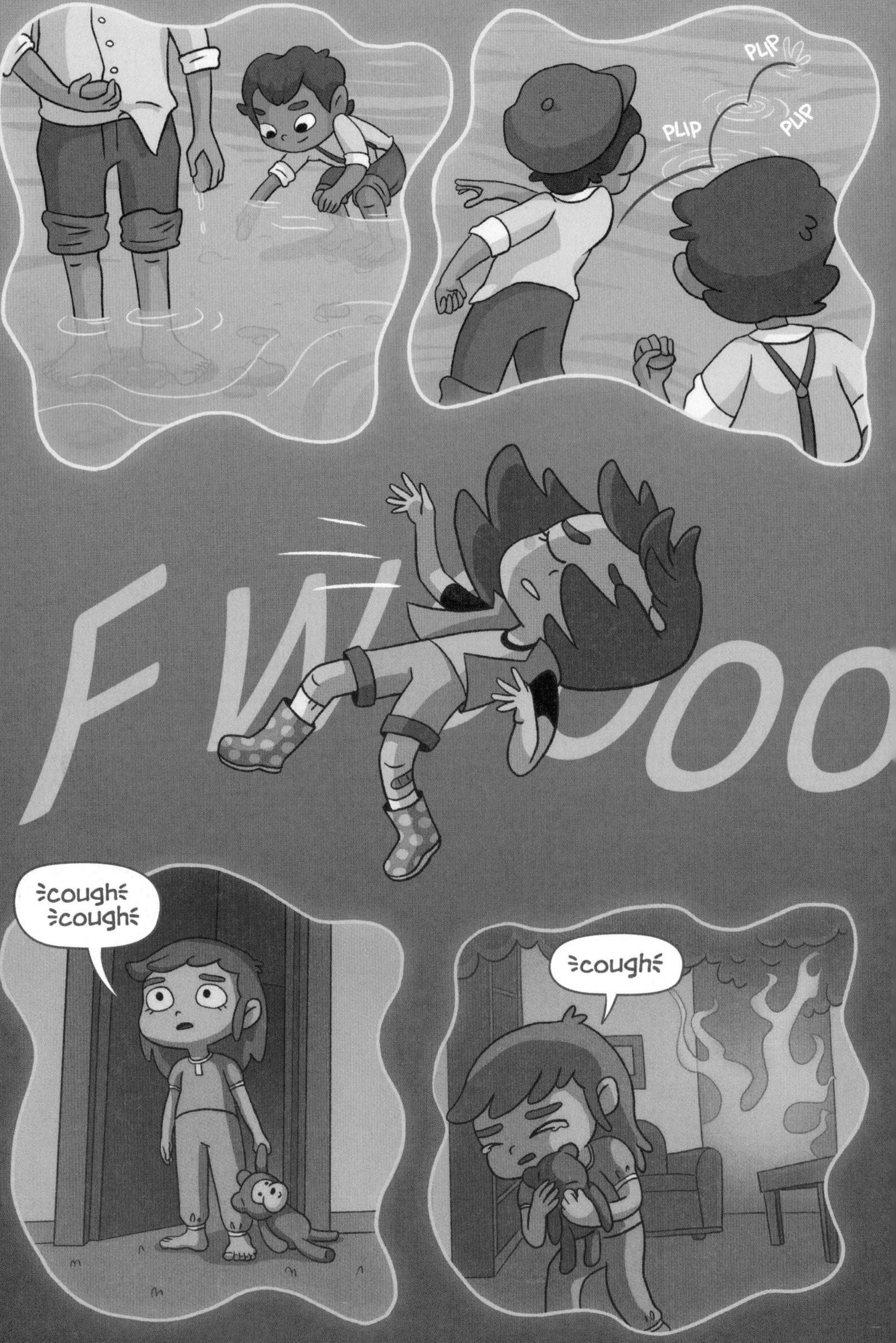
PLIP
PLIP
PLIP
FWOOO
cough cough
cough

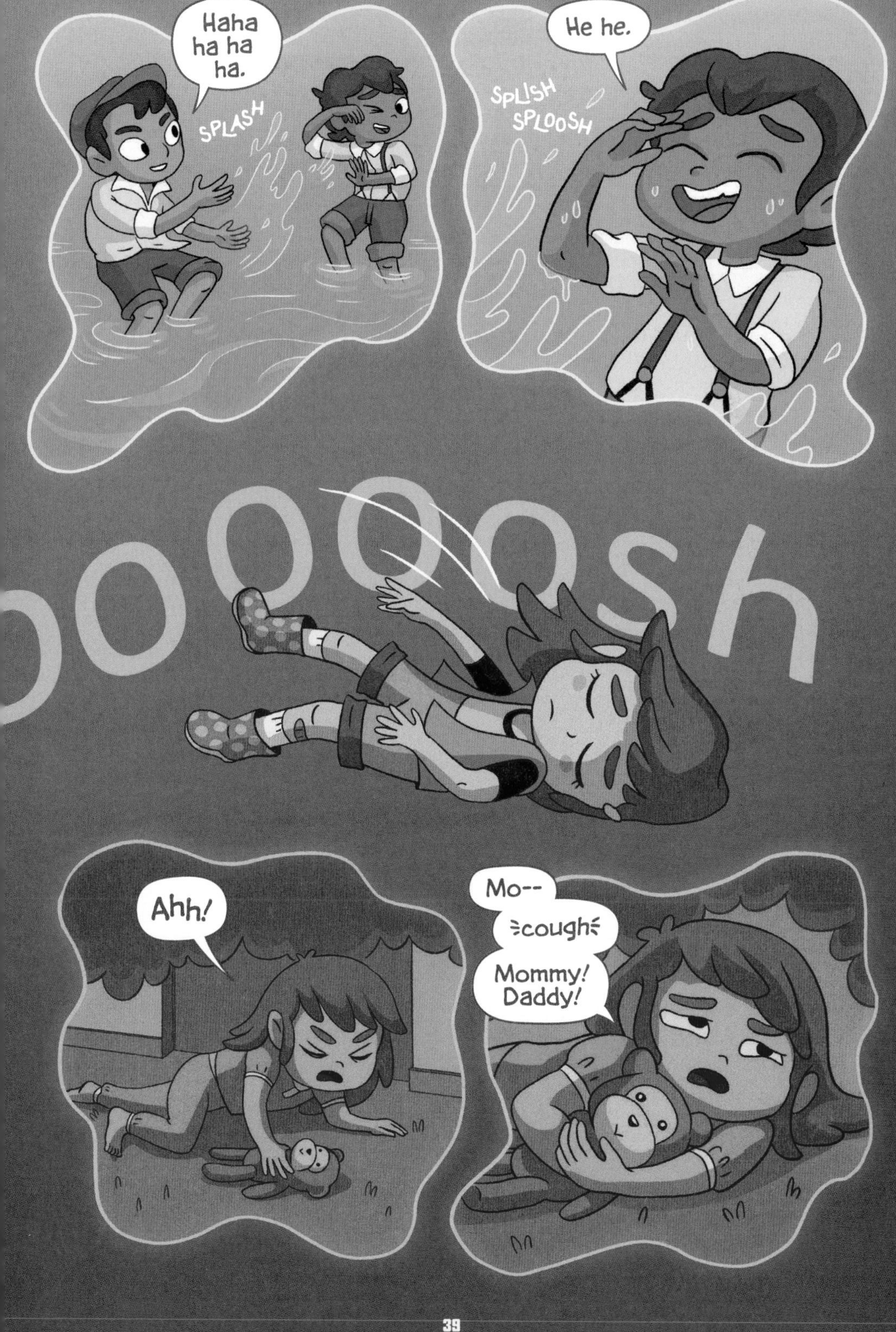
Haha ha ha ha.
SPLASH
He he.
SPLISH
SPLOOSH
oooOOsh
Ahh!
Mo--
cough
Mommy! Daddy!

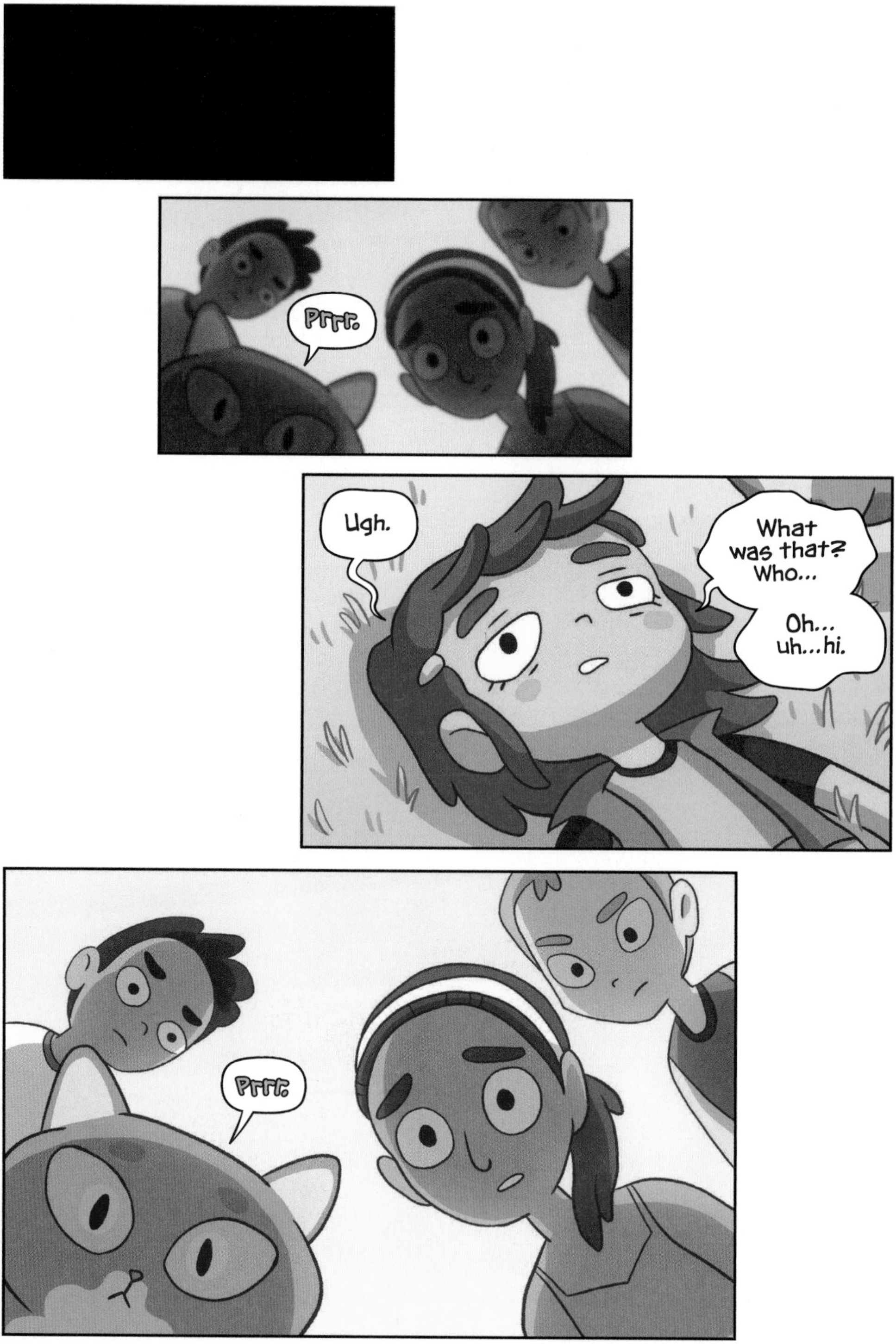
Prrr.
Ugh.
What was that? Who...
Oh... uh...hi.
Prrr.

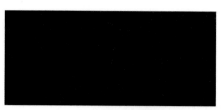

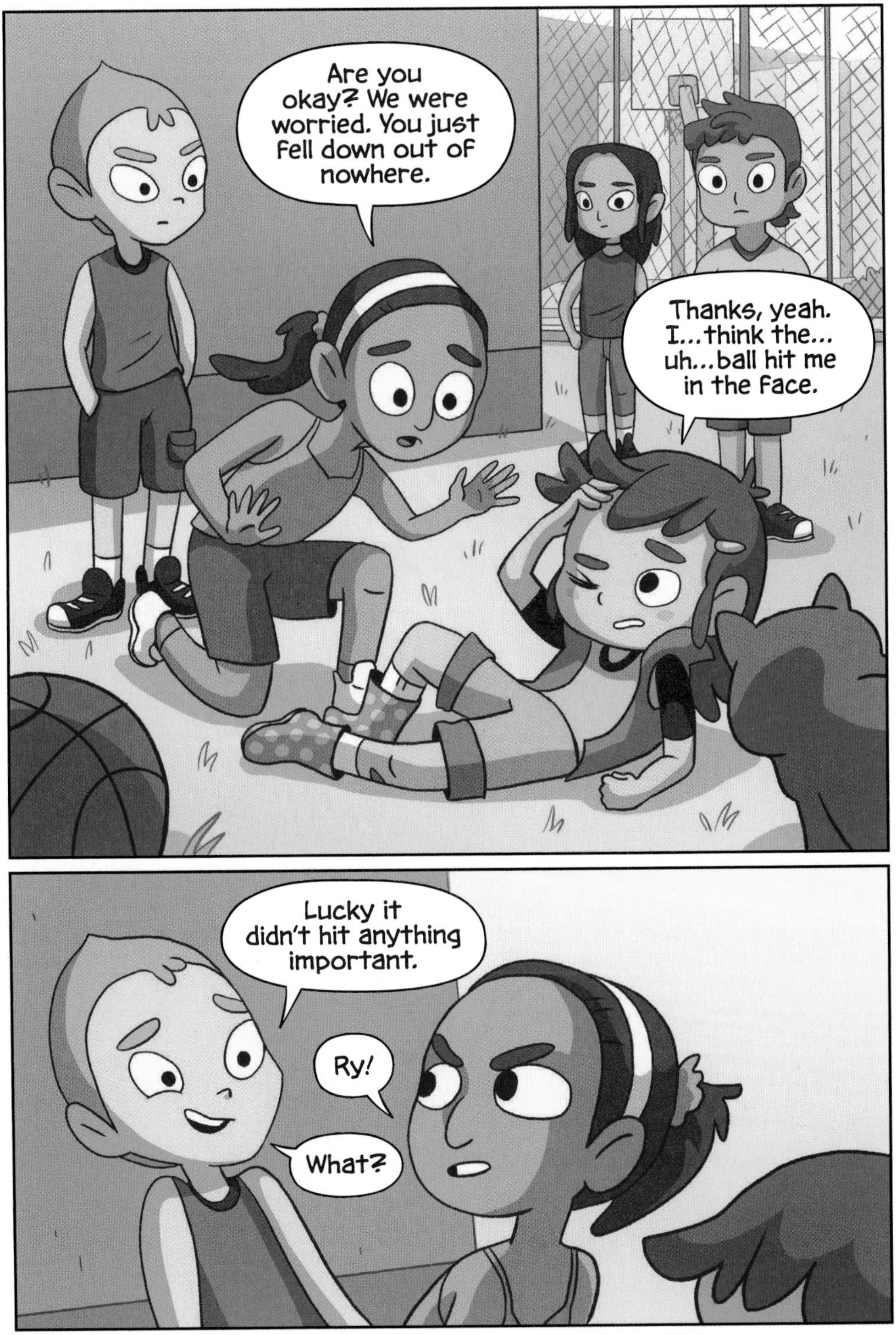
Are you okay? We were worried. You just fell down out of nowhere.
Thanks, yeah. I...think the... uh...ball hit me in the face.
Lucky it didn't hit anything important.
Ry!
What?

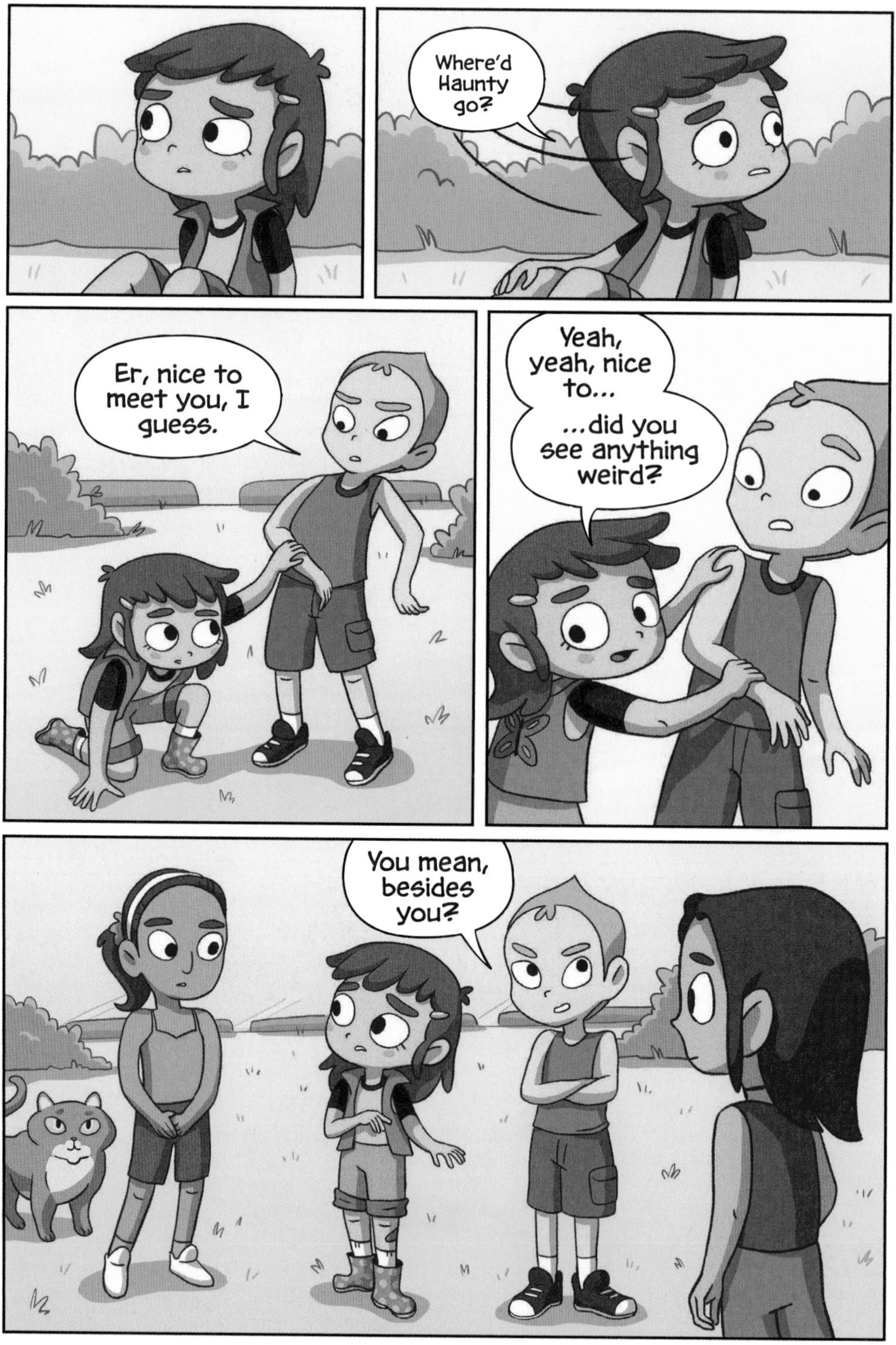
Where'd Haunty go?
Er, nice to meet you, I guess.
Yeah, yeah, nice to...
...did you see anything weird?
You mean, besides you?

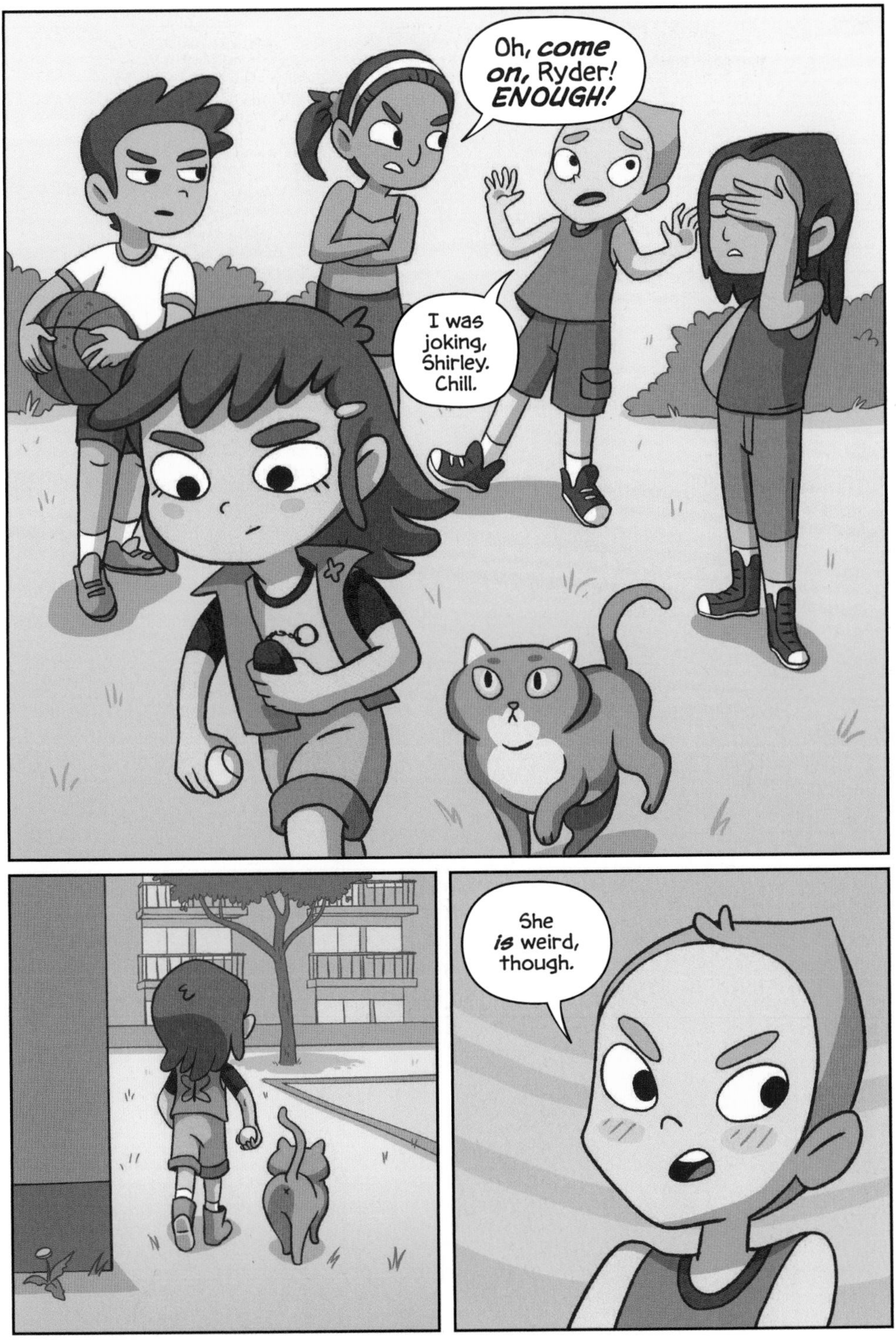
Oh, *come on*, Ryder! ***ENOUGH!***
I was joking, Shirley. Chill.
She *is* weird, though.

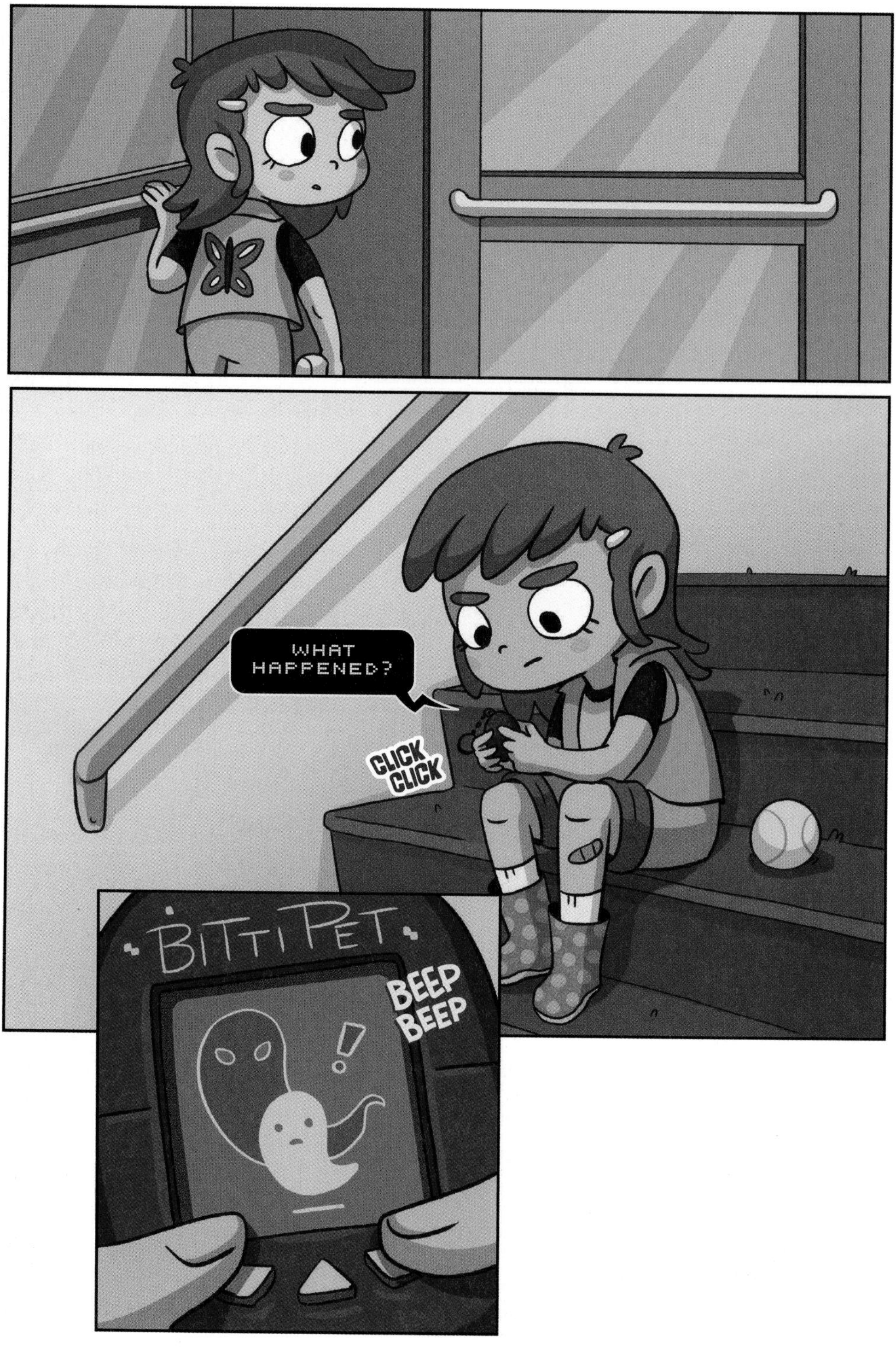
WHAT HAPPENED?
CLICK CLICK
BITTIPET
BEEP BEEP

CHAPTER THREE.

RUUUMBLE

CRUNCH
CRUNCH

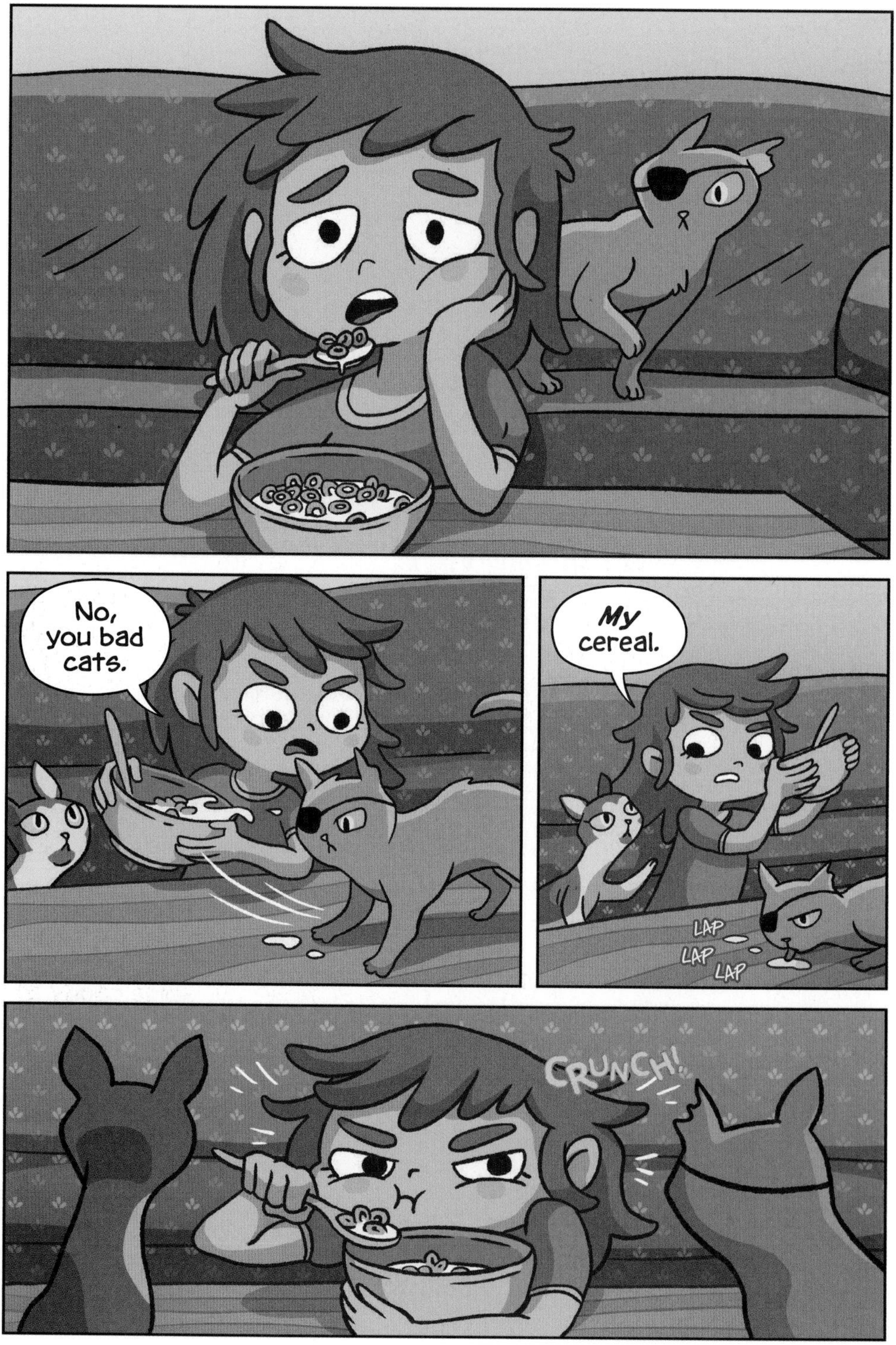

No, you bad cats.
My cereal.
LAP
LAP
LAP
CRUNCH!

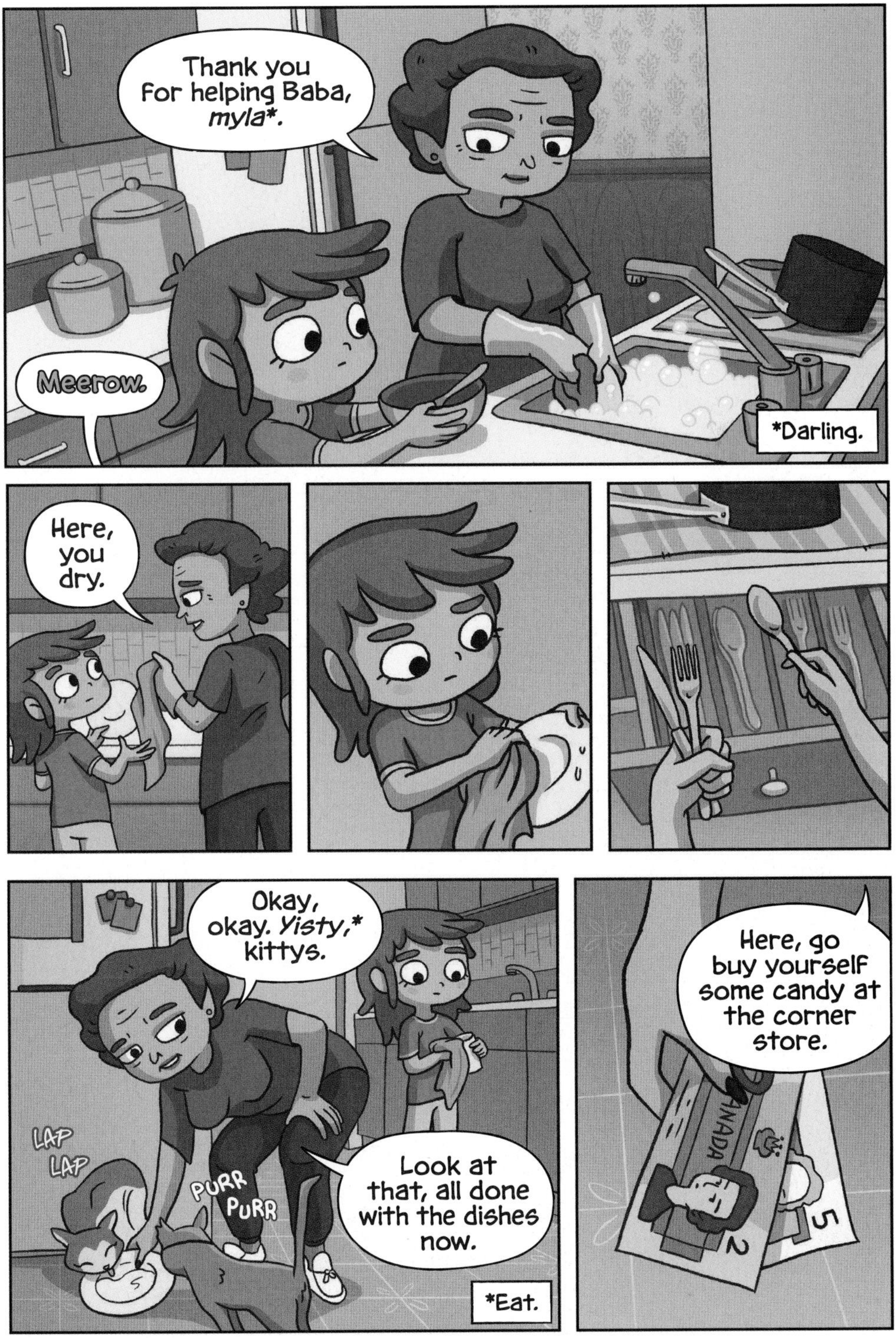
Thank you for helping Baba, *myla**.
Meerow.
*Darling.
Here, you dry.
Okay, okay. *Yisty,** kittys.
LAP LAP
PURR PURR
Look at that, all done with the dishes now.
*Eat.
Here, go buy yourself some candy at the corner store.

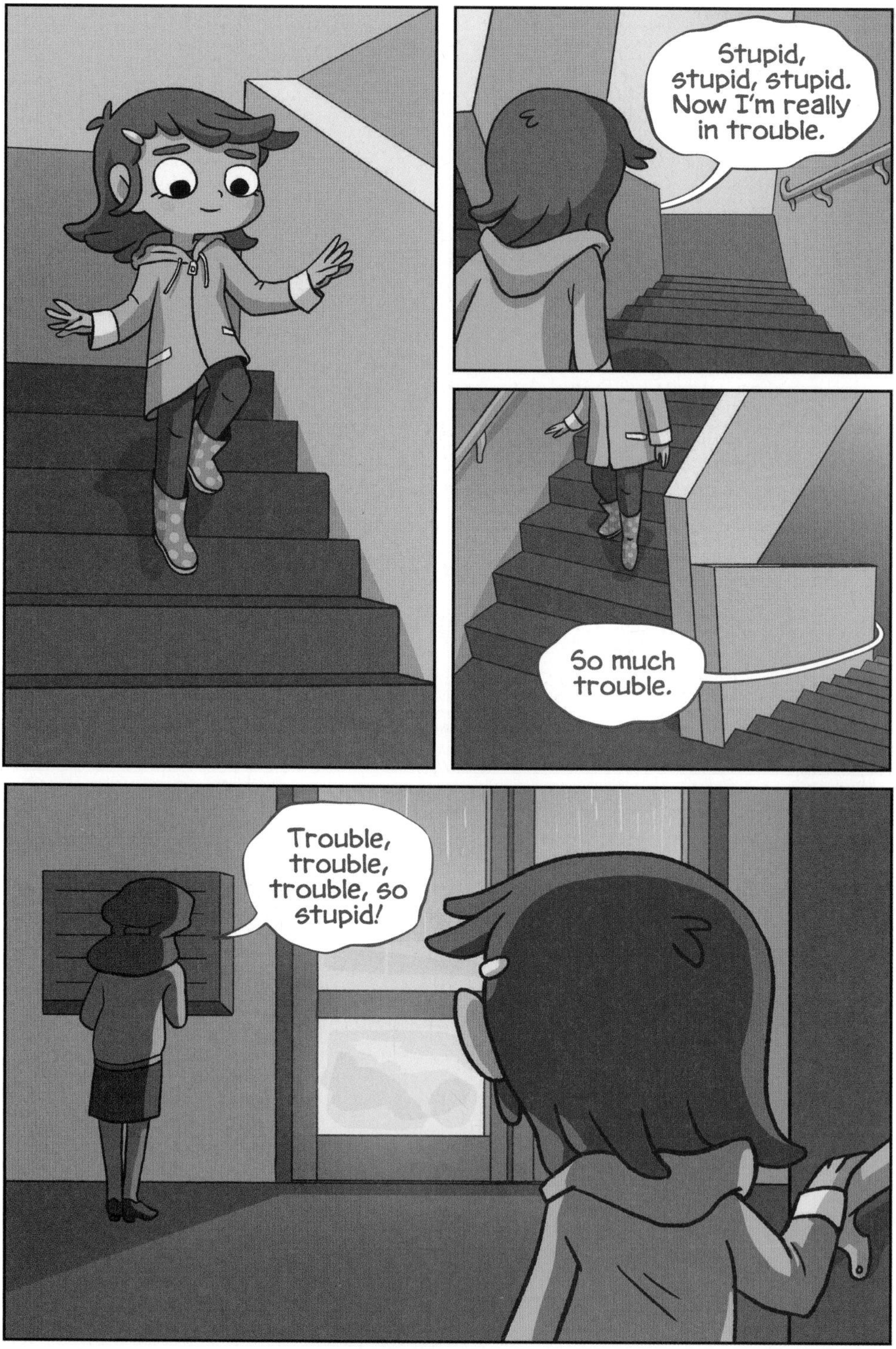
Stupid, stupid, stupid. Now I'm really in trouble.
So much trouble.
Trouble, trouble, trouble, so stupid!

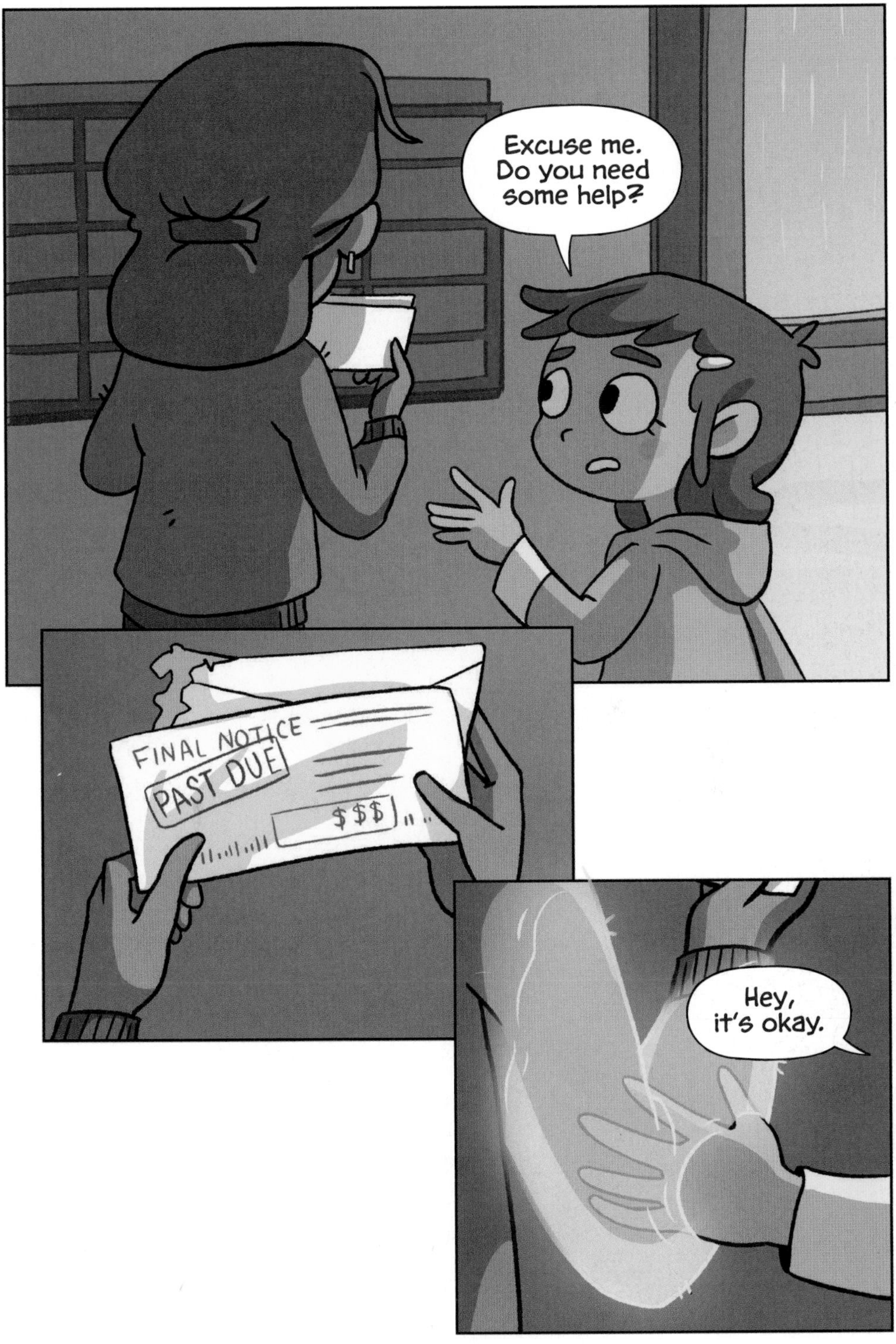
Excuse me. Do you need some help?
FINAL NOTICE
PAST DUE
$$$
Hey, it's okay.

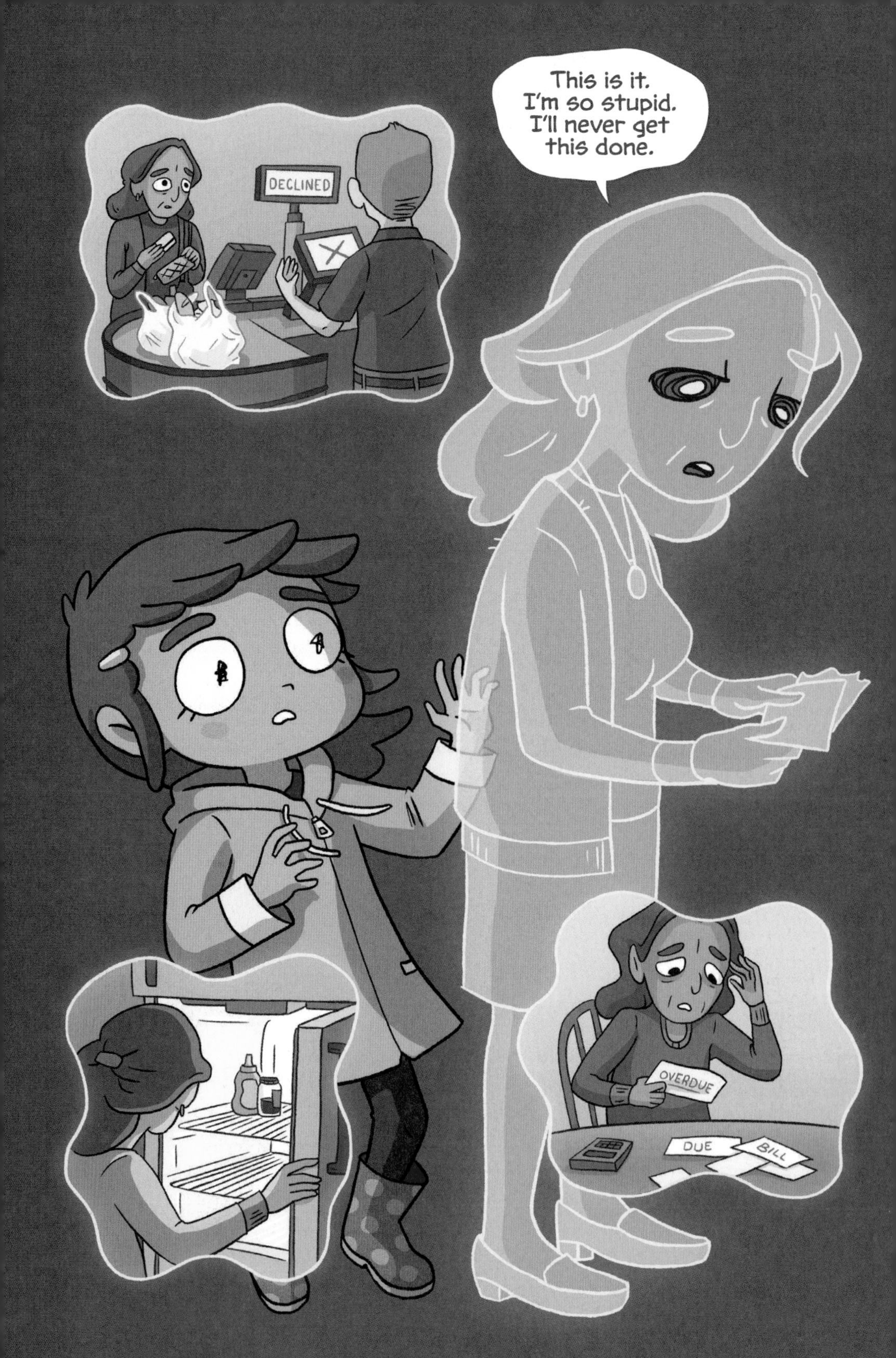
This is it.
I'm so stupid.
I'll never get
this done.
DECLINED
OVERDUE
DUE
BILL

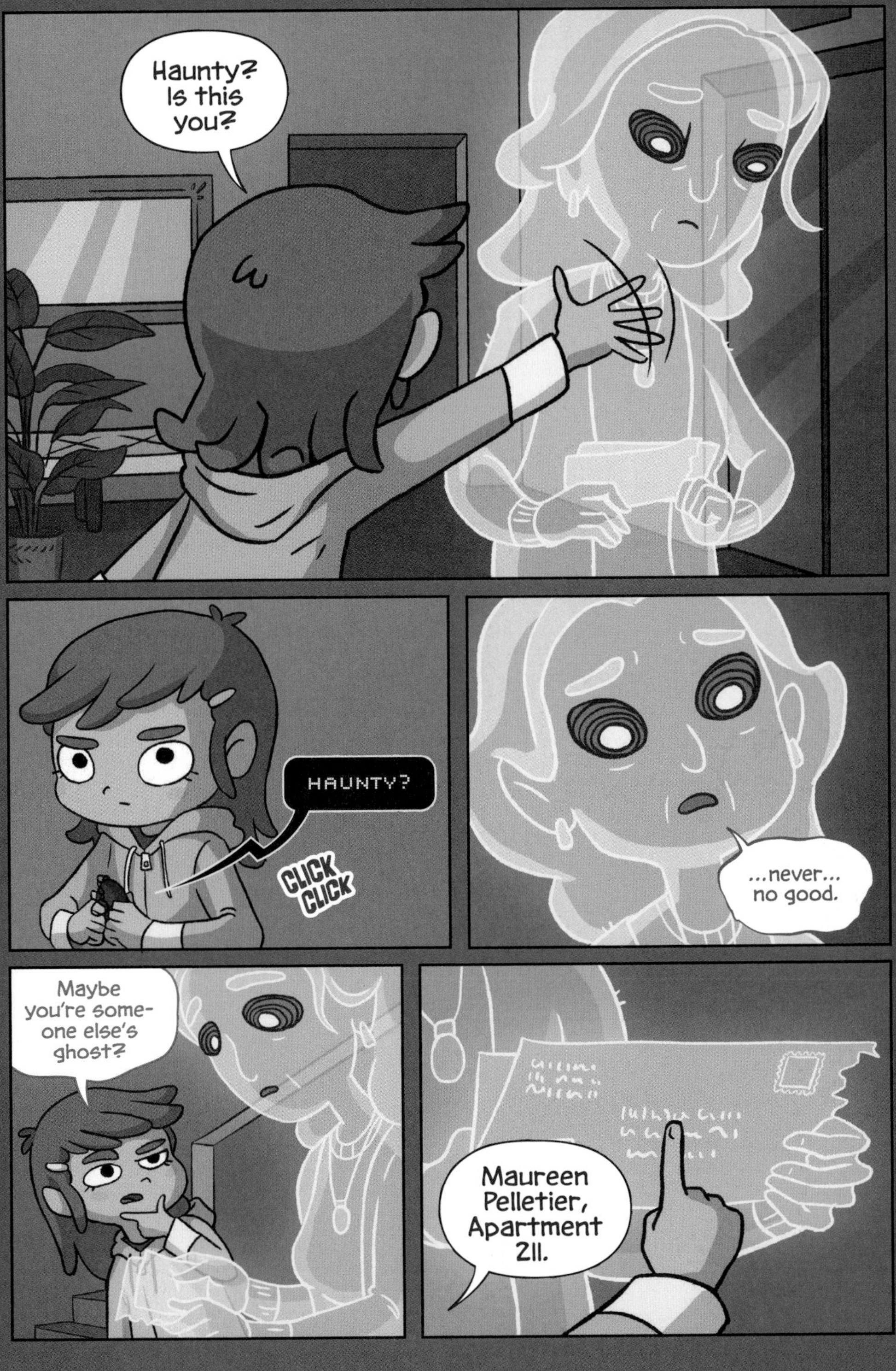

Haunty? Is this you?
HAUNTY?
CLICK CLICK
...never... no good.
Maybe you're some-one else's ghost?
Maureen Pelletier, Apartment 211.

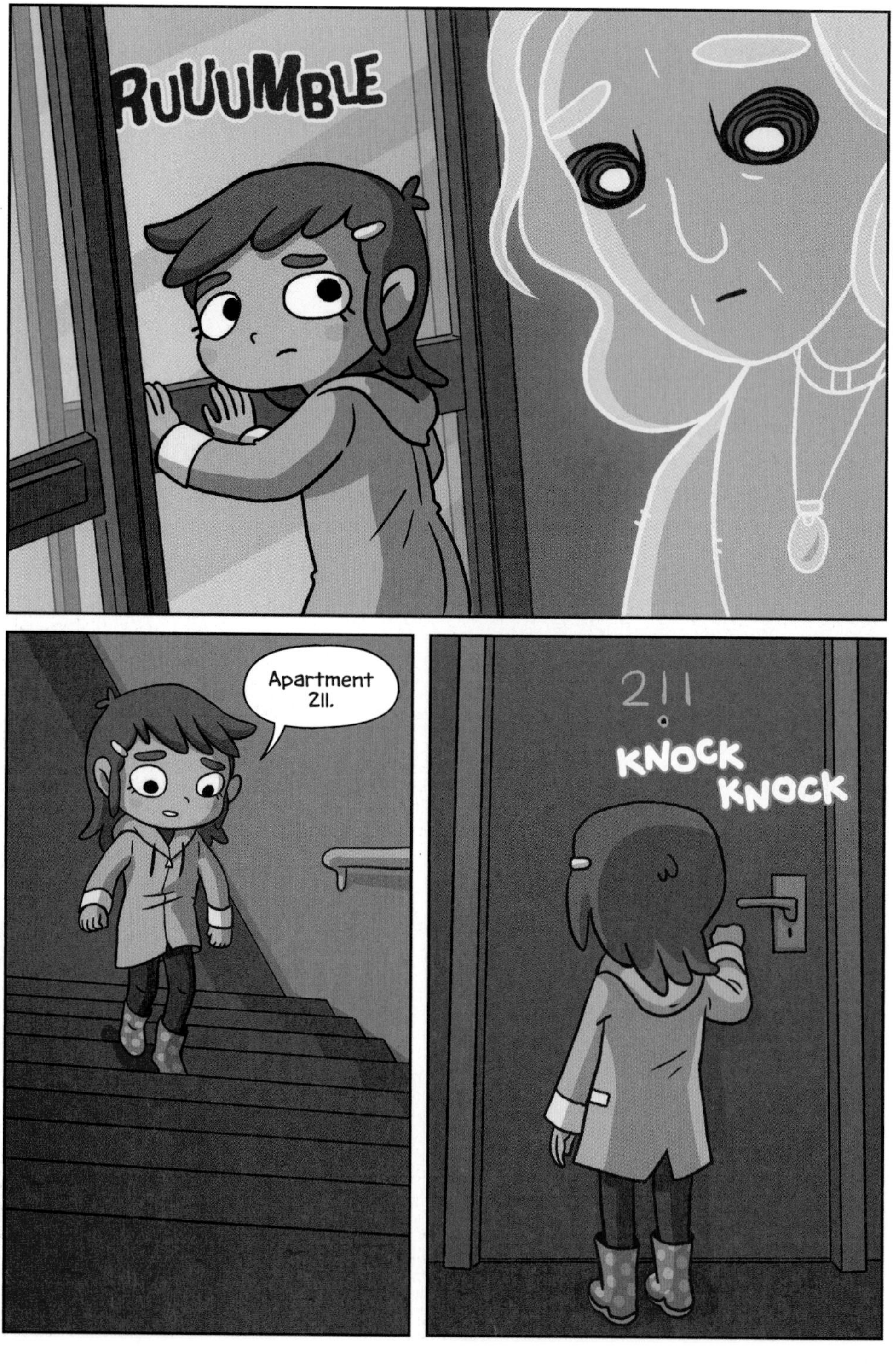
RUUUMBLE
Apartment 211.
211
KNOCK KNOCK

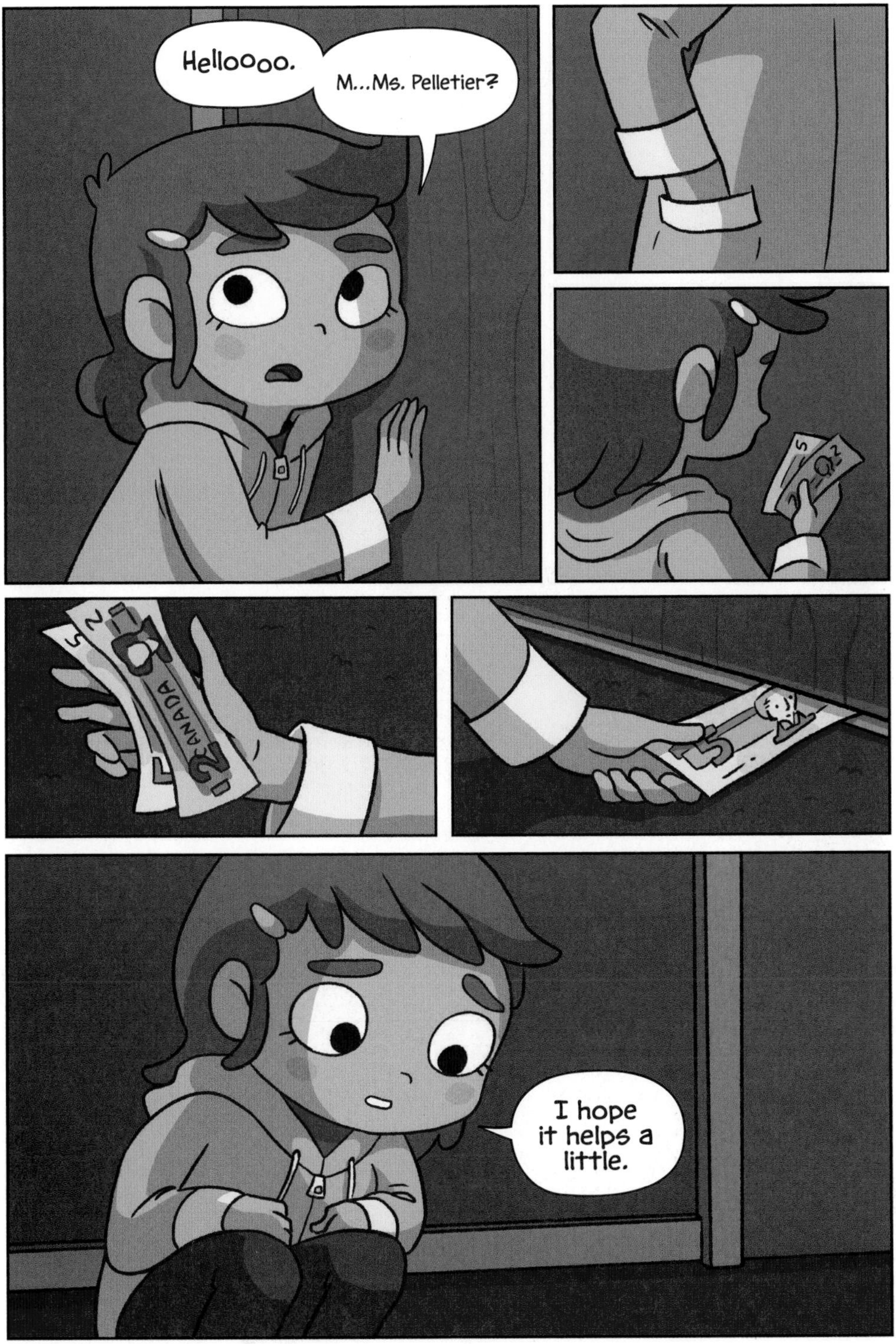
Hellooooo.
M...Ms. Pelletier?
CANADA
I hope it helps a little.

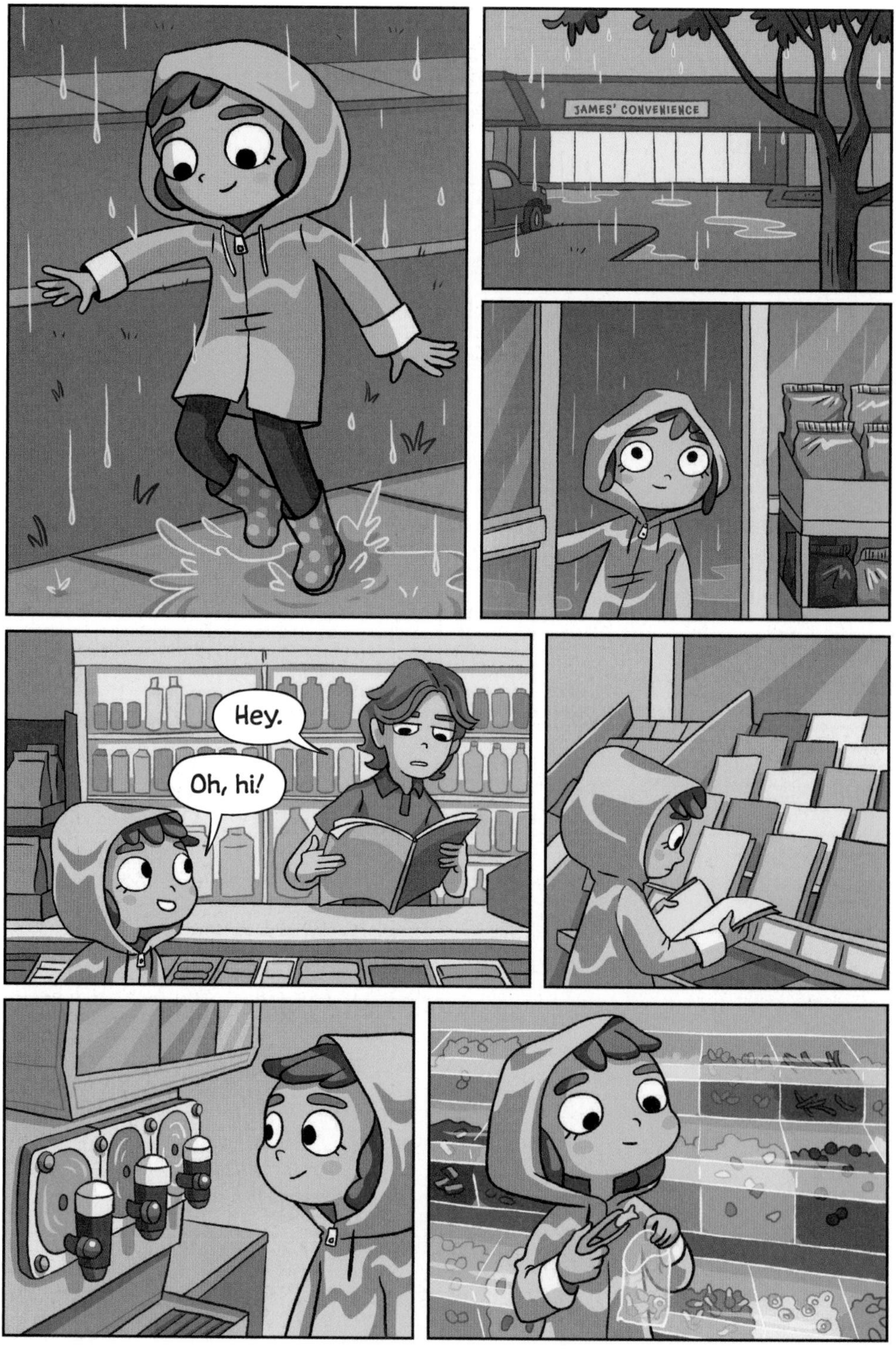
JAMES' CONVENIENCE
Oh, hi!
Hey.

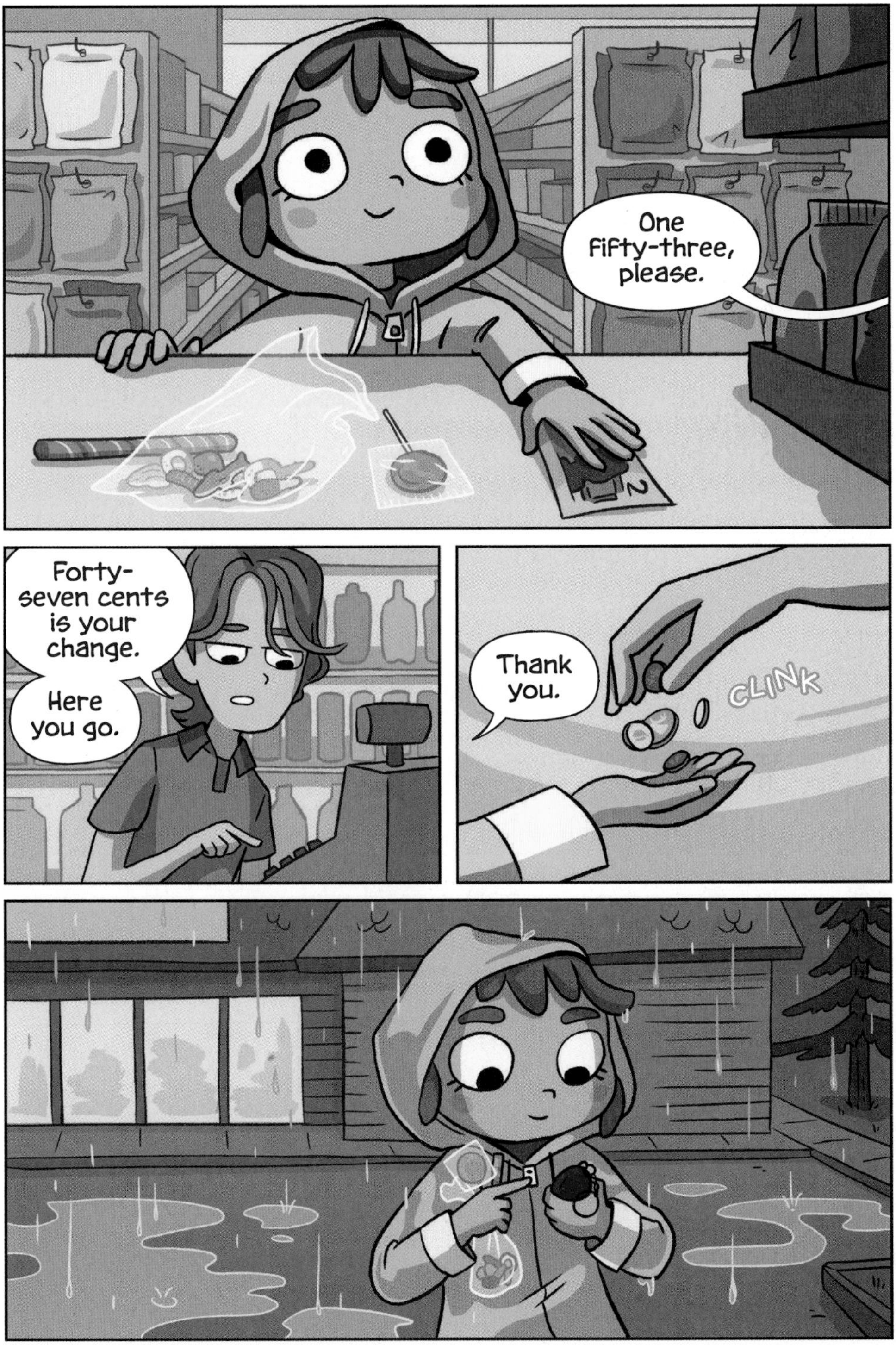
One fifty-three, please.
Forty-seven cents is your change.
Here you go.
Thank you.
CLINK

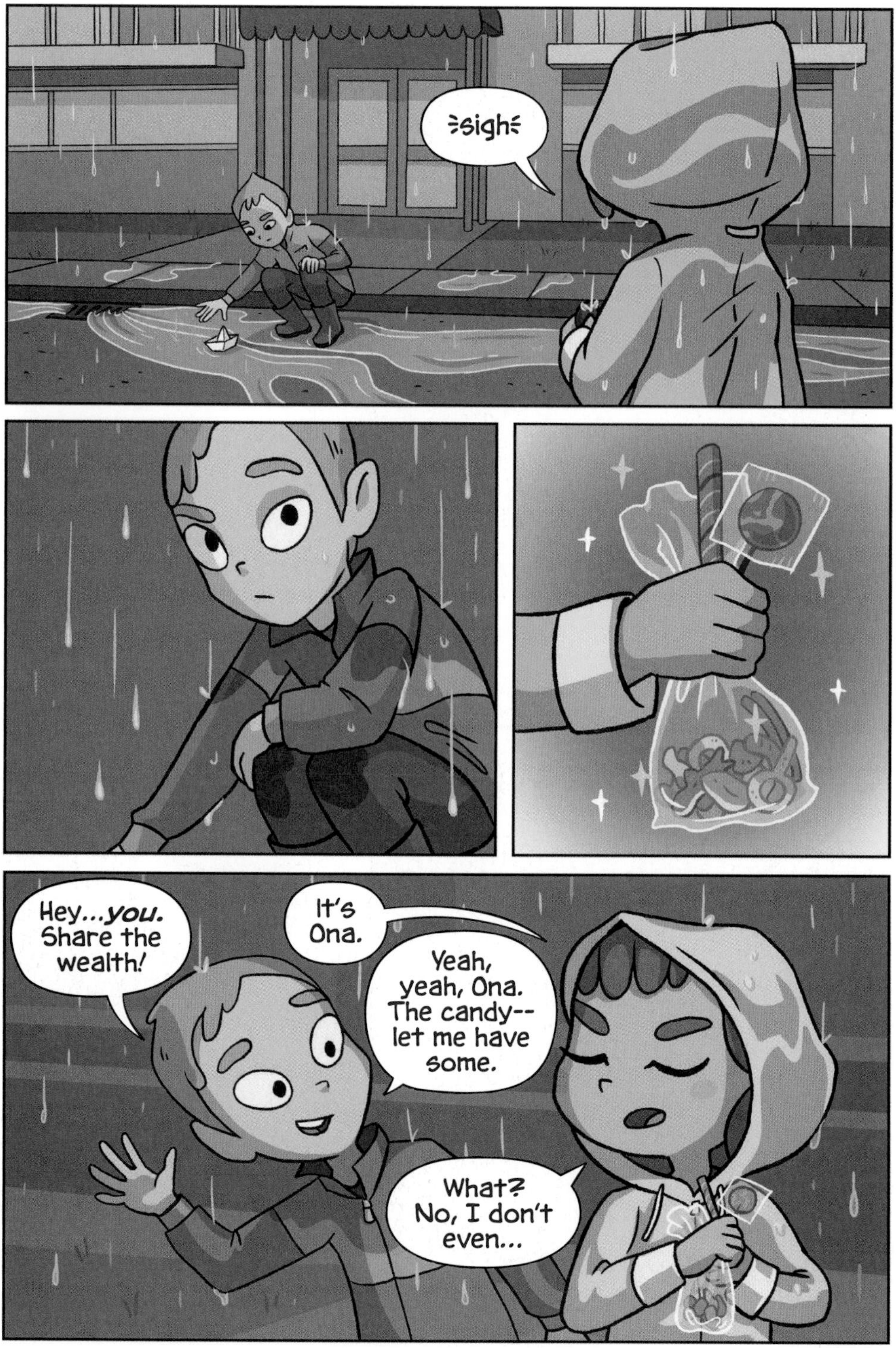

≋sigh≋
Hey...*you.* Share the wealth!
It's Ona.
Yeah, yeah, Ona. The candy-- let me have some.
What? No, I don't even...

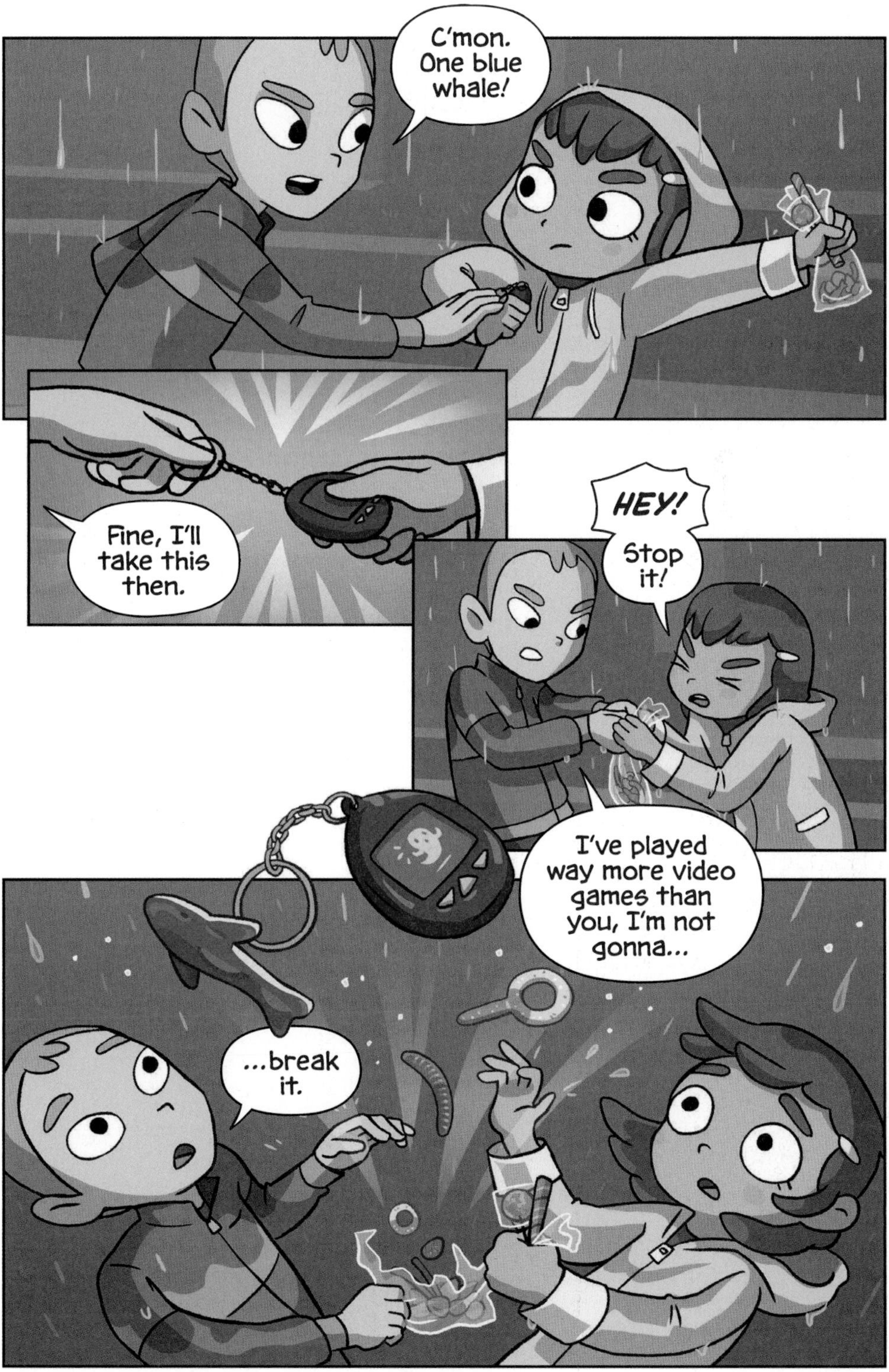

C'mon. One blue whale!
Fine, I'll take this then.
HEY!
Stop it!
I've played way more video games than you, I'm not gonna...
...break it.

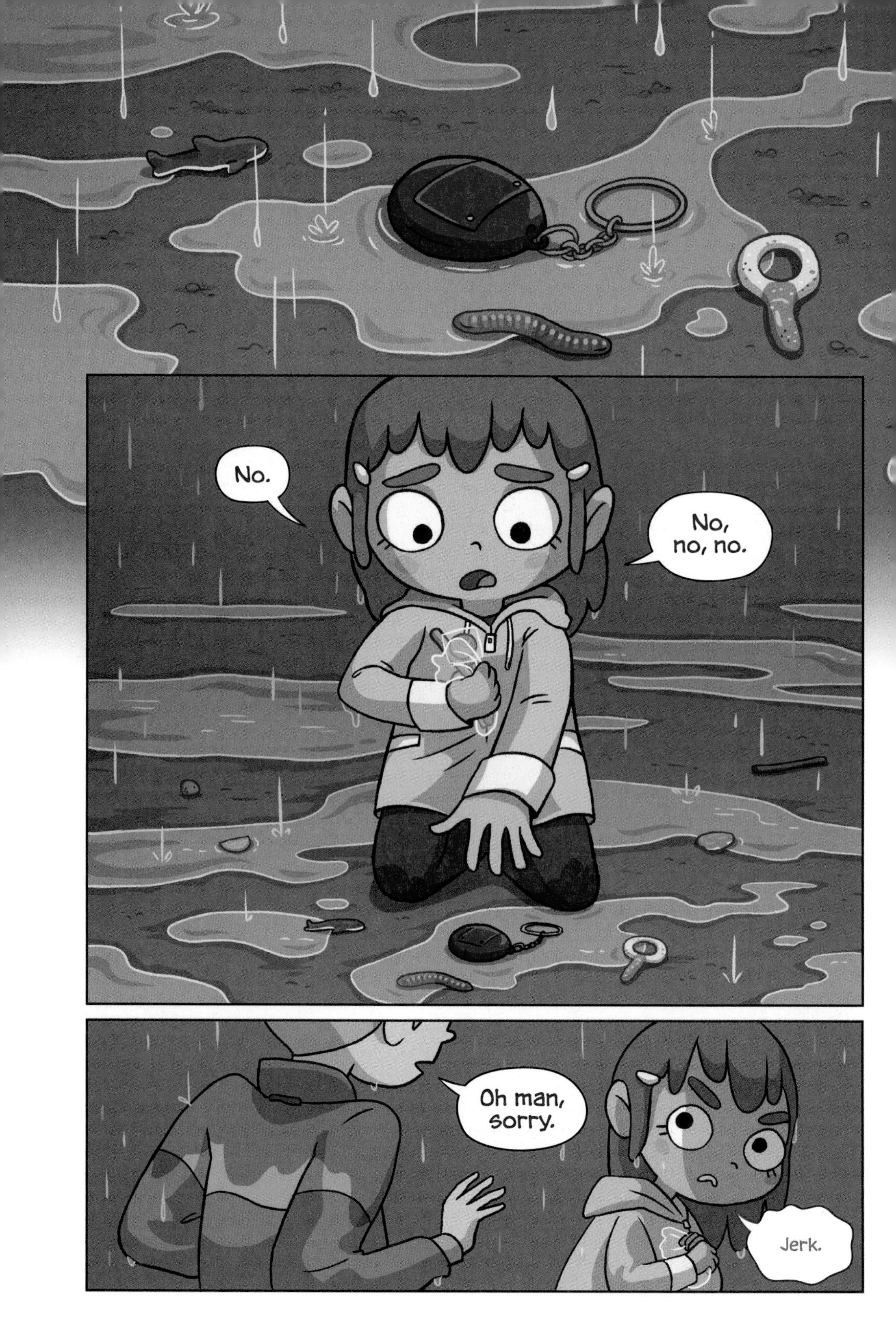
No.
No, no, no.
Oh man, sorry.
Jerk.

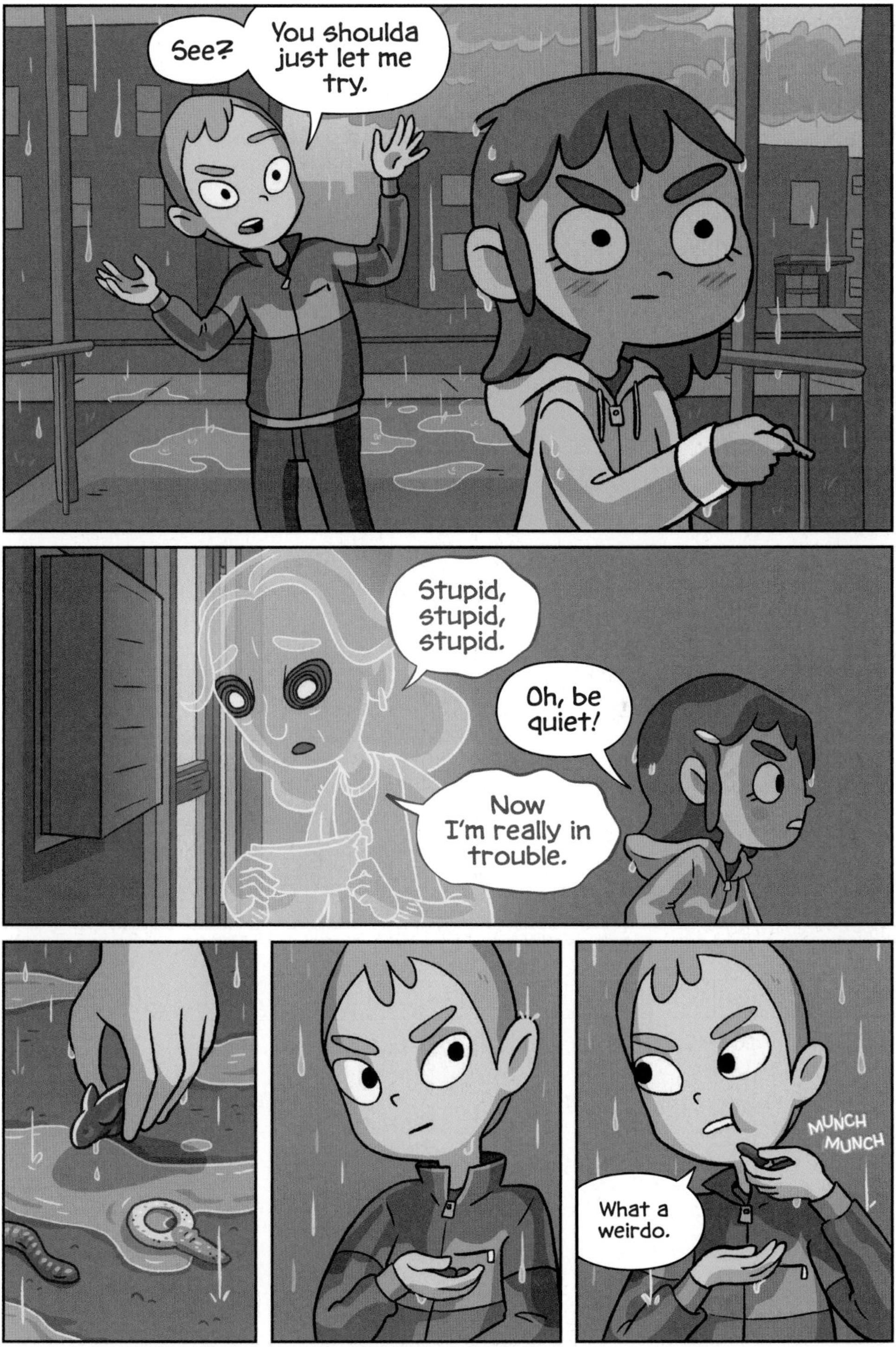
See?
You shoulda just let me try.
Stupid, stupid, stupid.
Oh, be quiet!
Now I'm really in trouble.
MUNCH MUNCH
What a weirdo.

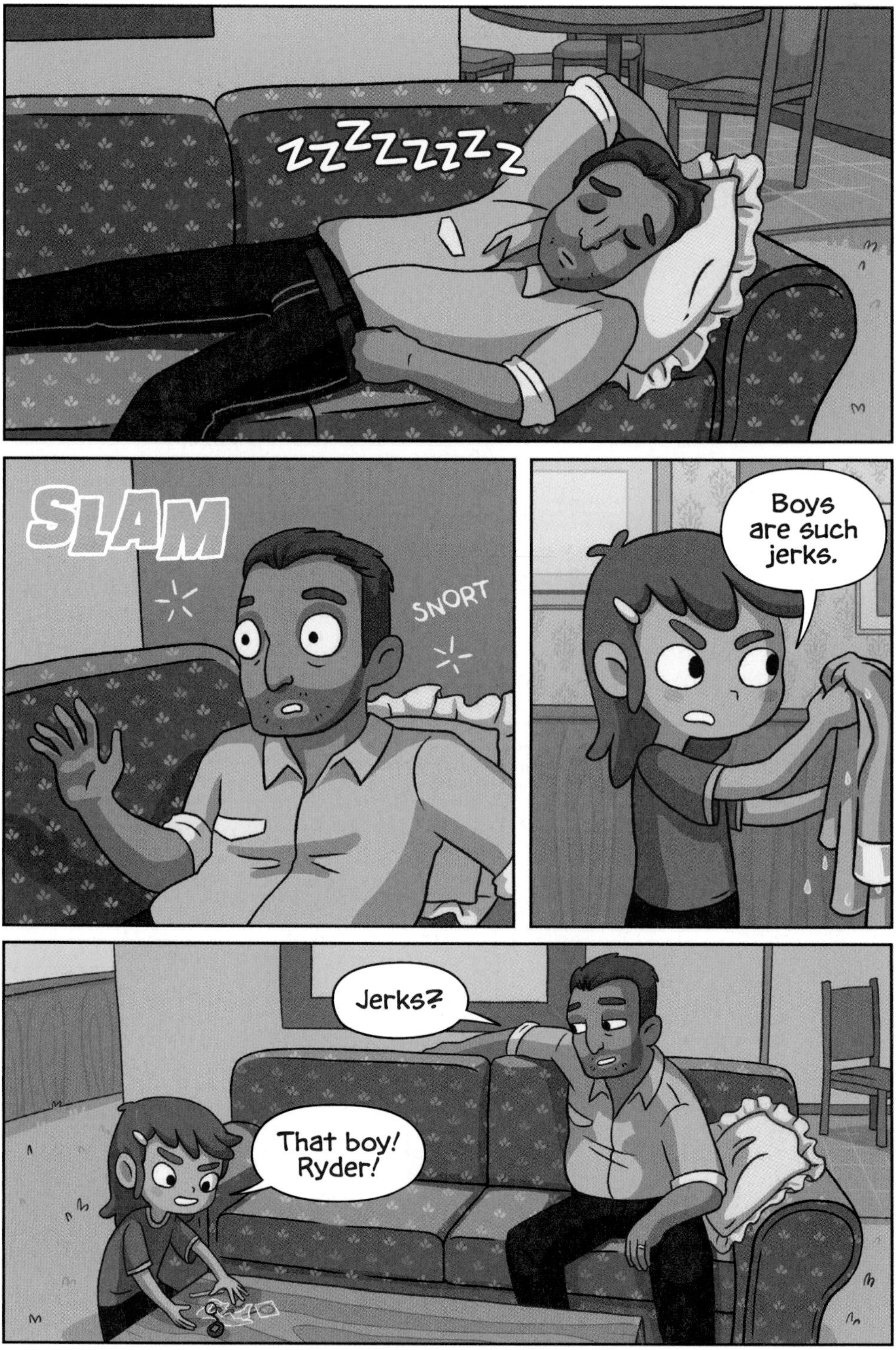
ZZZZZZZZ
SLAM
SNORT
Boys are such jerks.
Jerks?
That boy! Ryder!

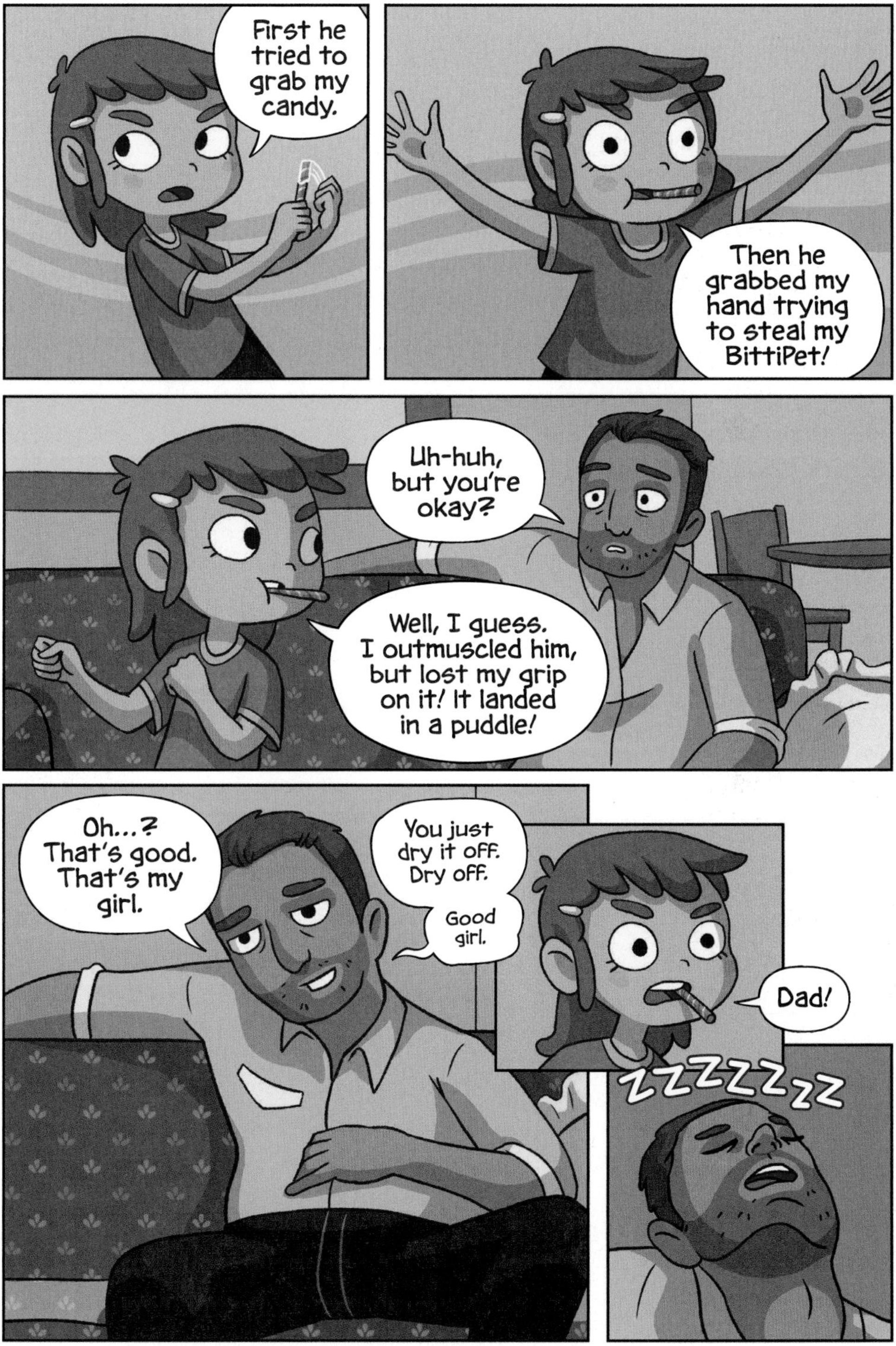
First he tried to grab my candy.
Then he grabbed my hand trying to steal my BittiPet!
Uh-huh, but you're okay?
Well, I guess. I outmuscled him, but lost my grip on it! It landed in a puddle!
Oh...? That's good. That's my girl.
You just dry it off. Dry off.
Good girl.
Dad!
ZZZZZZzZ

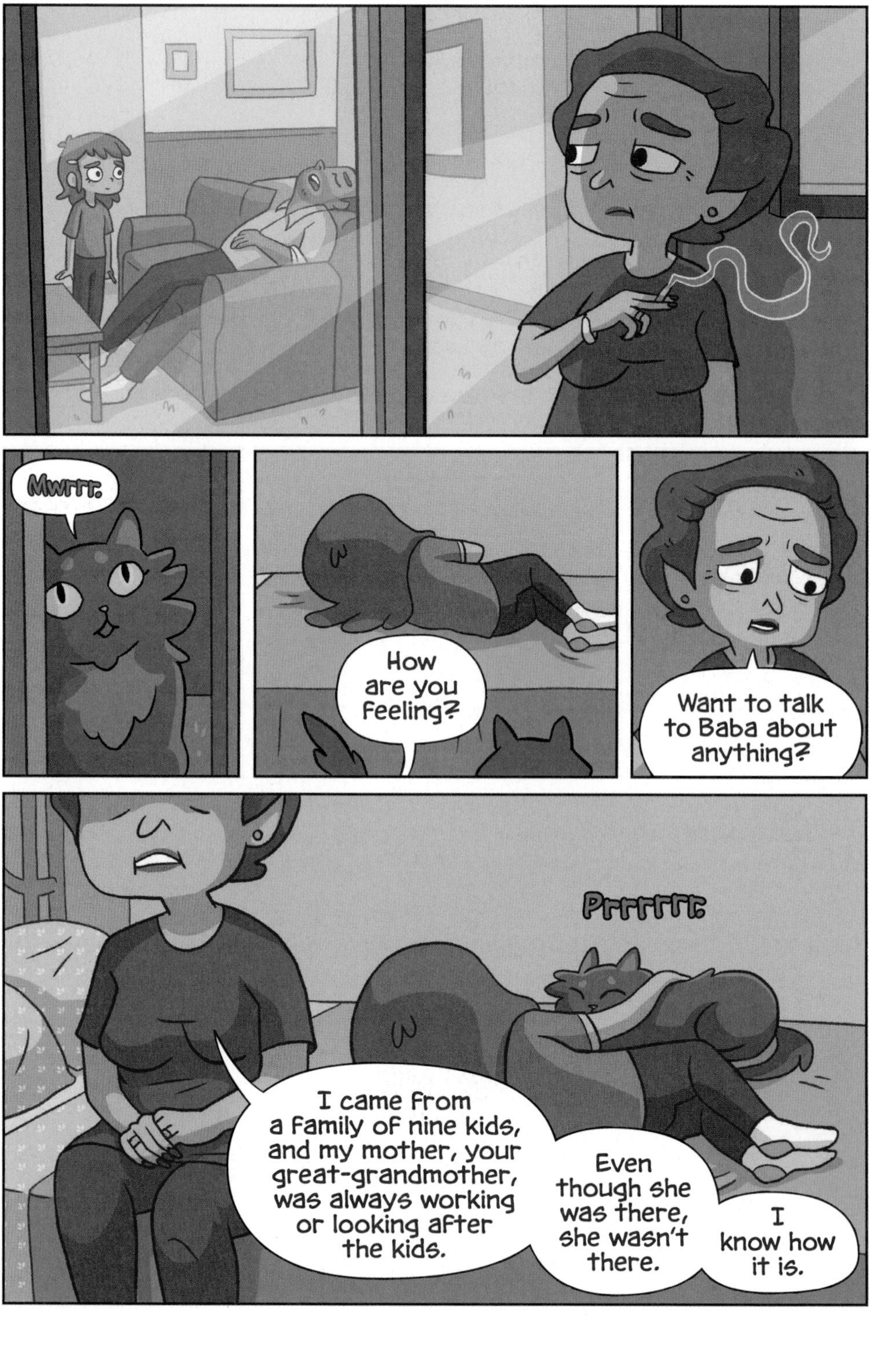
Mwrrr.
How are you feeling?
Want to talk to Baba about anything?
Prrrrrr.
I came from a family of nine kids, and my mother, your great-grandmother, was always working or looking after the kids.
Even though she was there, she wasn't there.
I know how it is.

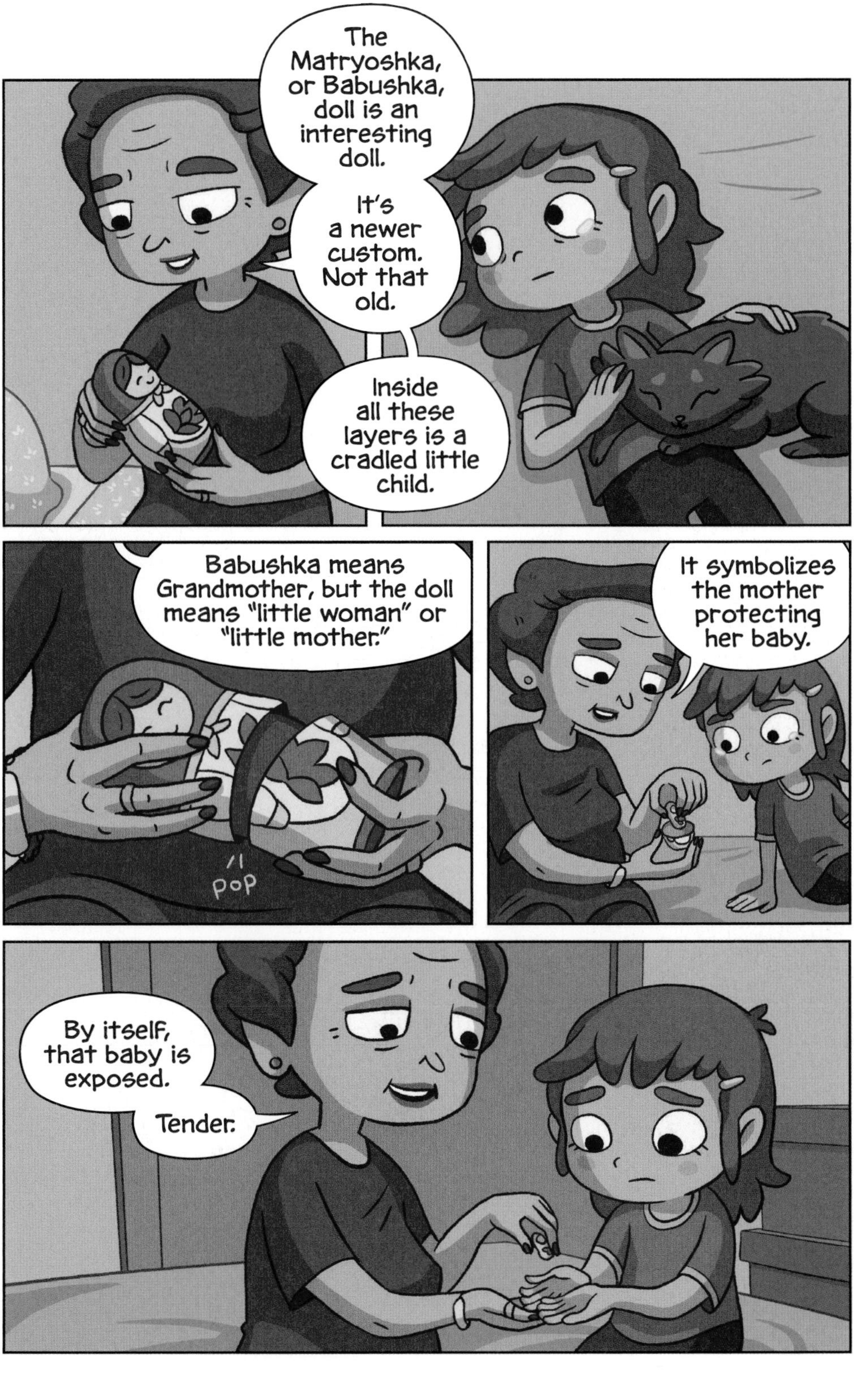
The Matryoshka, or Babushka, doll is an interesting doll.
It's a newer custom. Not that old.
Inside all these layers is a cradled little child.
Babushka means Grandmother, but the doll means "little woman" or "little mother."
POP
It symbolizes the mother protecting her baby.
By itself, that baby is exposed.
Tender.

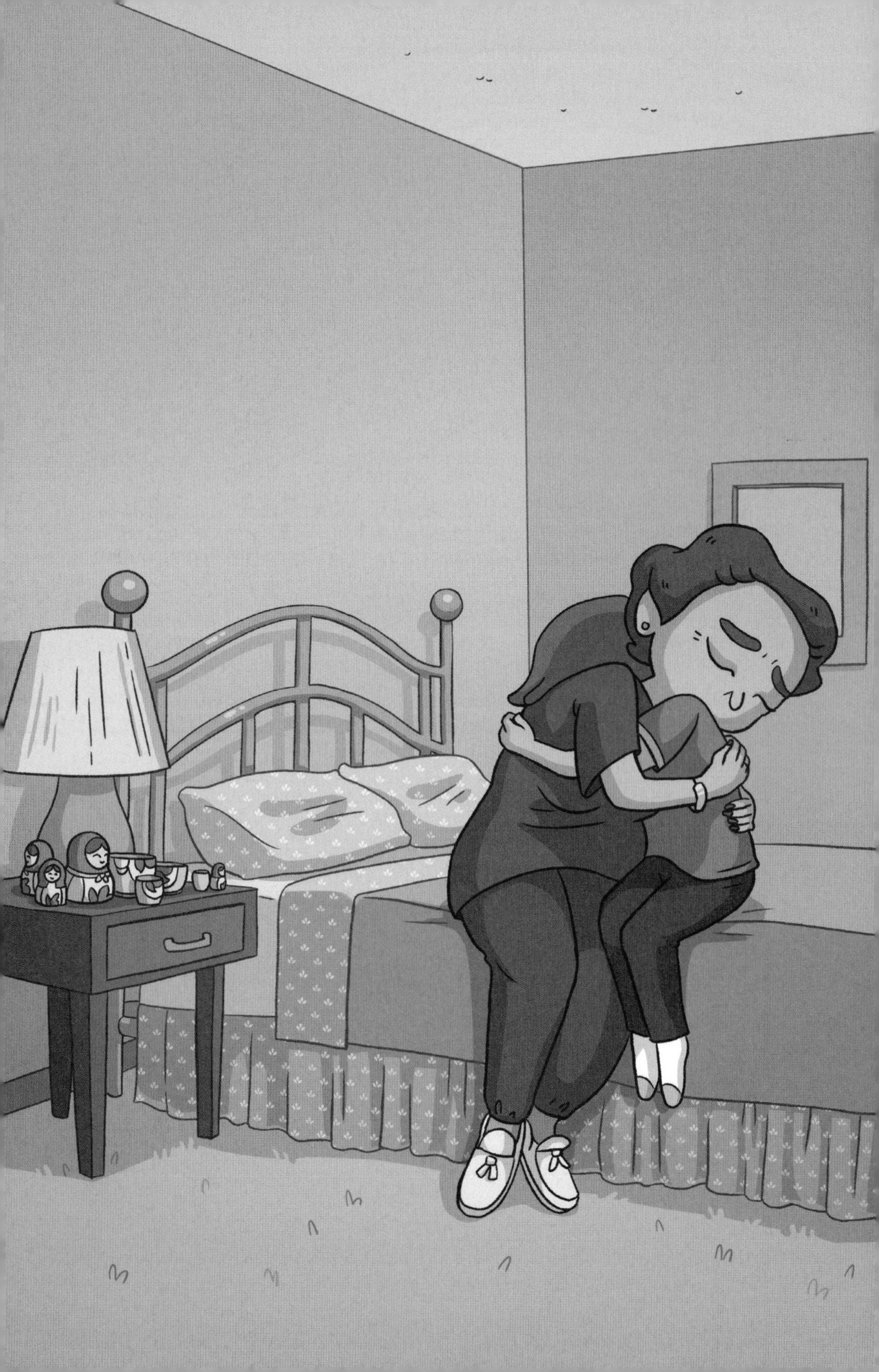

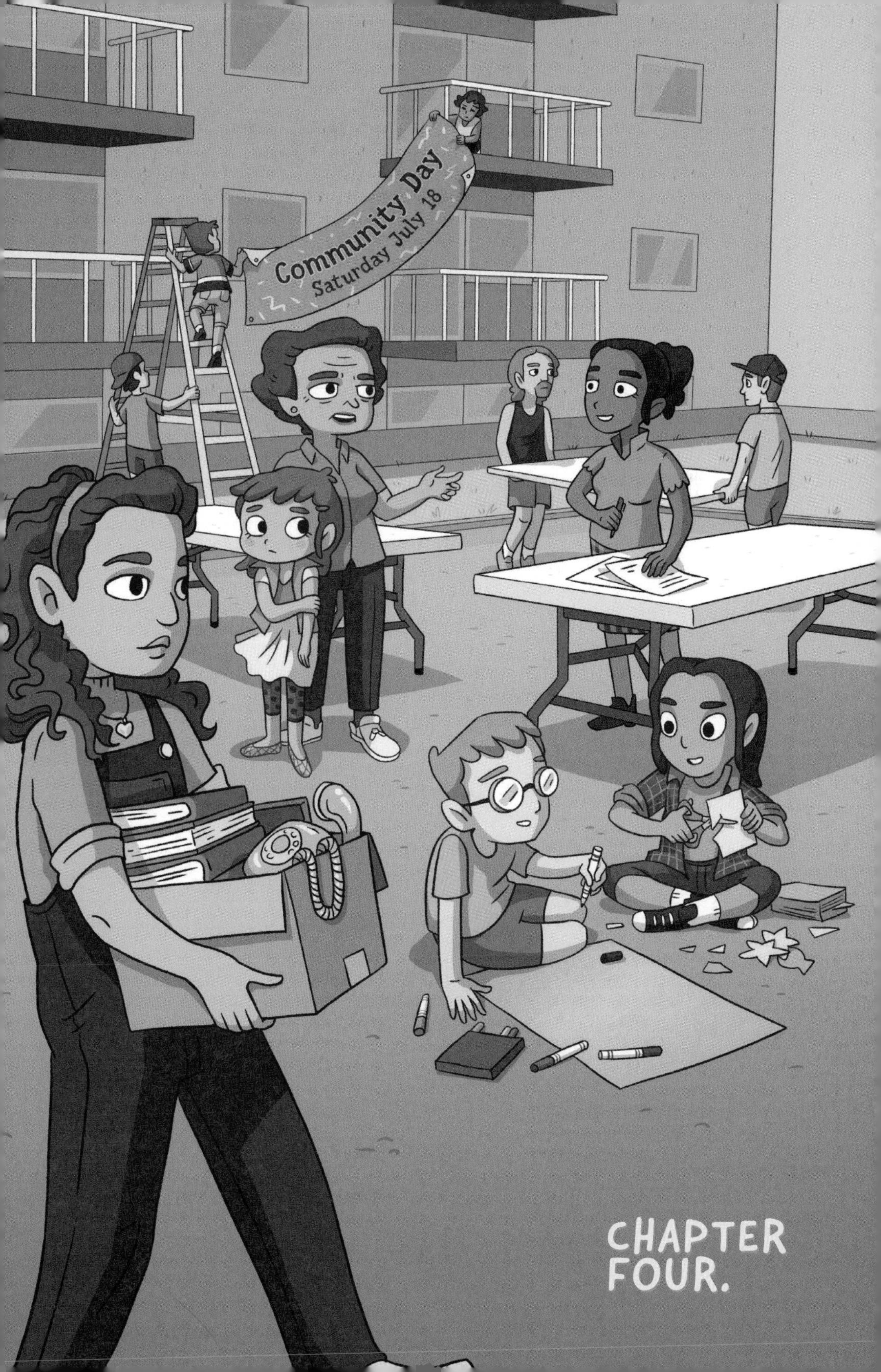
Community Day
Saturday July 18

CHAPTER FOUR.

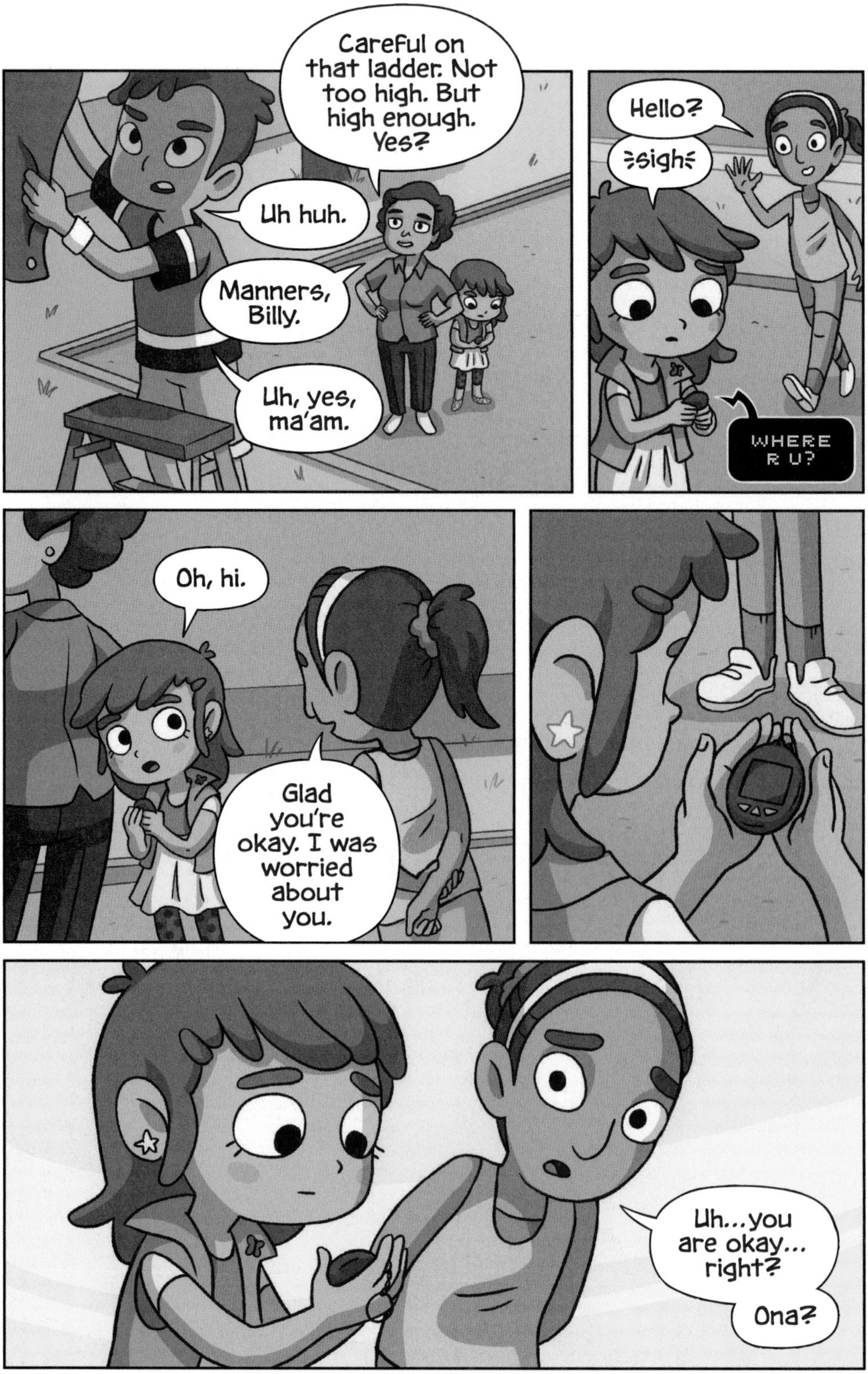
Careful on that ladder. Not too high. But high enough. Yes?
Uh huh.
Manners, Billy.
Uh, yes, ma'am.
Hello?
sigh
WHERE R U?
Oh, hi.
Glad you're okay. I was worried about you.
Uh...you are okay... right?
Ona?

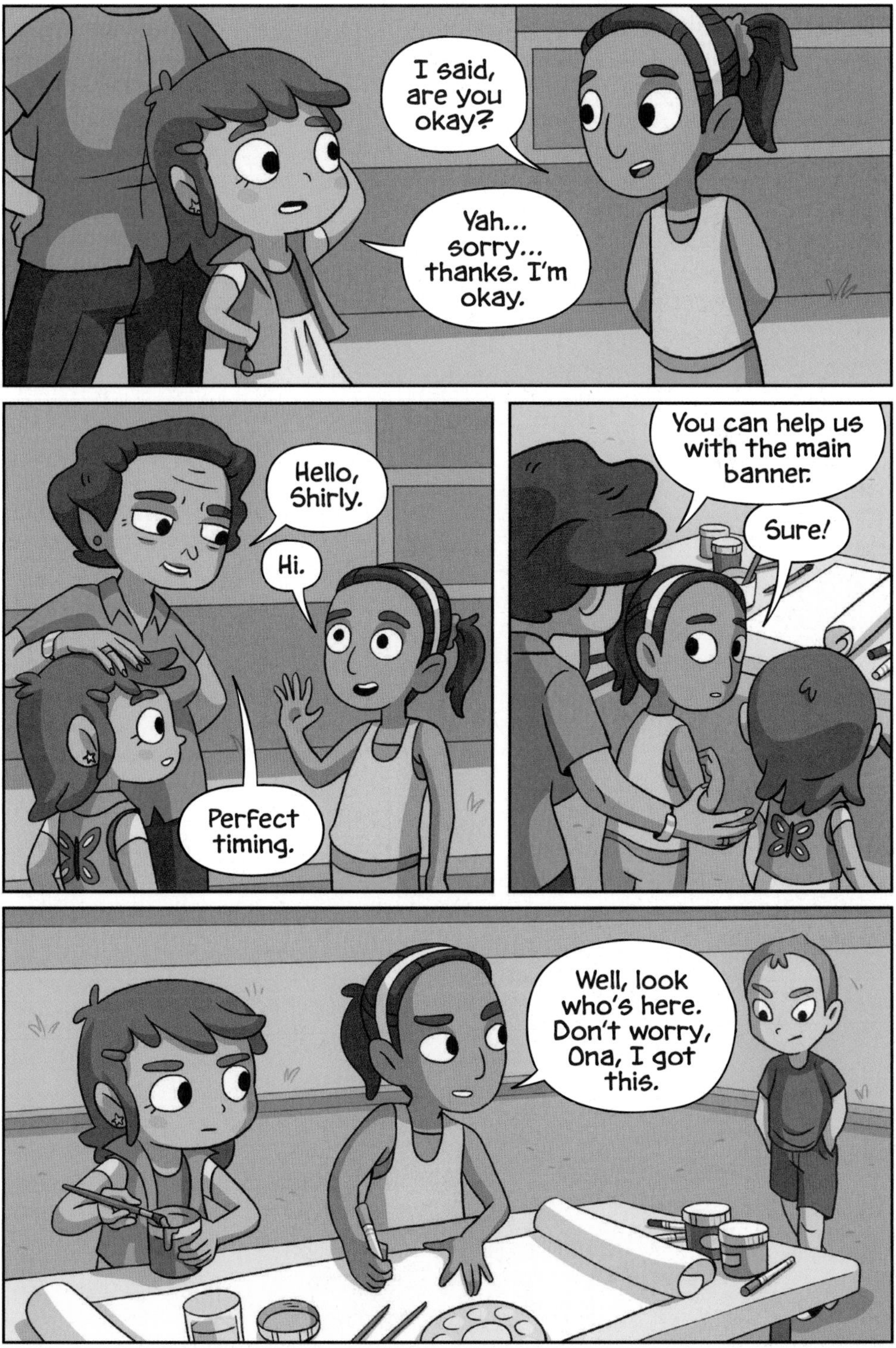

I said, are you okay?
Yah... sorry... thanks. I'm okay.
Hello, Shirly.
Hi.
Perfect timing.
You can help us with the main banner.
Sure!
Well, look who's here. Don't worry, Ona, I got this.

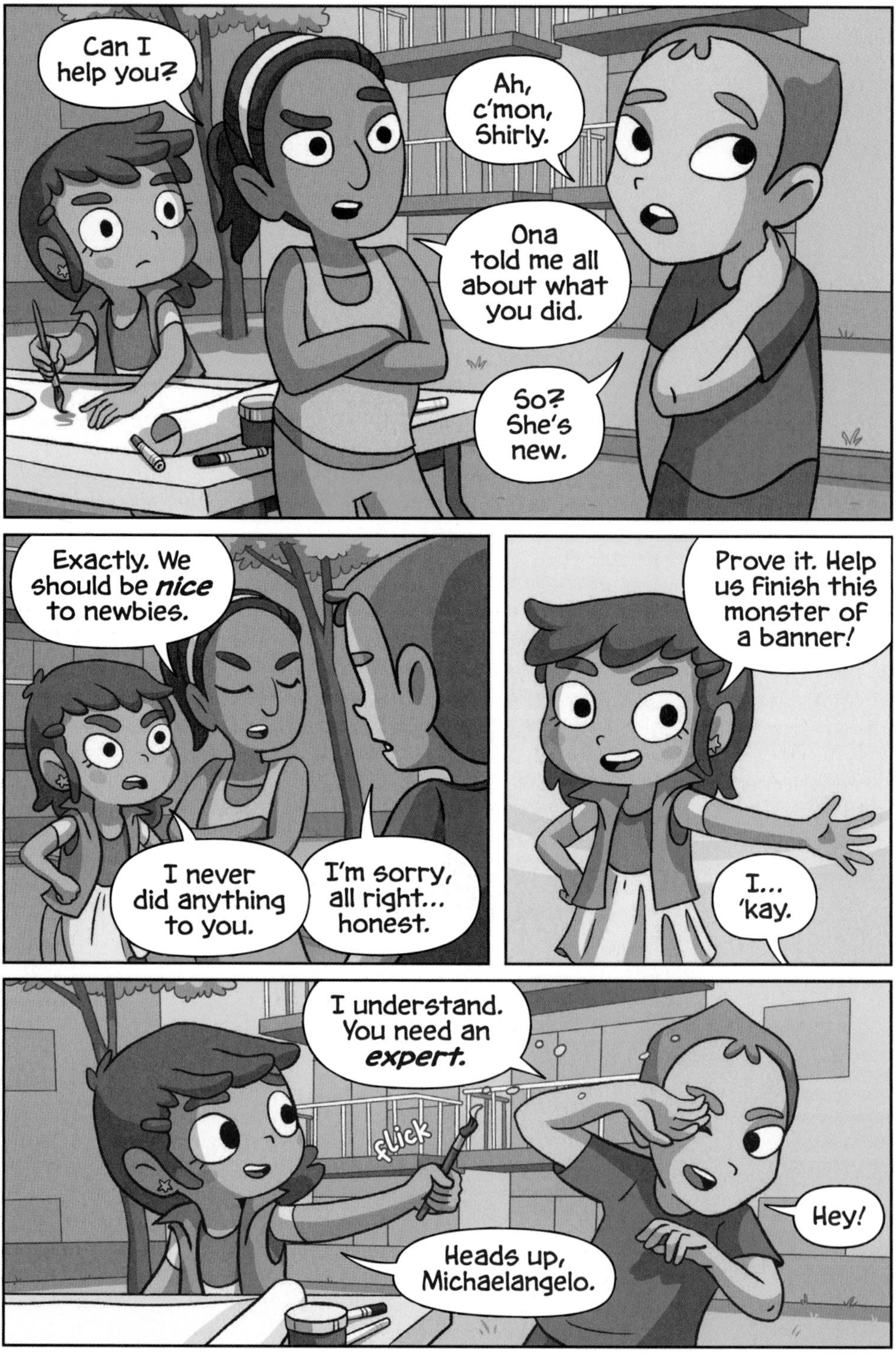
Can I help you?
Ah, c'mon, Shirly.
Ona told me all about what you did.
So? She's new.
Exactly. We should be *nice* to newbies.
I never did anything to you.
I'm sorry, all right... honest.
Prove it. Help us finish this monster of a banner!
I... 'kay.
I understand. You need an *expert*.
flick
Hey!
Heads up, Michaelangelo.

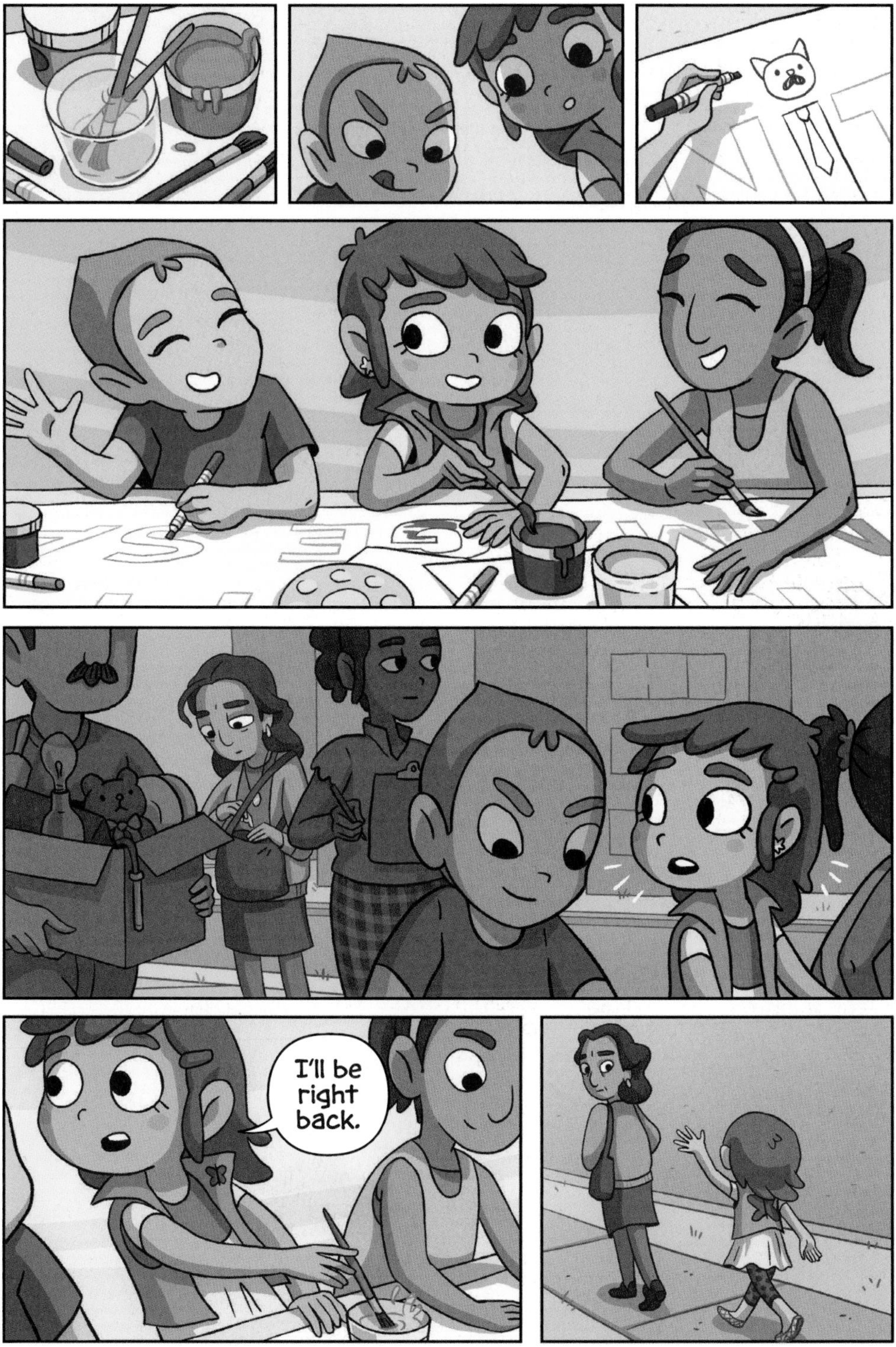
I'll be right back.

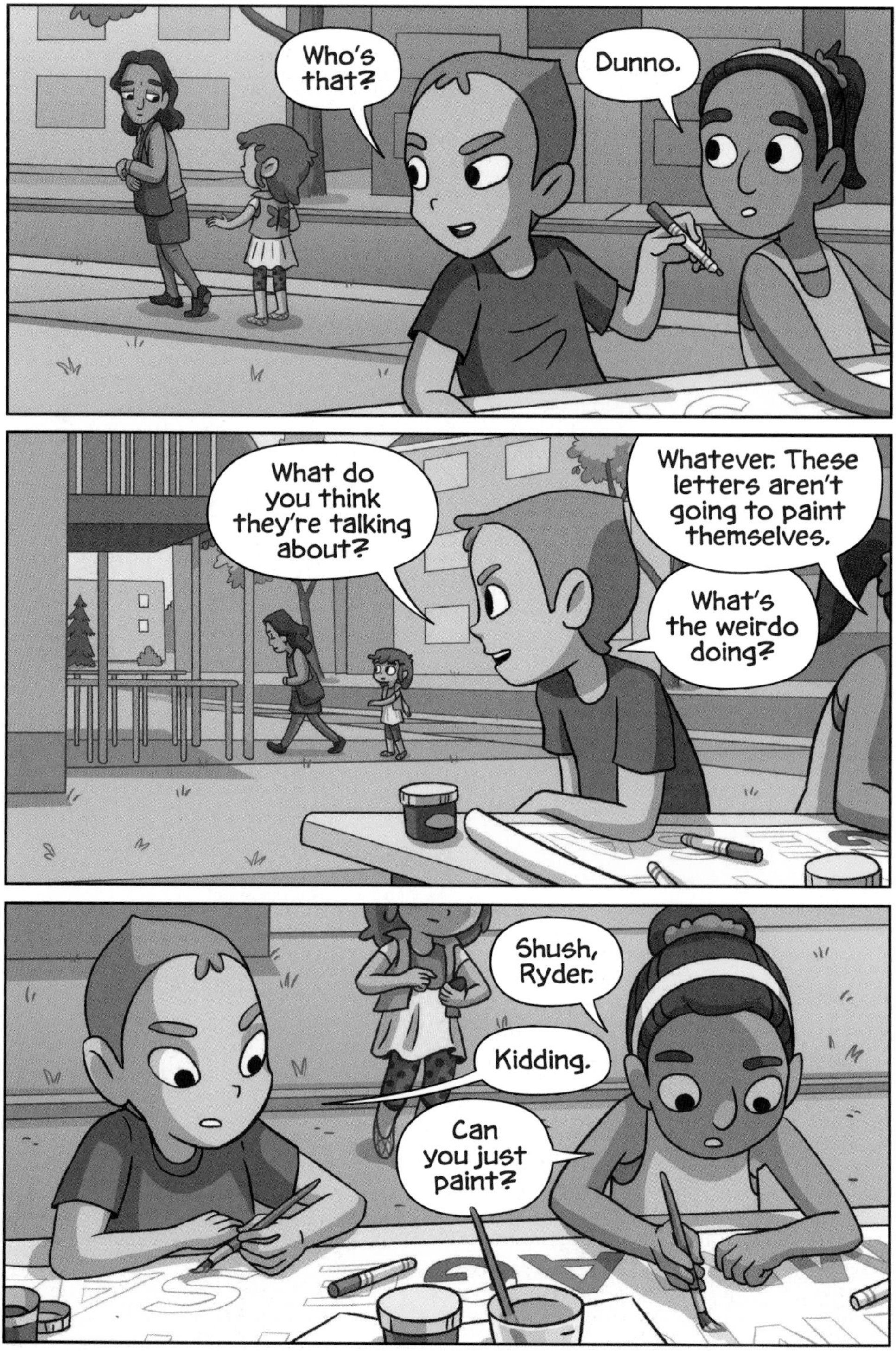
Who's that?
Dunno.
What do you think they're talking about?
Whatever. These letters aren't going to paint themselves.
What's the weirdo doing?
Shush, Ryder.
Kidding.
Can you just paint?

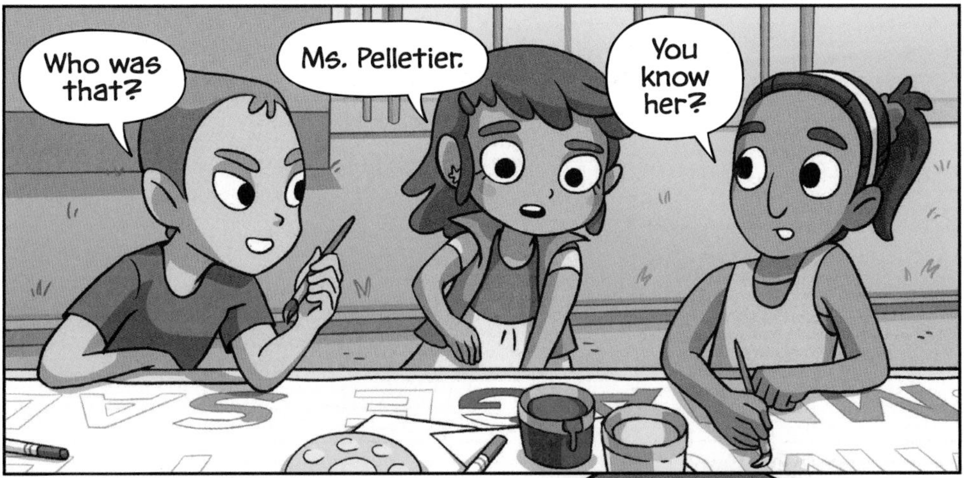
Who was that?
Ms. Pelletier.
You know her?

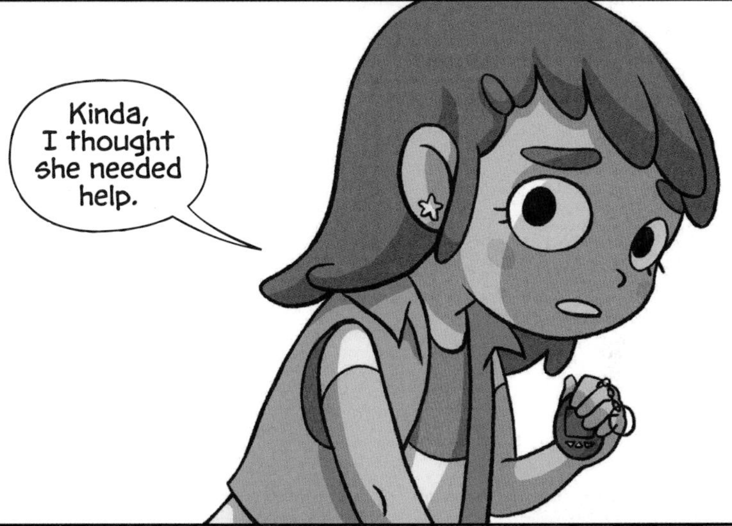
Kinda, I thought she needed help.

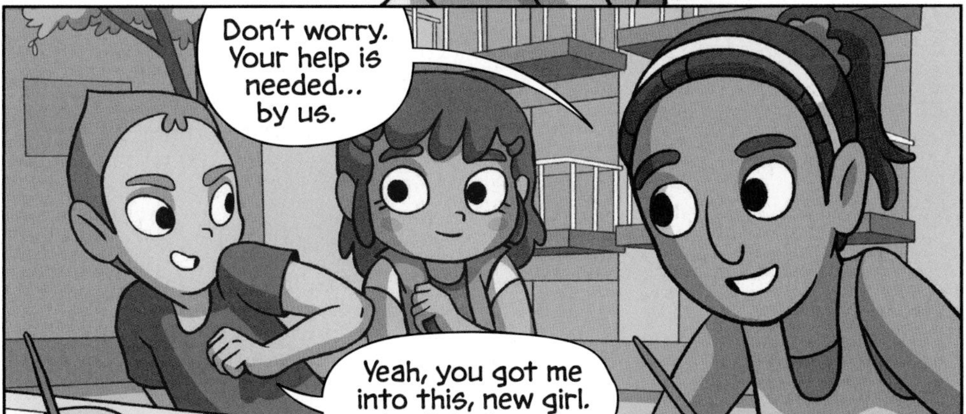
Don't worry. Your help is needed... by us.
Yeah, you got me into this, new girl. Can't bail now.

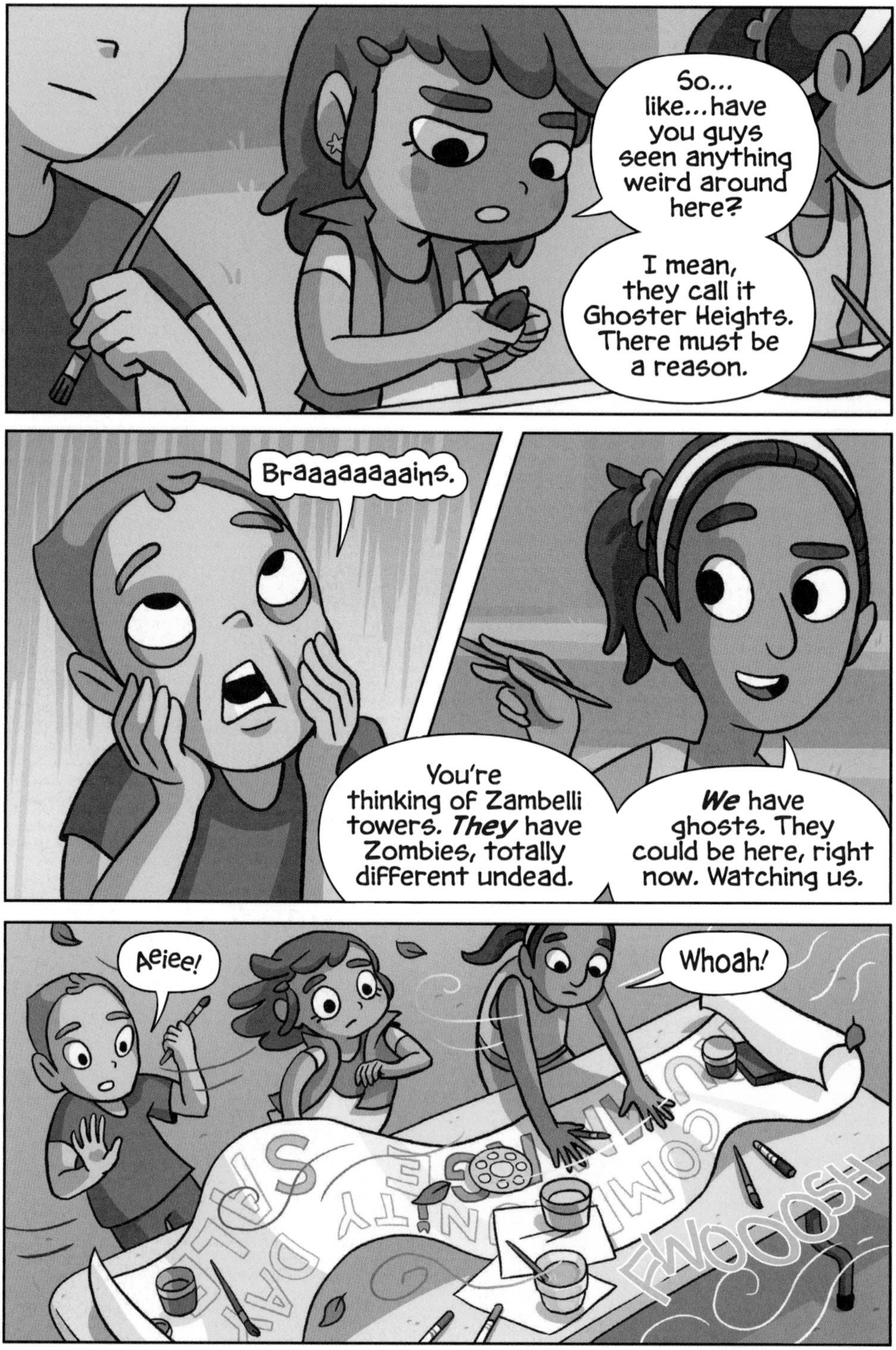
So... like...have you guys seen anything weird around here?
I mean, they call it Ghoster Heights. There must be a reason.
Braaaaaaaains.
You're thinking of Zambelli towers. *They* have Zombies, totally different undead.
We have ghosts. They could be here, right now. Watching us.
Aeiee!
Whoah!
FWOOOSH

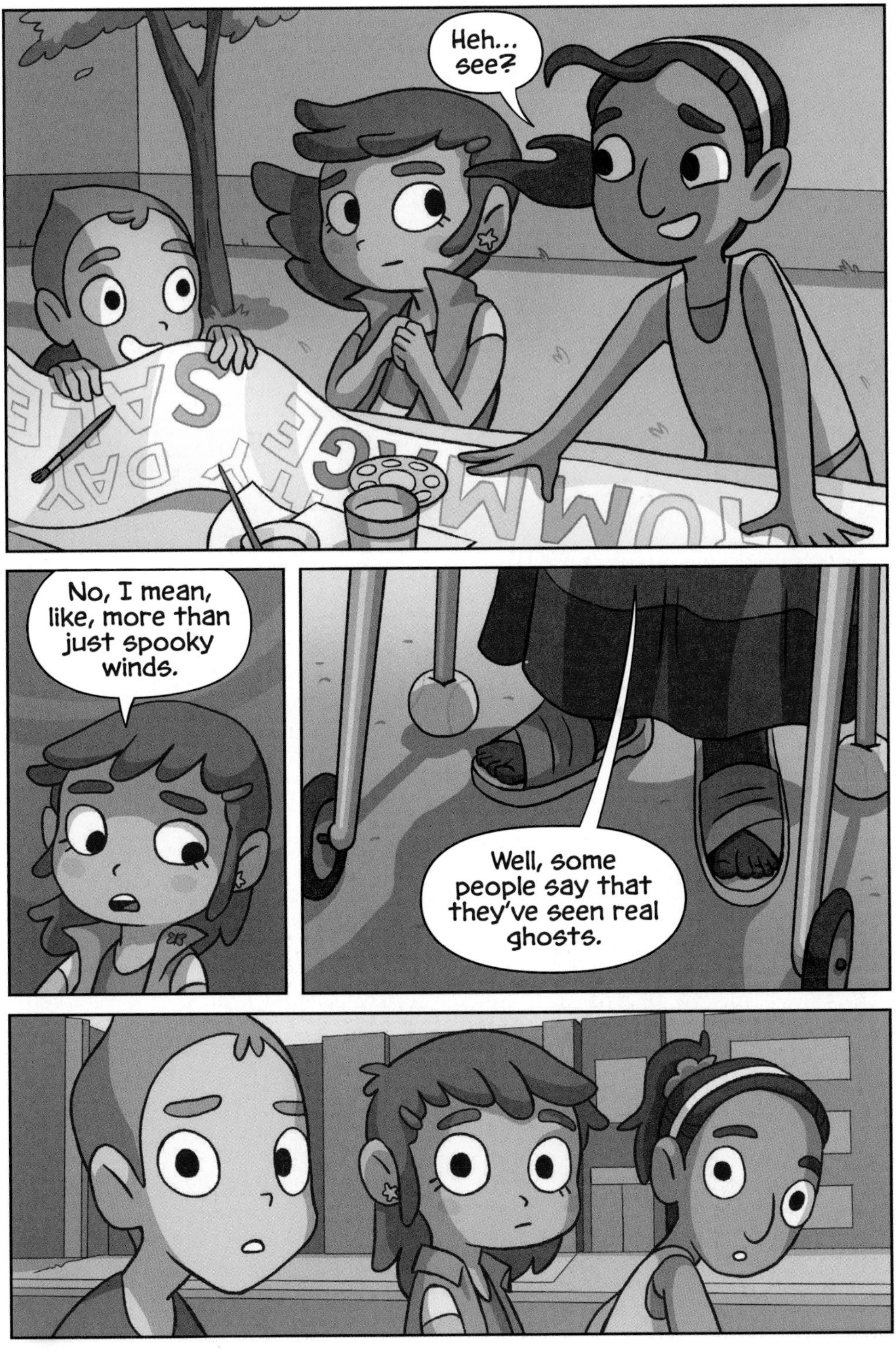
Heh... see?
No, I mean, like, more than just spooky winds.
Well, some people say that they've seen real ghosts.

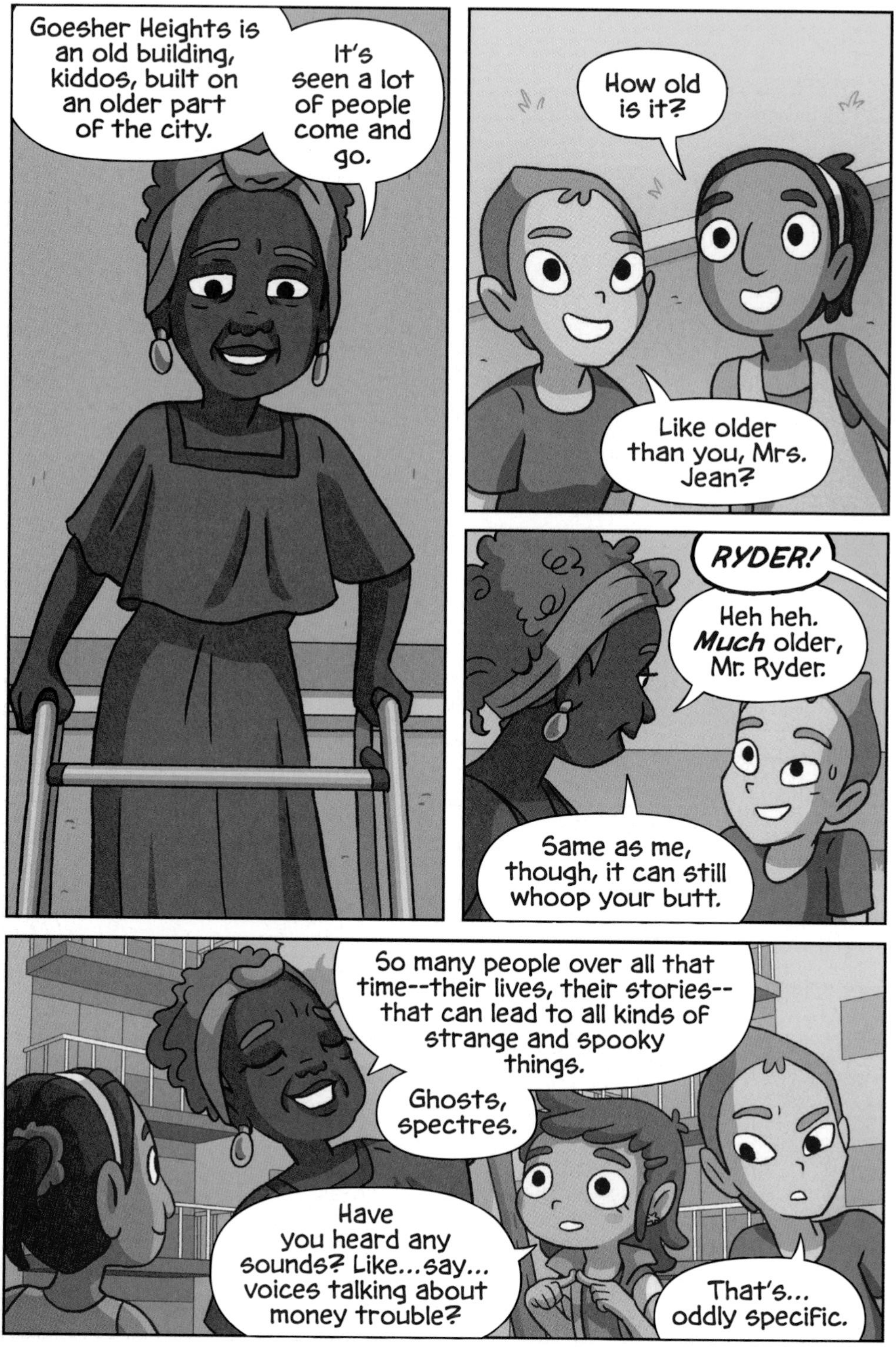
Goesher Heights is an old building, kiddos, built on an older part of the city.
It's seen a lot of people come and go.
How old is it?
Like older than you, Mrs. Jean?
RYDER!
Heh heh. *Much* older, Mr. Ryder.
Same as me, though, it can still whoop your butt.
So many people over all that time--their lives, their stories--that can lead to all kinds of strange and spooky things.
Ghosts, spectres.
Have you heard any sounds? Like...say... voices talking about money trouble?
That's... oddly specific.

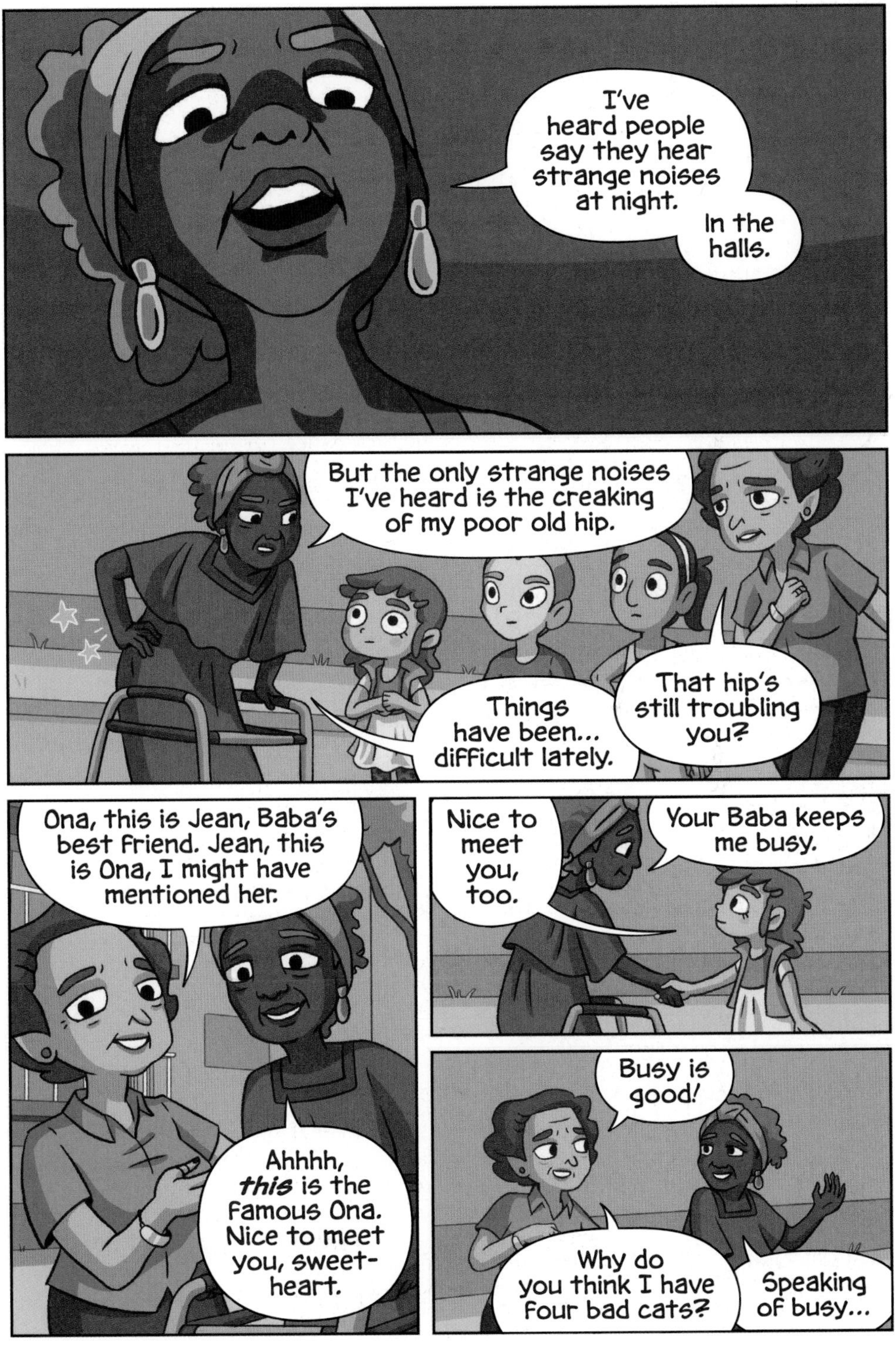
I've heard people say they hear strange noises at night.
In the halls.
But the only strange noises I've heard is the creaking of my poor old hip.
That hip's still troubling you?
Things have been... difficult lately.
Ona, this is Jean, Baba's best friend. Jean, this is Ona, I might have mentioned her.
Ahhhh, *this* is the famous Ona. Nice to meet you, sweet-heart.
Nice to meet you, too.
Your Baba keeps me busy.
Busy is good!
Why do you think I have four bad cats?
Speaking of busy...

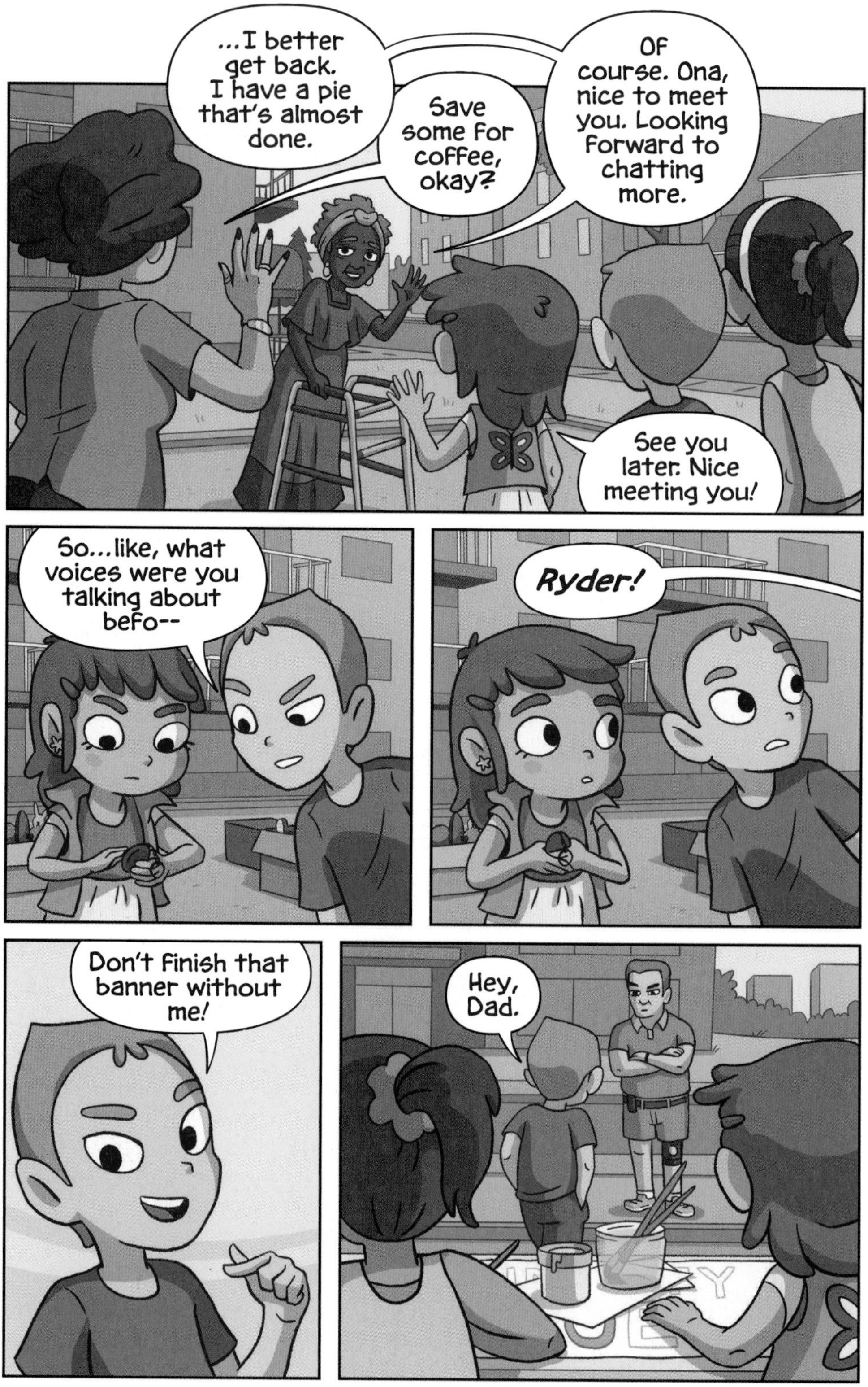
...I better get back. I have a pie that's almost done.
Save some for coffee, okay?
Of course. Ona, nice to meet you. Looking forward to chatting more.
See you later. Nice meeting you!
So...like, what voices were you talking about befo--
Ryder!
Don't finish that banner without me!
Hey, Dad.

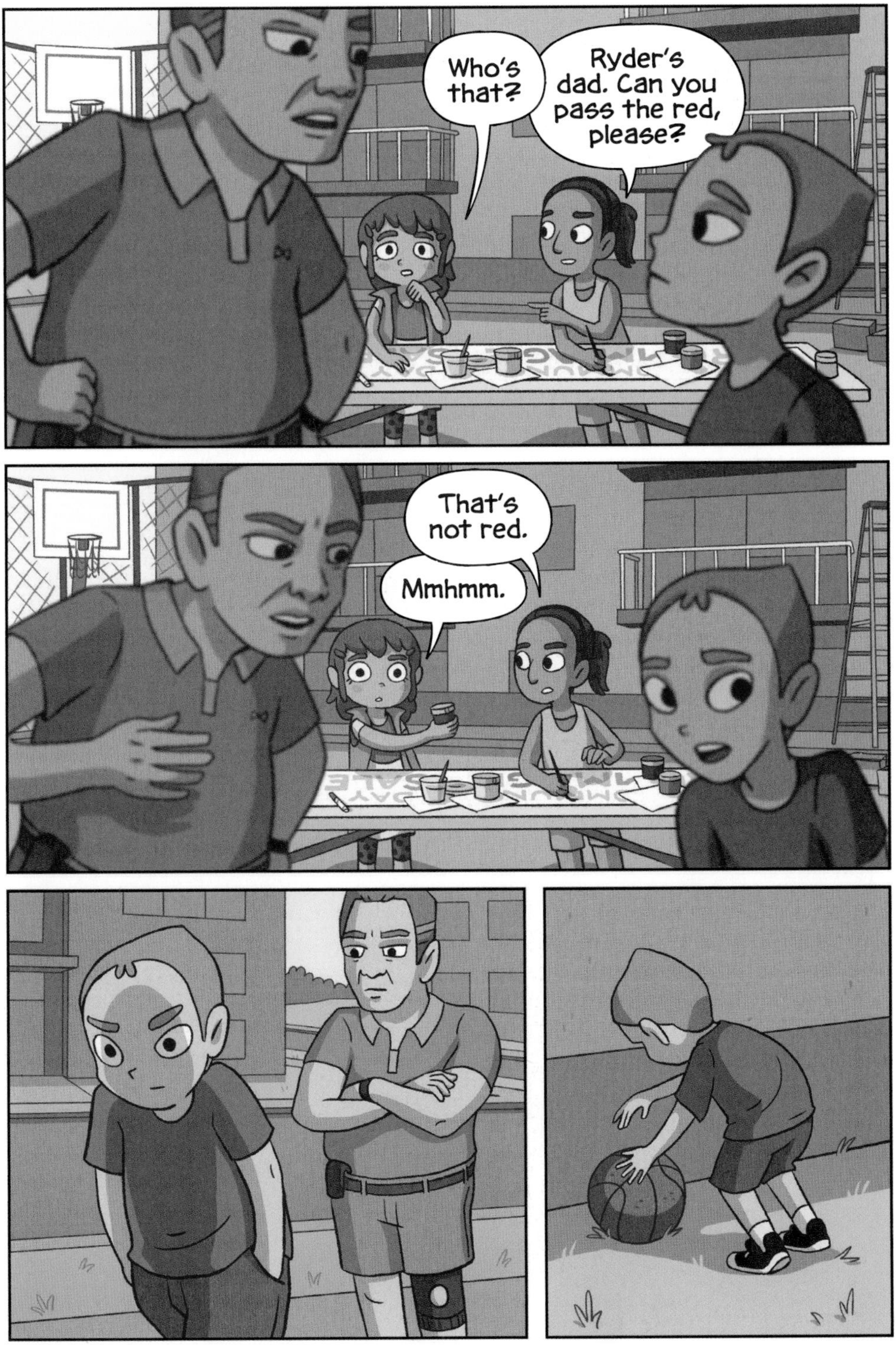
Who's that?
Ryder's dad. Can you pass the red, please?
That's not red.
Mmhmm.

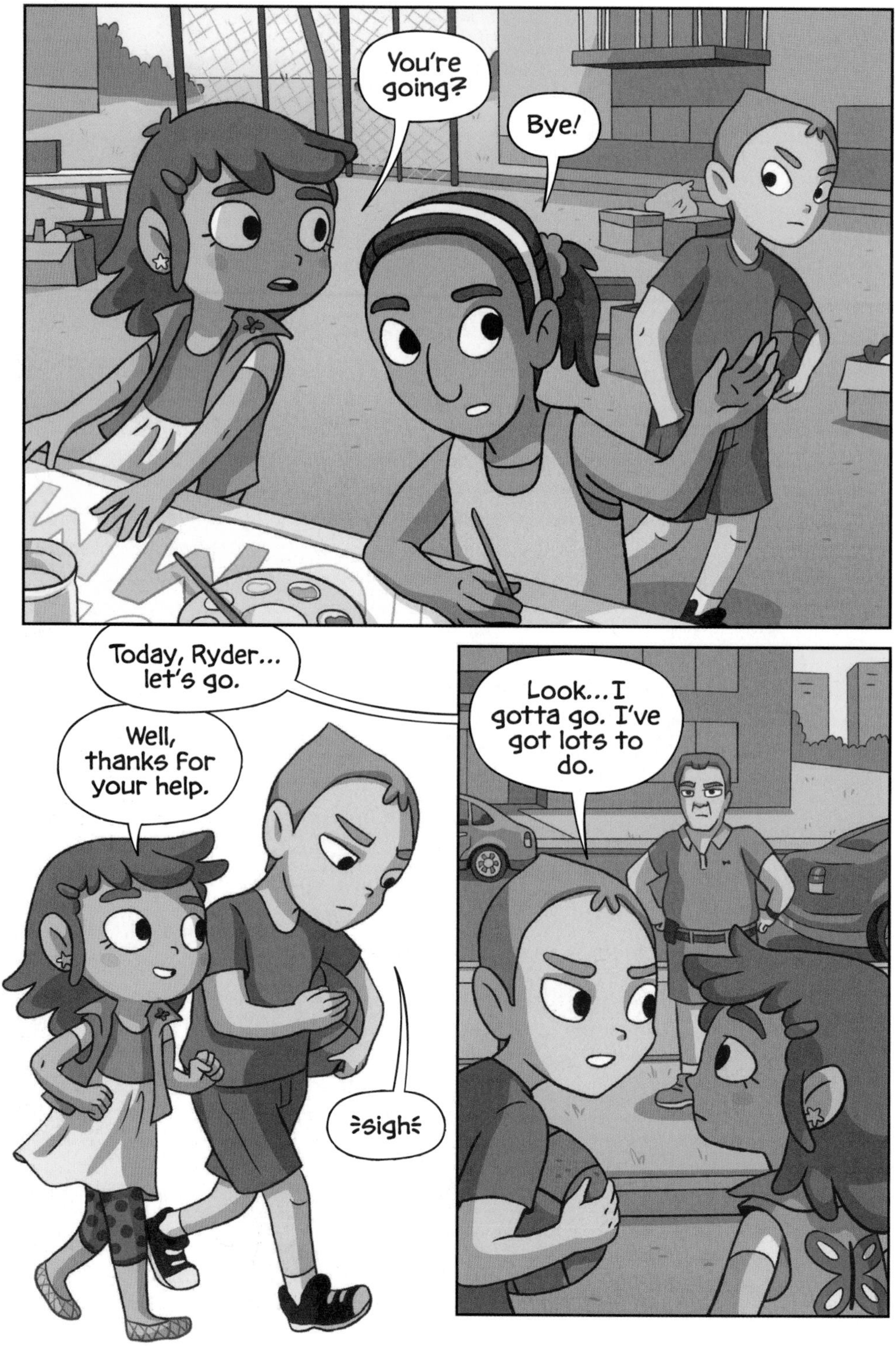
You're going?
Bye!
Today, Ryder... let's go.
Well, thanks for your help.
Look...I gotta go. I've got lots to do.
sigh

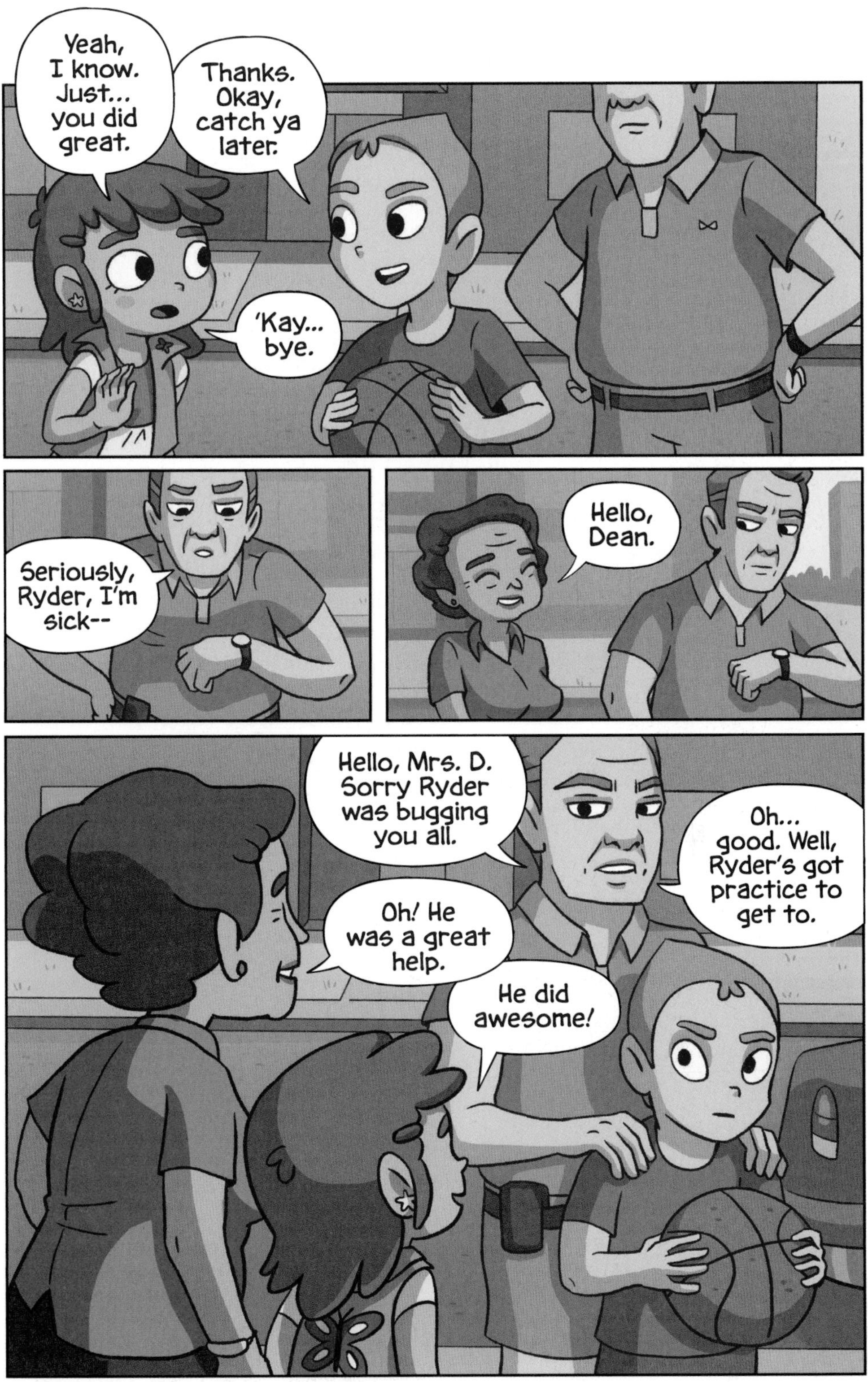
Yeah, I know. Just... you did great.
Thanks. Okay, catch ya later.
'Kay... bye.
Seriously, Ryder, I'm sick--
Hello, Dean.
Hello, Mrs. D. Sorry Ryder was bugging you all.
Oh! He was a great help.
He did awesome!
Oh... good. Well, Ryder's got practice to get to.

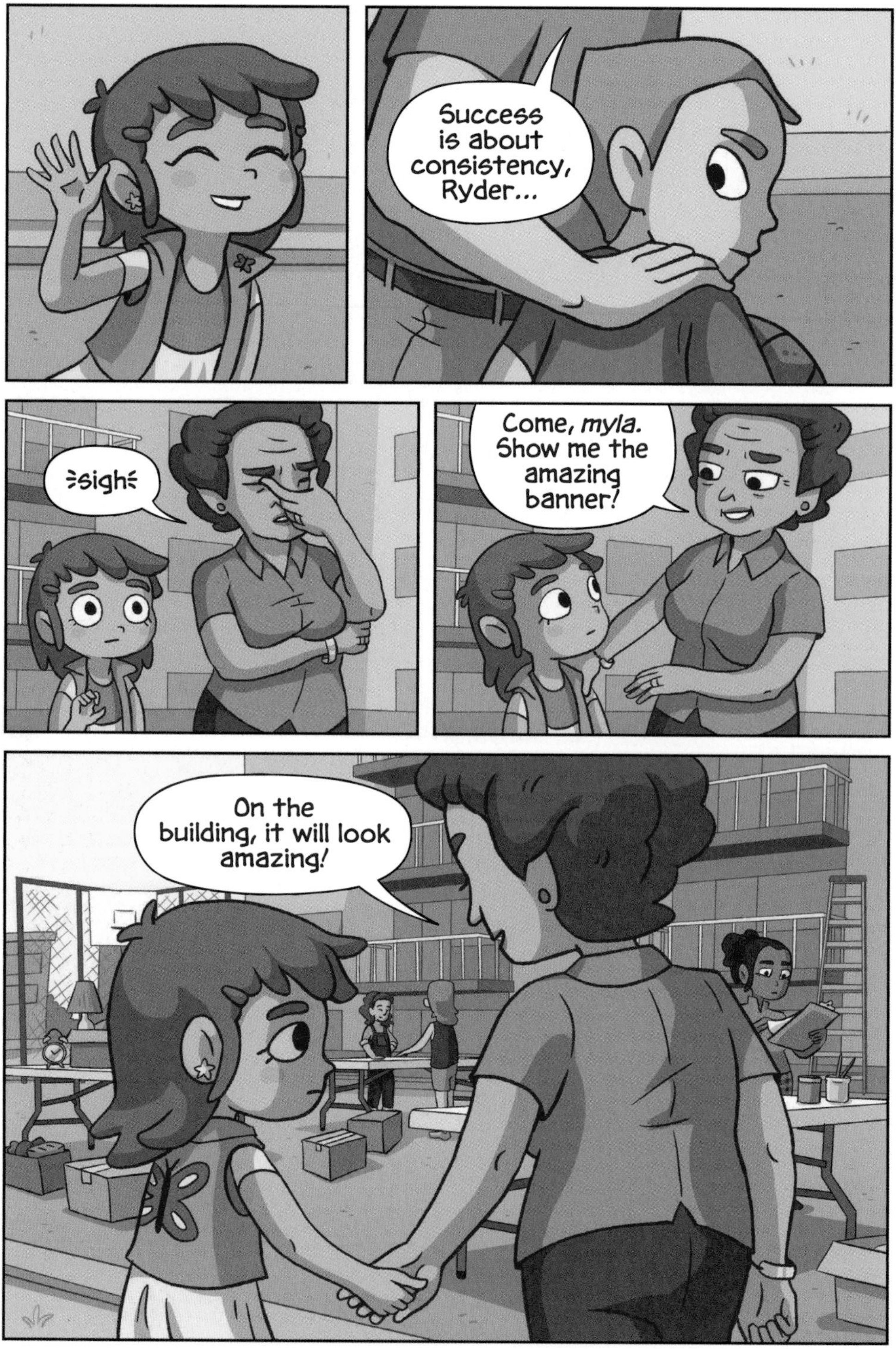
Success is about consistency, Ryder...
≑sigh≑
Come, *myla.* Show me the amazing banner!
On the building, it will look amazing!

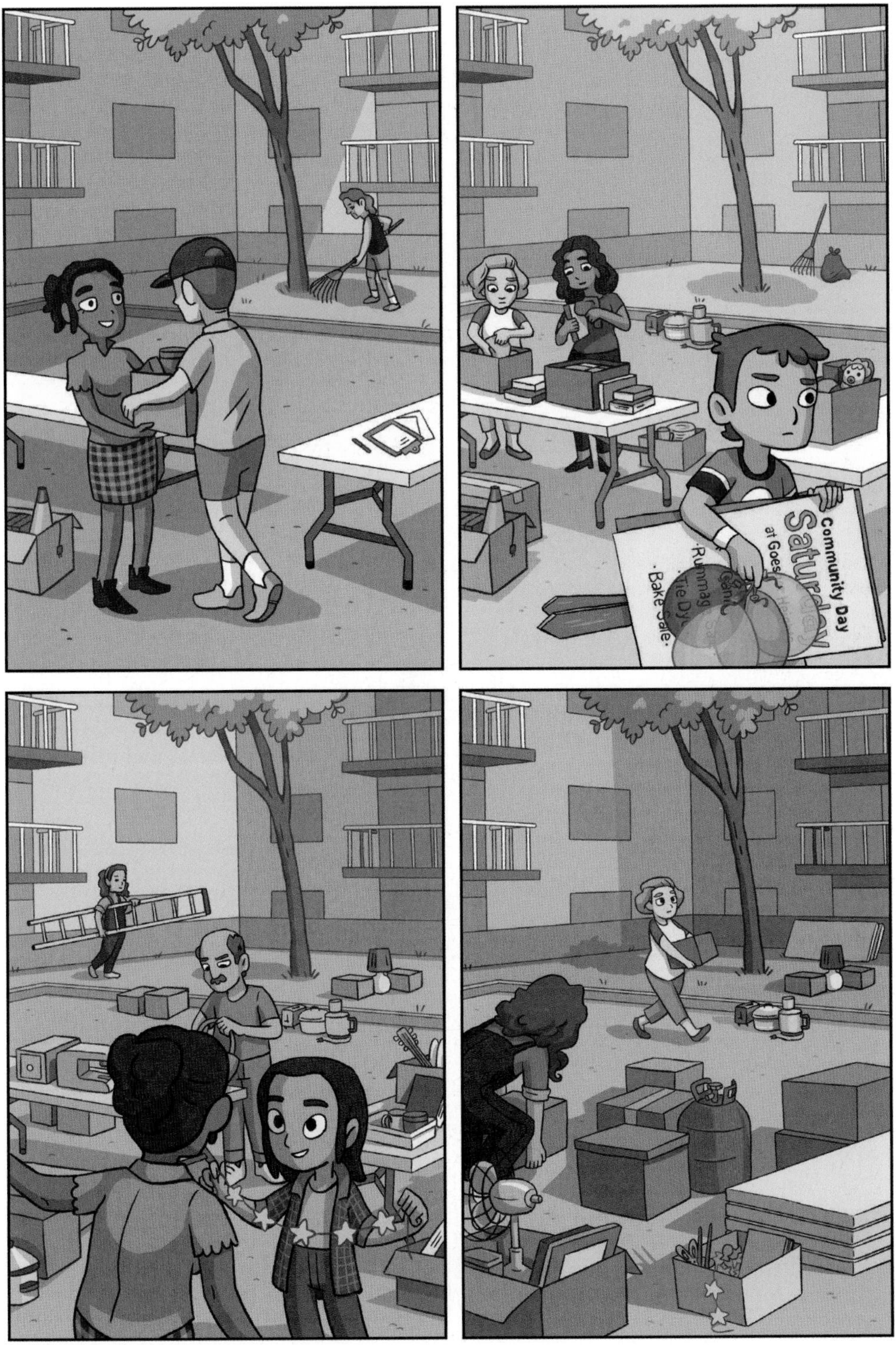
Community Day
Saturday
·Bake Sale·

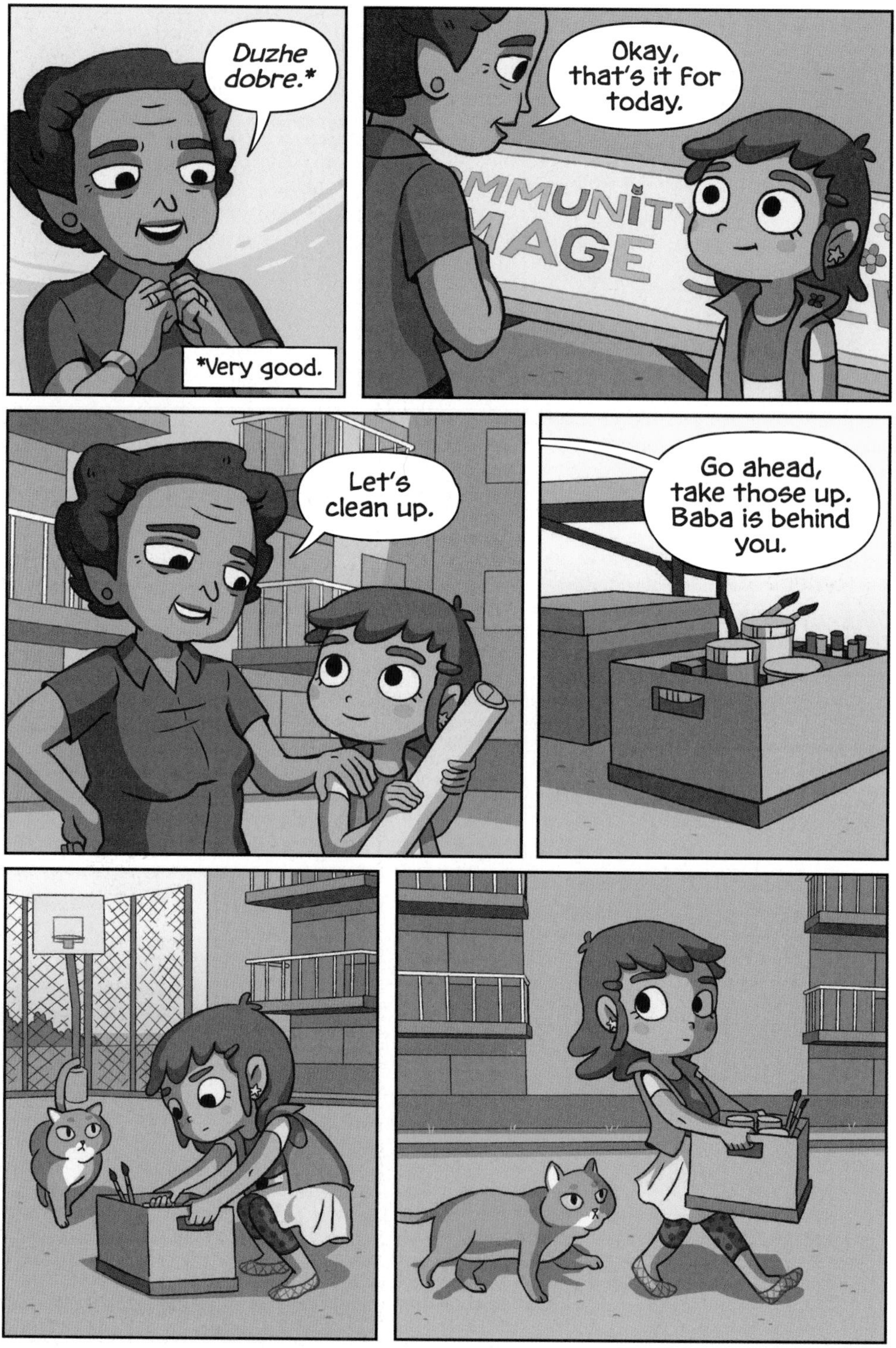

Duzhe dobre.*
*Very good.
Okay, that's it for today.
MMUNITY
AGE
Let's clean up.
Go ahead, take those up. Baba is behind you.

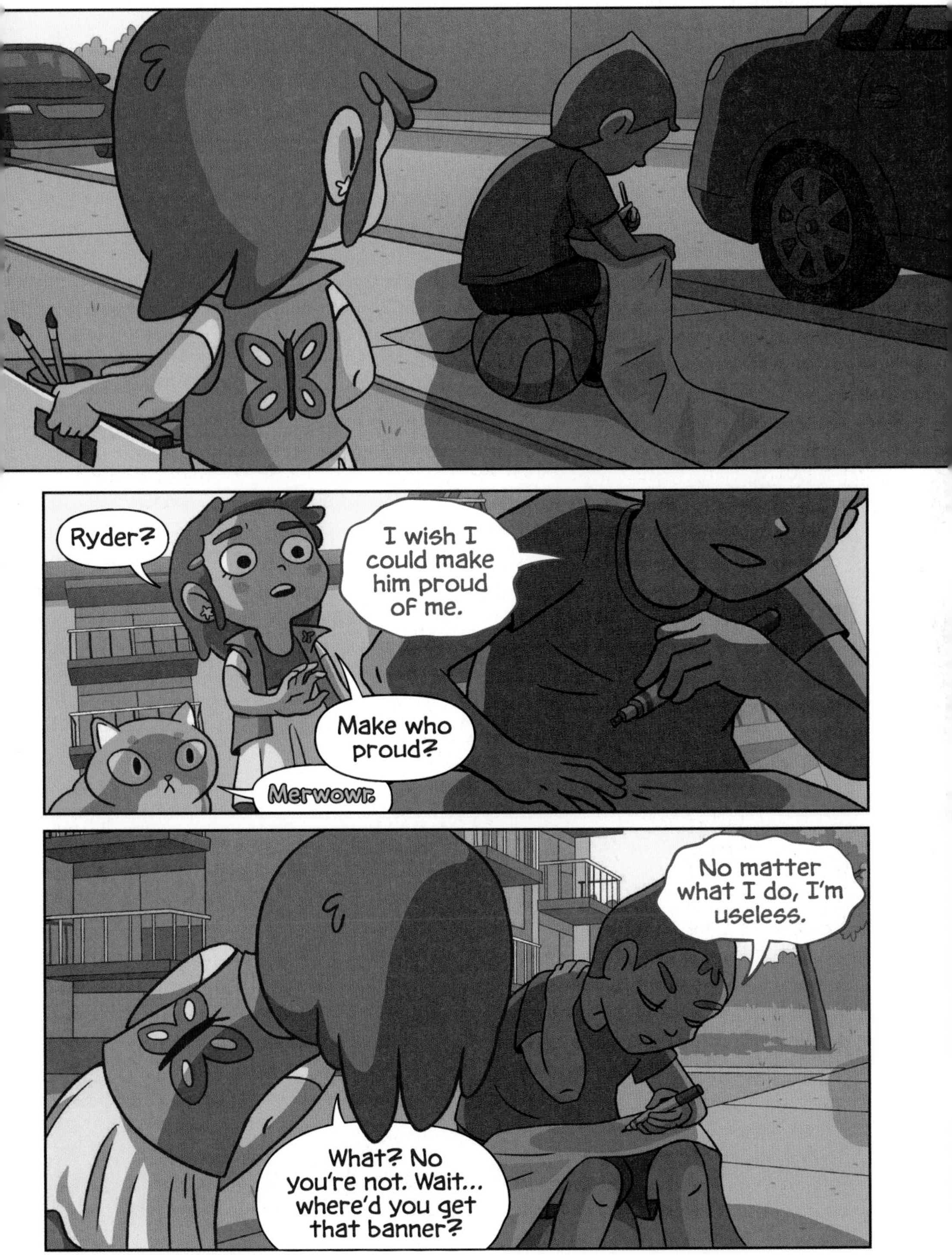
Ryder?
I wish I could make him proud of me.
Make who proud?
Merwowr.
No matter what I do, I'm useless.
What? No you're not. Wait... where'd you get that banner?

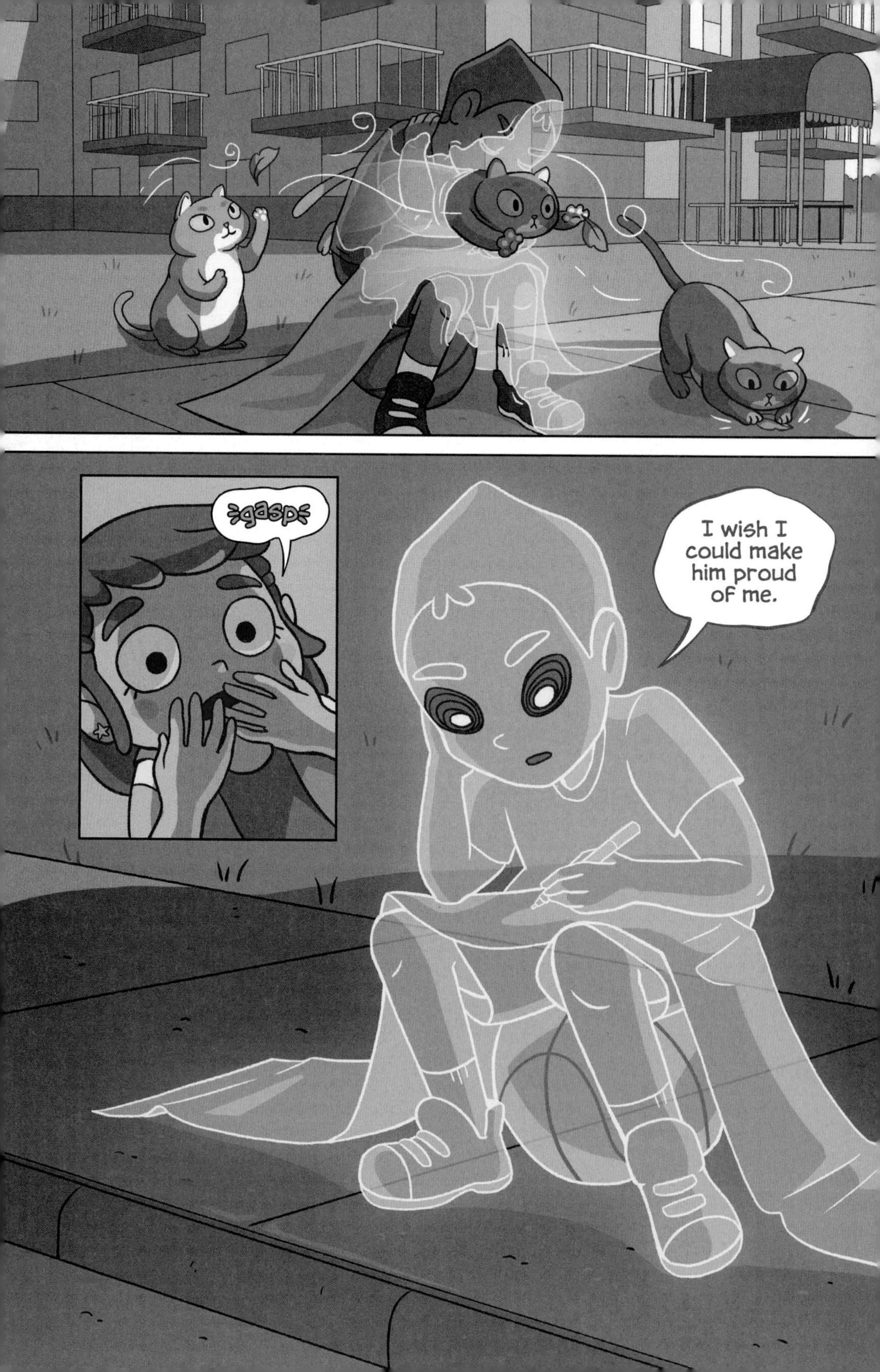
gasp
I wish I could make him proud of me.

CHAPTER
FIVE.

Ryder?
Ryder are
you...

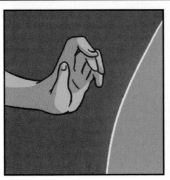

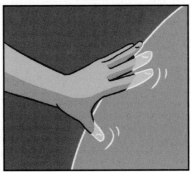

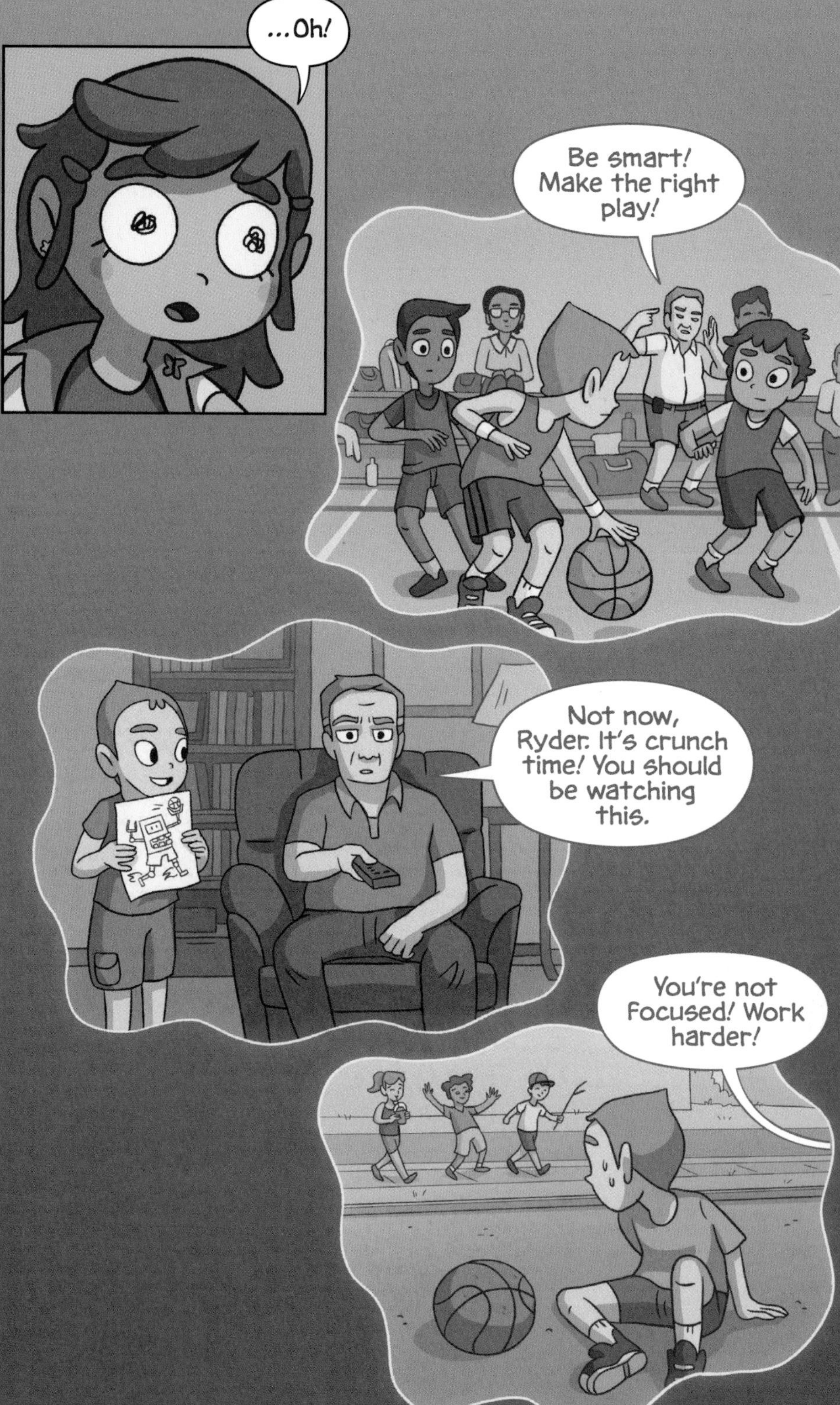
...Oh!
Be smart! Make the right play!
Not now, Ryder. It's crunch time! You should be watching this.
You're not focused! Work harder!

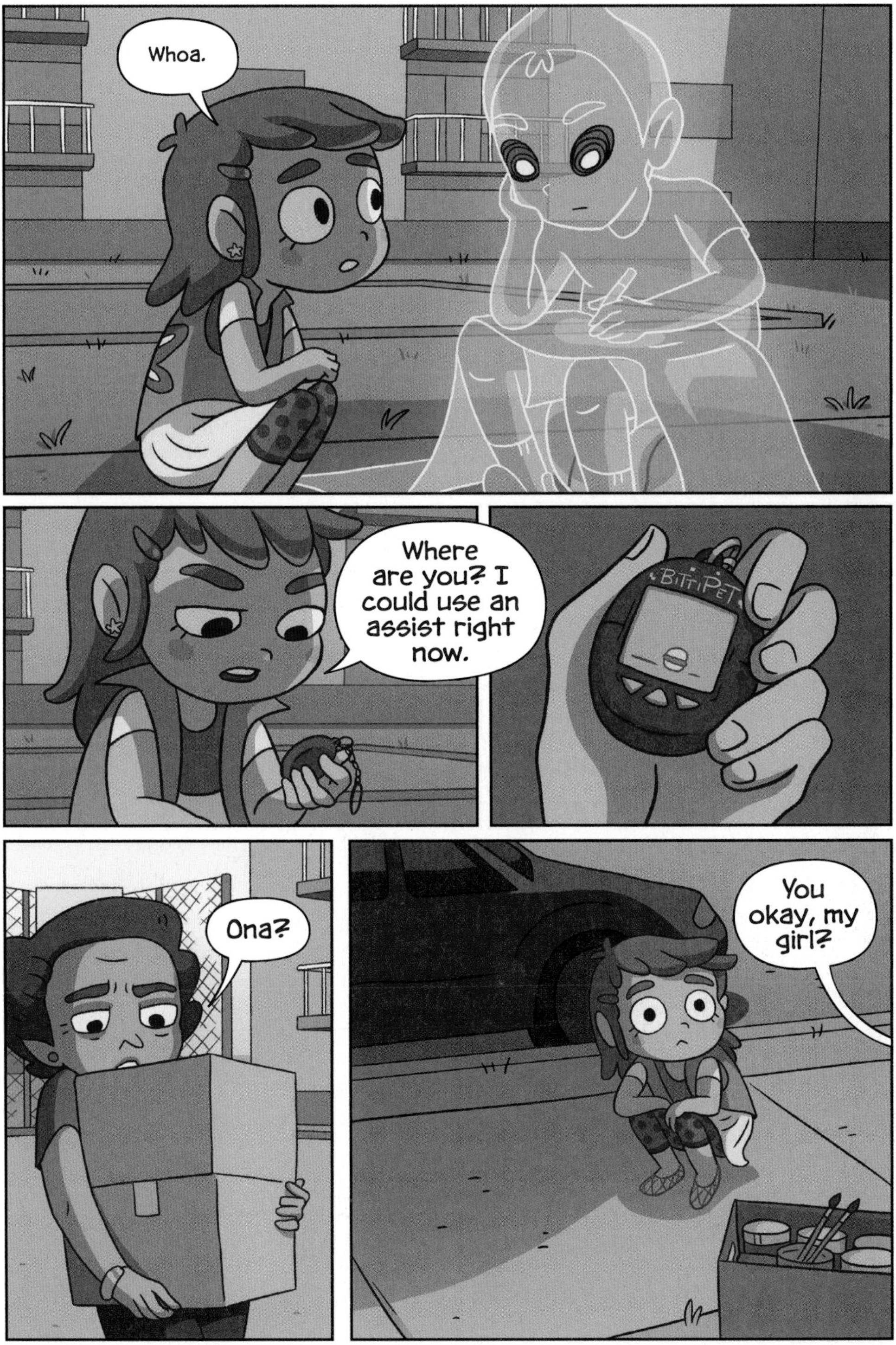
Whoa.
Where are you? I could use an assist right now.
BITTIPET
Ona?
You okay, my girl?

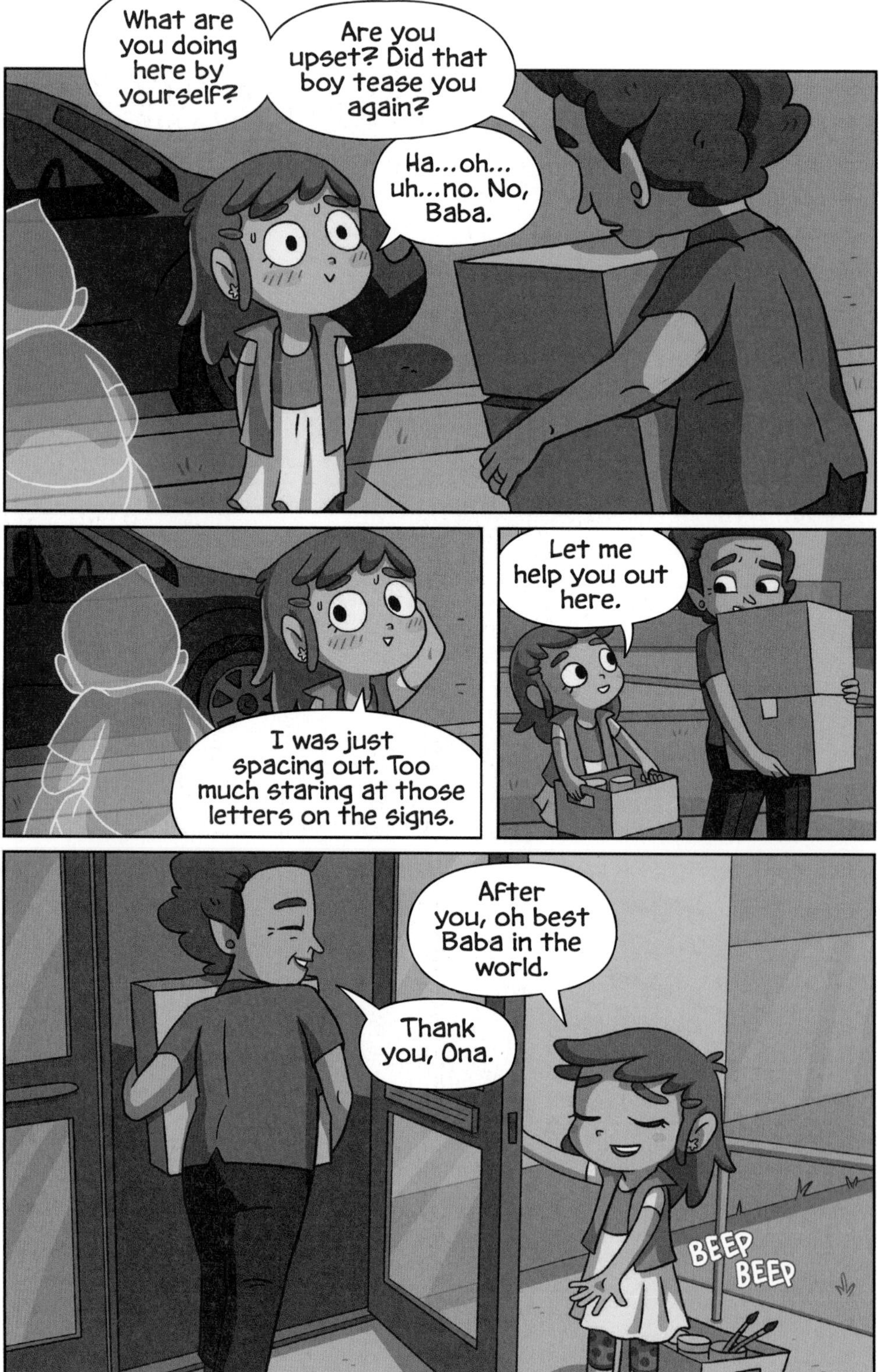
What are you doing here by yourself?
Are you upset? Did that boy tease you again?
Ha...oh... uh...no. No, Baba.
I was just spacing out. Too much staring at those letters on the signs.
Let me help you out here.
After you, oh best Baba in the world.
Thank you, Ona.
BEEP BEEP

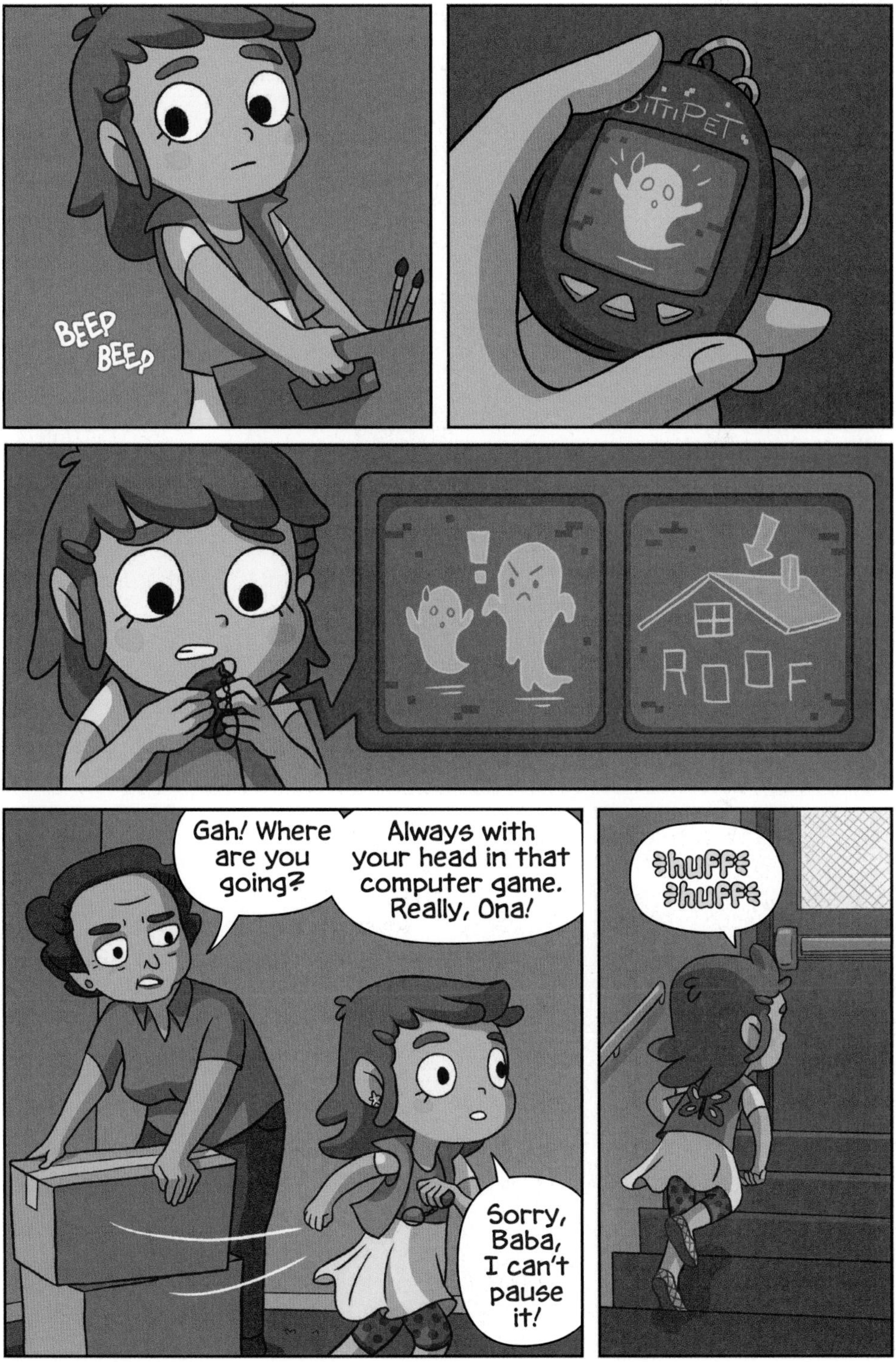
BEEP BEEP
BITTIPET
ROOF
Gah! Where are you going?
Always with your head in that computer game. Really, Ona!
Sorry, Baba, I can't pause it!
huff huff

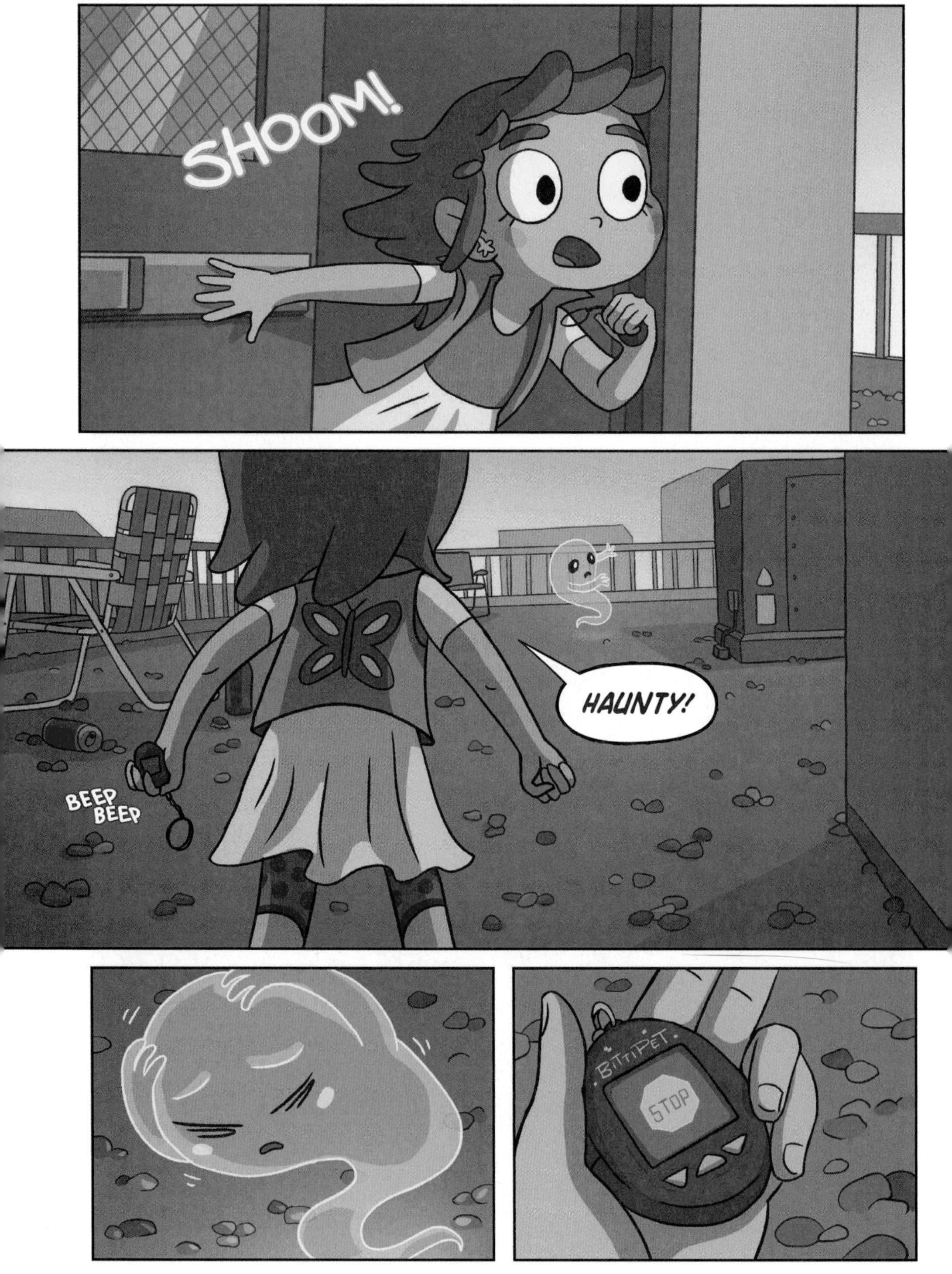
SHOOM!
HAUNTY!
BEEP BEEP
BITTIPET
STOP

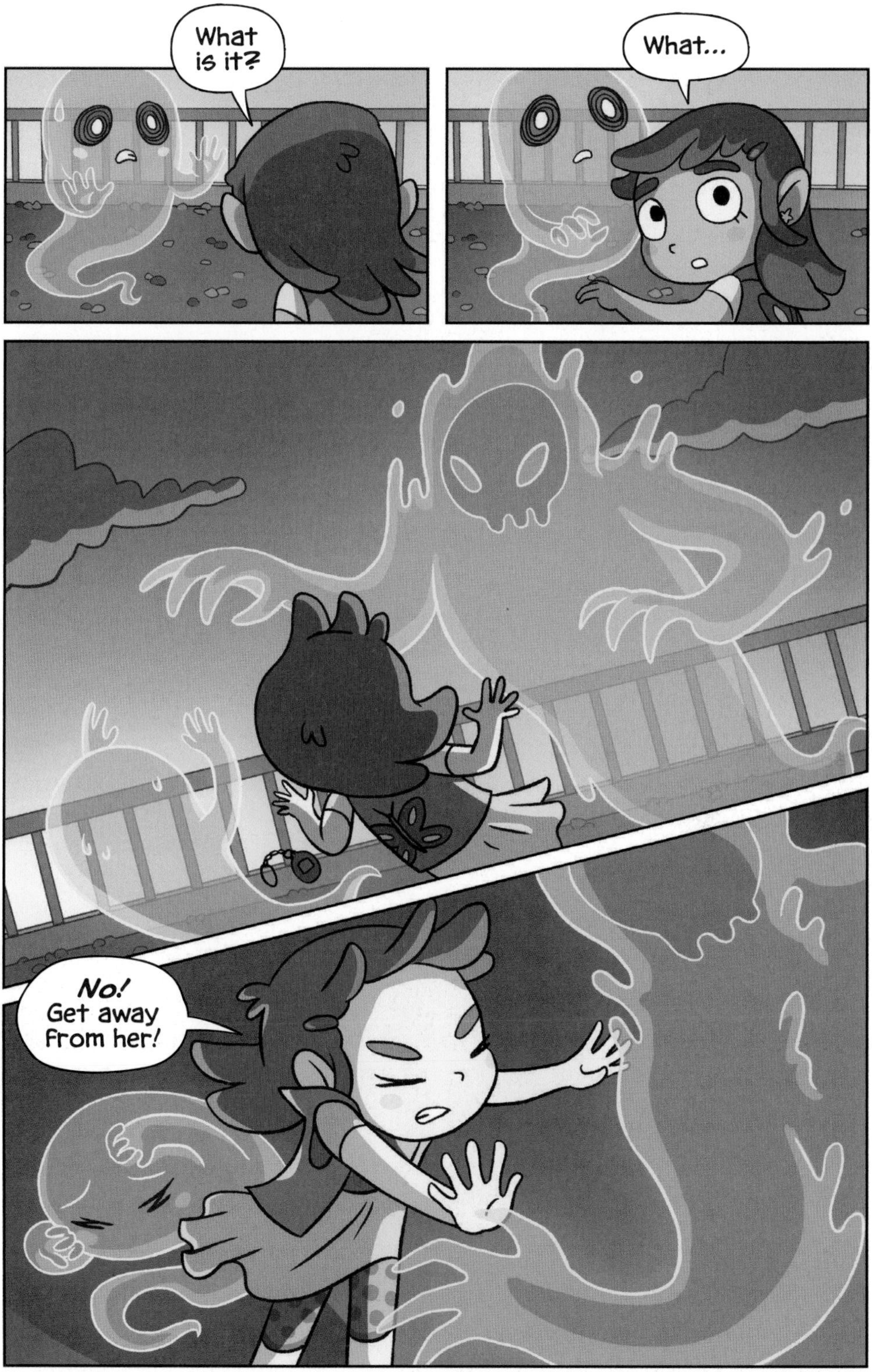
What is it?
What...
No! Get away from her!

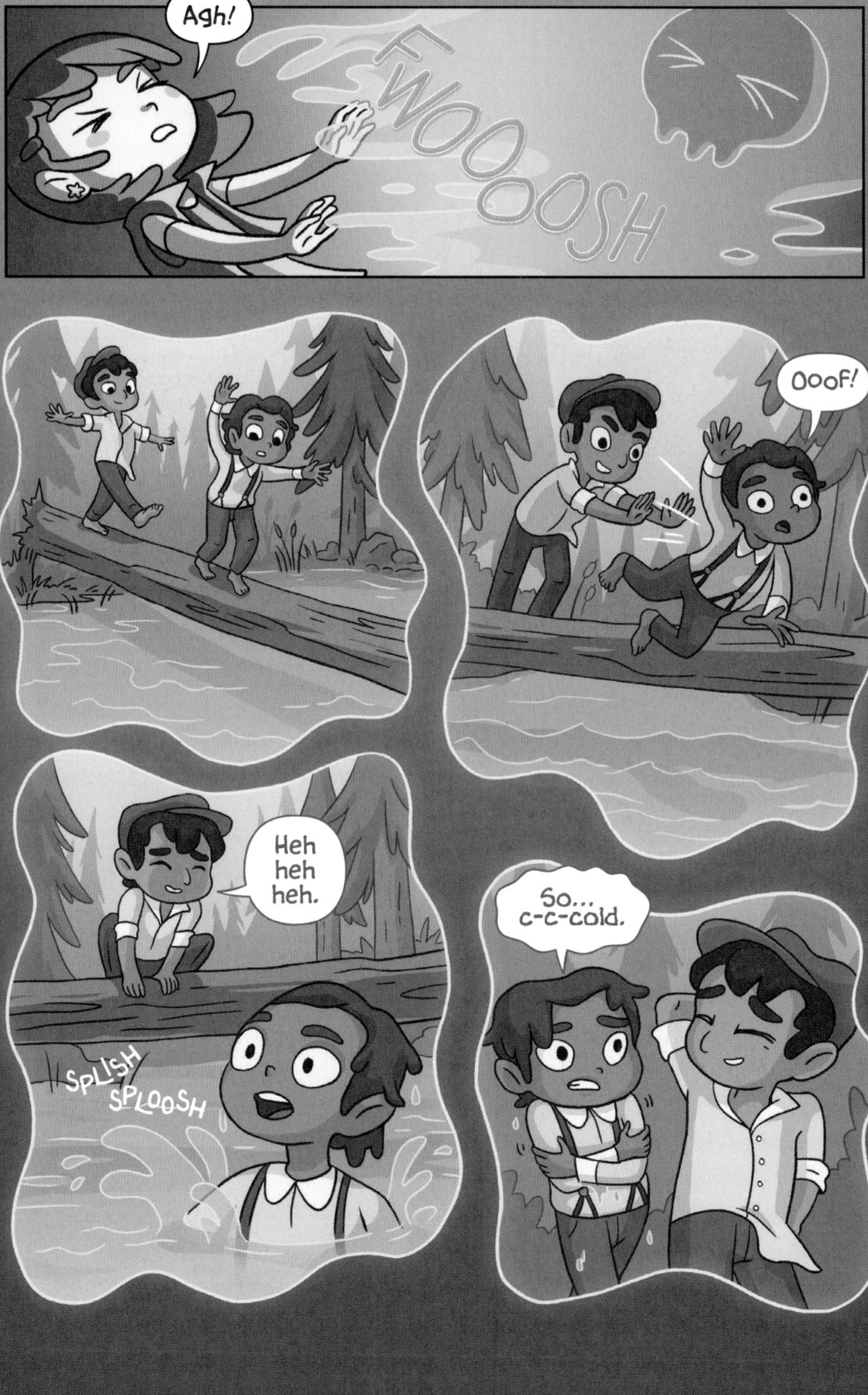
Agh!
FWOOOOSH
OOOF!
Heh heh heh.
SPLISH SPLOOSH
So... c-c-cold.

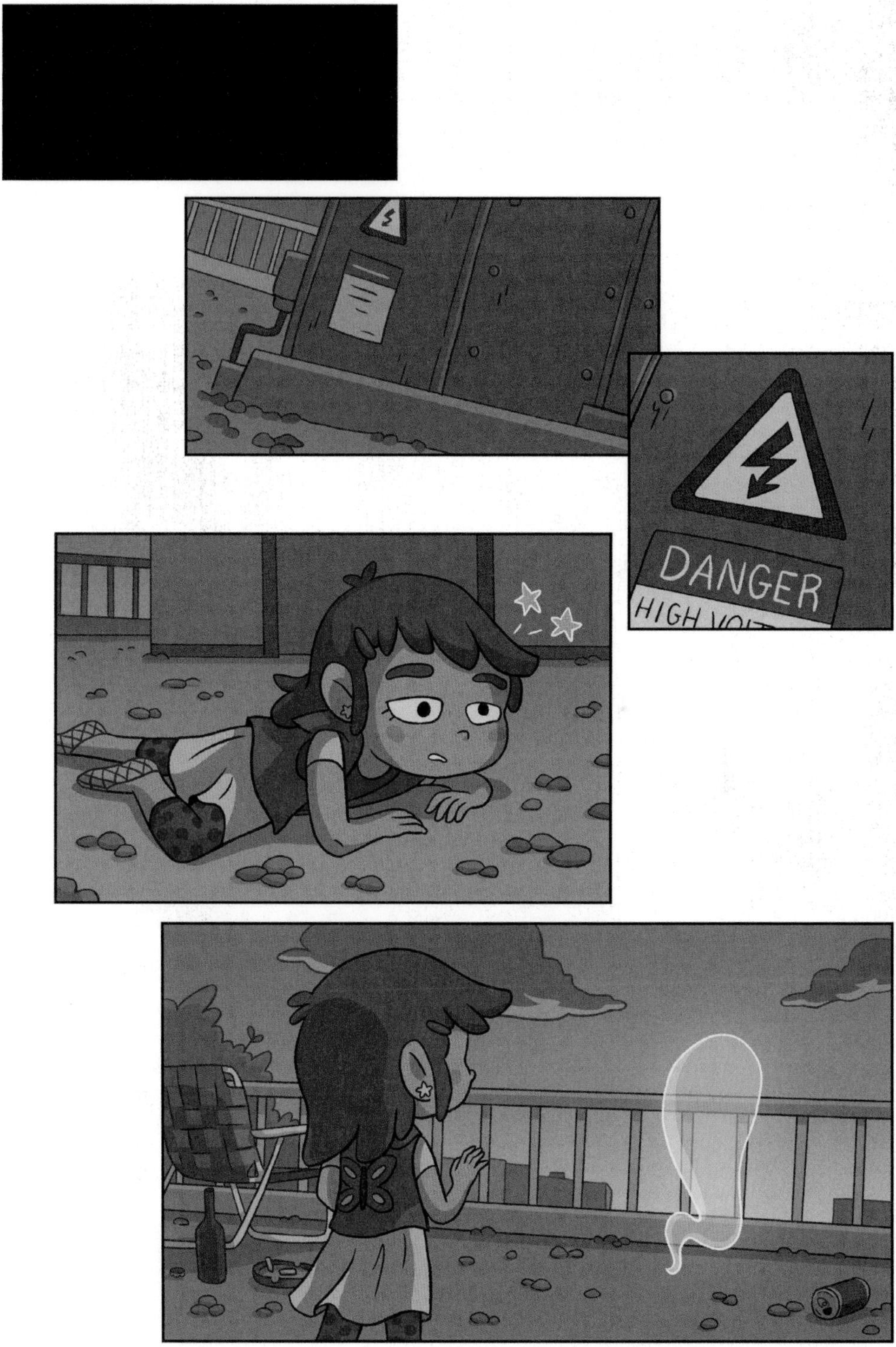
DANGER
HIGH

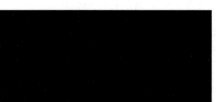

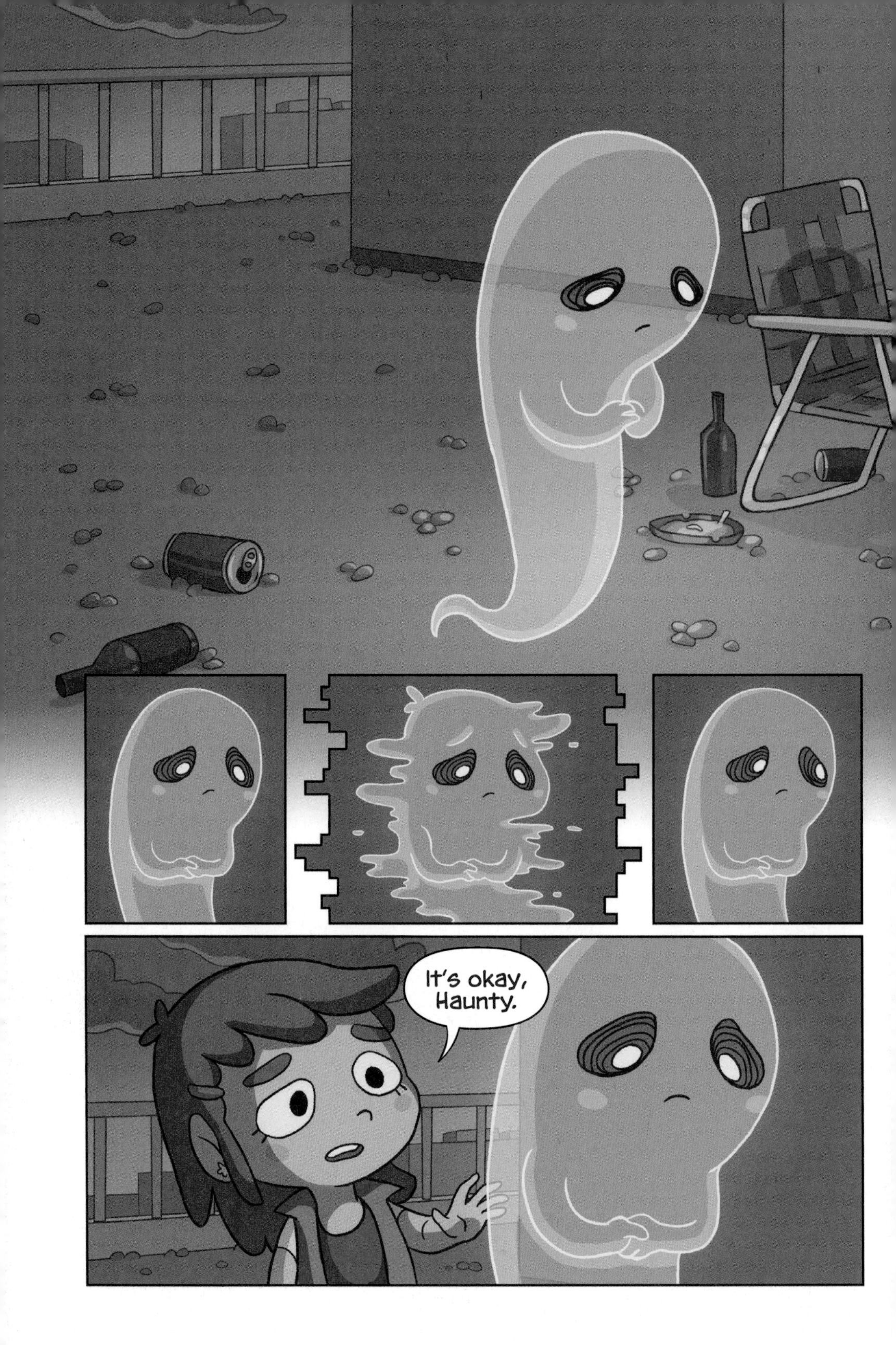
It's okay, Haunty.

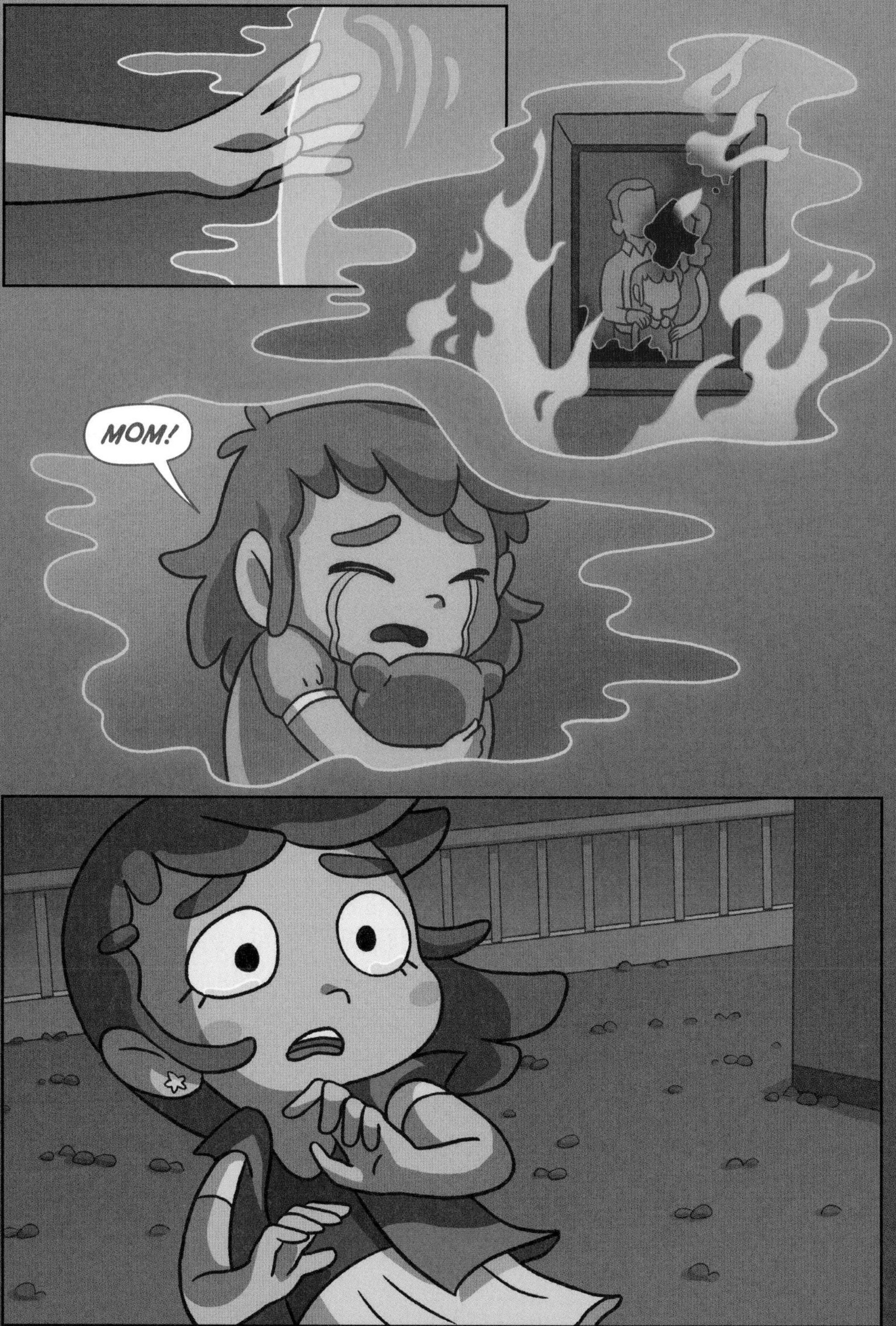
MOM!

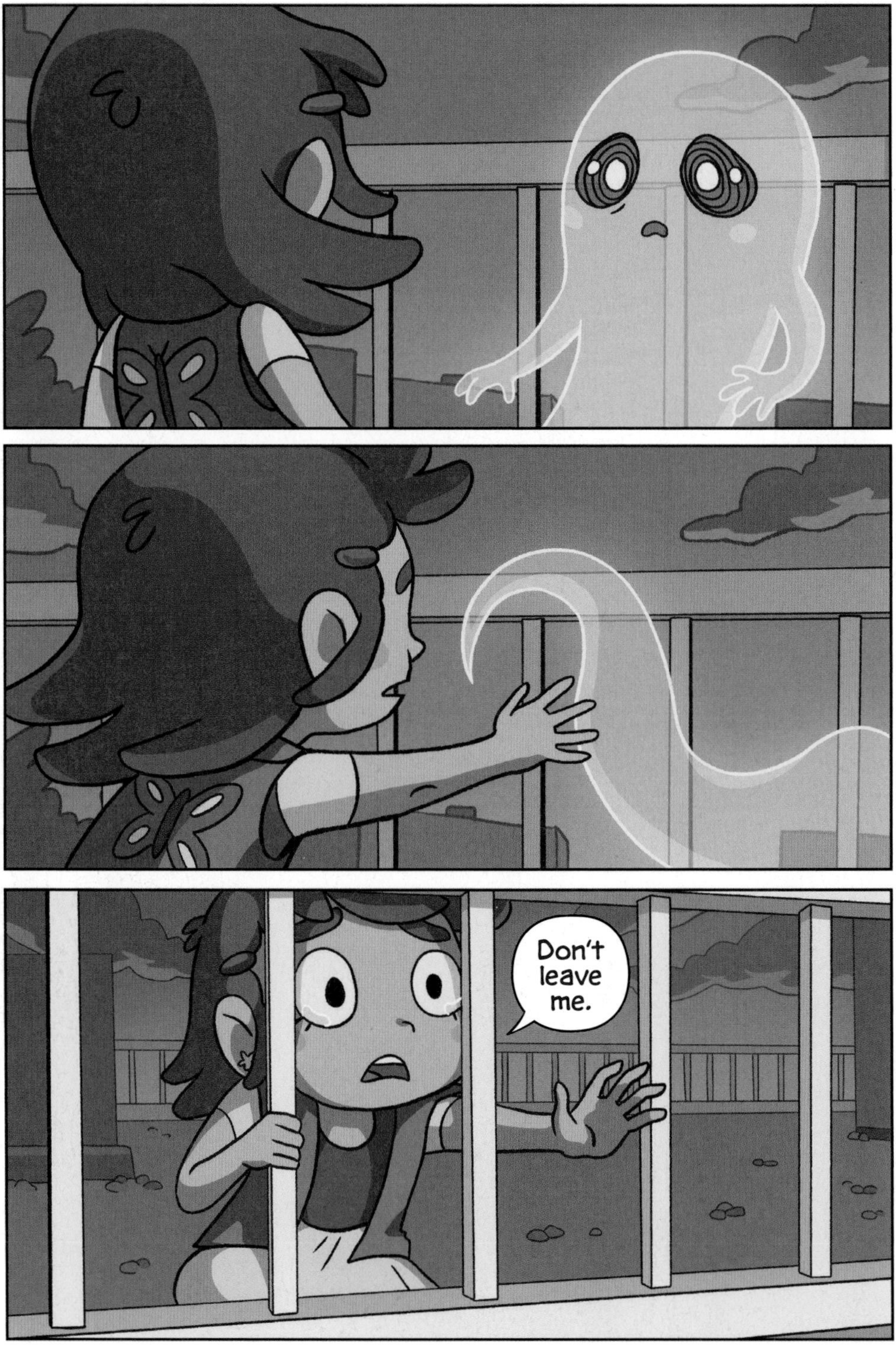
Don't leave me.

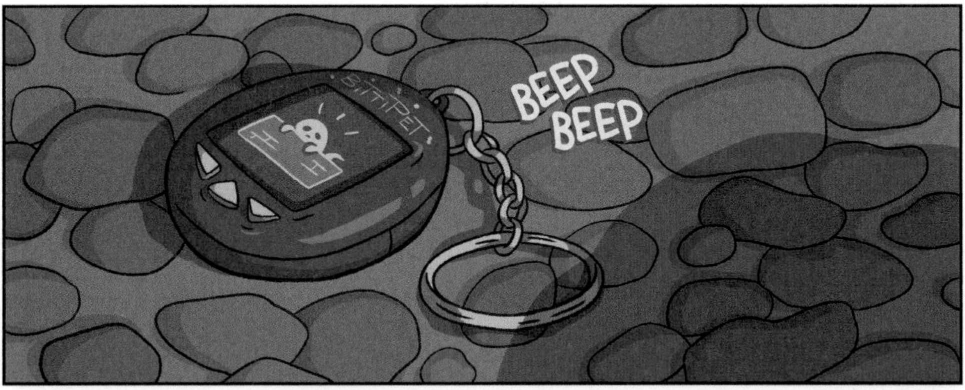
BITTIPET
BEEP BEEP

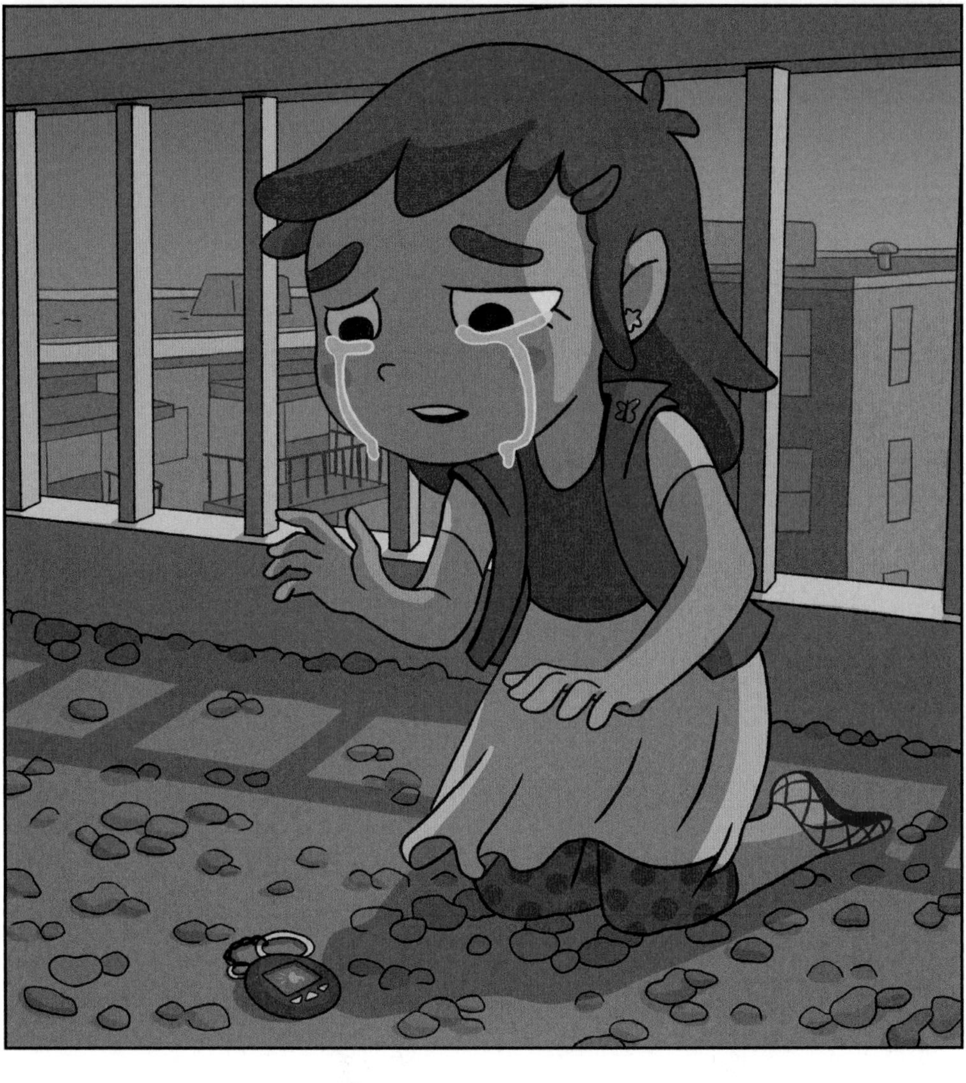

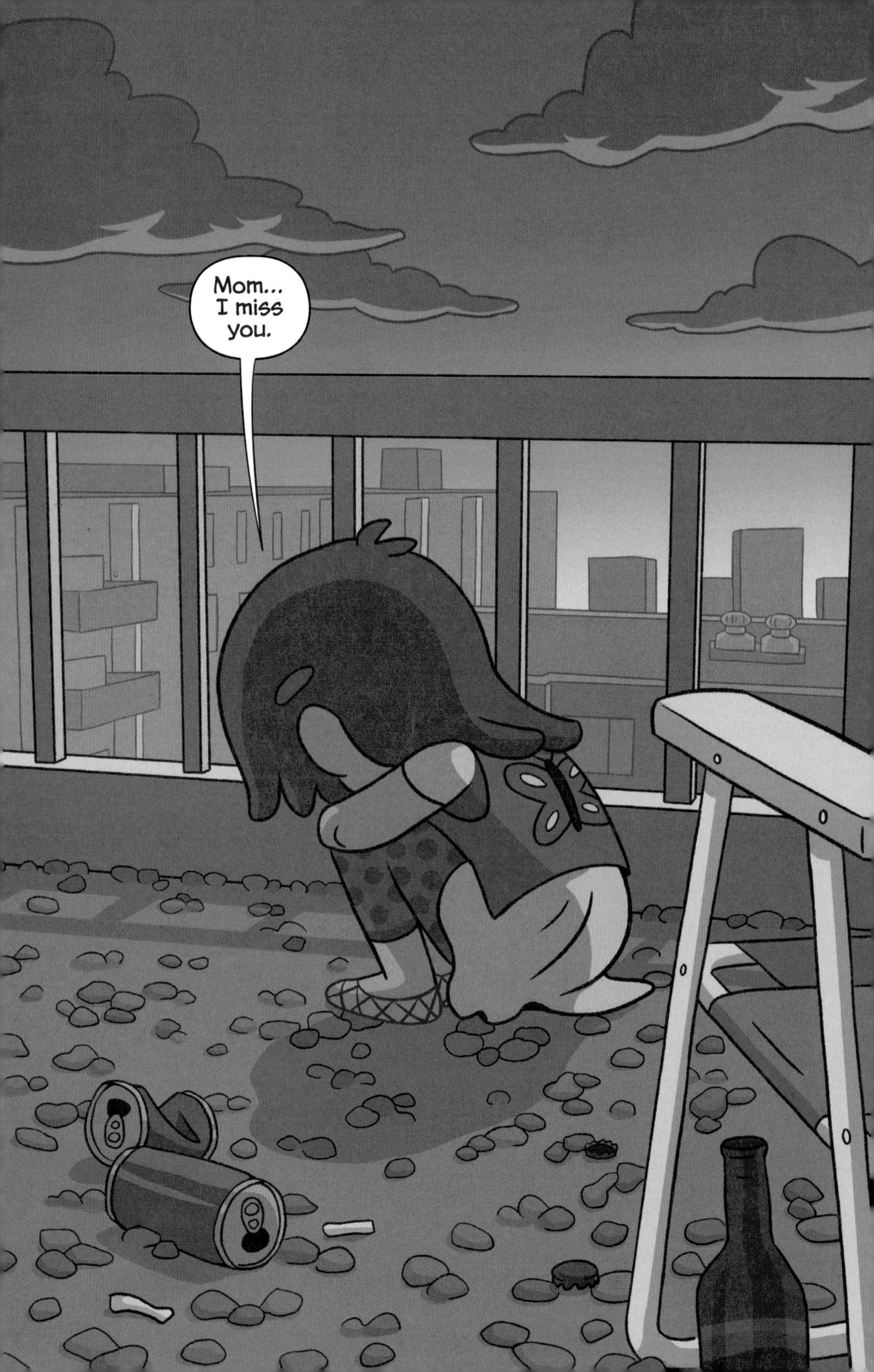
Mom... I miss you.

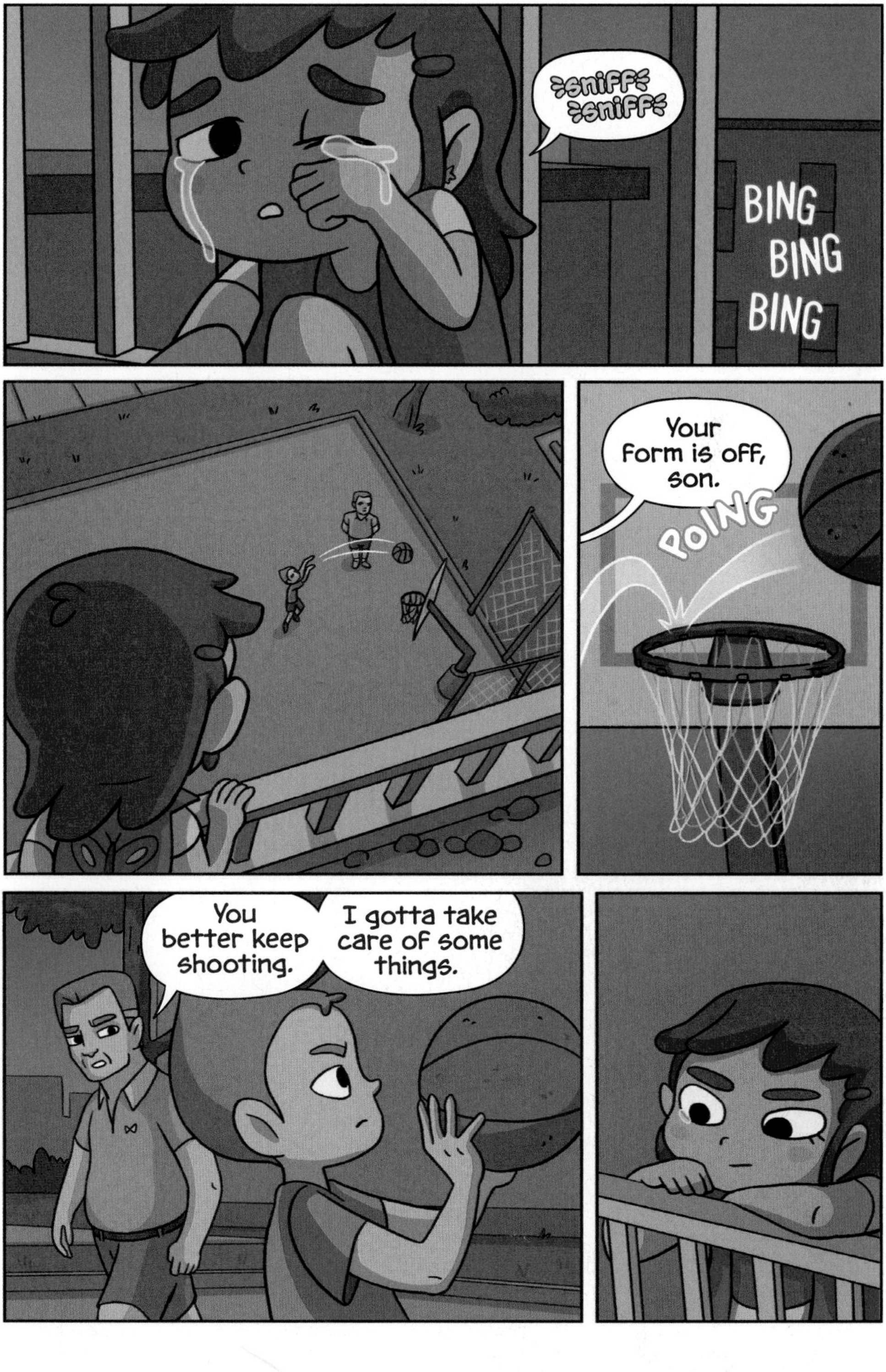

SNIFF SNIFF
BING BING BING
Your form is off, son.
POING
You better keep shooting.
I gotta take care of some things.

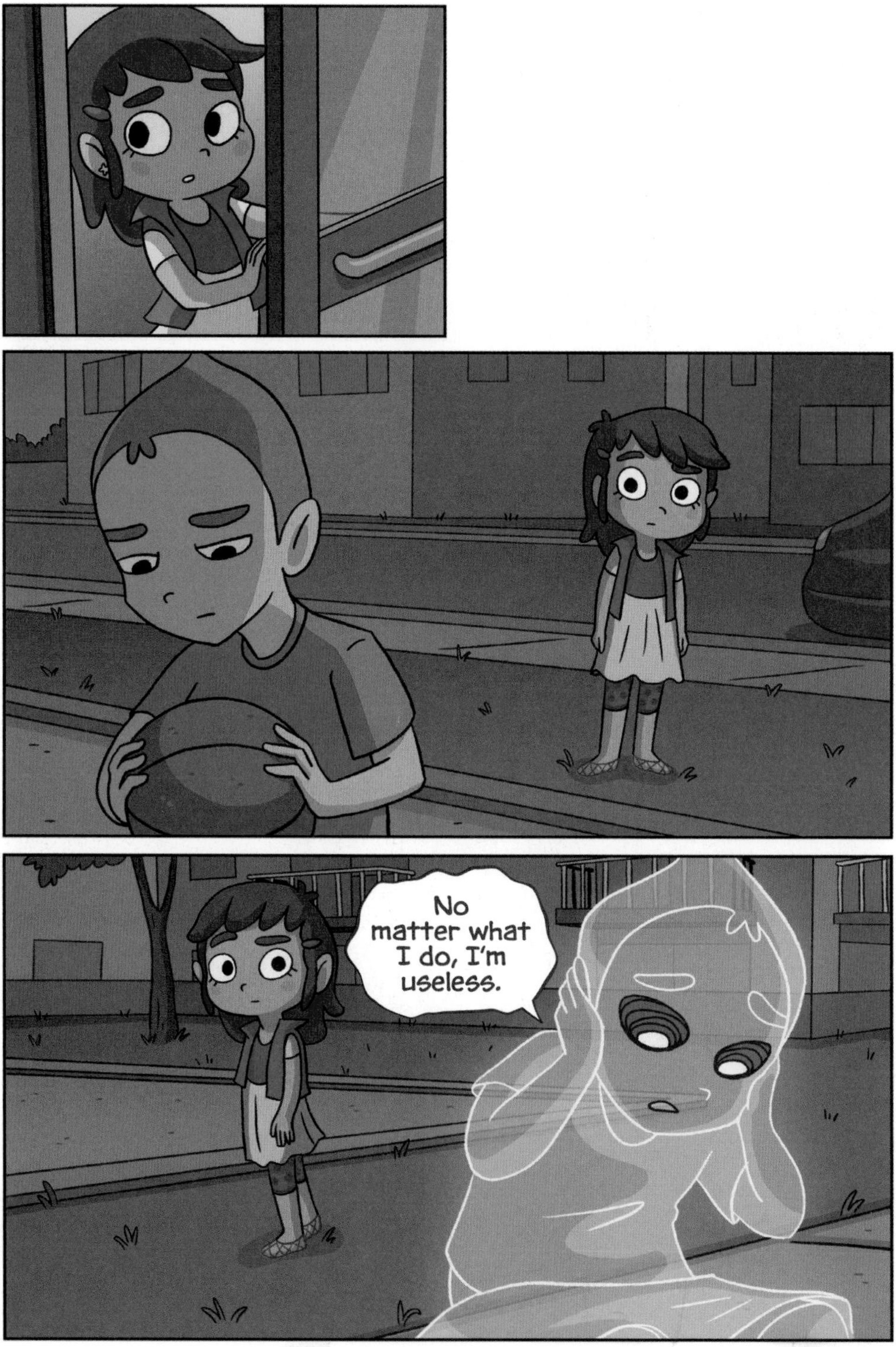
No matter what I do, I'm useless.

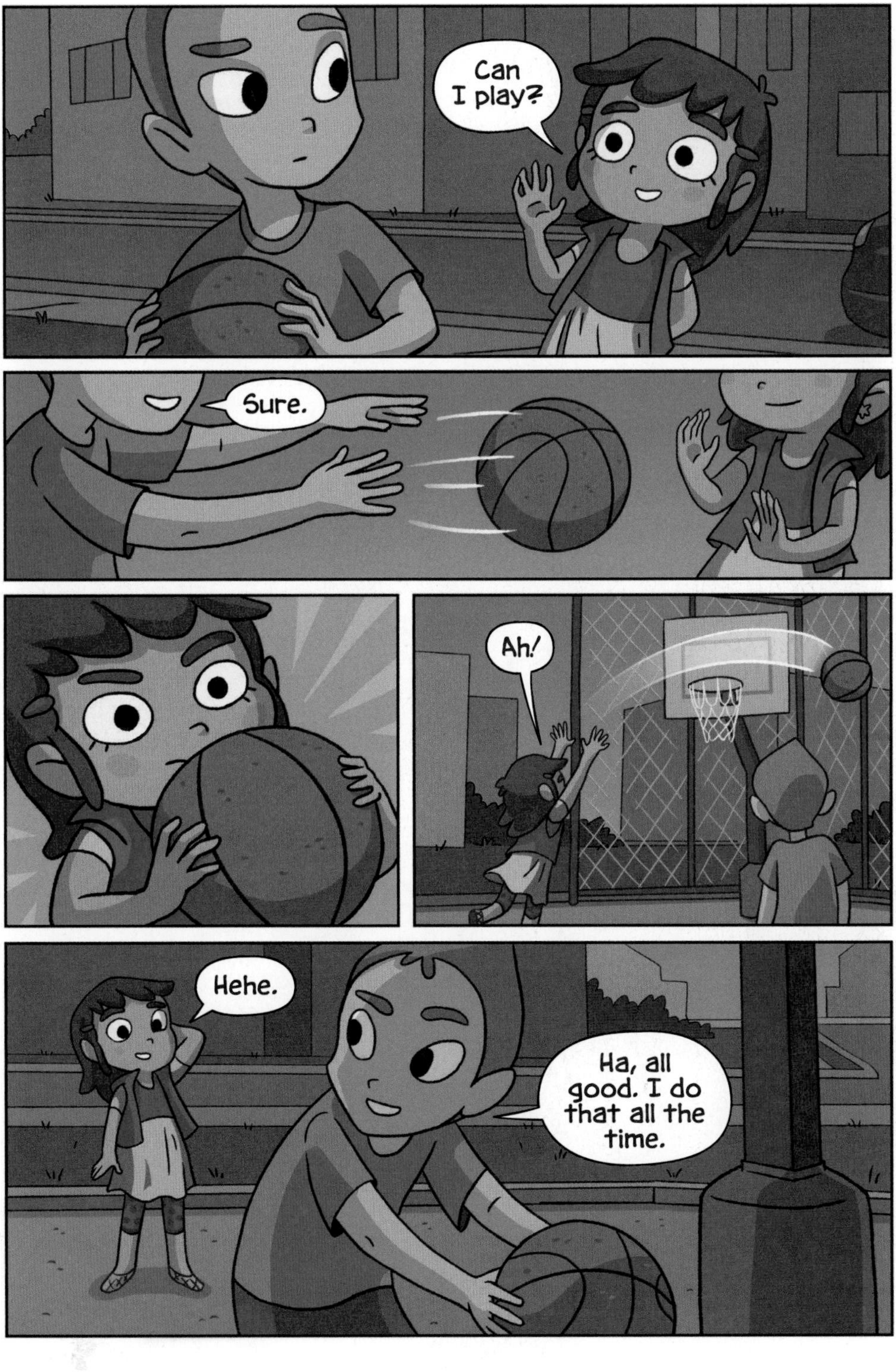
Can I play?
Sure.
Ah!
Hehe.
Ha, all good. I do that all the time.

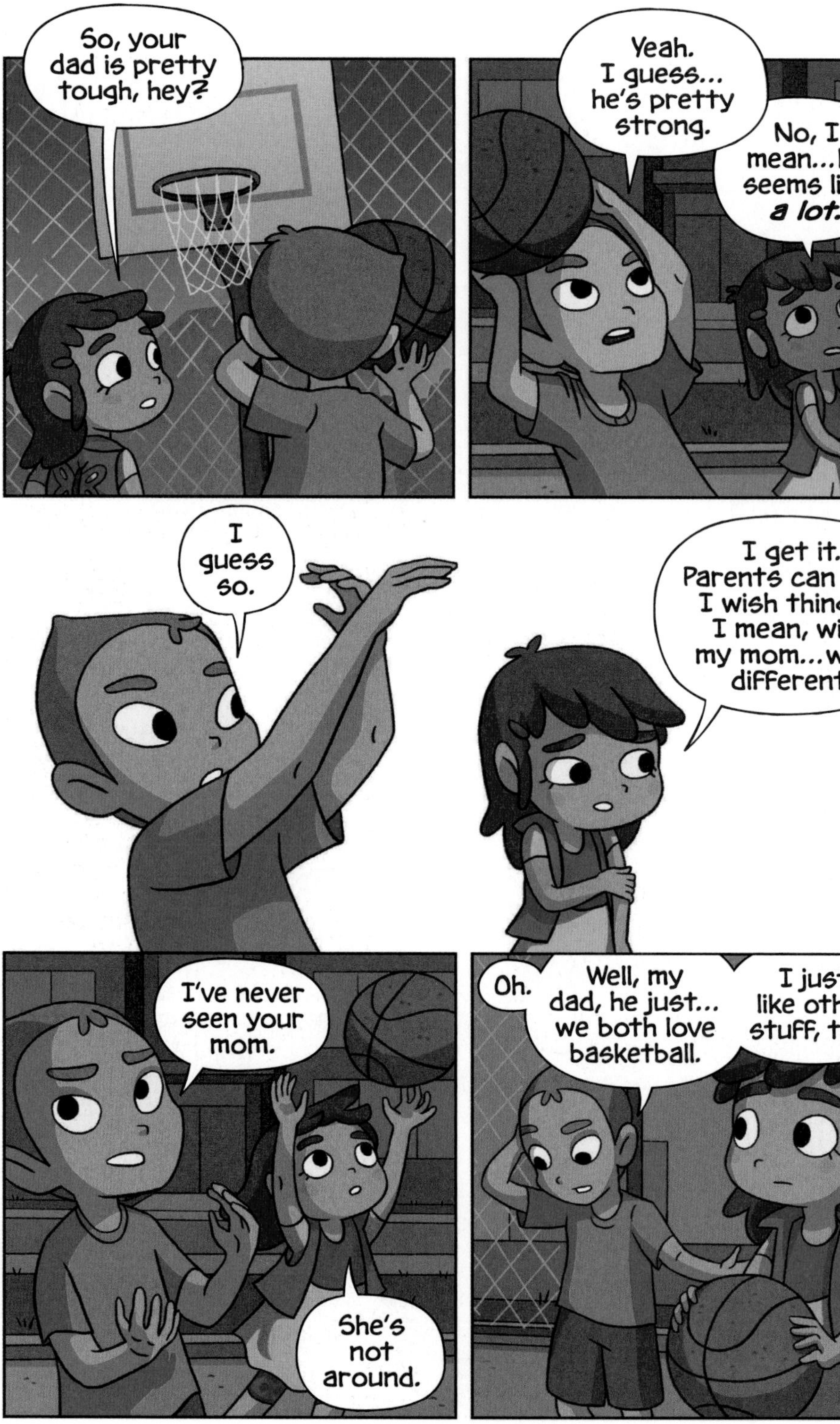
So, your dad is pretty tough, hey?
Yeah. I guess... he's pretty strong.
No, I mean...he seems like *a lot.*
I guess so.
I get it. Parents can be... I wish things... I mean, with my mom...were different.
I've never seen your mom.
She's not around.
Oh.
Well, my dad, he just... we both love basketball.
I just like other stuff, too.

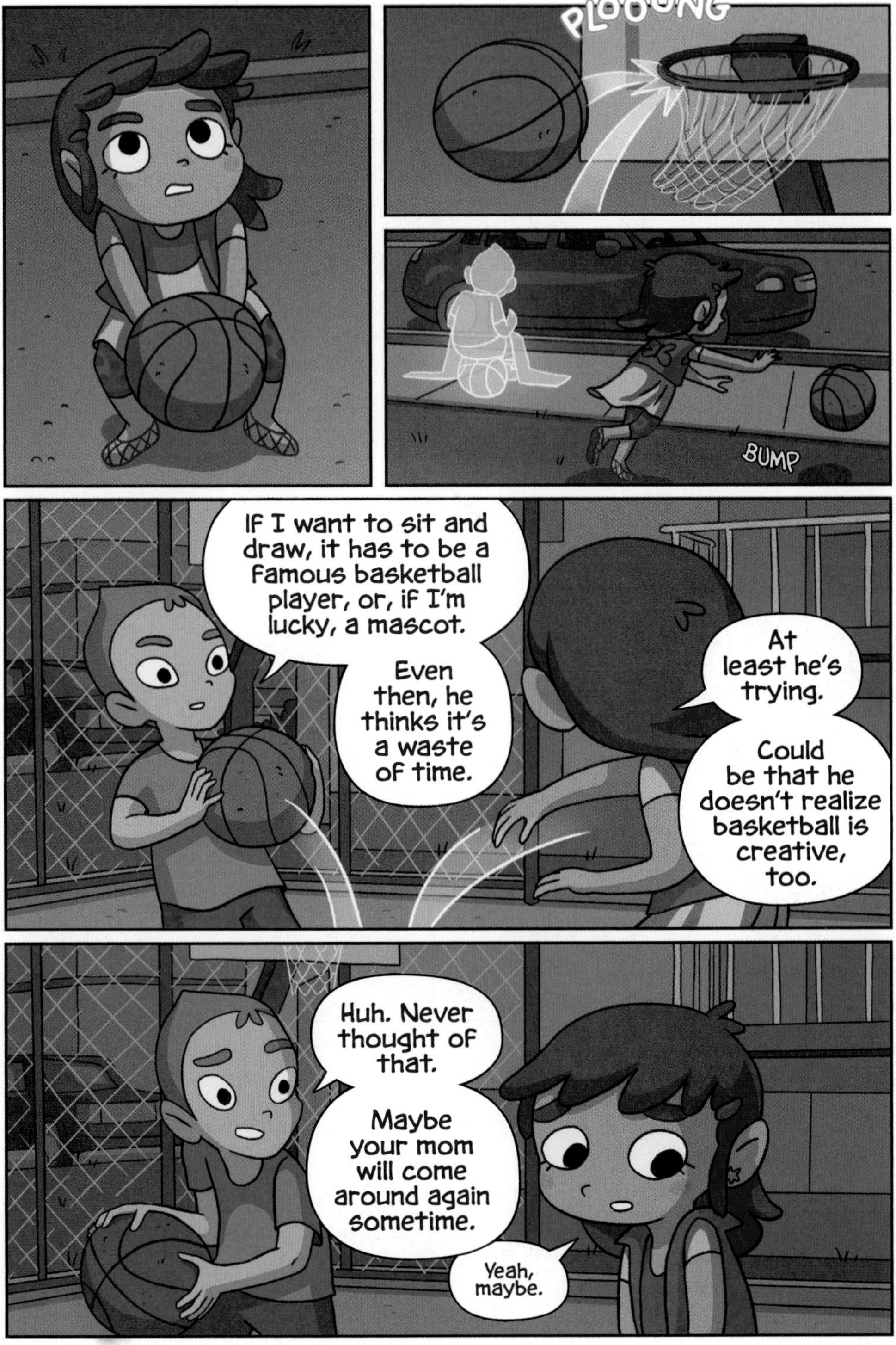
PLOOONG
BUMP
If I want to sit and draw, it has to be a famous basketball player, or, if I'm lucky, a mascot.
Even then, he thinks it's a waste of time.
At least he's trying.
Could be that he doesn't realize basketball is creative, too.
Huh. Never thought of that.
Maybe your mom will come around again sometime.
Yeah, maybe.

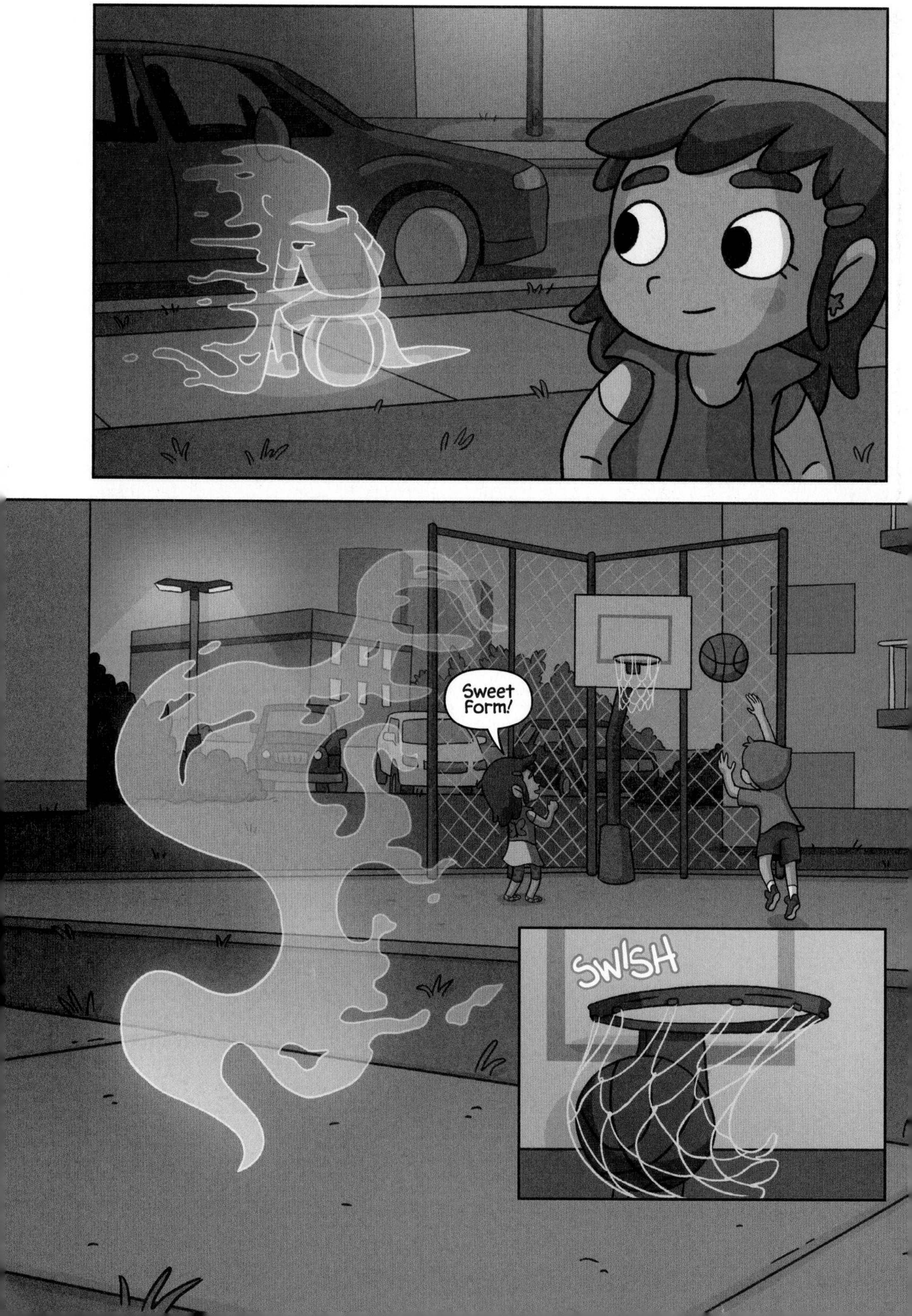
Sweet form!
SWISH

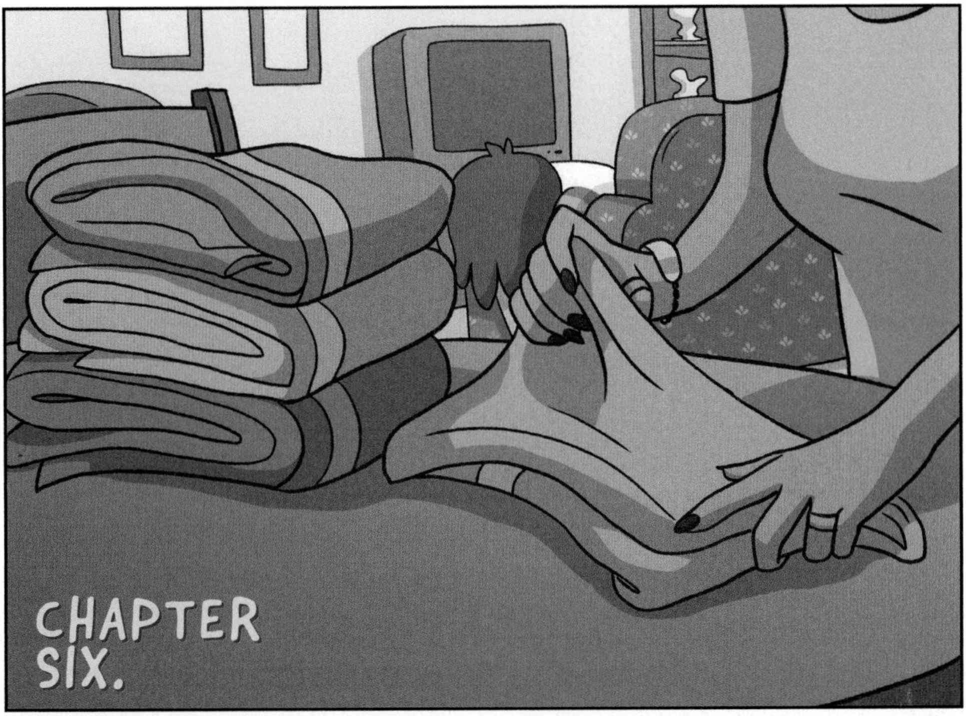
CHAPTER
SIX.

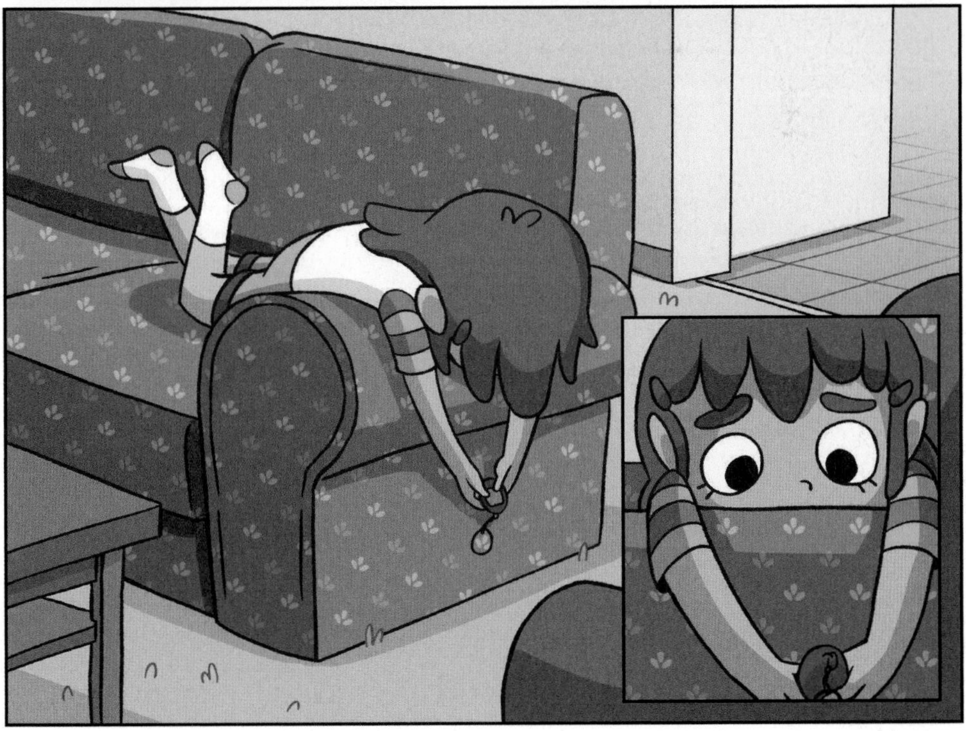

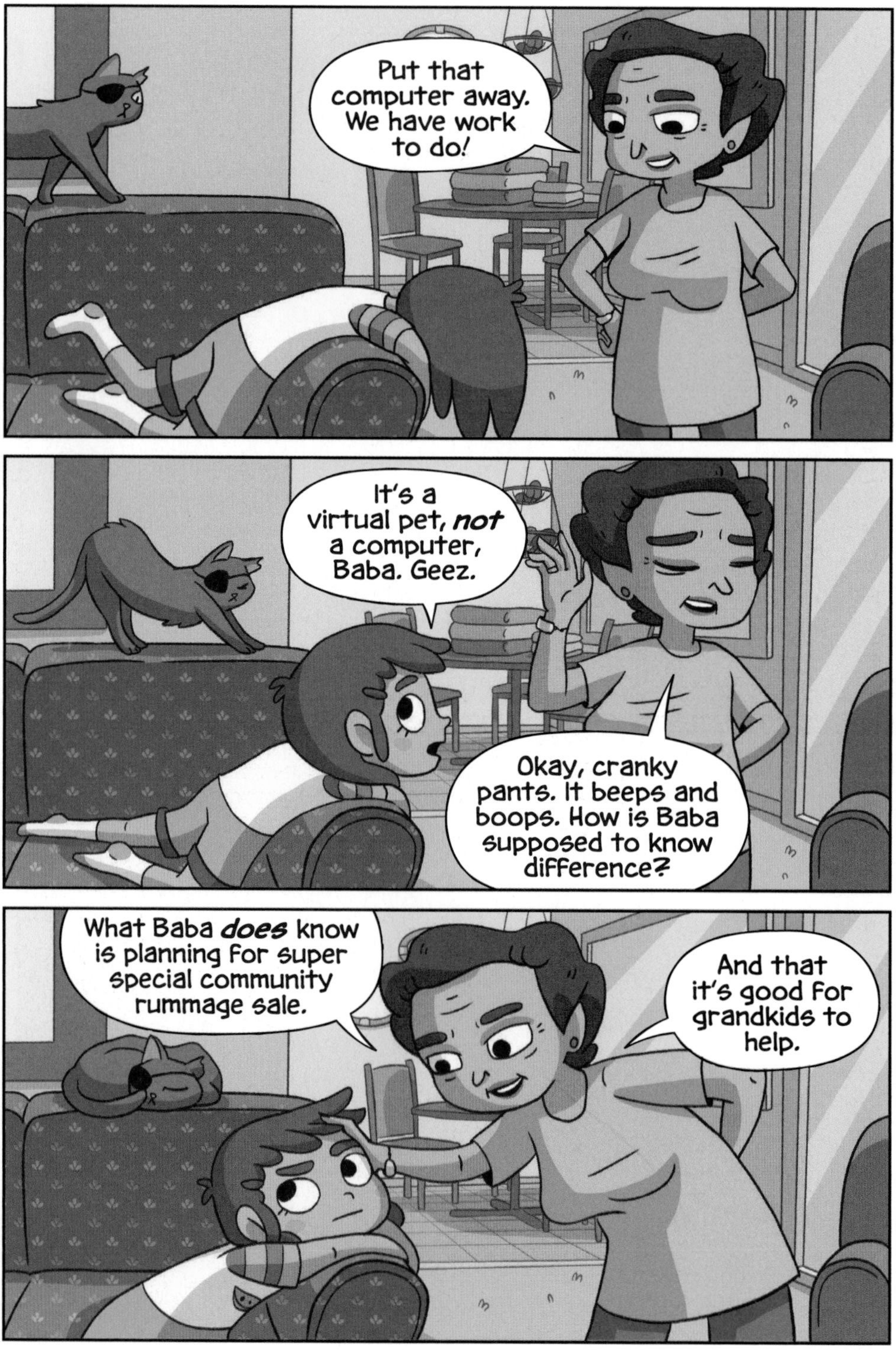

Put that computer away. We have work to do!
It's a virtual pet, *not* a computer, Baba. Geez.
Okay, cranky pants. It beeps and boops. How is Baba supposed to know difference?
What Baba *does* know is planning for super special community rummage sale.
And that it's good for grandkids to help.

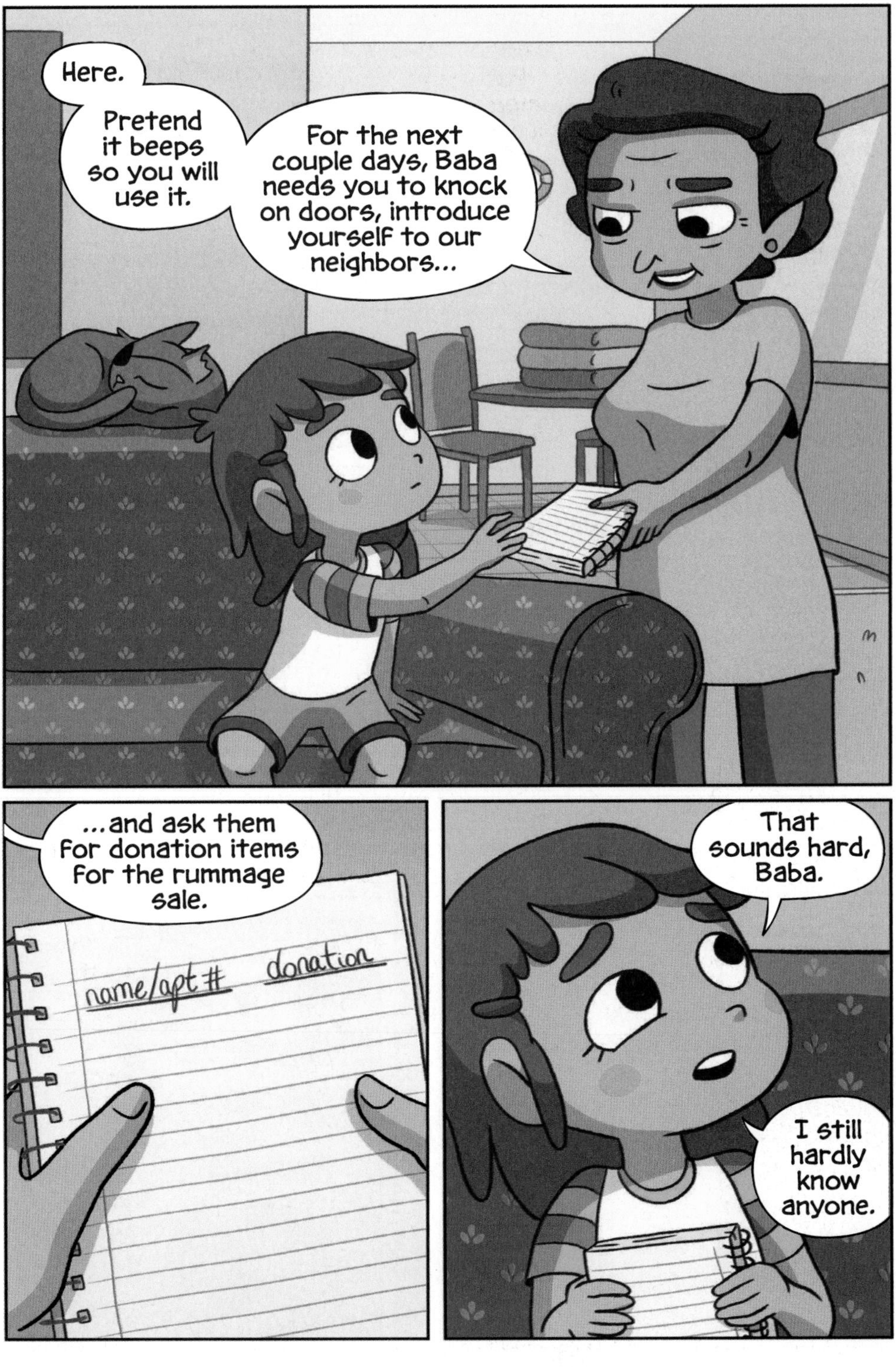
Here.
Pretend it beeps so you will use it.
For the next couple days, Baba needs you to knock on doors, introduce yourself to our neighbors...
...and ask them for donation items for the rummage sale.
name/apt #
donation
That sounds hard, Baba.
I still hardly know anyone.

You don't get to know people without talking to them.

They mostly know who you are and that you are helping Baba.

Plus, the notebook has a warm-up line for you. Look.

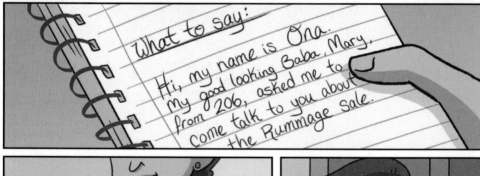

What to say:

Hi, my name is Ona. My good looking Baba, Mary, from 206, asked me to come talk to you about the Rummage Sale.

Heh. Okay, Baba.

Good girl. I'm going to run some errands for the sale.

See you soon. Good luck.

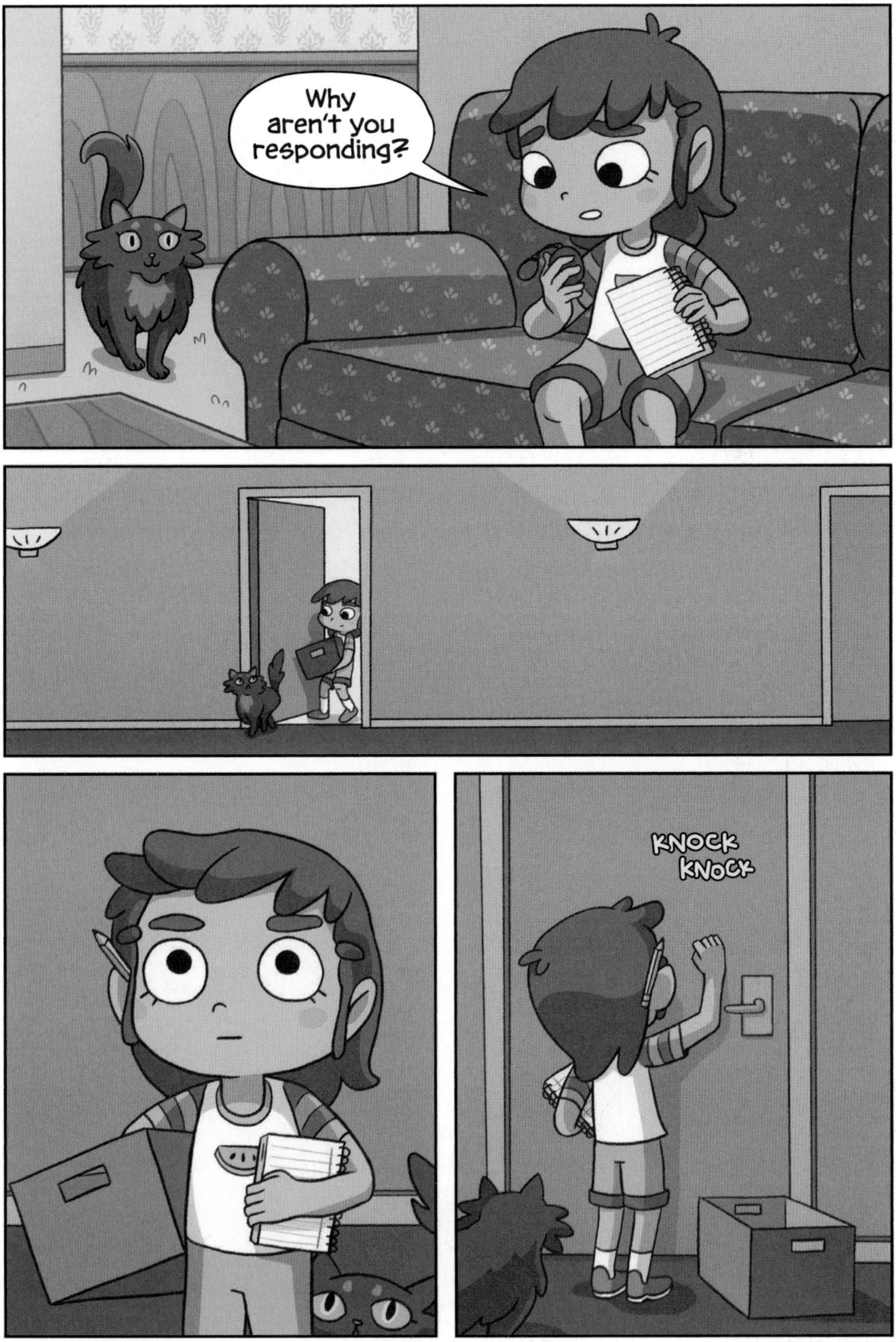
Why aren't you responding?
KNOCK
KNOCK

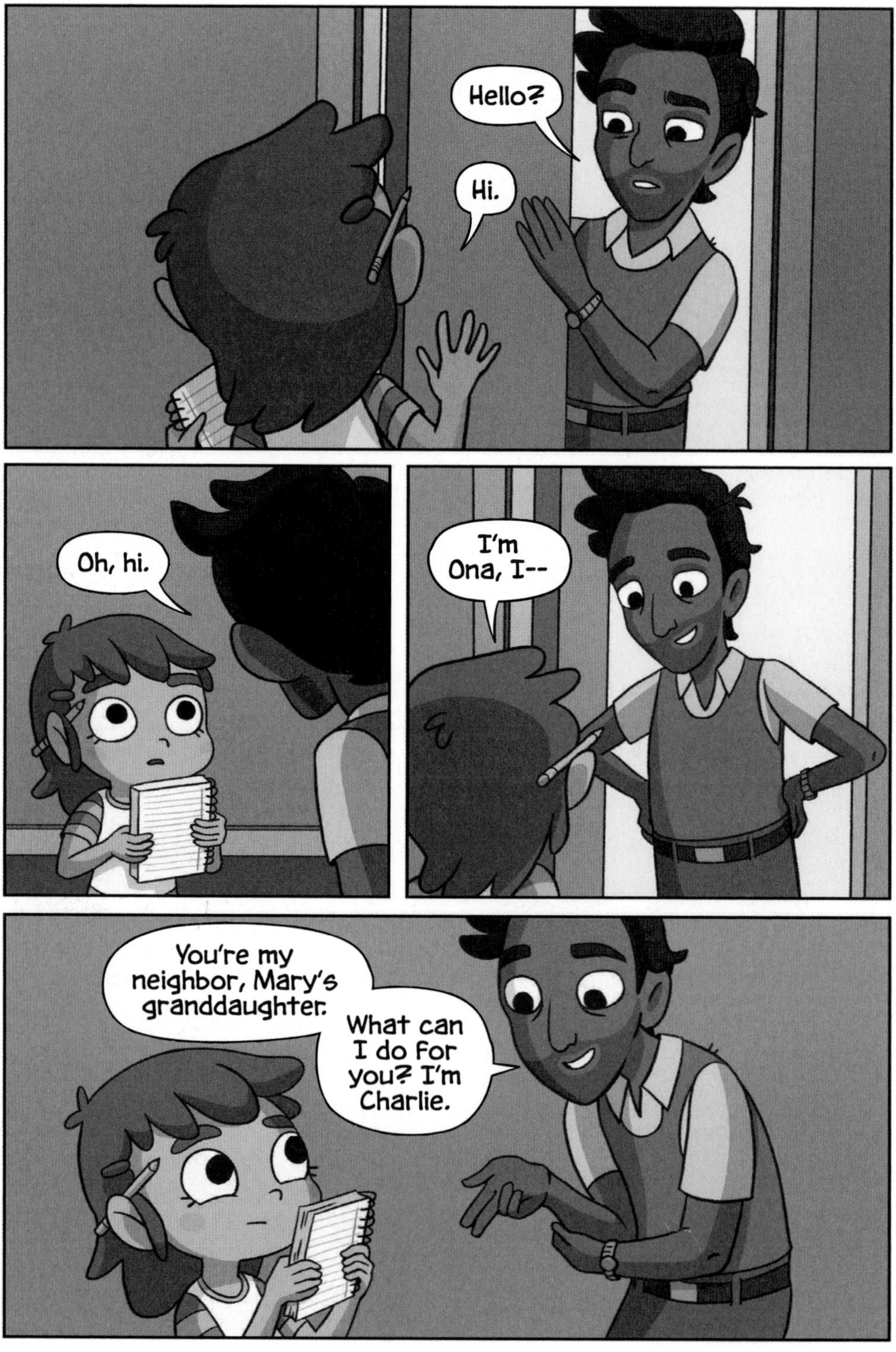
Hello?
Hi.
Oh, hi.
I'm Ona, I--
You're my neighbor, Mary's granddaughter.
What can I do for you? I'm Charlie.

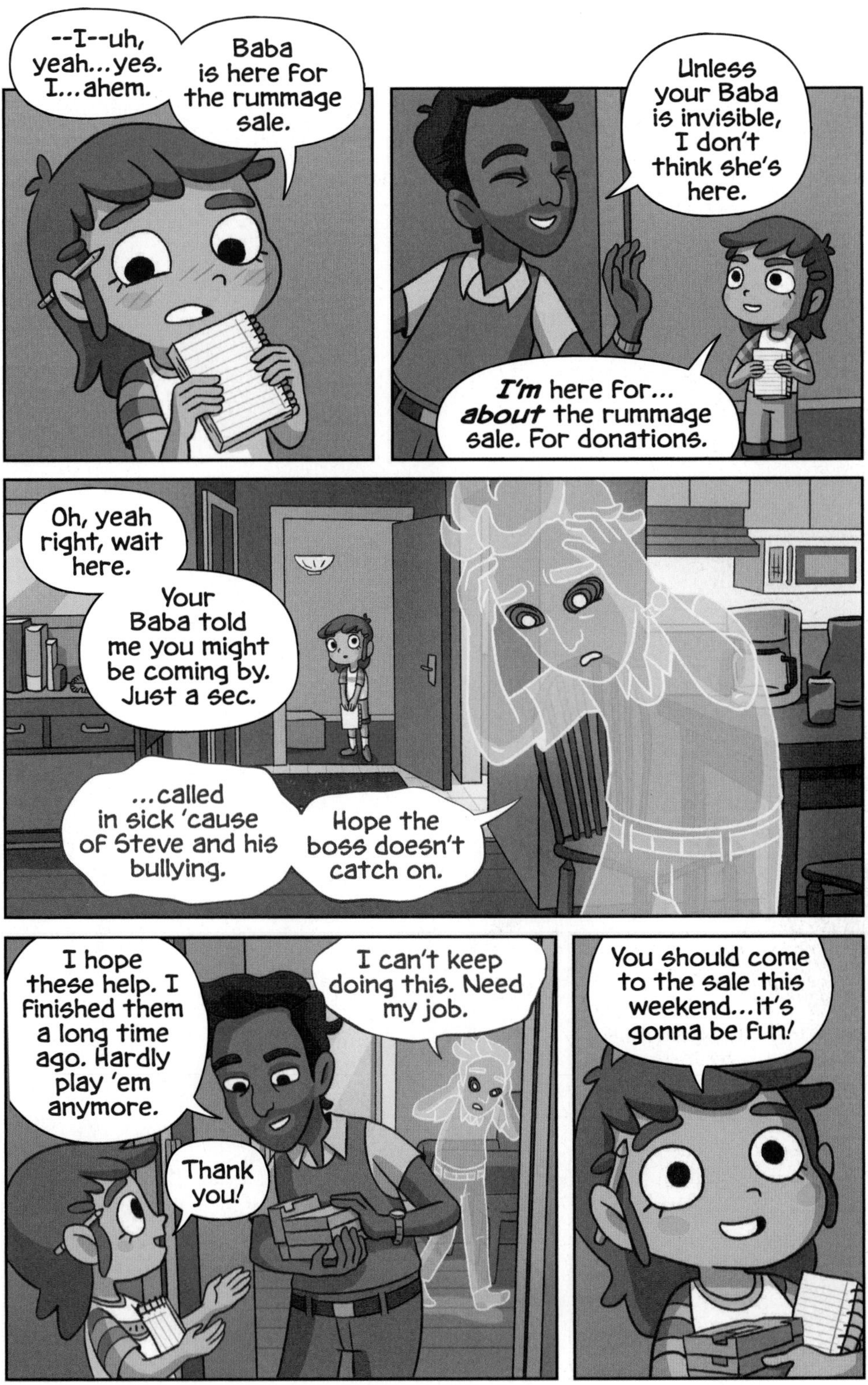
--I--uh, yeah...yes. I...ahem.
Baba is here for the rummage sale.
Unless your Baba is invisible, I don't think she's here.
I'm here for... *about* the rummage sale. For donations.
Oh, yeah right, wait here.
Your Baba told me you might be coming by. Just a sec.
...called in sick 'cause of Steve and his bullying.
Hope the boss doesn't catch on.
I hope these help. I finished them a long time ago. Hardly play 'em anymore.
I can't keep doing this. Need my job.
Thank you!
You should come to the sale this weekend...it's gonna be fun!

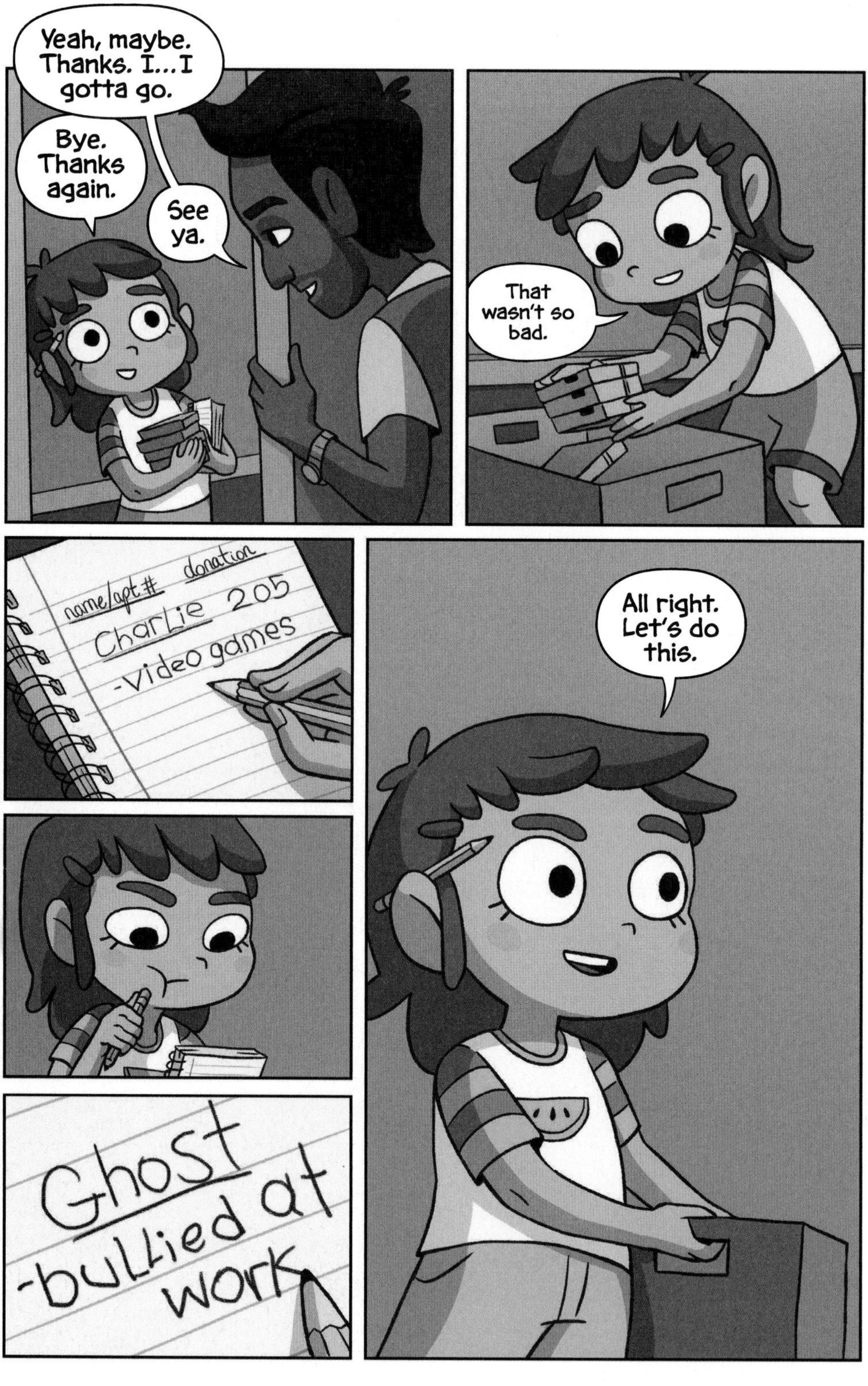
Yeah, maybe. Thanks. I...I gotta go.
Bye. Thanks again.
See ya.
That wasn't so bad.
name/apt # donation
Charlie 205
-video games
Ghost
-bullied at work
All right. Let's do this.

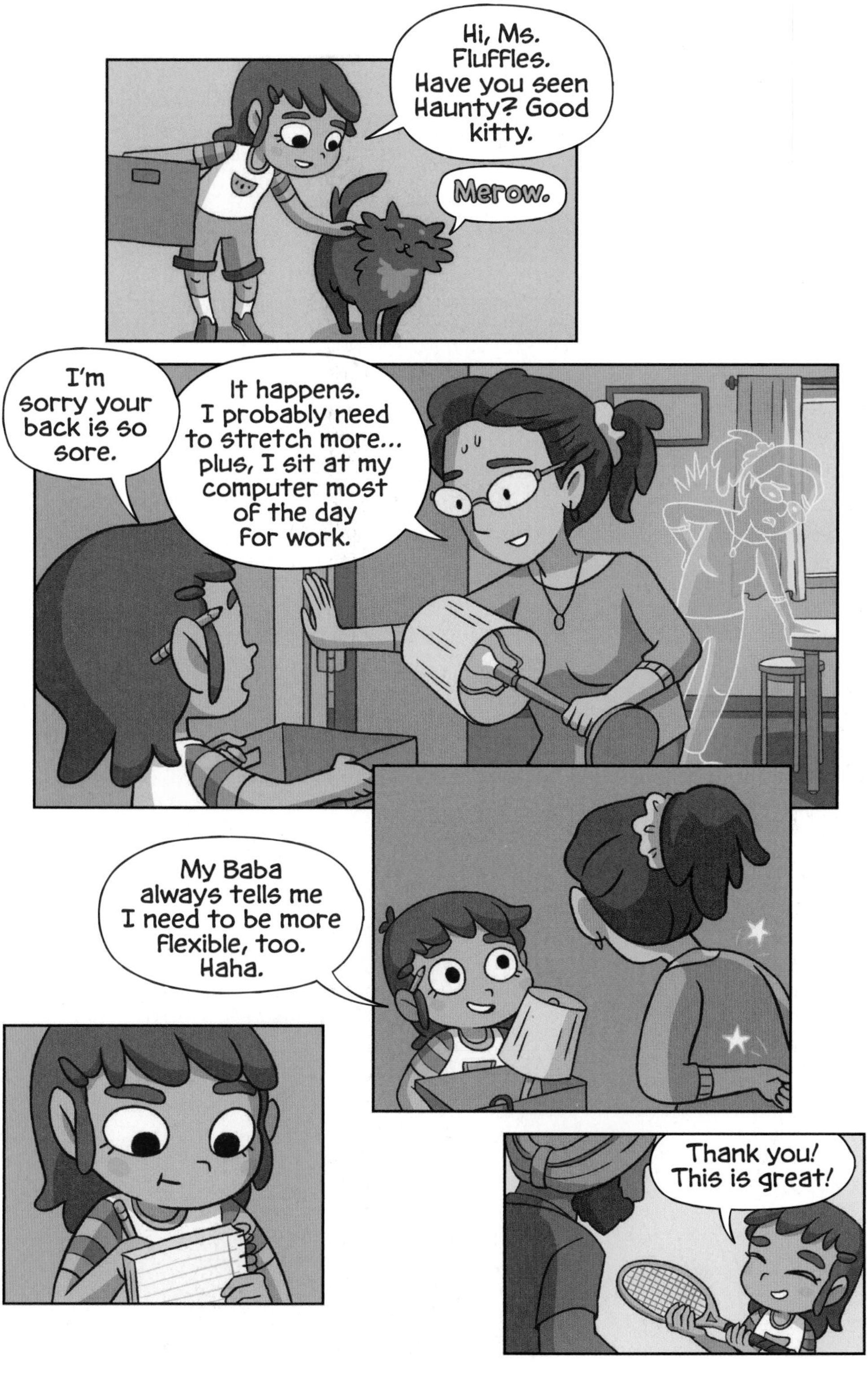
Hi, Ms. Fluffles. Have you seen Haunty? Good kitty.
Merow.
I'm sorry your back is so sore.
It happens. I probably need to stretch more... plus, I sit at my computer most of the day for work.
My Baba always tells me I need to be more flexible, too. Haha.
Thank you! This is great!

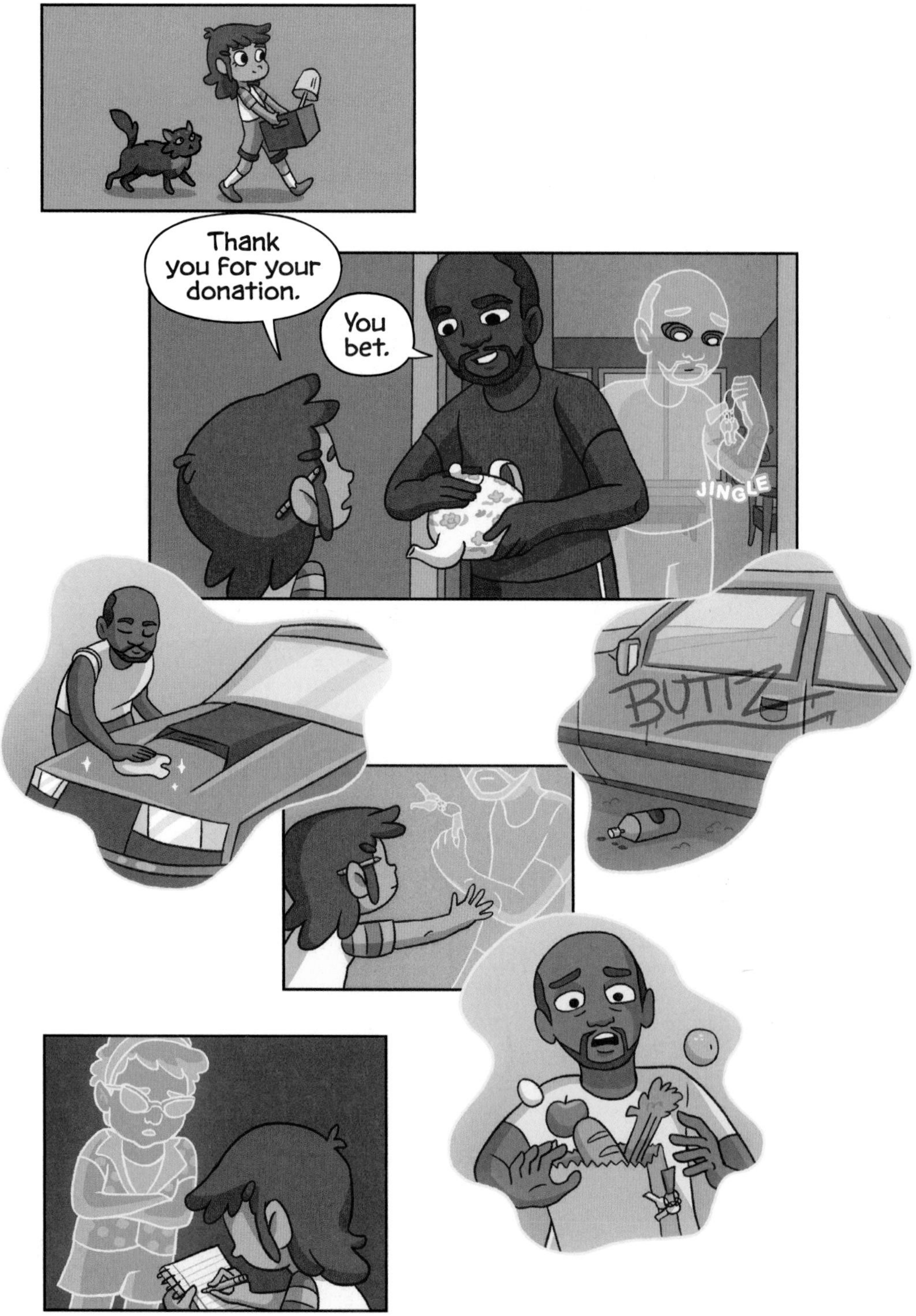
Thank you for your donation.
You bet.
JINGLE
BUTTZ

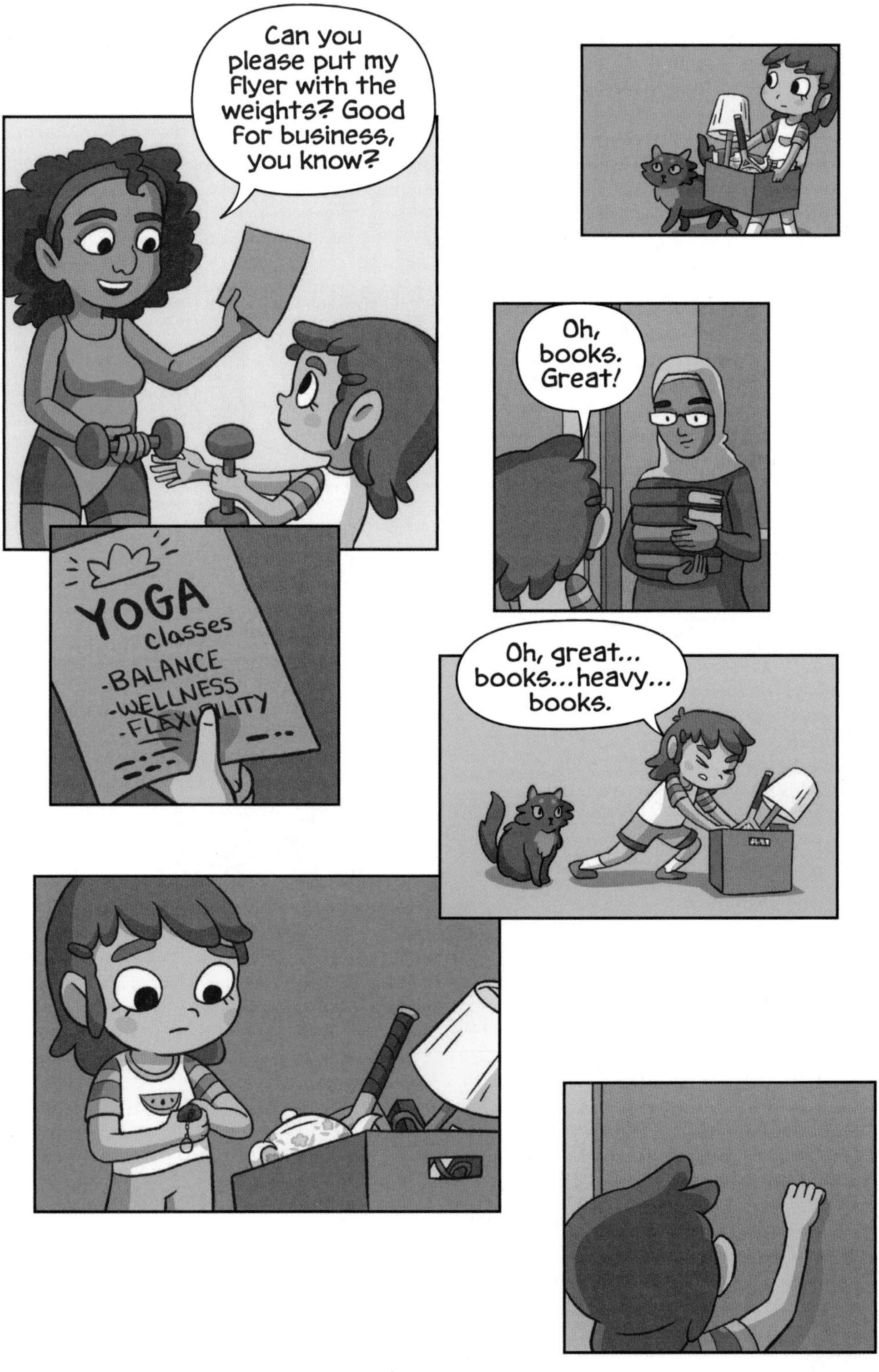
Can you please put my flyer with the weights? Good for business, you know?
YOGA
classes
-BALANCE
-WELLNESS
-FLEXIBILITY
Oh, books. Great!
Oh, great... books...heavy... books.

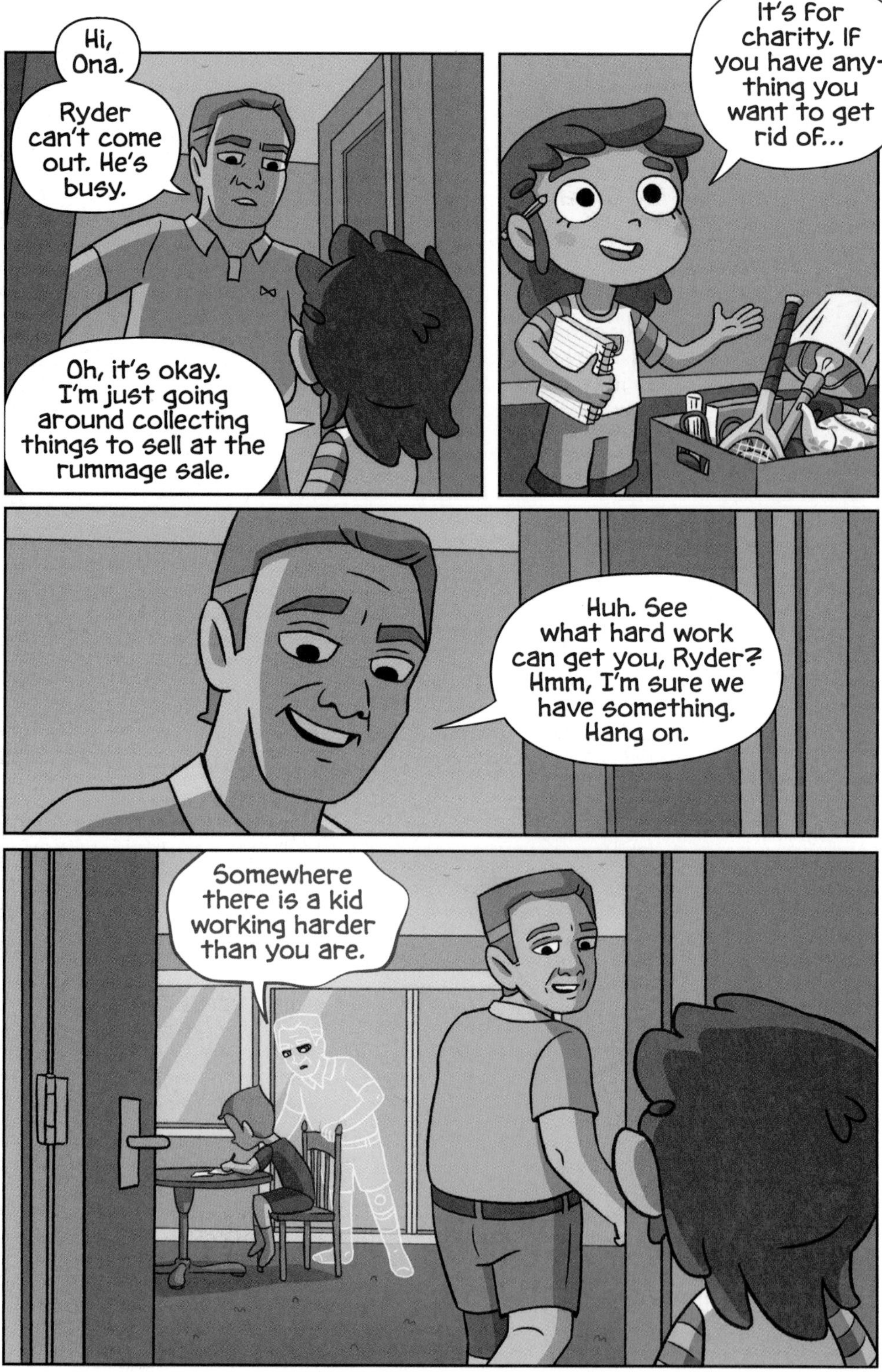

Hi, Ona.
Ryder can't come out. He's busy.
Oh, it's okay. I'm just going around collecting things to sell at the rummage sale.
It's for charity. If you have anything you want to get rid of...
Huh. See what hard work can get you, Ryder? Hmm, I'm sure we have something. Hang on.
Somewhere there is a kid working harder than you are.

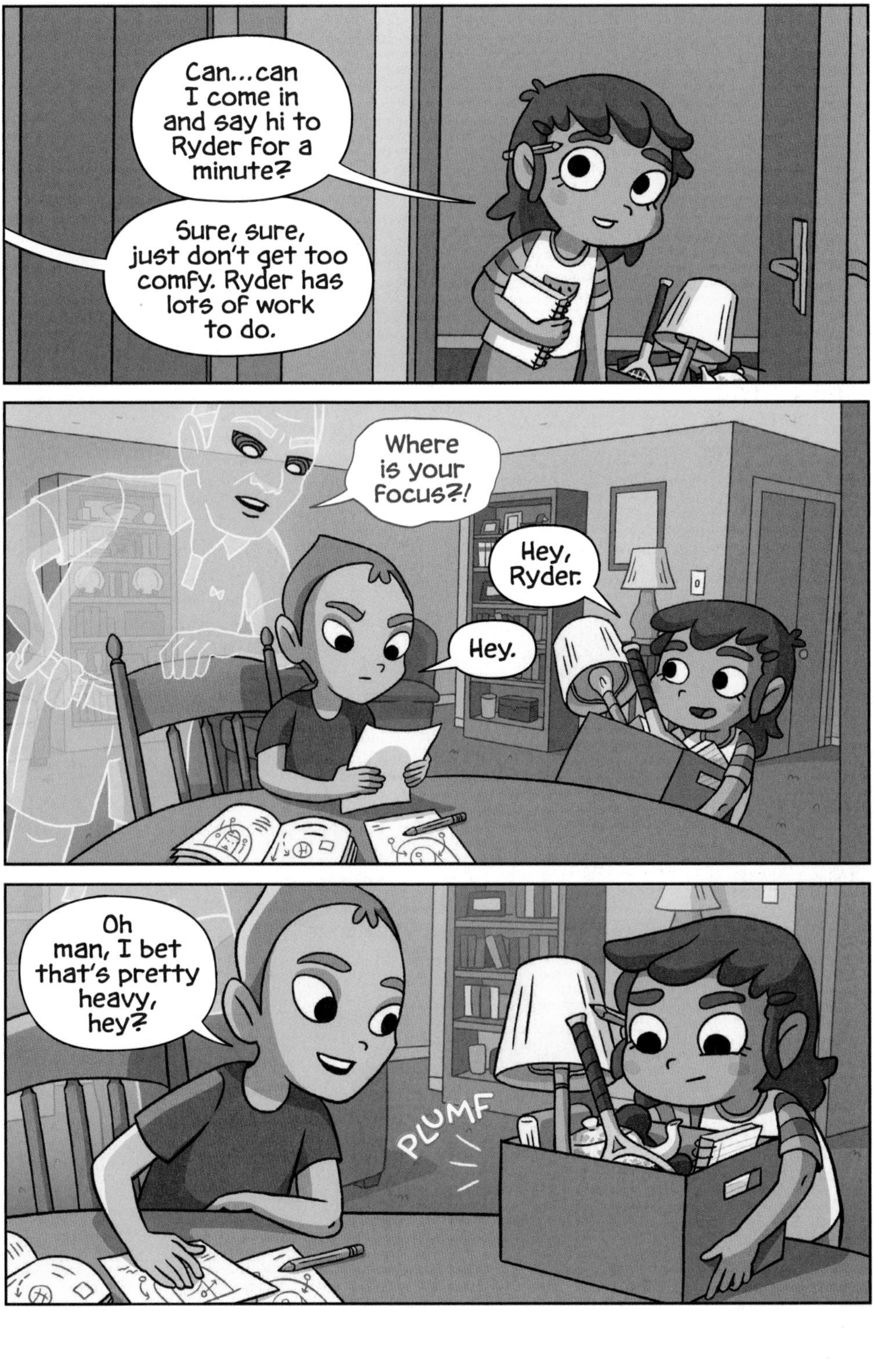
Can...can I come in and say hi to Ryder for a minute?
Sure, sure, just don't get too comfy. Ryder has lots of work to do.
Where is your focus?!
Hey, Ryder.
Hey.
Oh man, I bet that's pretty heavy, hey?
PLUMF

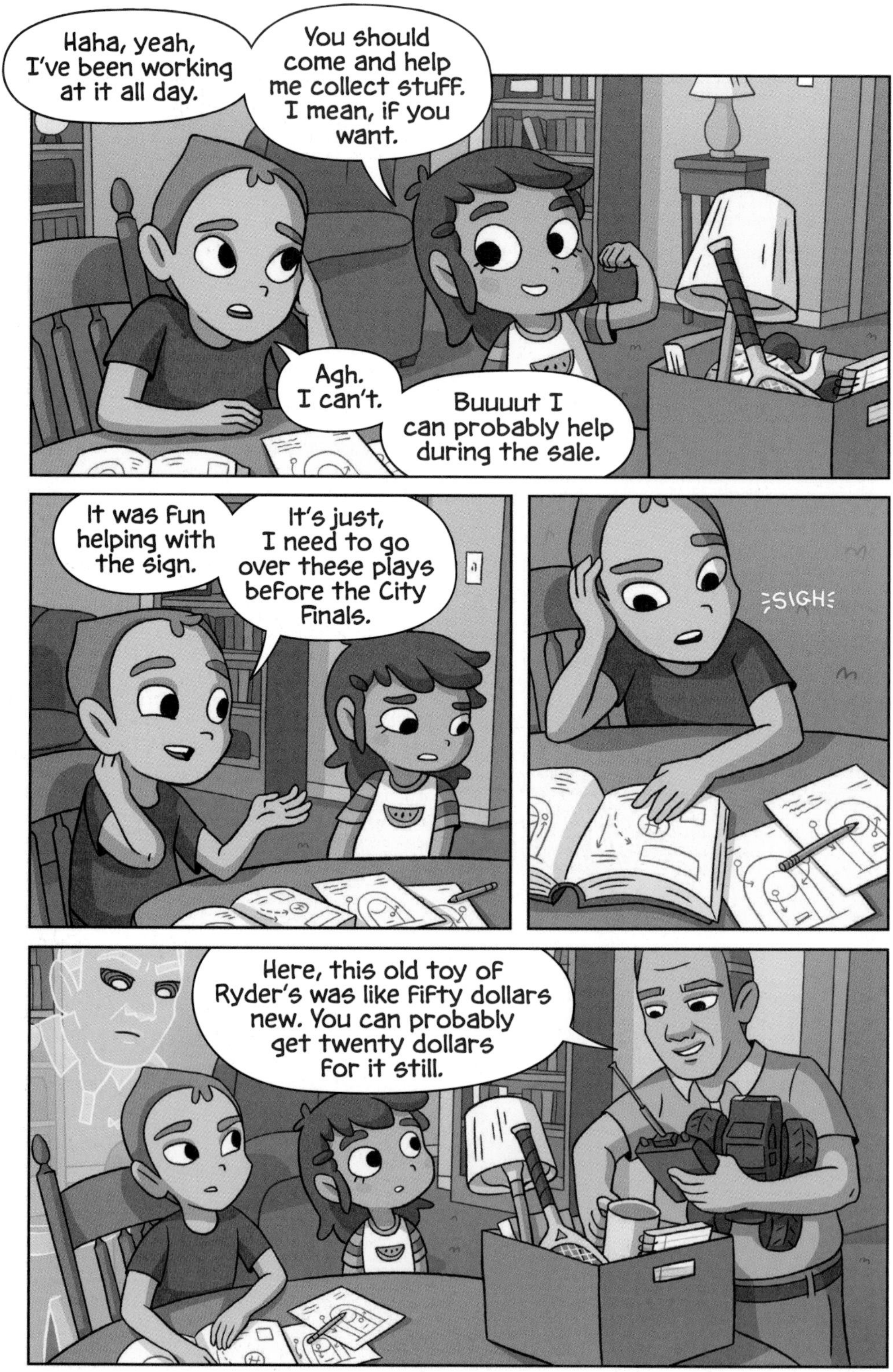
Haha, yeah, I've been working at it all day.
You should come and help me collect stuff. I mean, if you want.
Agh. I can't.
Buuuut I can probably help during the sale.
It was fun helping with the sign.
It's just, I need to go over these plays before the City Finals.
SIGH
Here, this old toy of Ryder's was like fifty dollars new. You can probably get twenty dollars for it still.

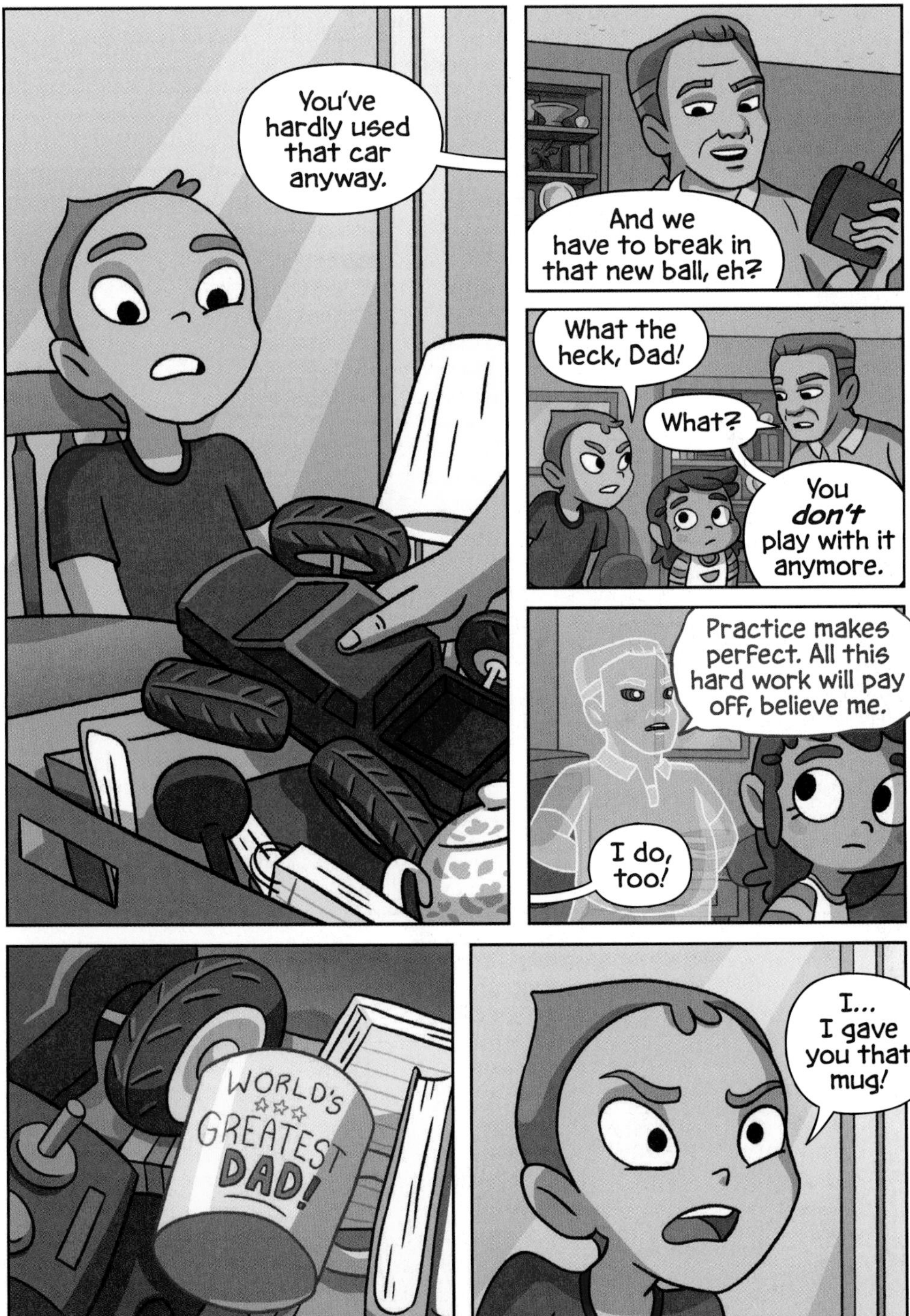
You've hardly used that car anyway.
And we have to break in that new ball, eh?
What the heck, Dad!
What?
You *don't* play with it anymore.
Practice makes perfect. All this hard work will pay off, believe me.
I do, too!
WORLD'S GREATEST DAD!
I... I gave you that mug!

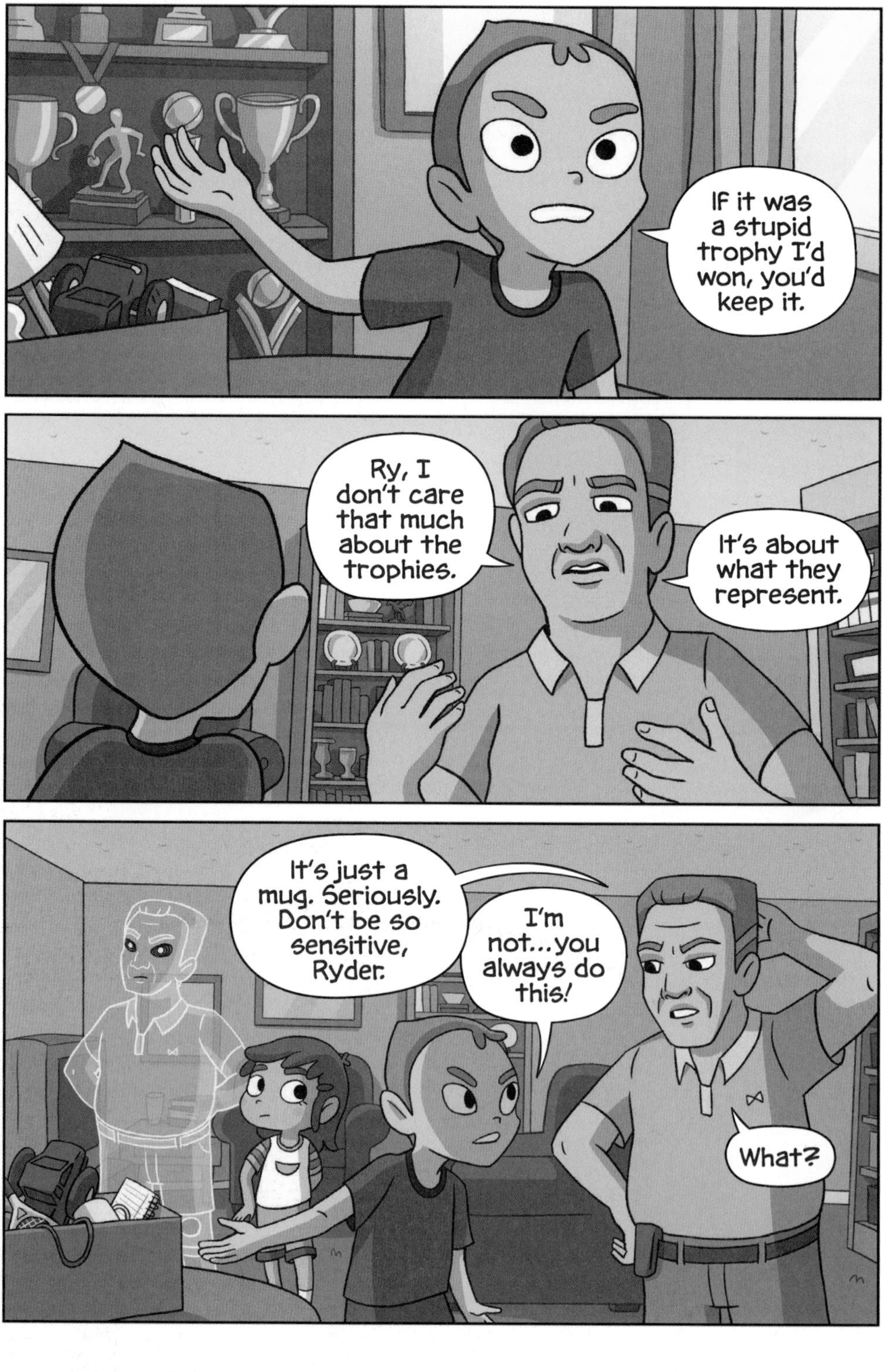
If it was a stupid trophy I'd won, you'd keep it.
Ry, I don't care that much about the trophies.
It's about what they represent.
It's just a mug. Seriously. Don't be so sensitive, Ryder.
I'm not...you always do this!
What?

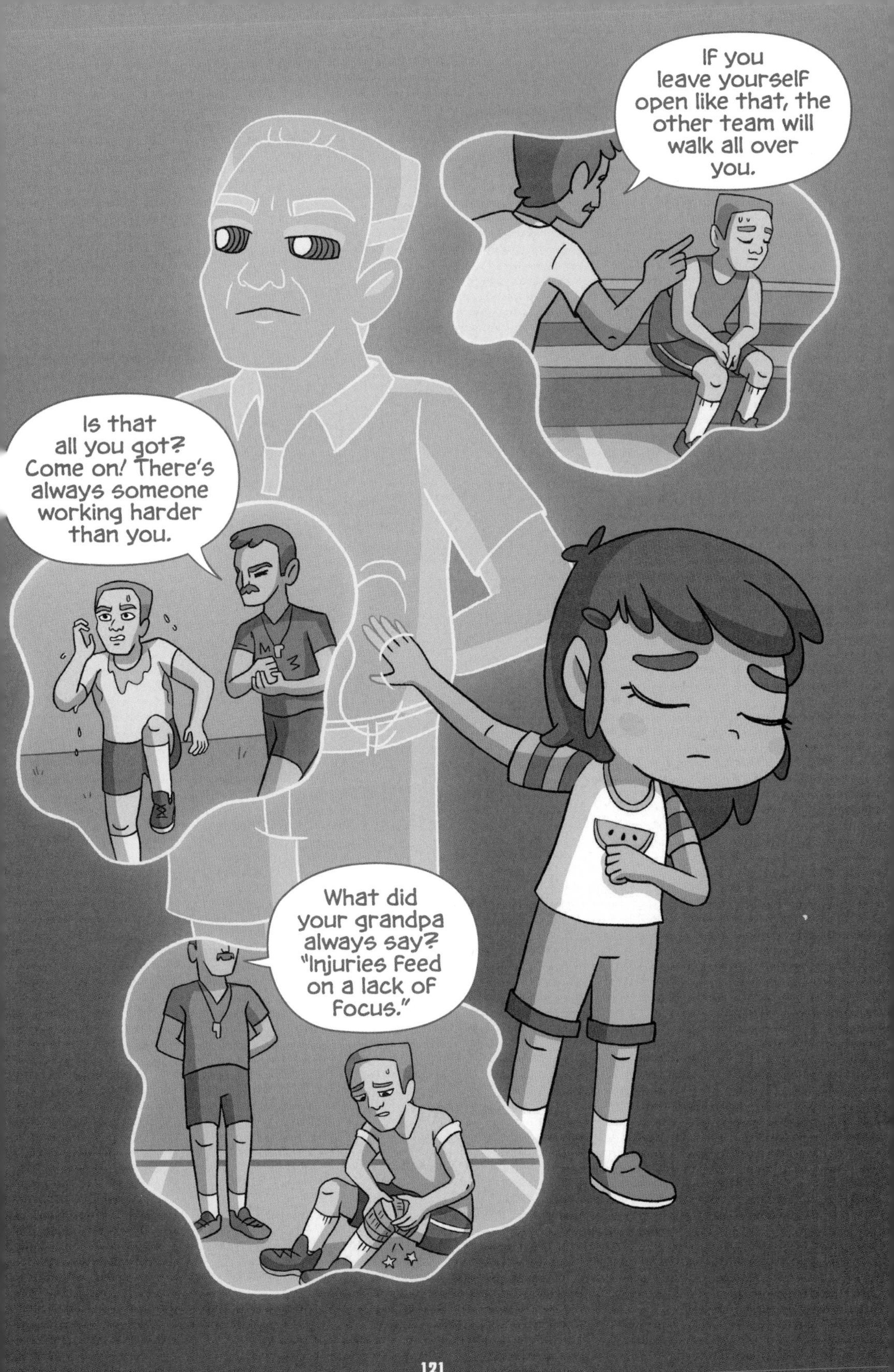
If you leave yourself open like that, the other team will walk all over you.
Is that all you got? Come on! There's always someone working harder than you.
What did your grandpa always say? "Injuries feed on a lack of focus."

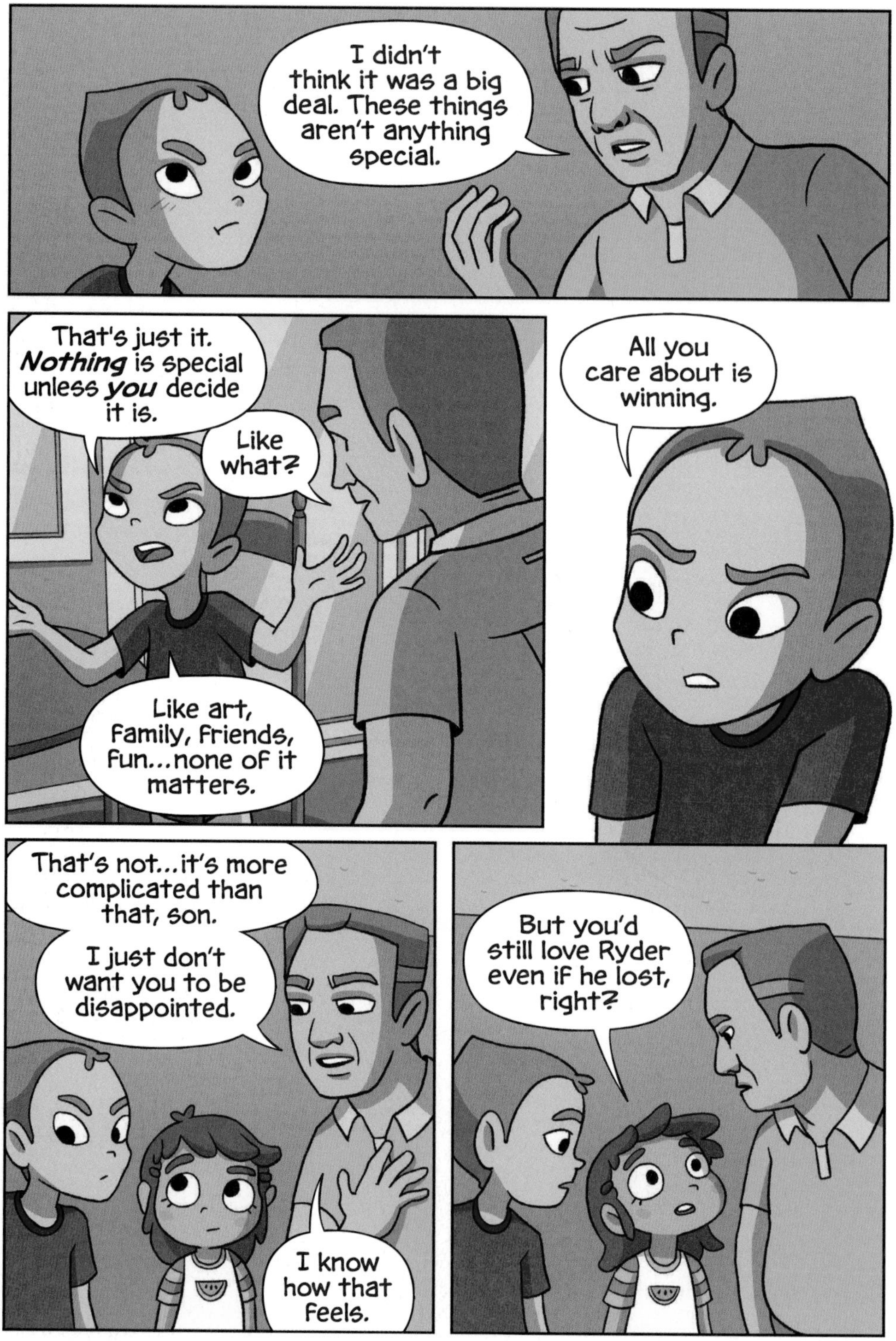
I didn't think it was a big deal. These things aren't anything special.
That's just it. *Nothing* is special unless *you* decide it is.
Like what?
Like art, family, friends, fun...none of it matters.
All you care about is winning.
That's not...it's more complicated than that, son.
I just don't want you to be disappointed.
I know how that feels.
But you'd still love Ryder even if he lost, right?

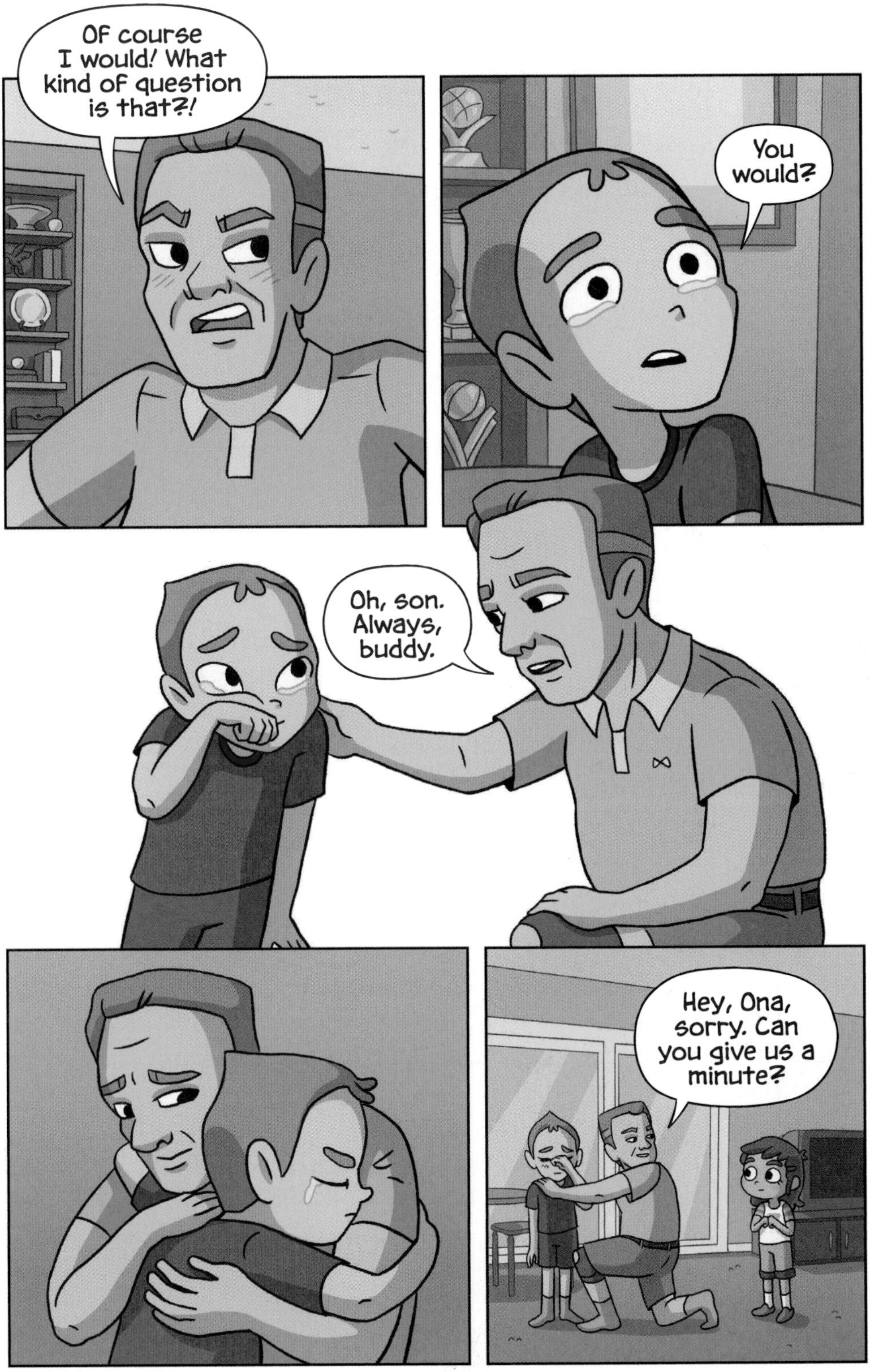
Of course I would! What kind of question is that?!
You would?
Oh, son. Always, buddy.
Hey, Ona, sorry. Can you give us a minute?

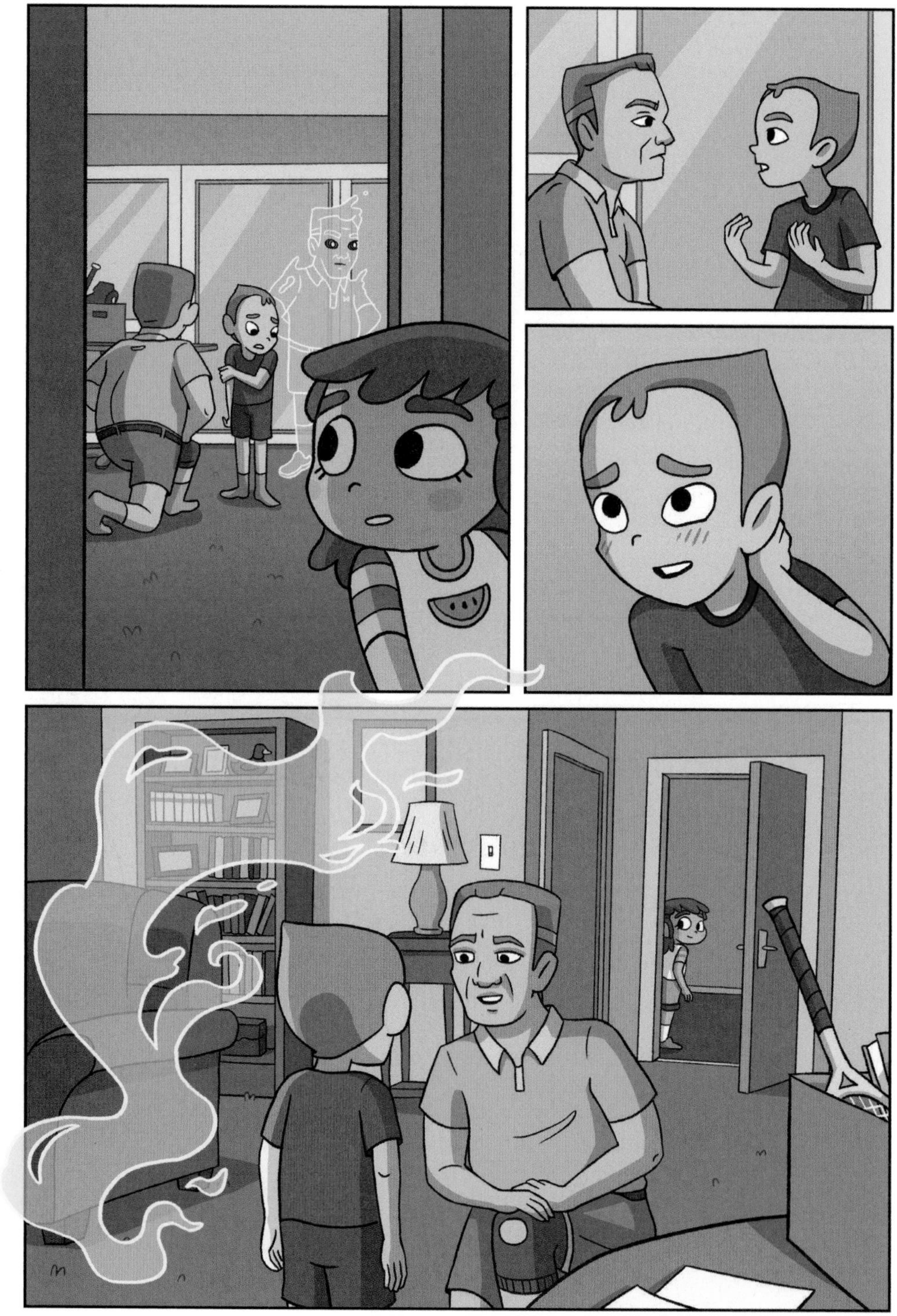

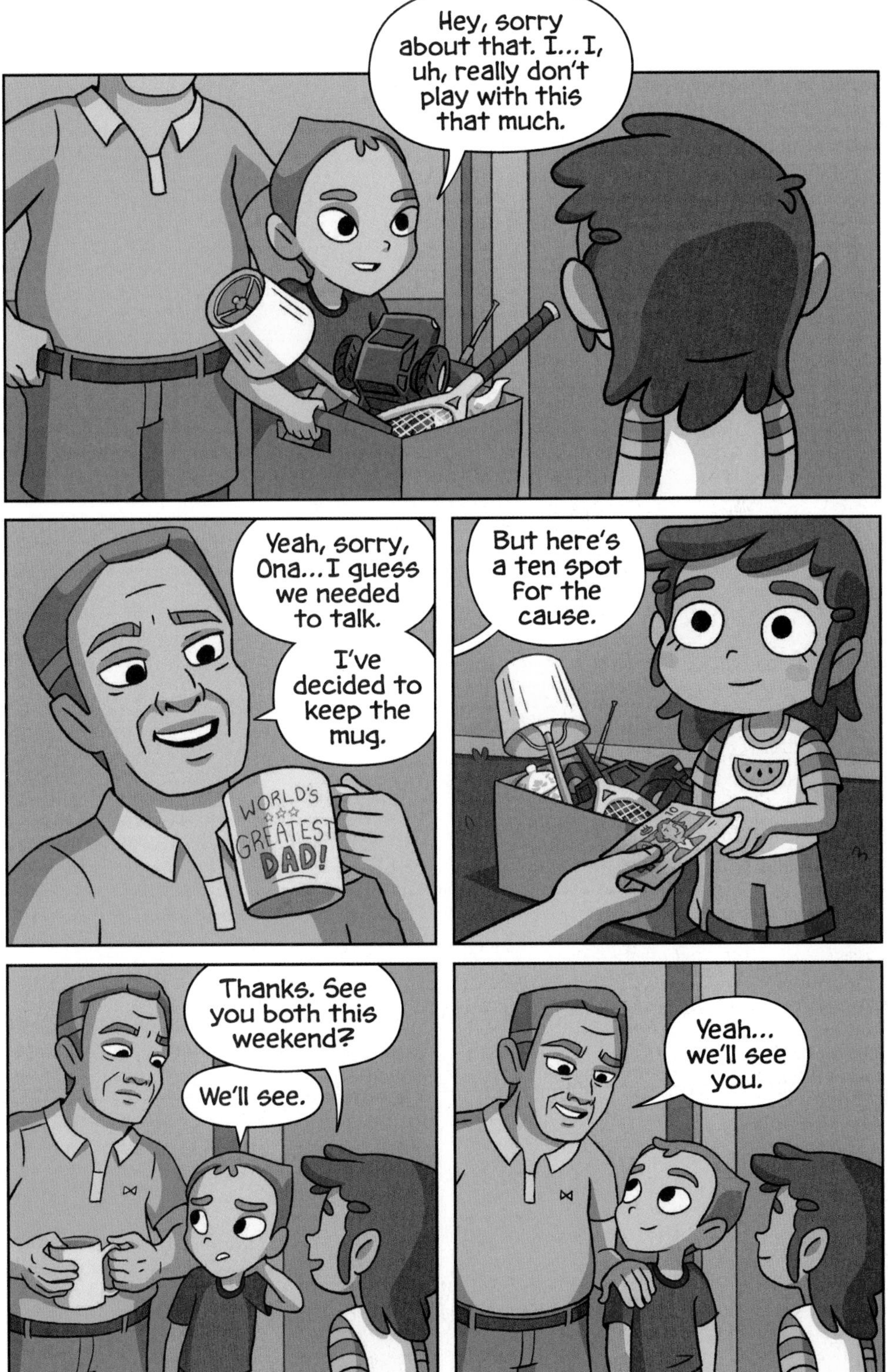

Hey, sorry about that. I...I, uh, really don't play with this that much.
Yeah, sorry, Ona...I guess we needed to talk.
I've decided to keep the mug.
WORLD'S GREATEST DAD!
But here's a ten spot for the cause.
Thanks. See you both this weekend?
We'll see.
Yeah... we'll see you.

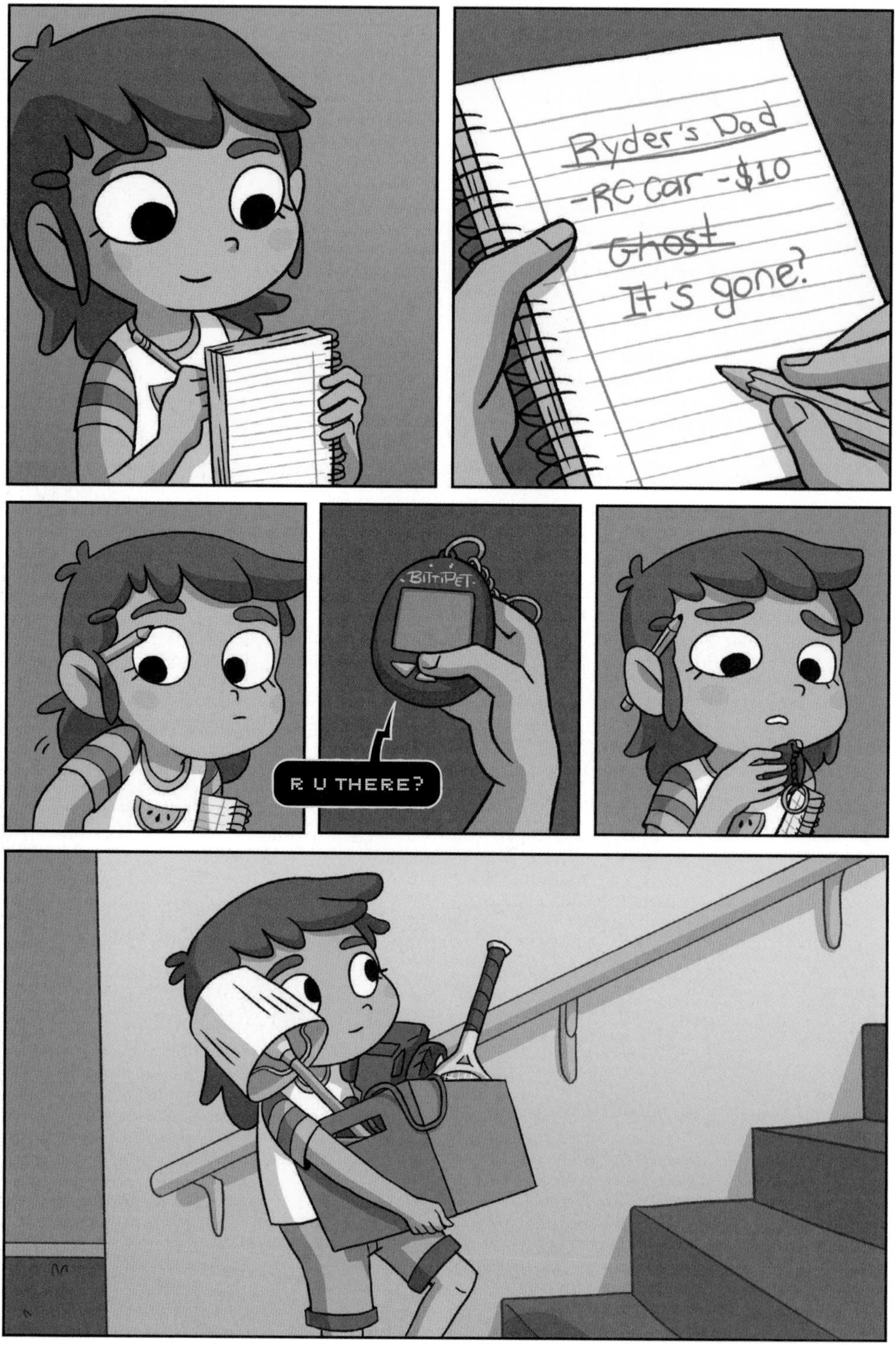
Ryder's Dad
-RC car -$10
Ghost
It's gone?
BITTIPET
R U THERE?

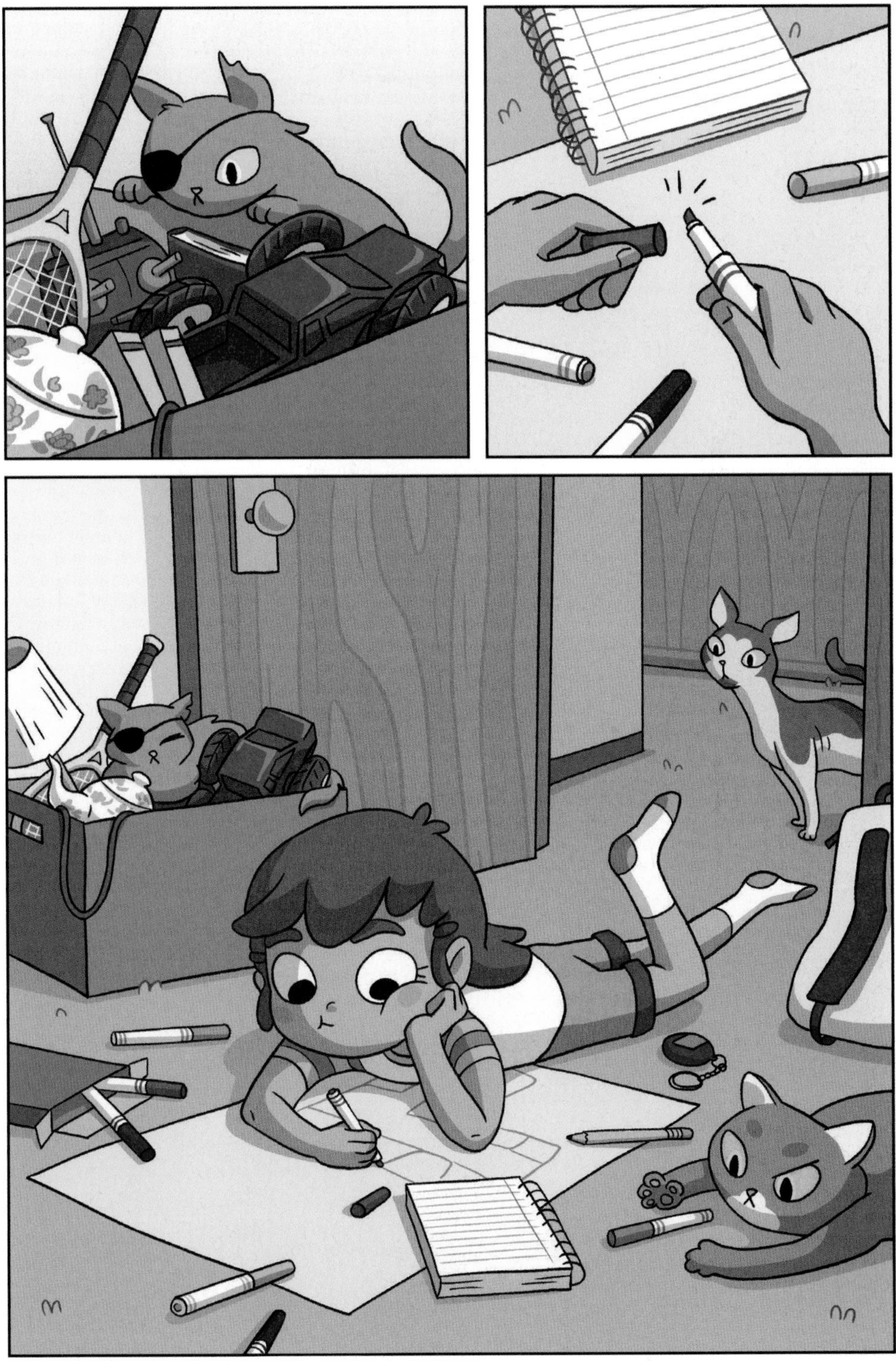

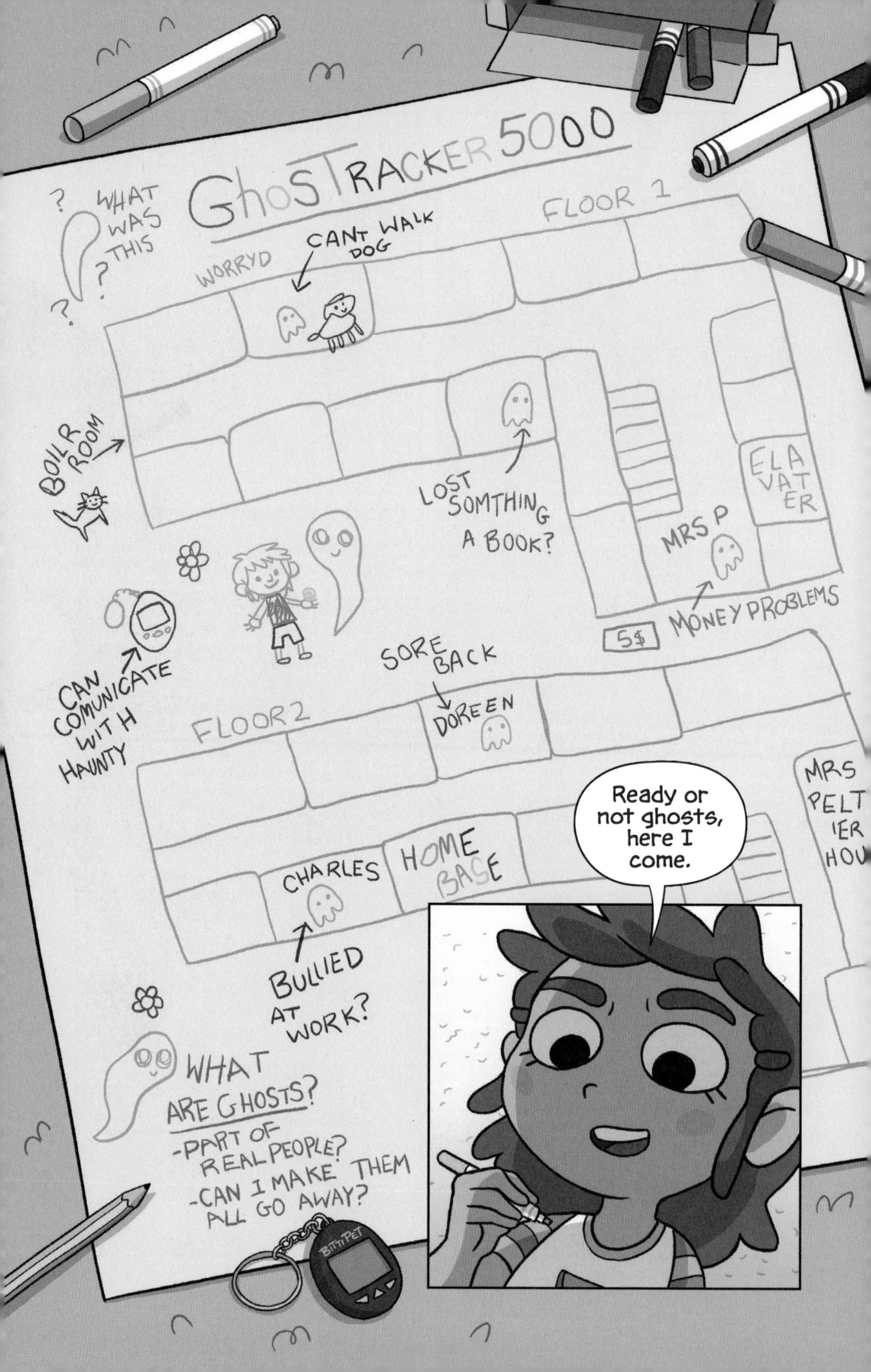
GhosTRACKER 5000
WHAT WAS THIS
FLOOR 1
WORRYD
CANT WALK DOG
BOILR ROOM
LOST SOMTHING A BOOK?
ELA VAT ER
MRS P
MONEY PROBLEMS
5$
CAN COMUNICATE WITH HAUNTY
SORE BACK
DOREEN
FLOOR2
CHARLES
HOME BASE
BULLIED AT WORK?
WHAT ARE GHOSTS?
-PART OF REAL PEOPLE?
-CAN I MAKE THEM ALL GO AWAY?
BITTIPET
Ready or not ghosts, here I come.

CHAPTER SEVEN.

Ona! Wake up! Breakfast is ready.

Yisty, yisty* it will stick to your ribs.

*Eat.

This brown sugar will make sure it sticks.

Heh...so good.

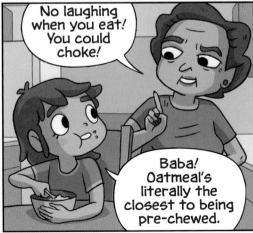

No laughing when you eat! You could choke!

Baba! Oatmeal's literally the closest to being pre-chewed.

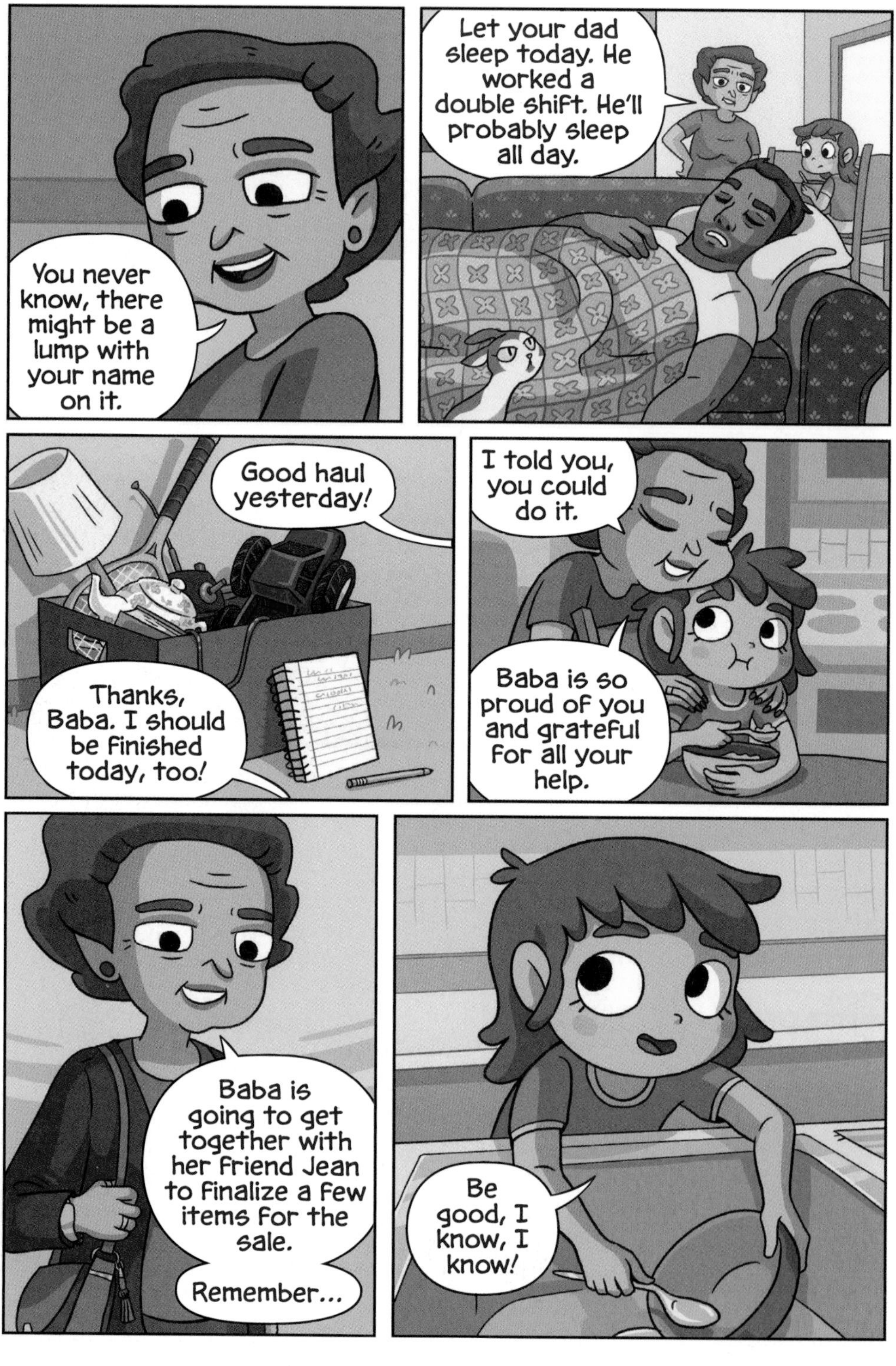
You never know, there might be a lump with your name on it.
Let your dad sleep today. He worked a double shift. He'll probably sleep all day.
Good haul yesterday!
Thanks, Baba. I should be finished today, too!
I told you, you could do it.
Baba is so proud of you and grateful for all your help.
Baba is going to get together with her friend Jean to finalize a few items for the sale.
Remember...
Be good, I know, I know!

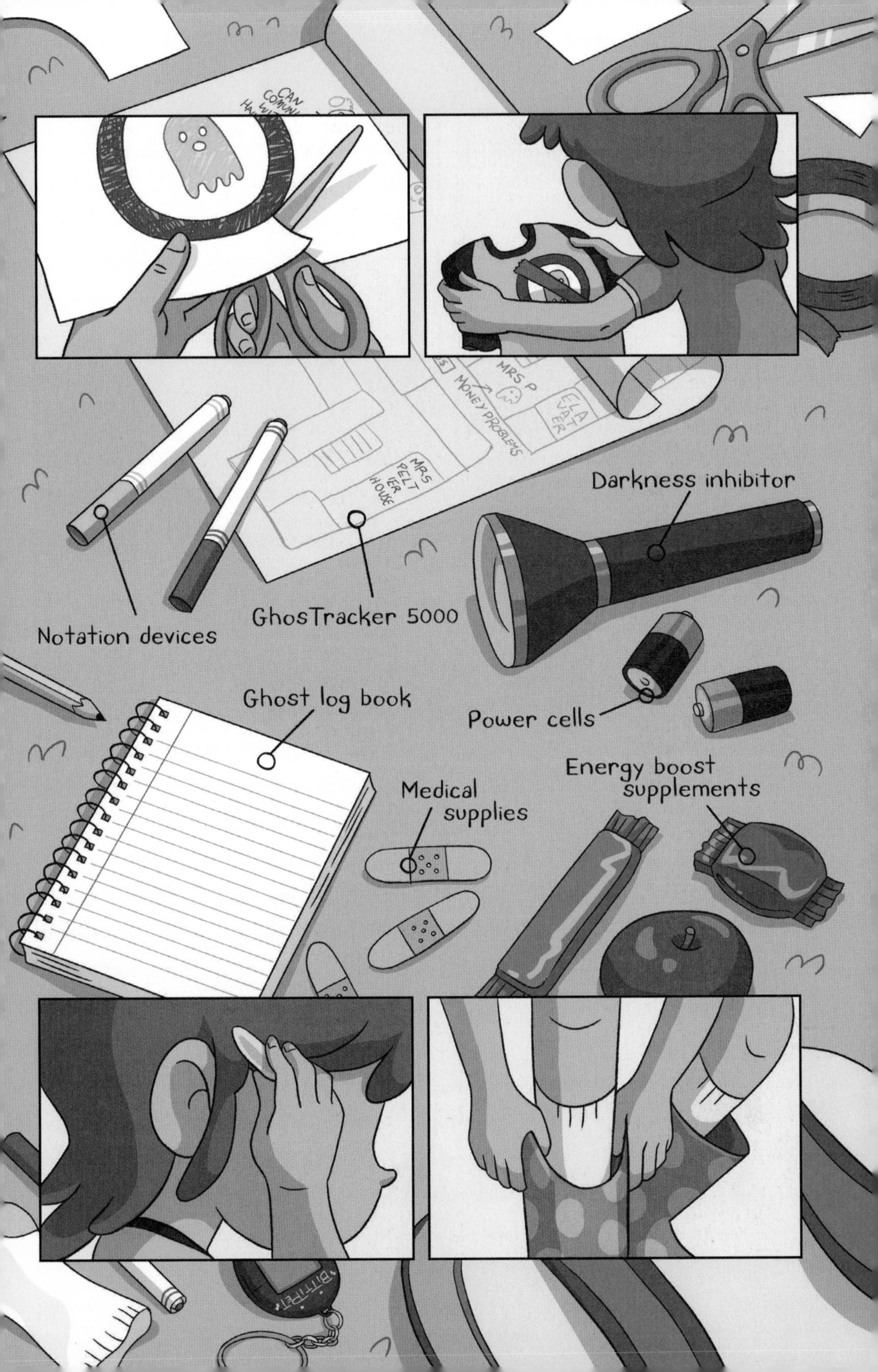
MRS P
MONEY PROBLEMS
ELA VAT ER
MRS PELT IER HOUSE
Darkness inhibitor
Notation devices
GhosTracker 5000
Ghost log book
Power cells
Energy boost supplements
Medical supplies
BITTIPET

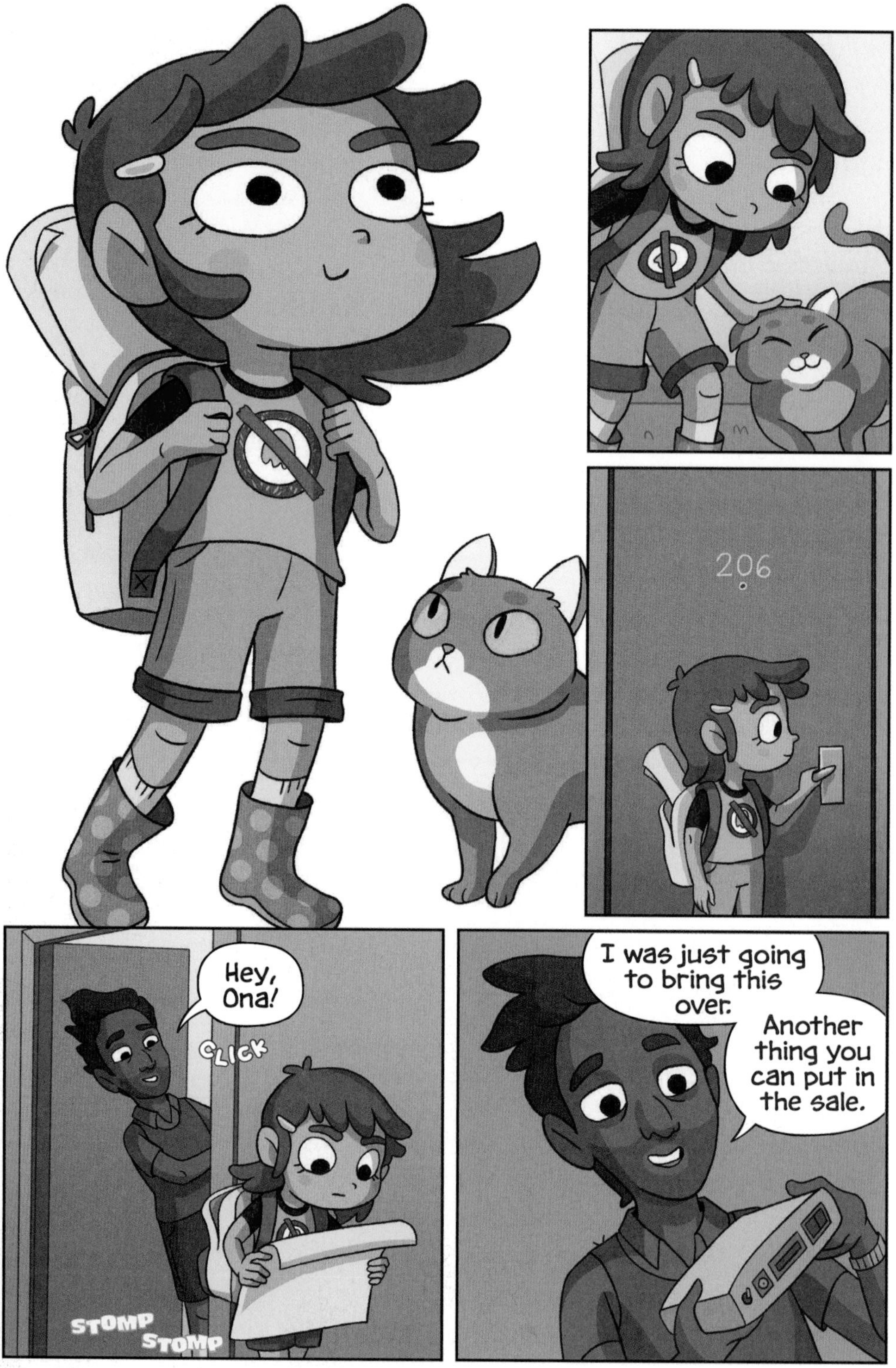
206
Hey, Ona!
CLICK
STOMP
STOMP
I was just going to bring this over.
Another thing you can put in the sale.

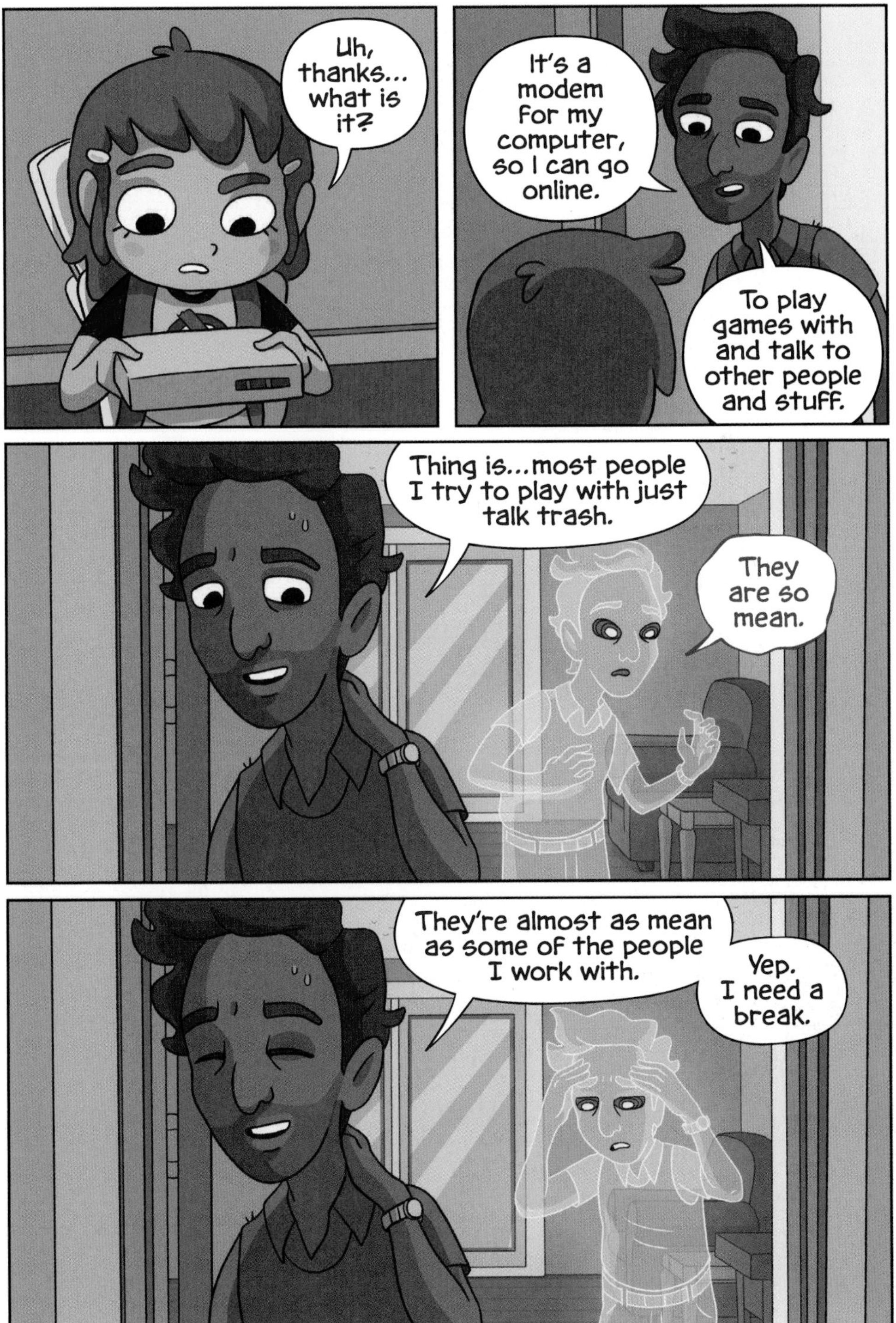
Uh, thanks... what is it?
It's a modem for my computer, so I can go online.
To play games with and talk to other people and stuff.
Thing is...most people I try to play with just talk trash.
They are so mean.
They're almost as mean as some of the people I work with.
Yep. I need a break.

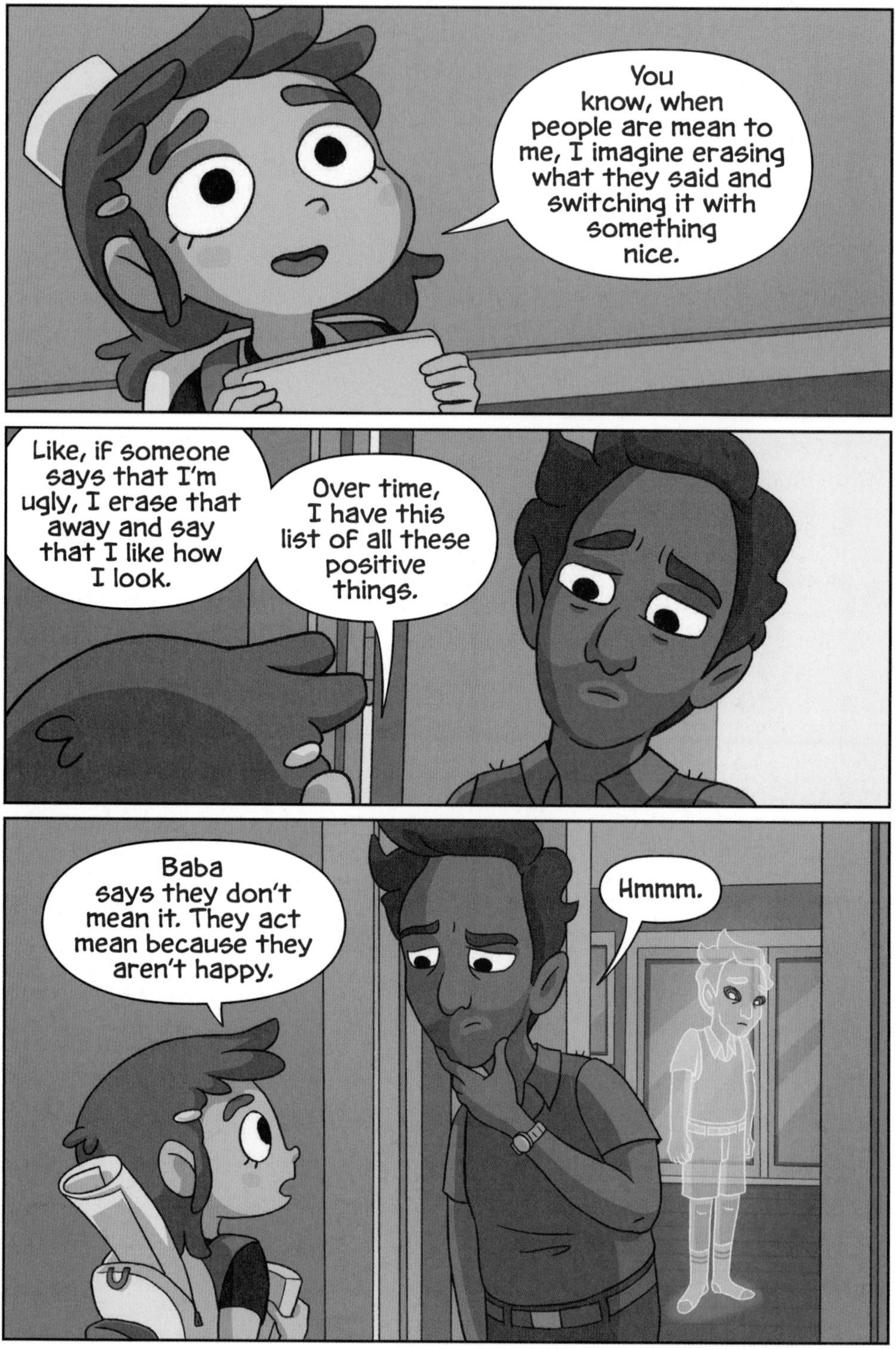
You know, when people are mean to me, I imagine erasing what they said and switching it with something nice.
Like, if someone says that I'm ugly, I erase that away and say that I like how I look.
Over time, I have this list of all these positive things.
Baba says they don't mean it. They act mean because they aren't happy.
Hmmm.

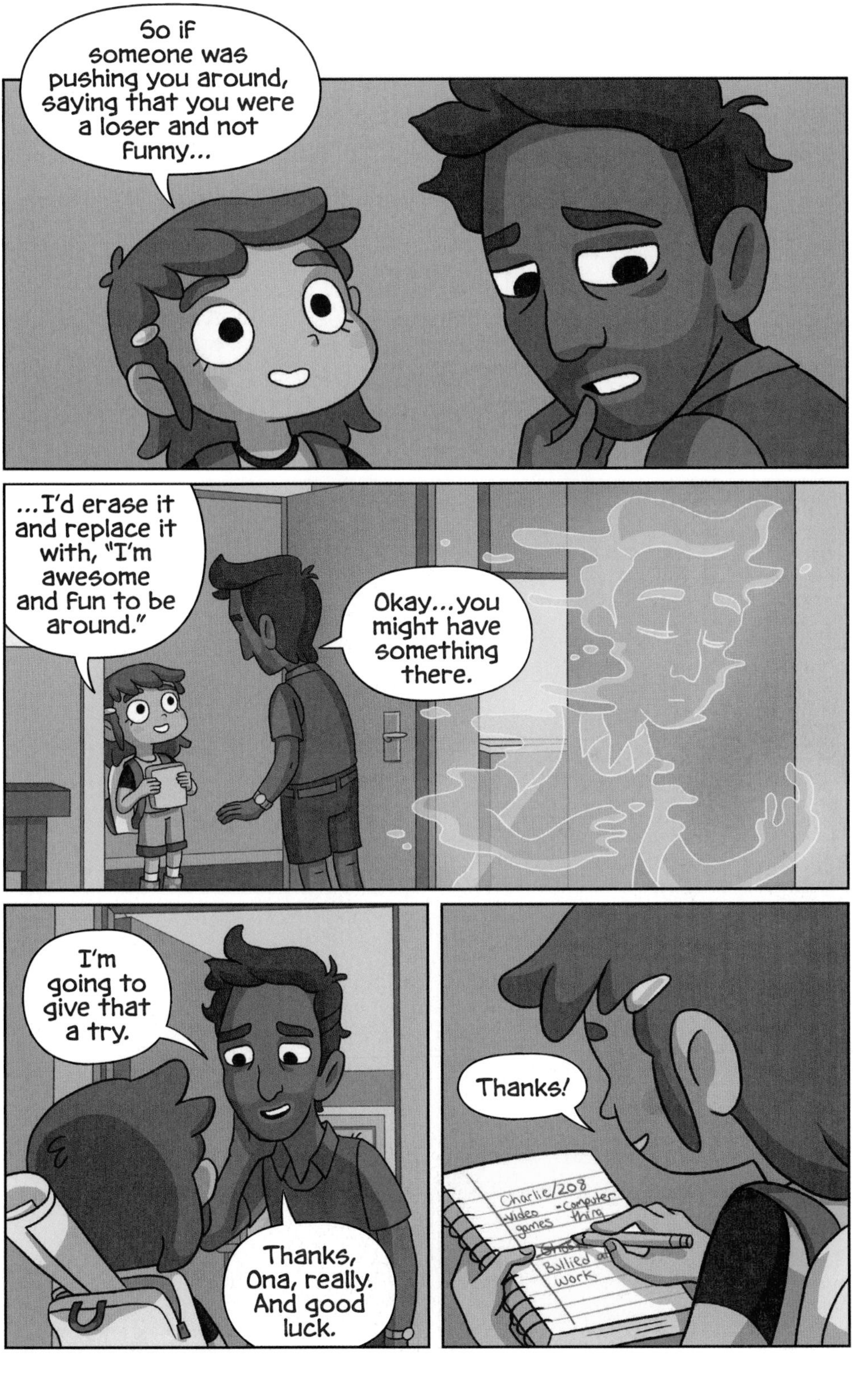
So if someone was pushing you around, saying that you were a loser and not funny...
...I'd erase it and replace it with, "I'm awesome and fun to be around."
Okay...you might have something there.
I'm going to give that a try.
Thanks, Ona, really. And good luck.
Thanks!
Charlie/208
-video games -computer thing
-Ghost Bullied at work

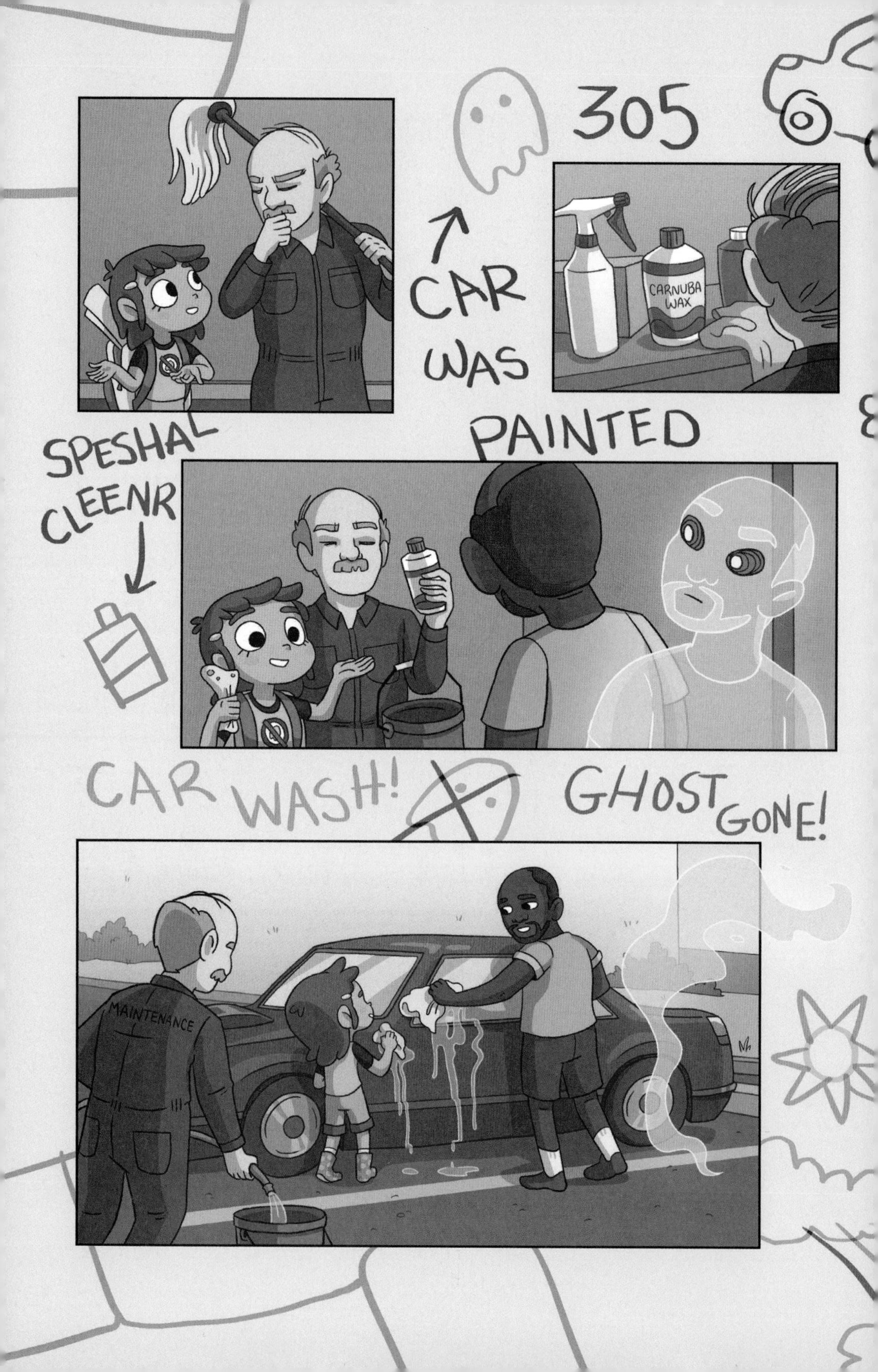
305
CAR WAS PAINTED
CARNUBA WAX
SPESHAL CLEENR
CAR WASH!
GHOST GONE!
MAINTENANCE

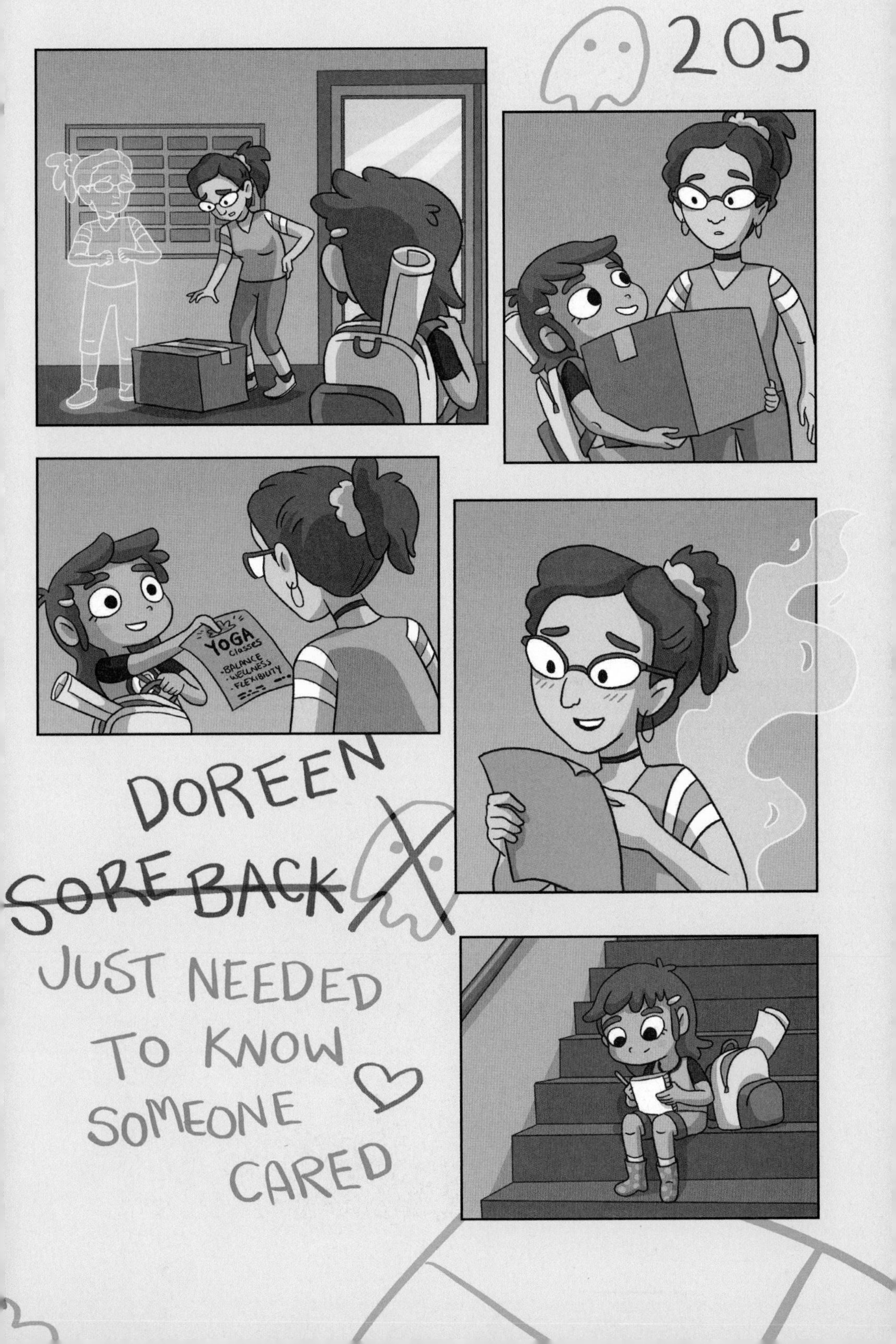
205
YOGA
classes
•BALANCE
•WELLNESS
•FLEXIBILITY
DOREEN
SORE BACK
JUST NEEDED
TO KNOW
SOMEONE
CARED

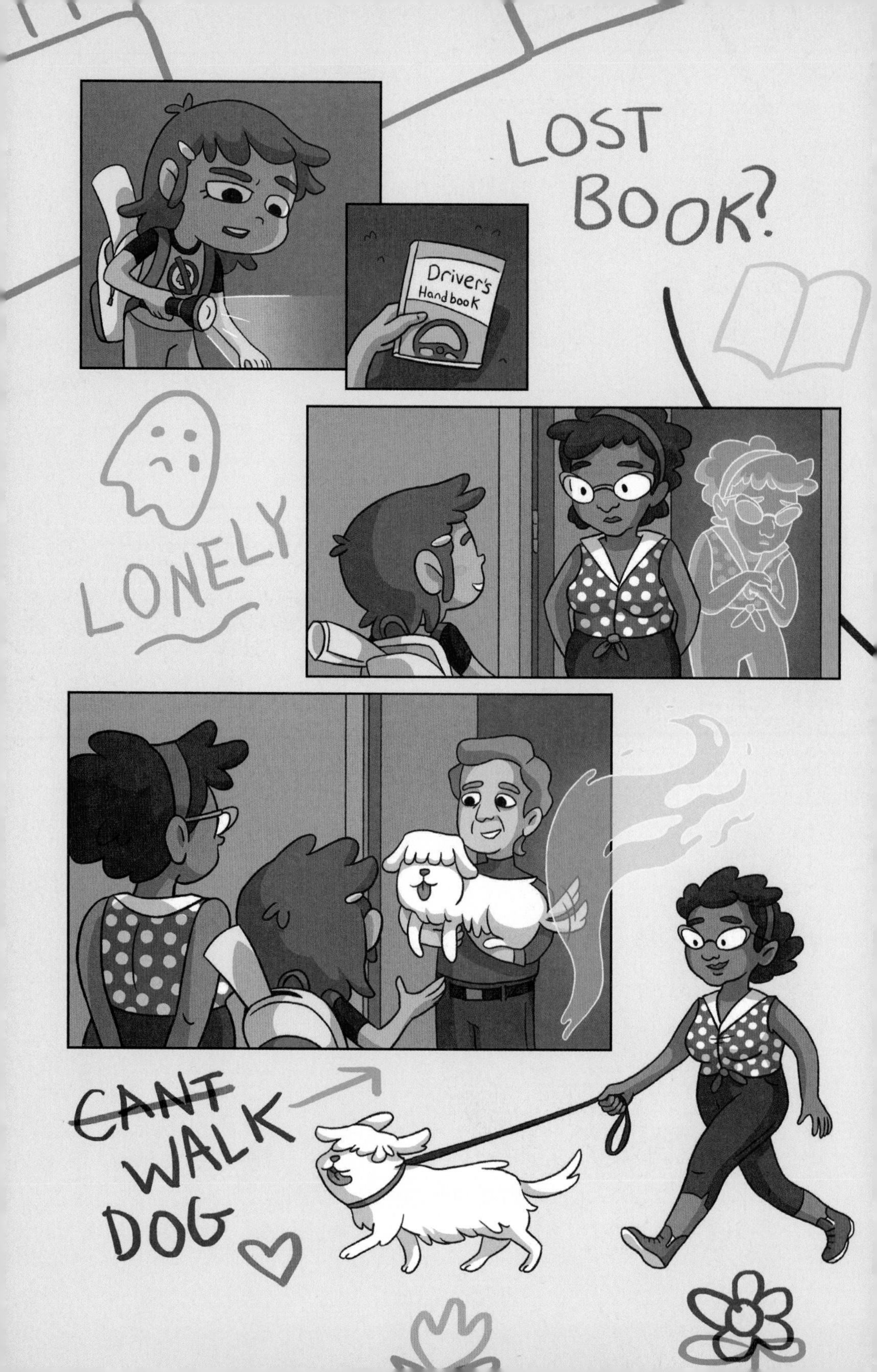
LOST BOOK?
Driver's Handbook
LONELY
CANT
WALK
DOG

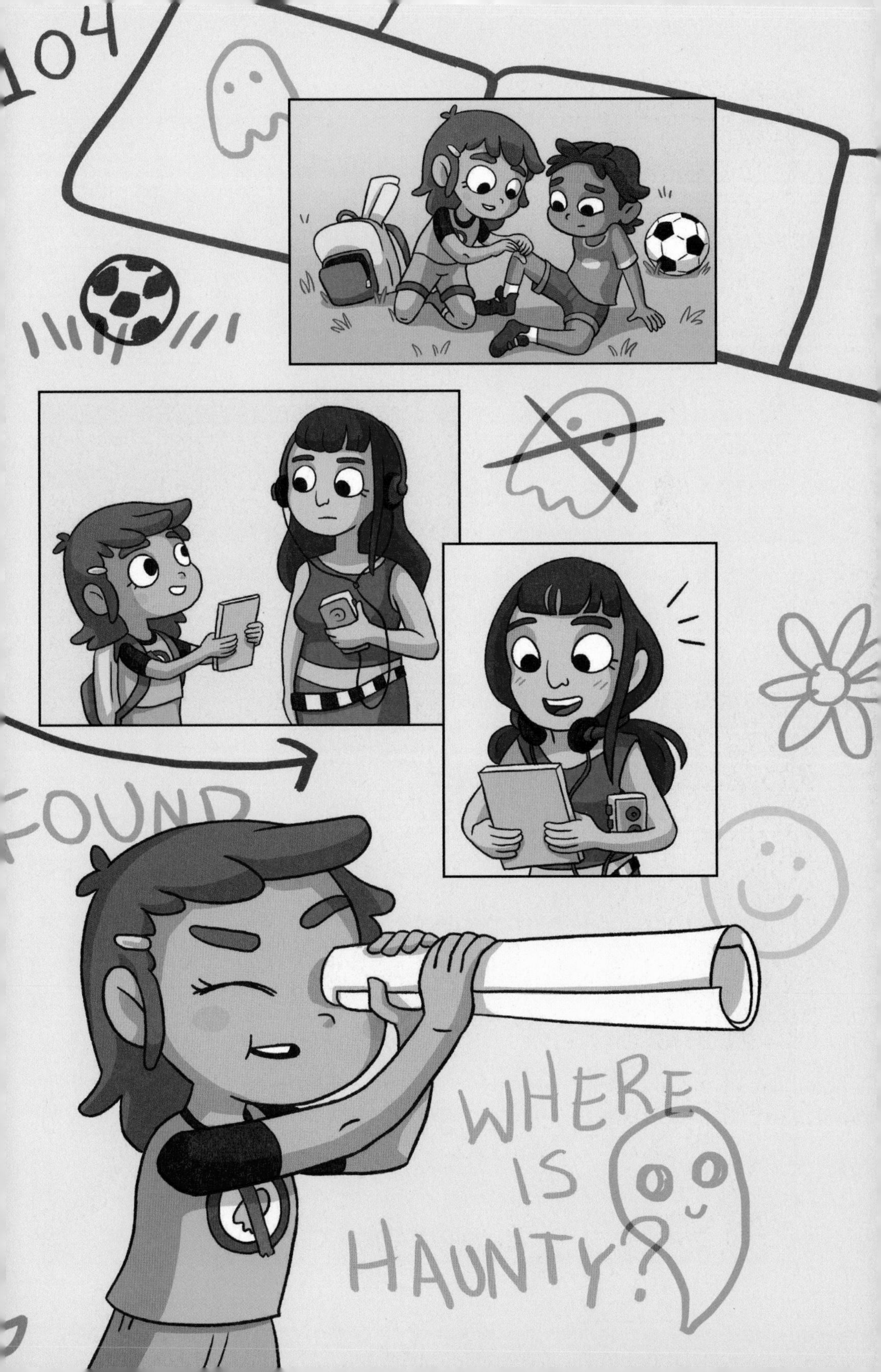
104
FOUND
WHERE IS HAUNTY?

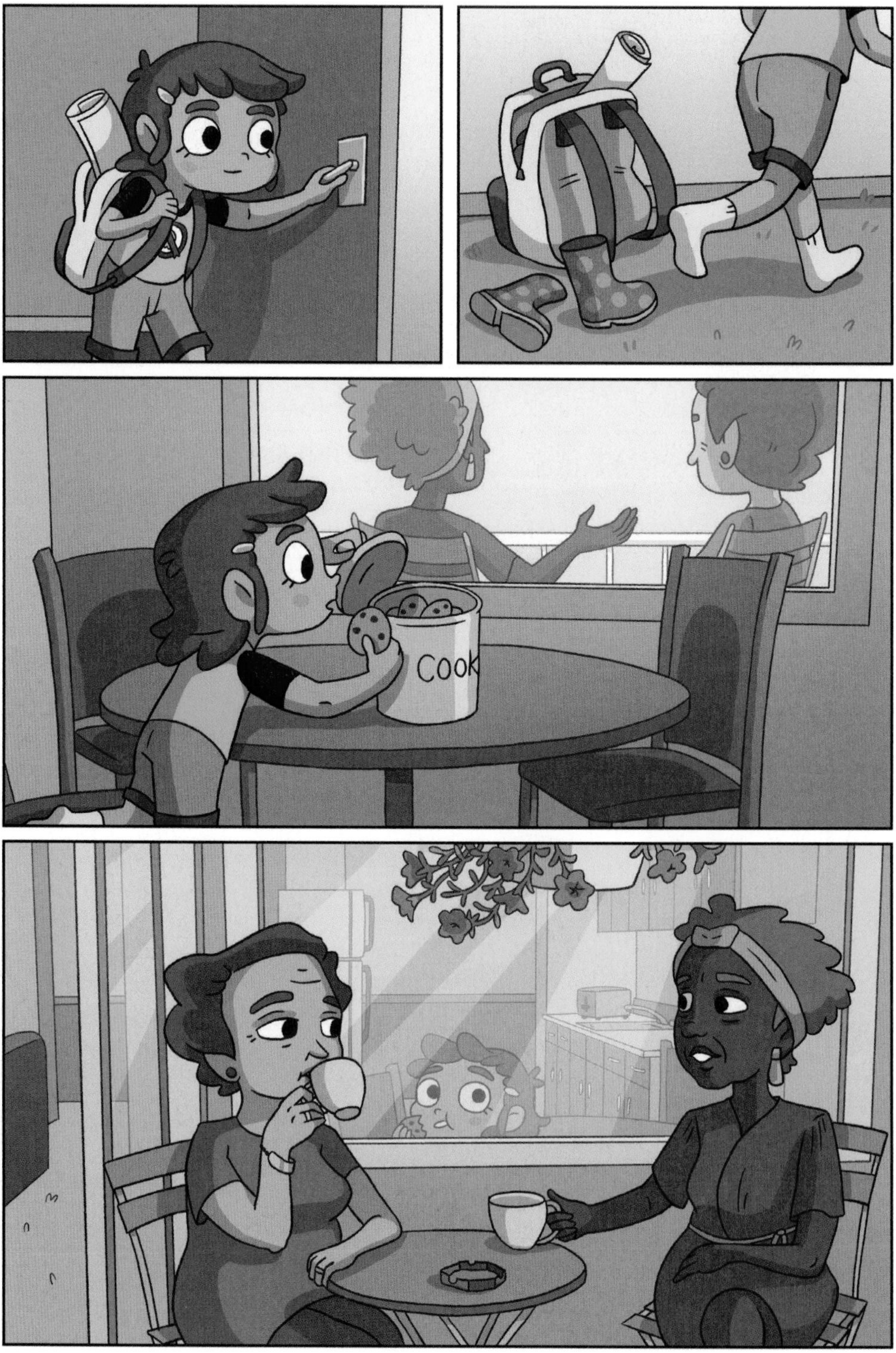
COOK

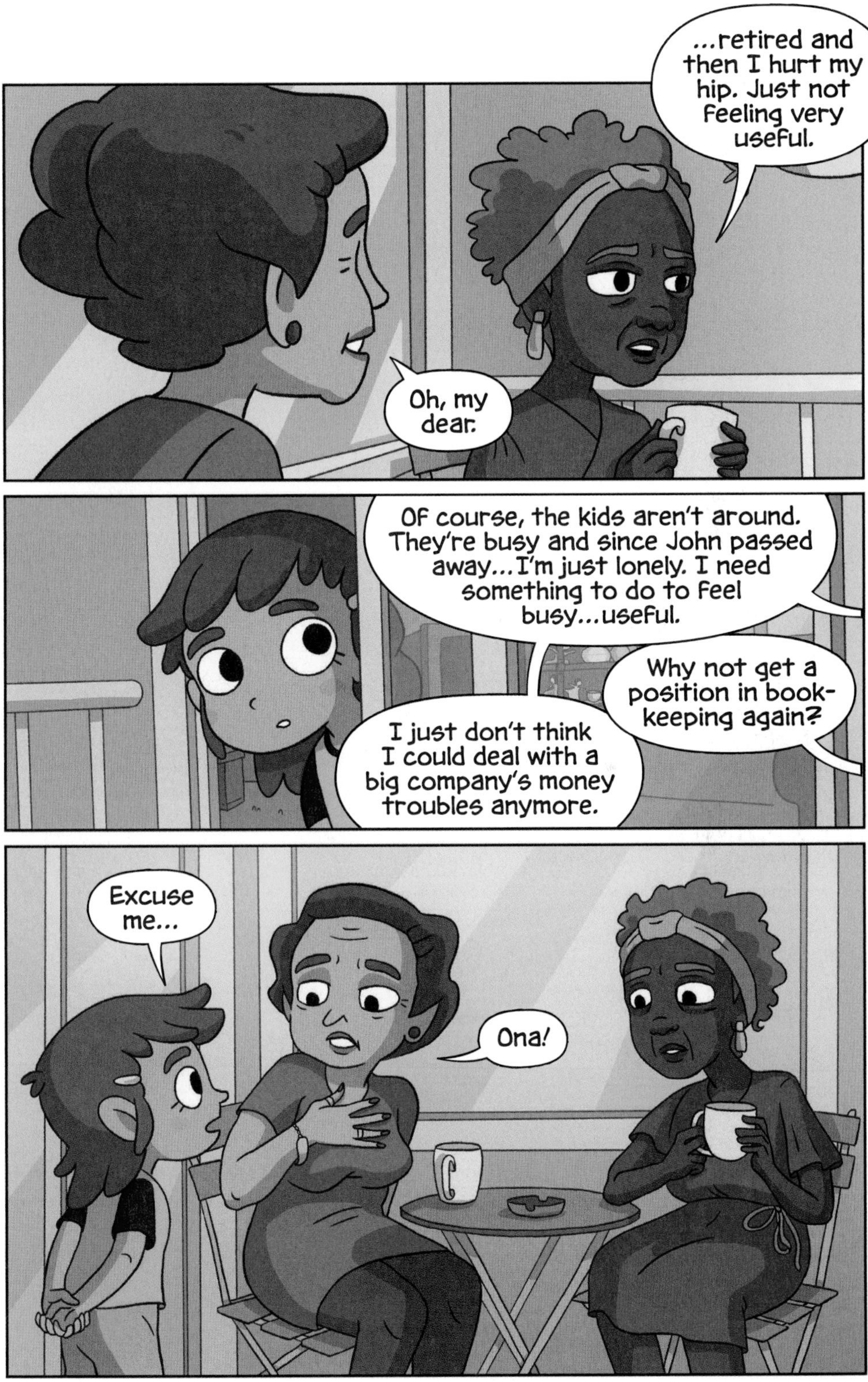
...retired and then I hurt my hip. Just not feeling very useful.
Oh, my dear.
Of course, the kids aren't around. They're busy and since John passed away... I'm just lonely. I need something to do to feel busy...useful.
Why not get a position in book-keeping again?
I just don't think I could deal with a big company's money troubles anymore.
Excuse me...
Ona!

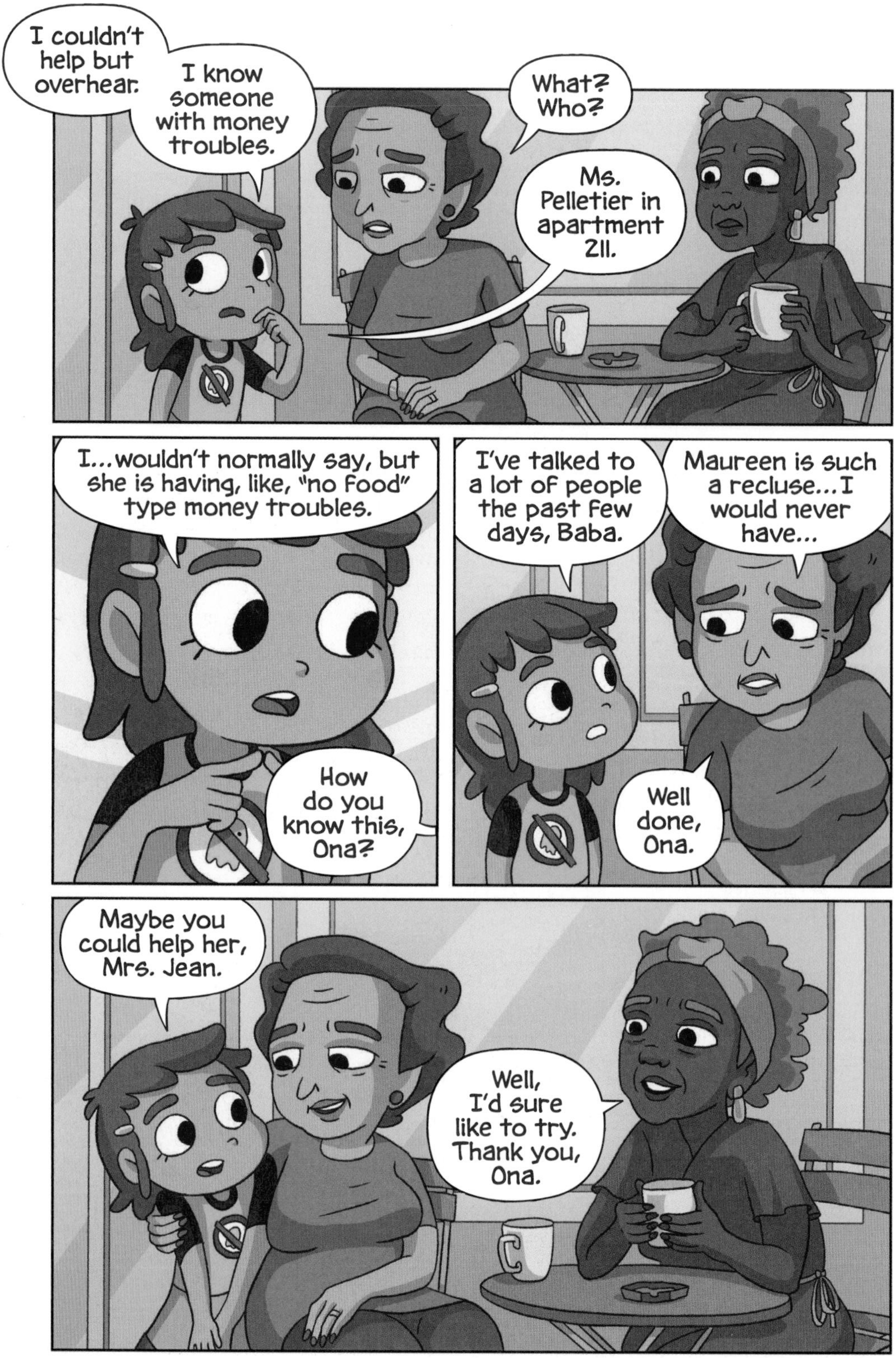
I couldn't help but overhear.
I know someone with money troubles.
What? Who?
Ms. Pelletier in apartment 211.
I...wouldn't normally say, but she is having, like, "no food" type money troubles.
How do you know this, Ona?
I've talked to a lot of people the past few days, Baba.
Maureen is such a recluse...I would never have...
Well done, Ona.
Maybe you could help her, Mrs. Jean.
Well, I'd sure like to try. Thank you, Ona.

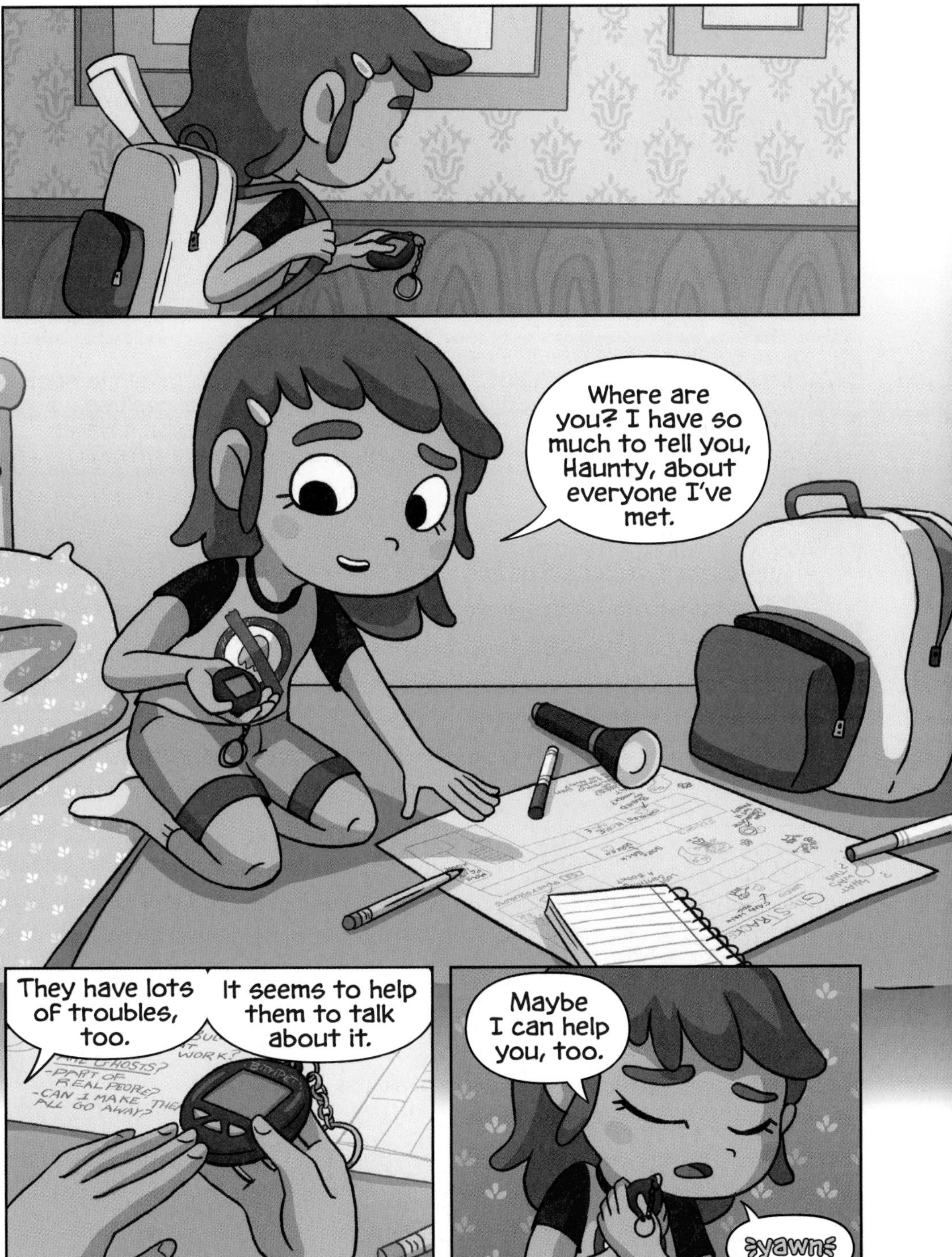
Where are you? I have so much to tell you, Haunty, about everyone I've met.
They have lots of troubles, too.
It seems to help them to talk about it.
Maybe I can help you, too.
yawn

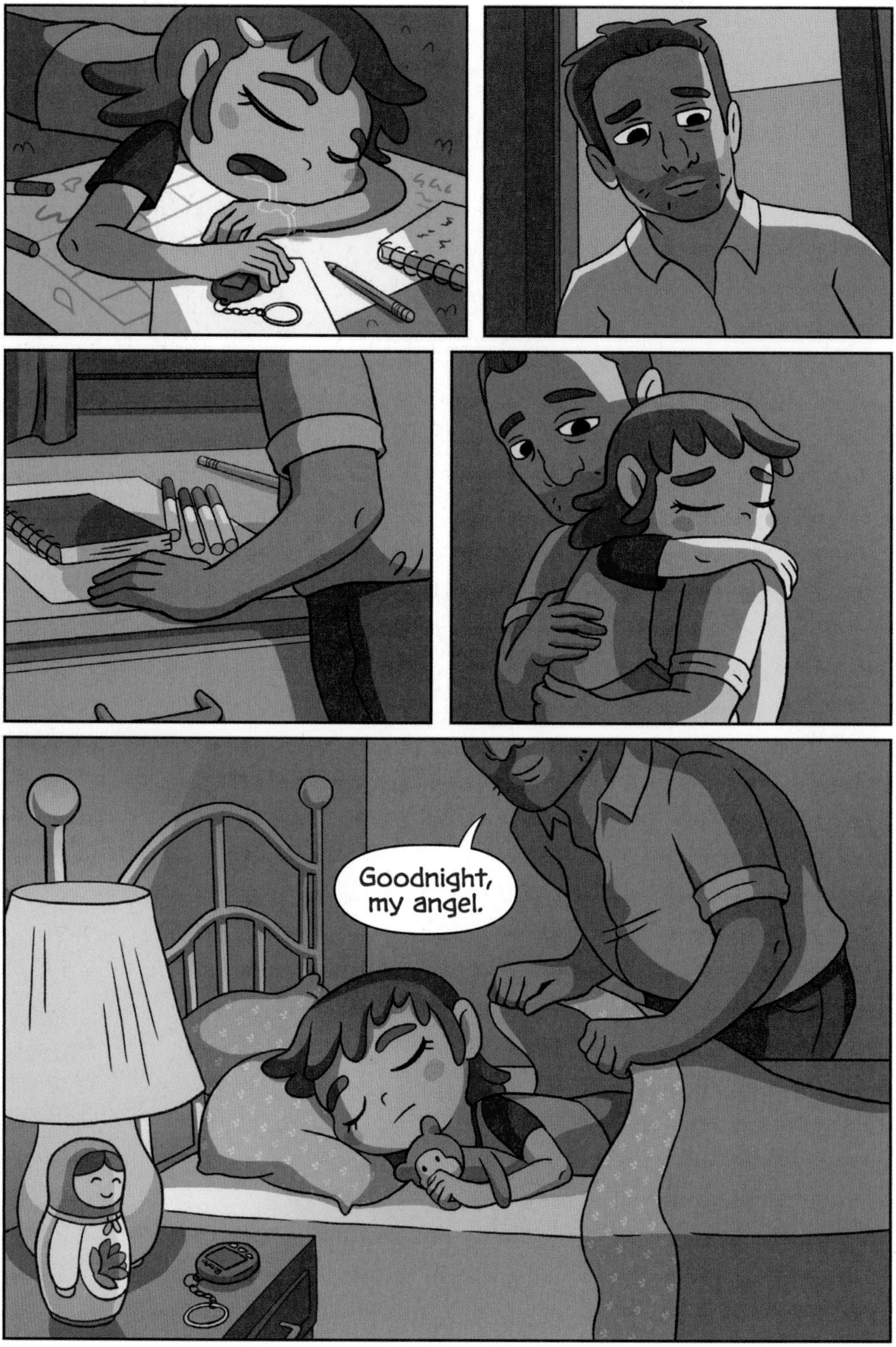
Goodnight,
my angel.

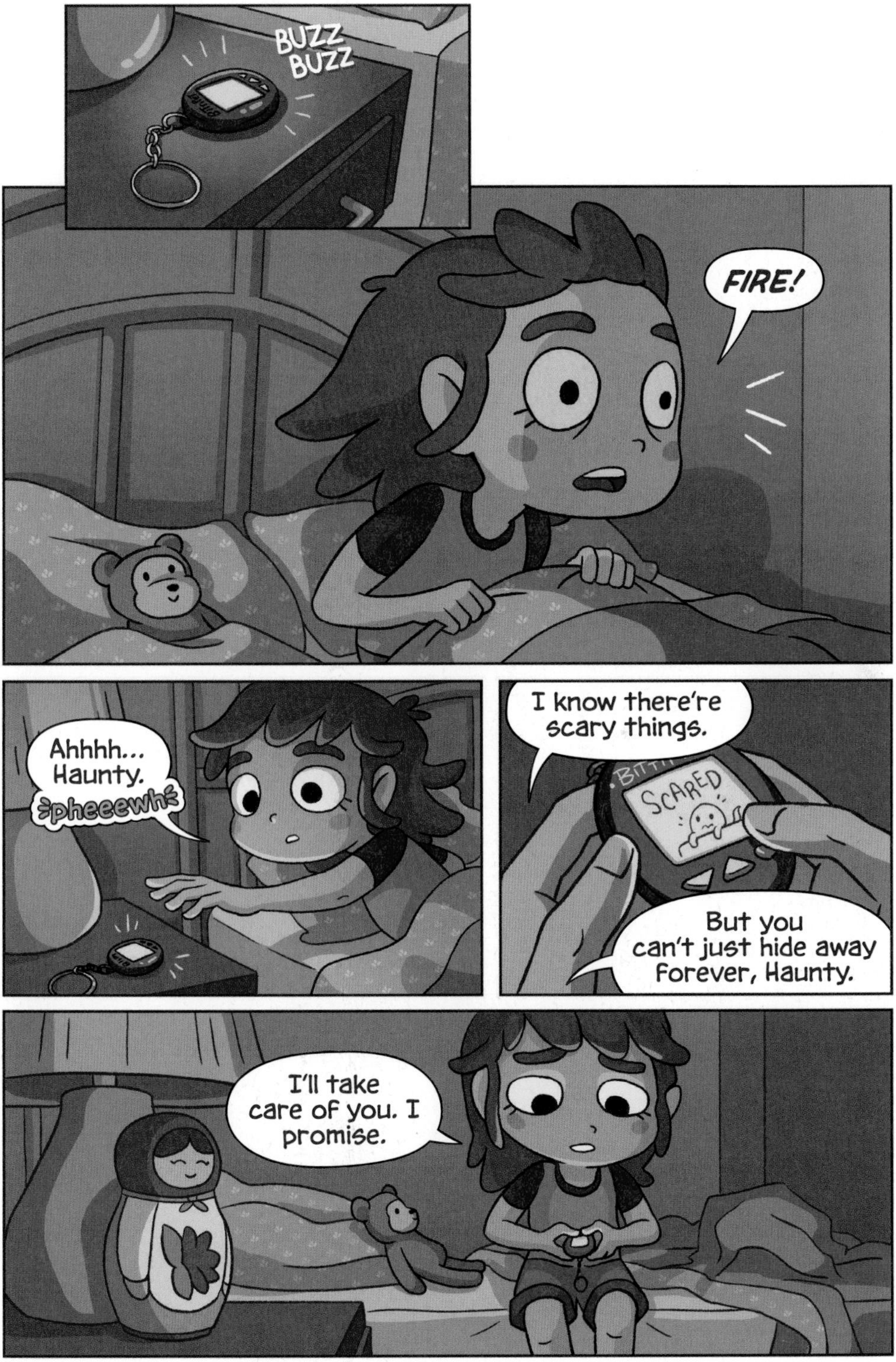
BUZZ BUZZ
FIRE!
Ahhhh... Haunty.
pheeewh
I know there're scary things.
SCARED
But you can't just hide away forever, Haunty.
I'll take care of you. I promise.

I'll find you.

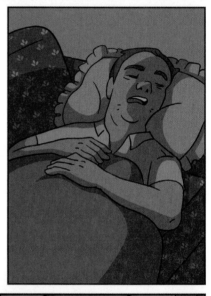

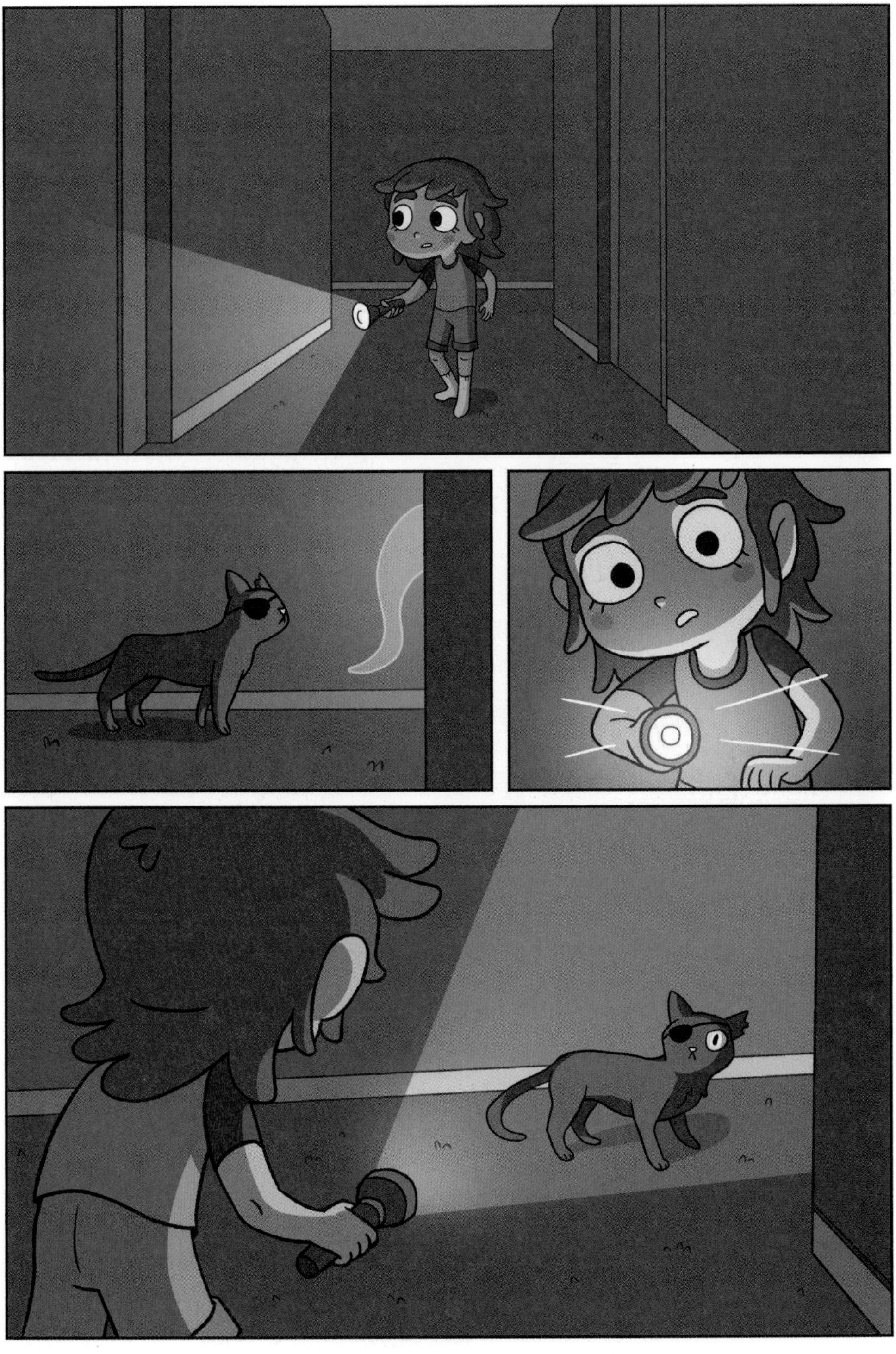

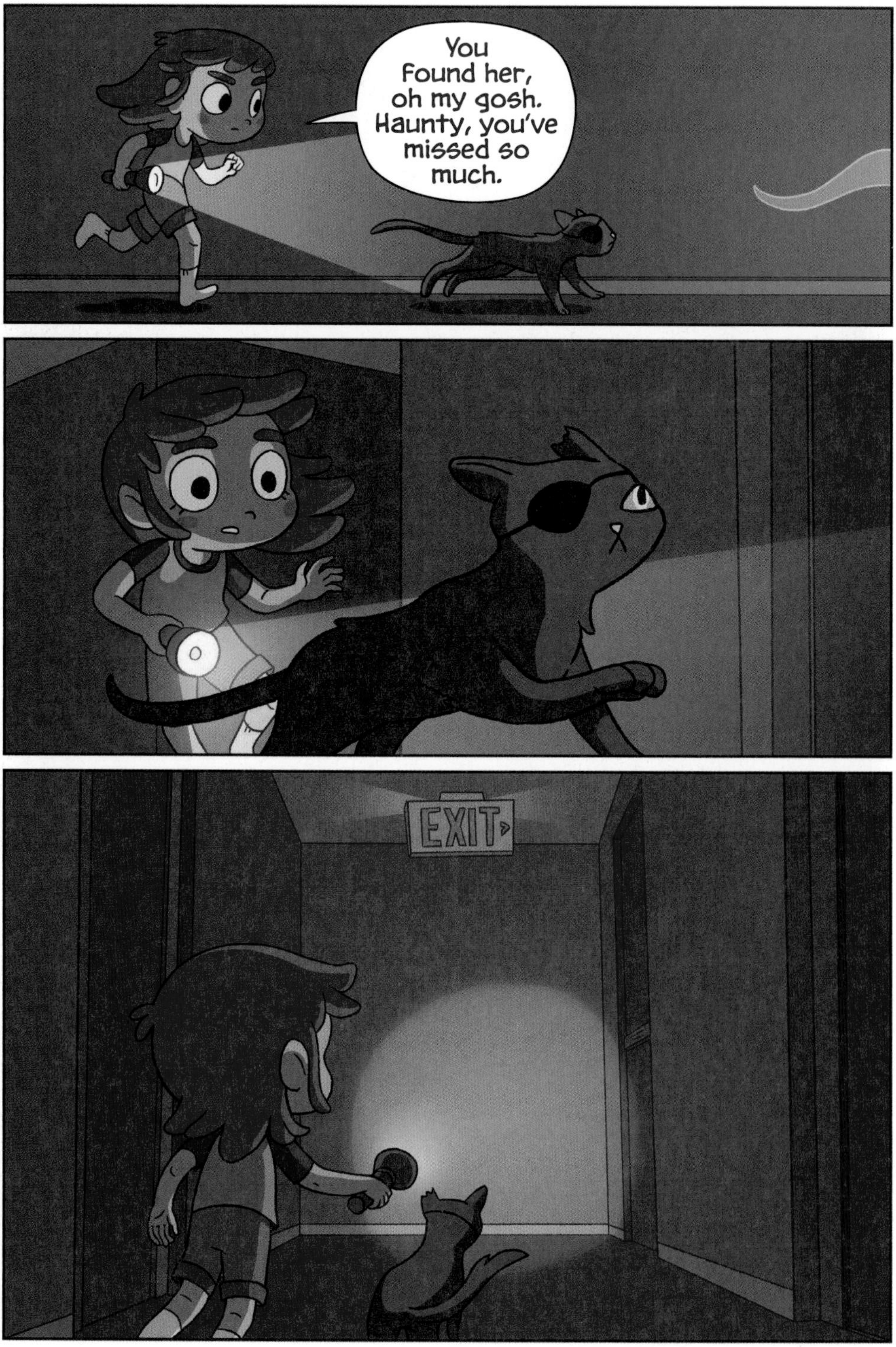
You found her, oh my gosh. Haunty, you've missed so much.
EXIT

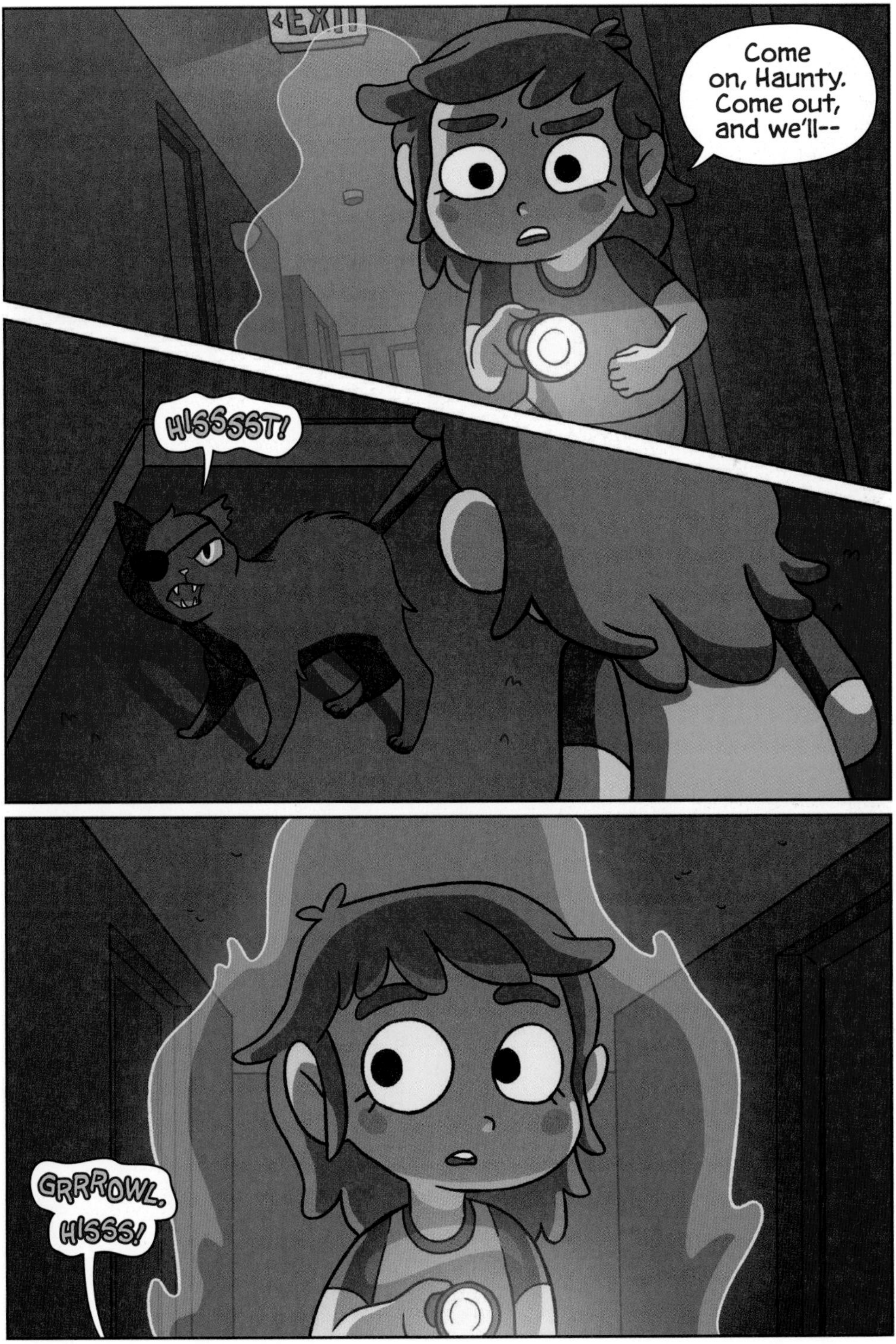

EXIT
Come on, Haunty. Come out, and we'll--
HISSSST!
GRRROWL. HISSS!

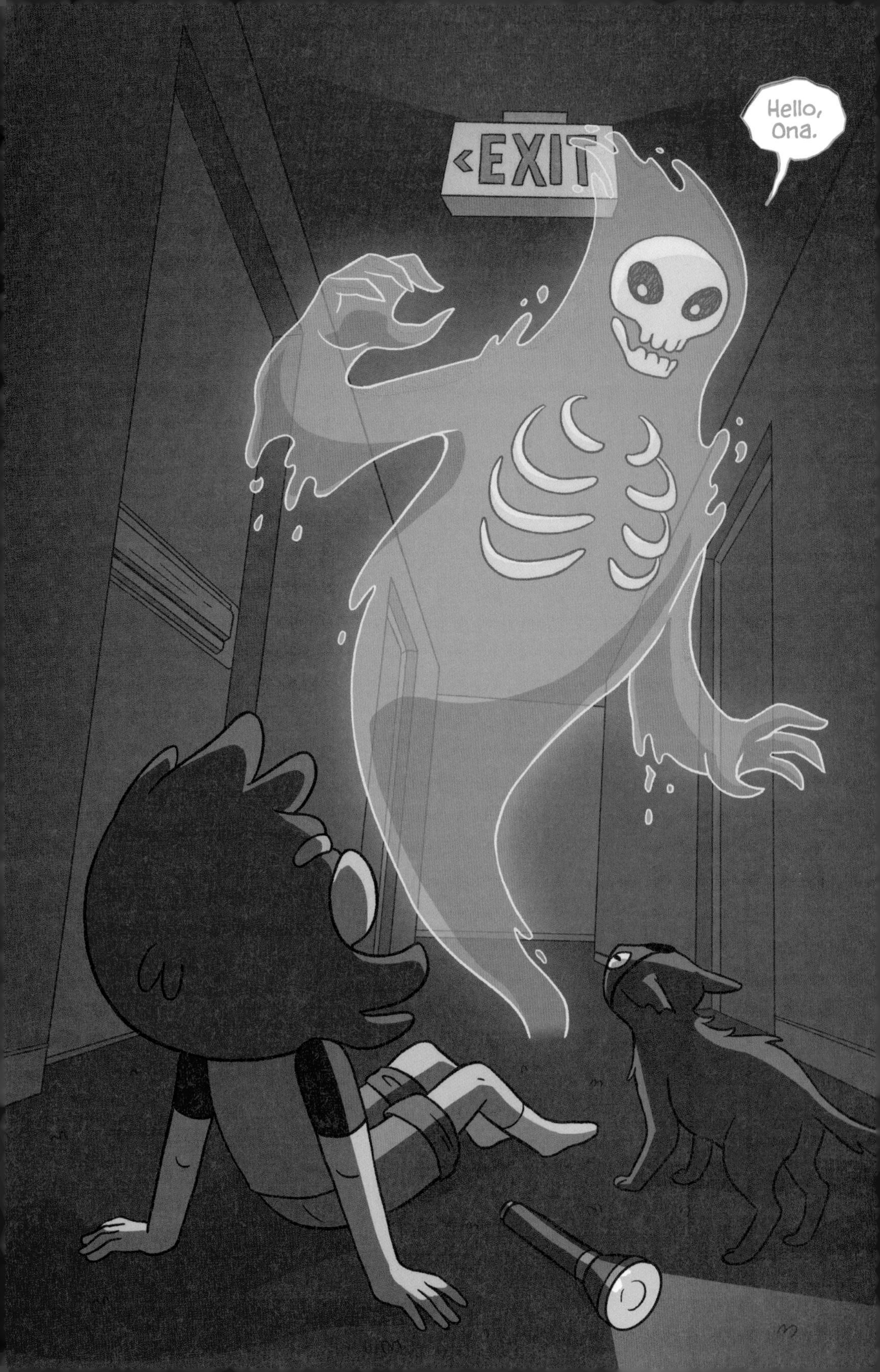
EXIT
Hello, Ona.

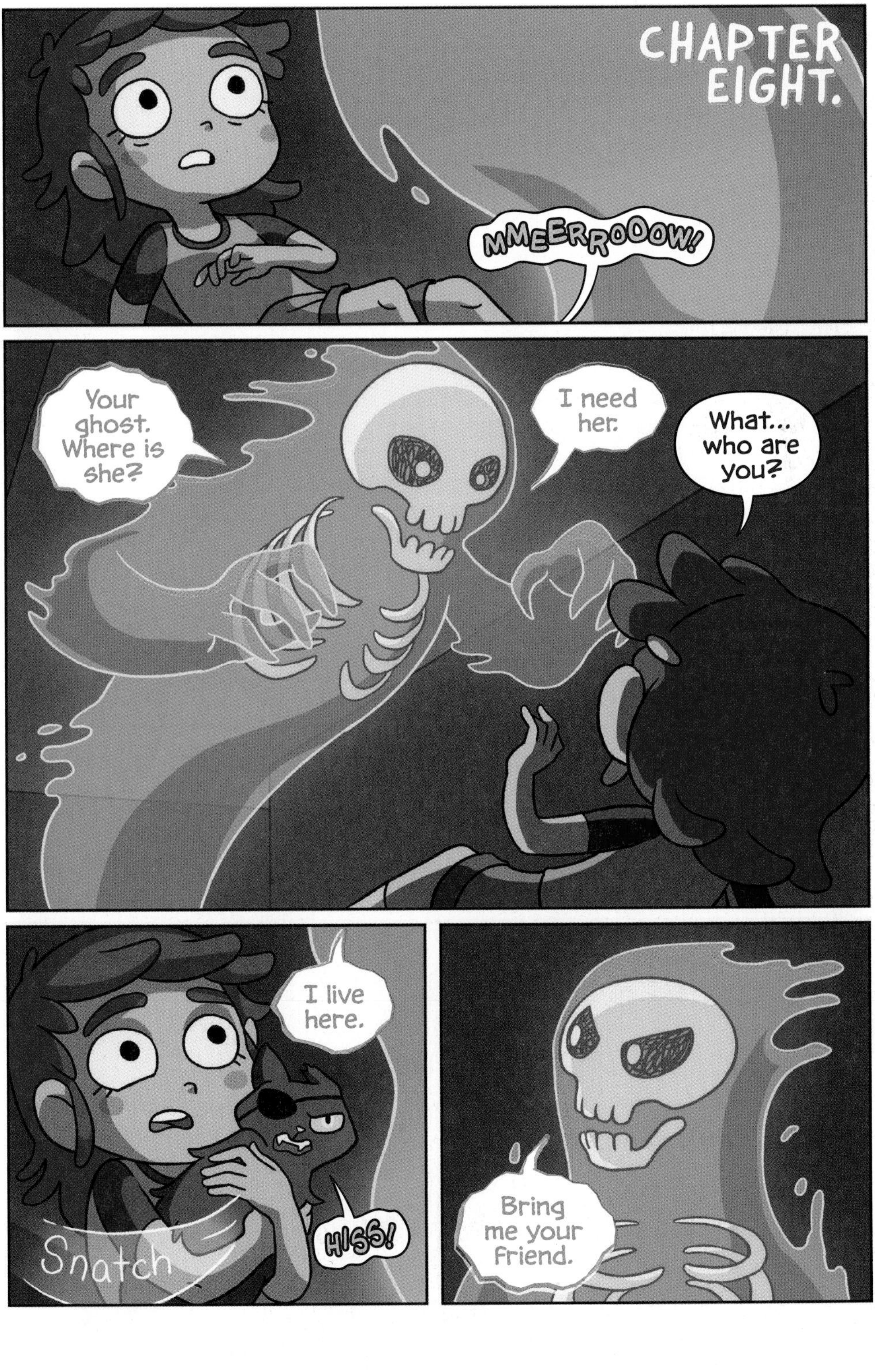
CHAPTER EIGHT.
MMEERROOOW!
Your ghost. Where is she?
I need her.
What... who are you?
I live here.
Snatch
HISS!
Bring me your friend.

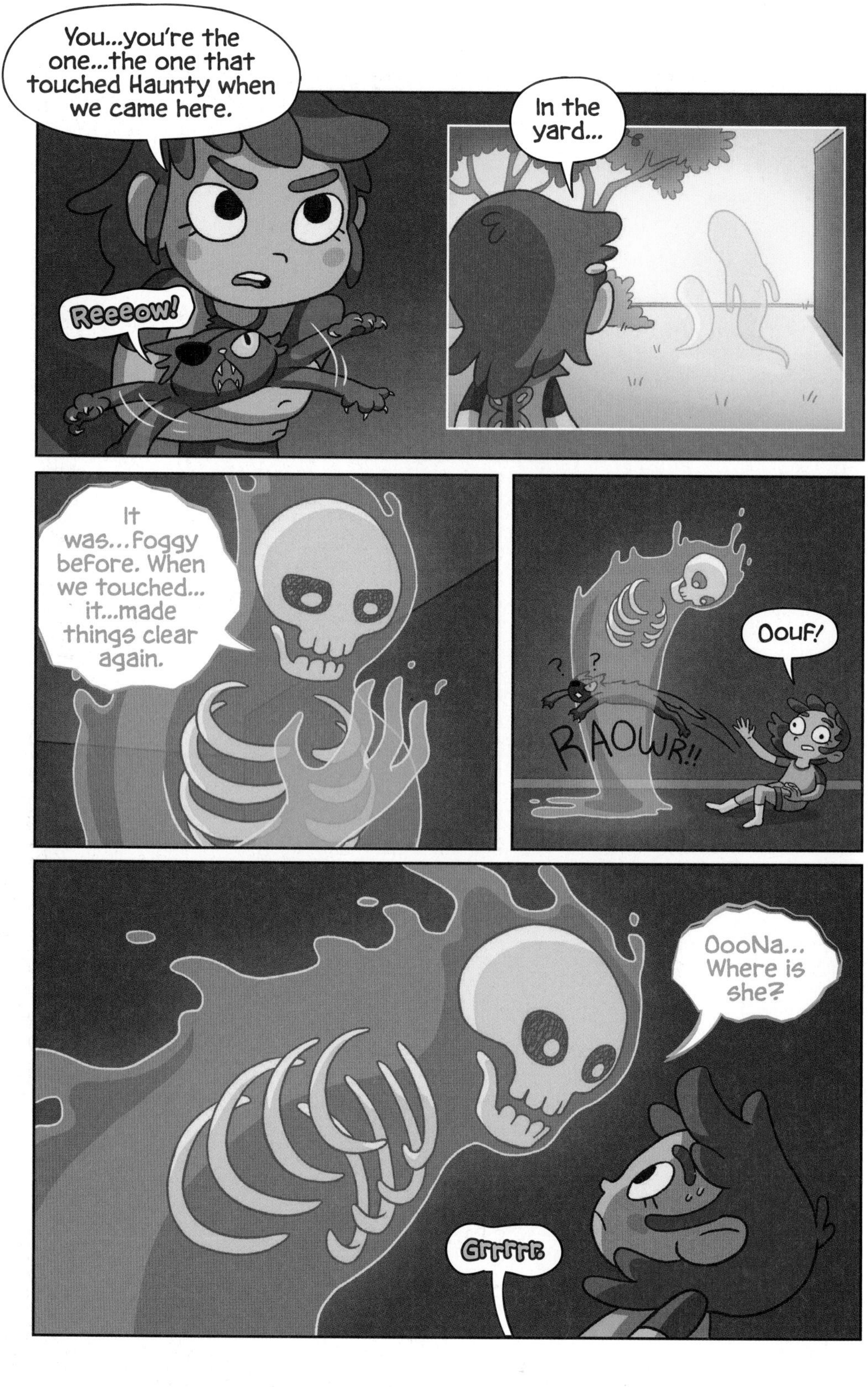
You...you're the one...the one that touched Haunty when we came here.
Reeeow!
In the yard...
It was...foggy before. When we touched... it...made things clear again.
Oouf!
RAOWR!!
OooNa... Where is she?
Grrrrr.

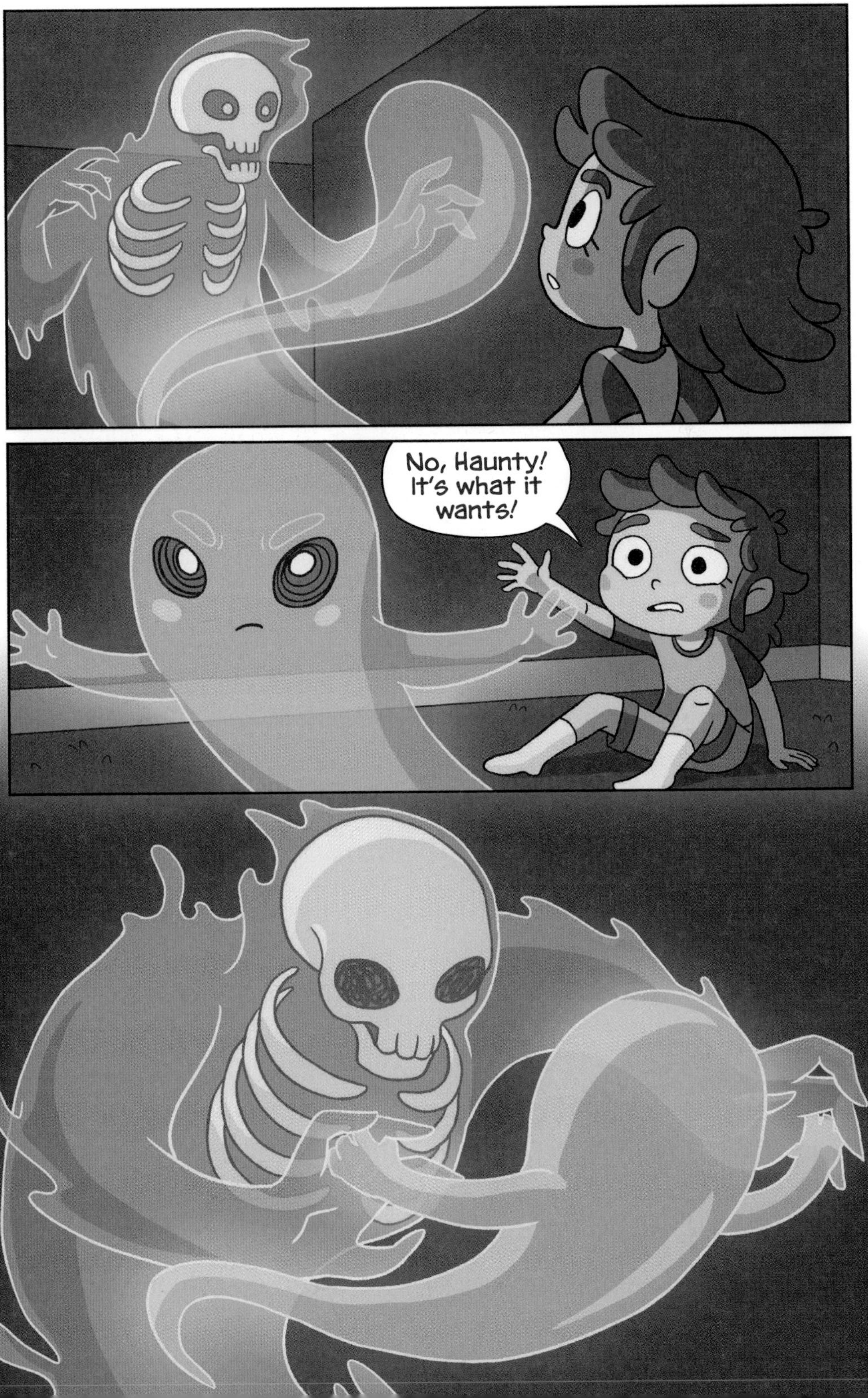
No, Haunty! It's what it wants!

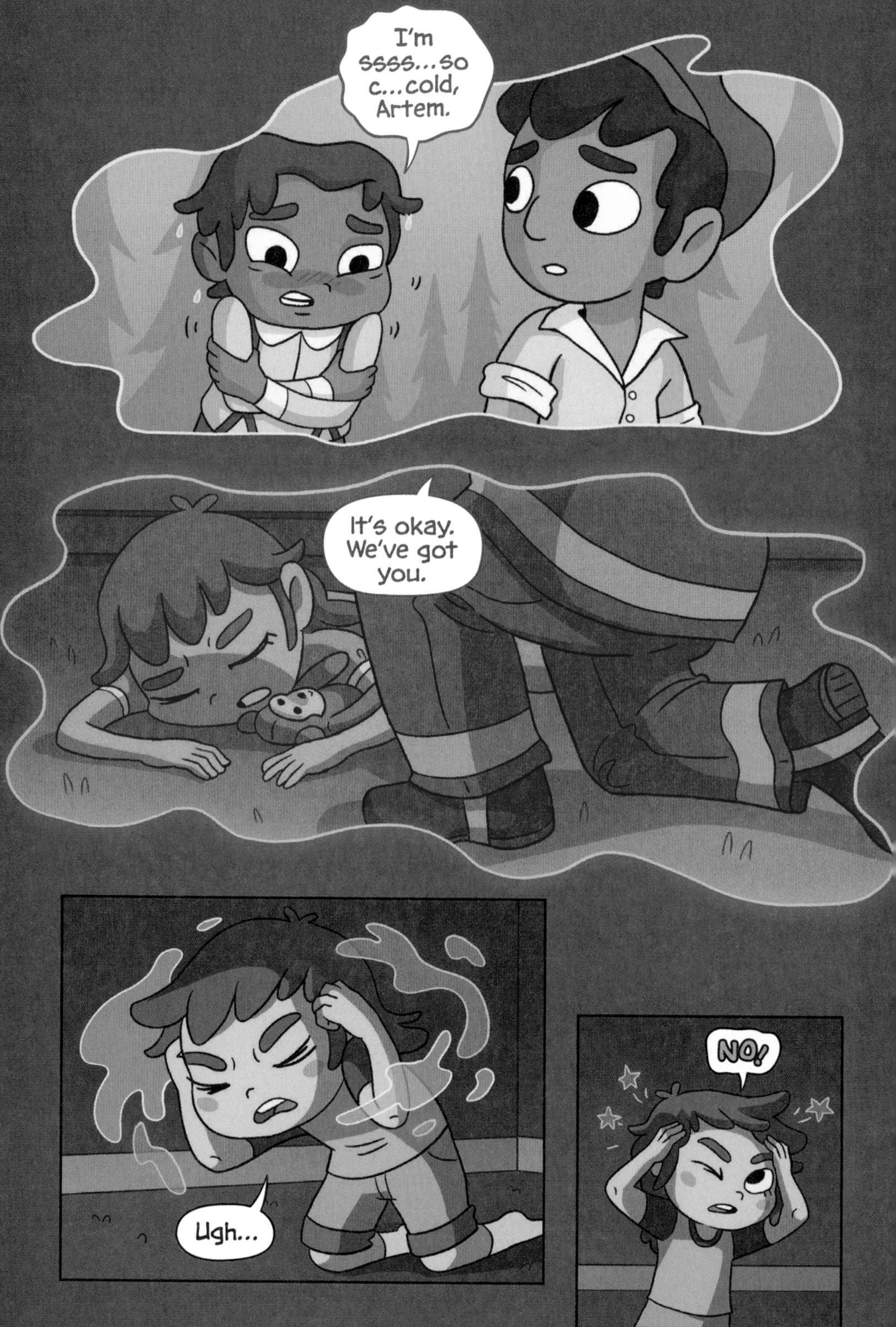
I'm ssss...so c...cold, Artem.
It's okay. We've got you.
Ugh...
NO!

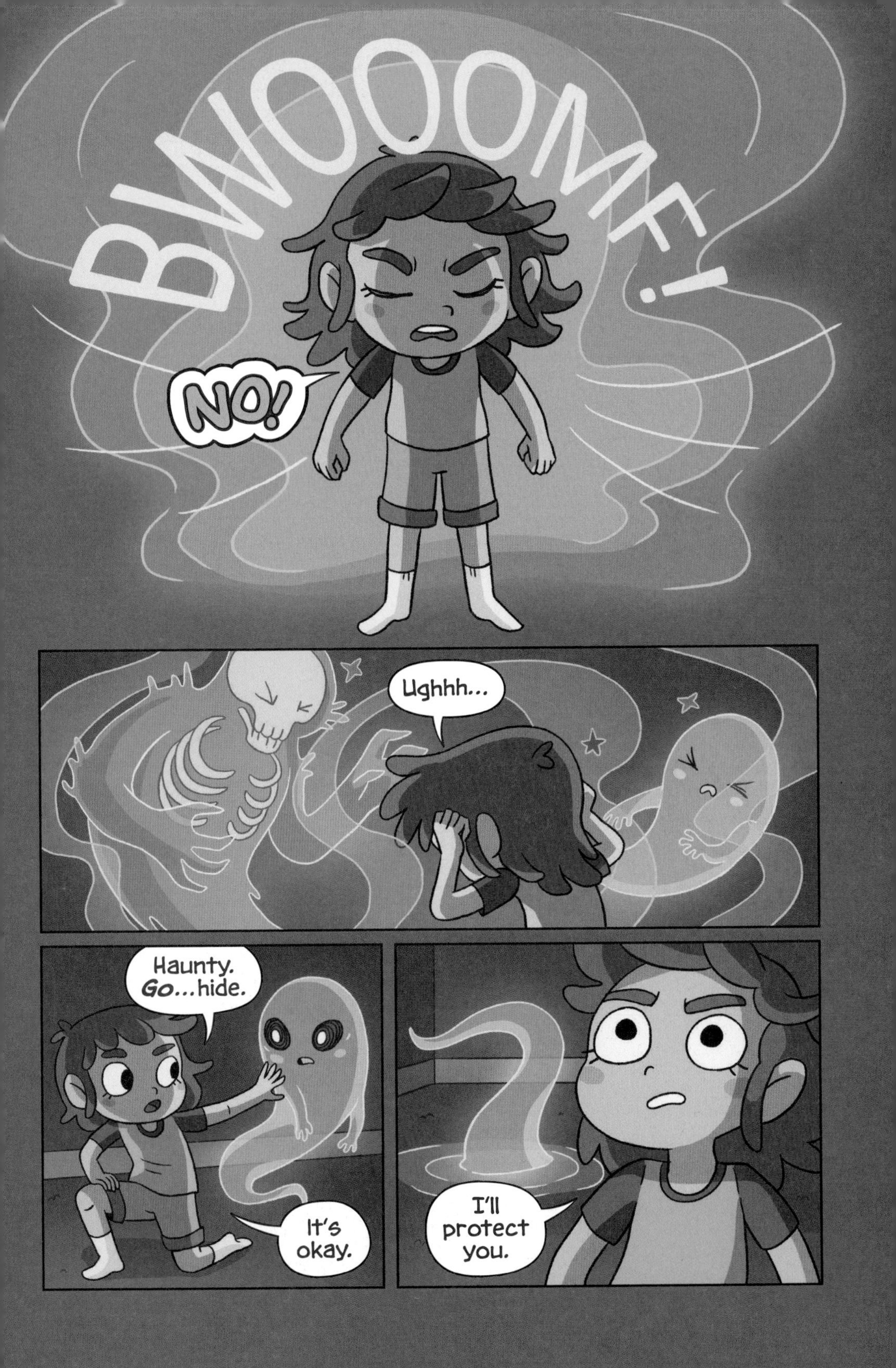
BWOOOMF!
NO!
Ughhh...
Haunty. Go...hide.
It's okay.
I'll protect you.

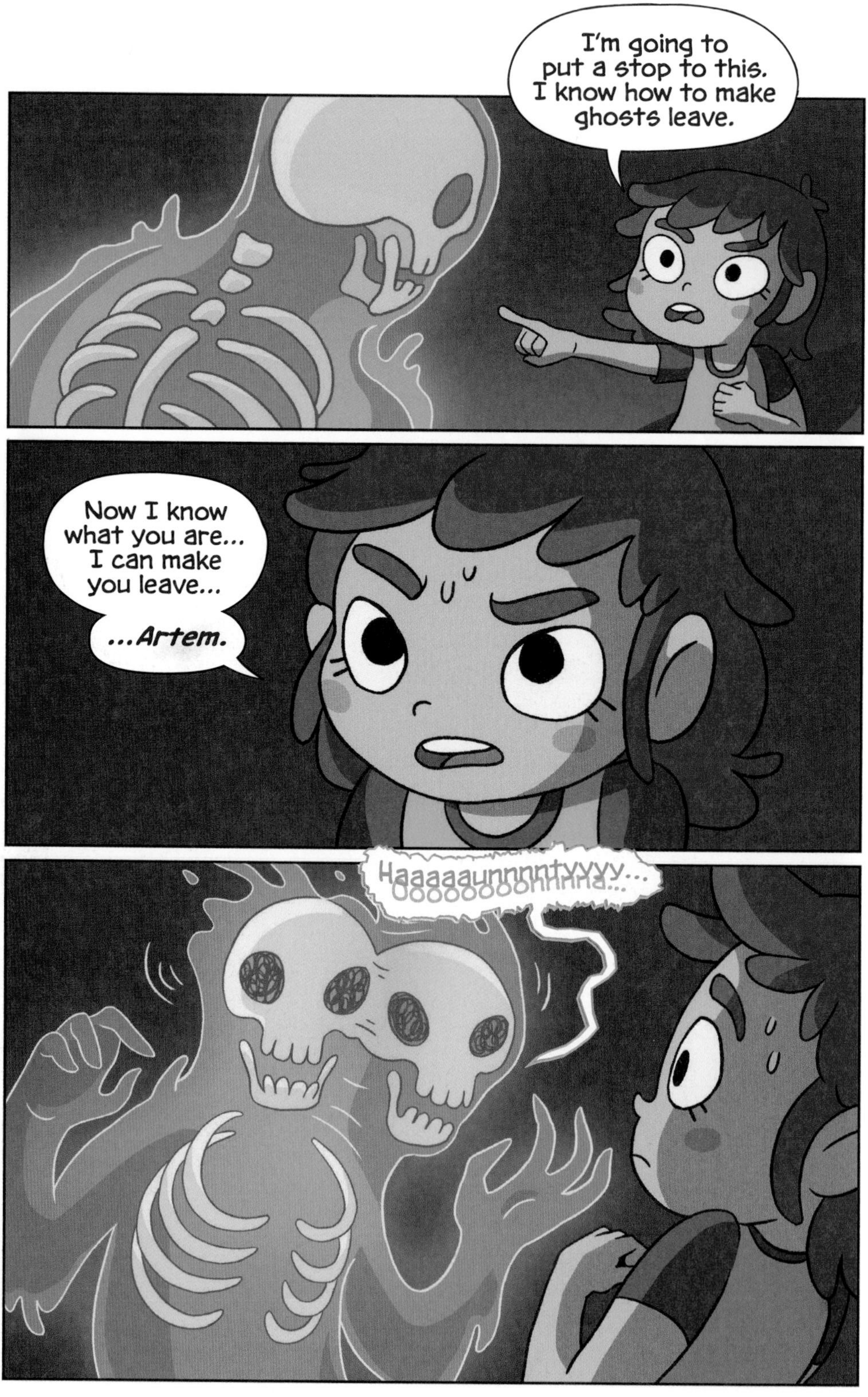
I'm going to put a stop to this. I know how to make ghosts leave.
Now I know what you are... I can make you leave...
...Artem.
Haaaaaunnnntyyyy...

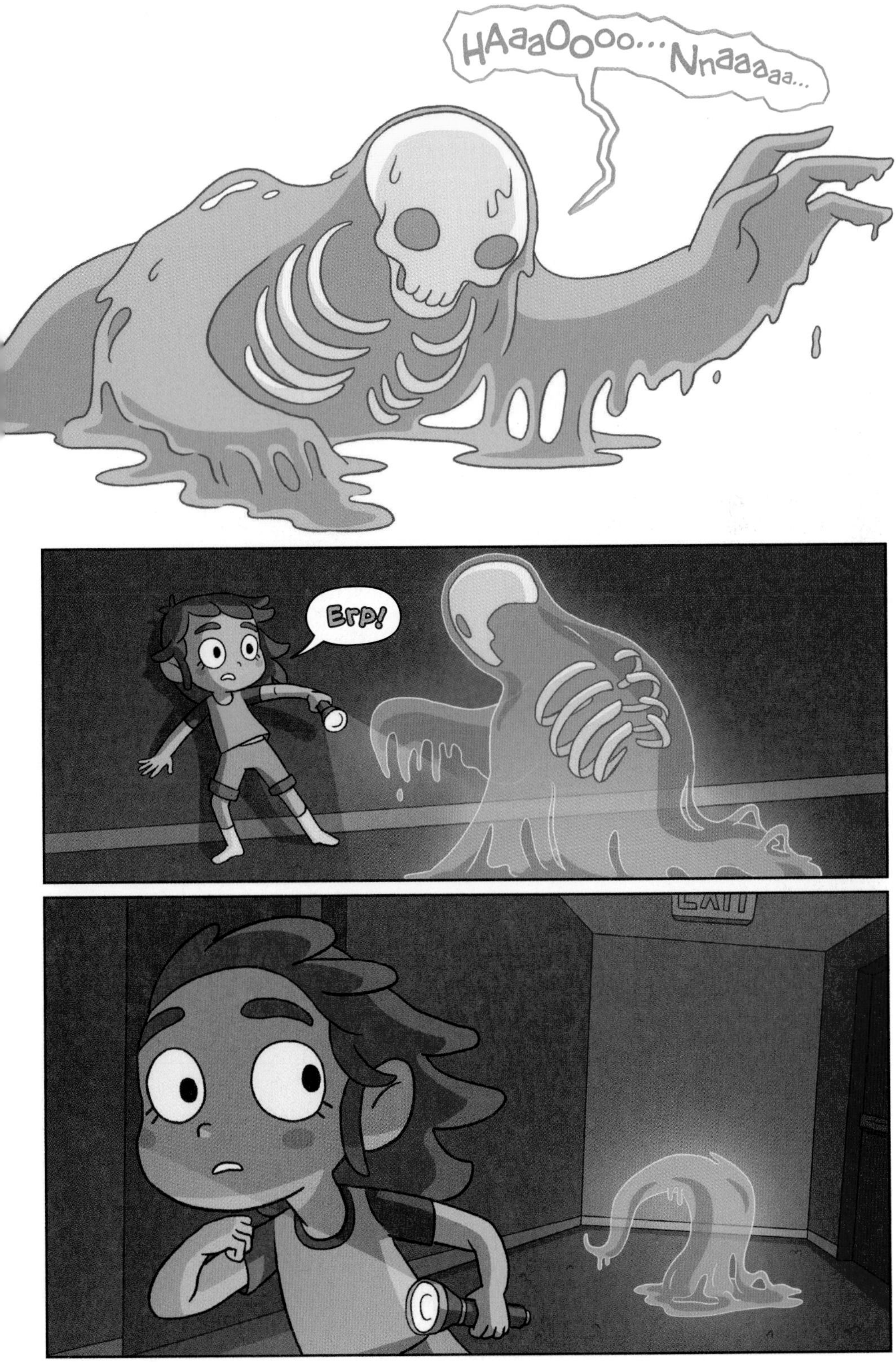
HAaaOooo...Nnaaaaa...
Erp!

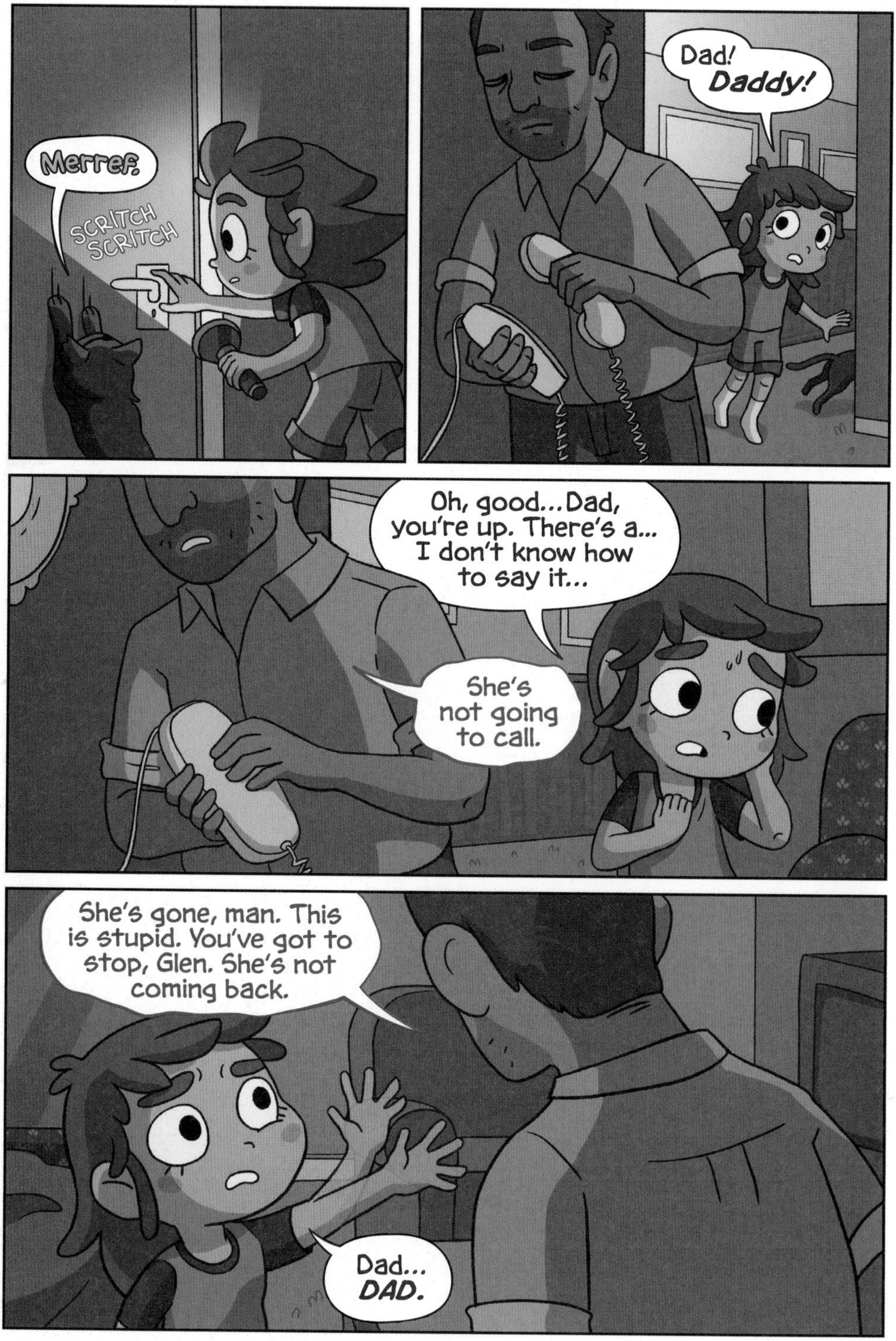
Merref.
SCRITCH SCRITCH
Dad!
Daddy!
Oh, good...Dad, you're up. There's a... I don't know how to say it...
She's not going to call.
She's gone, man. This is stupid. You've got to stop, Glen. She's not coming back.
Dad...
DAD.

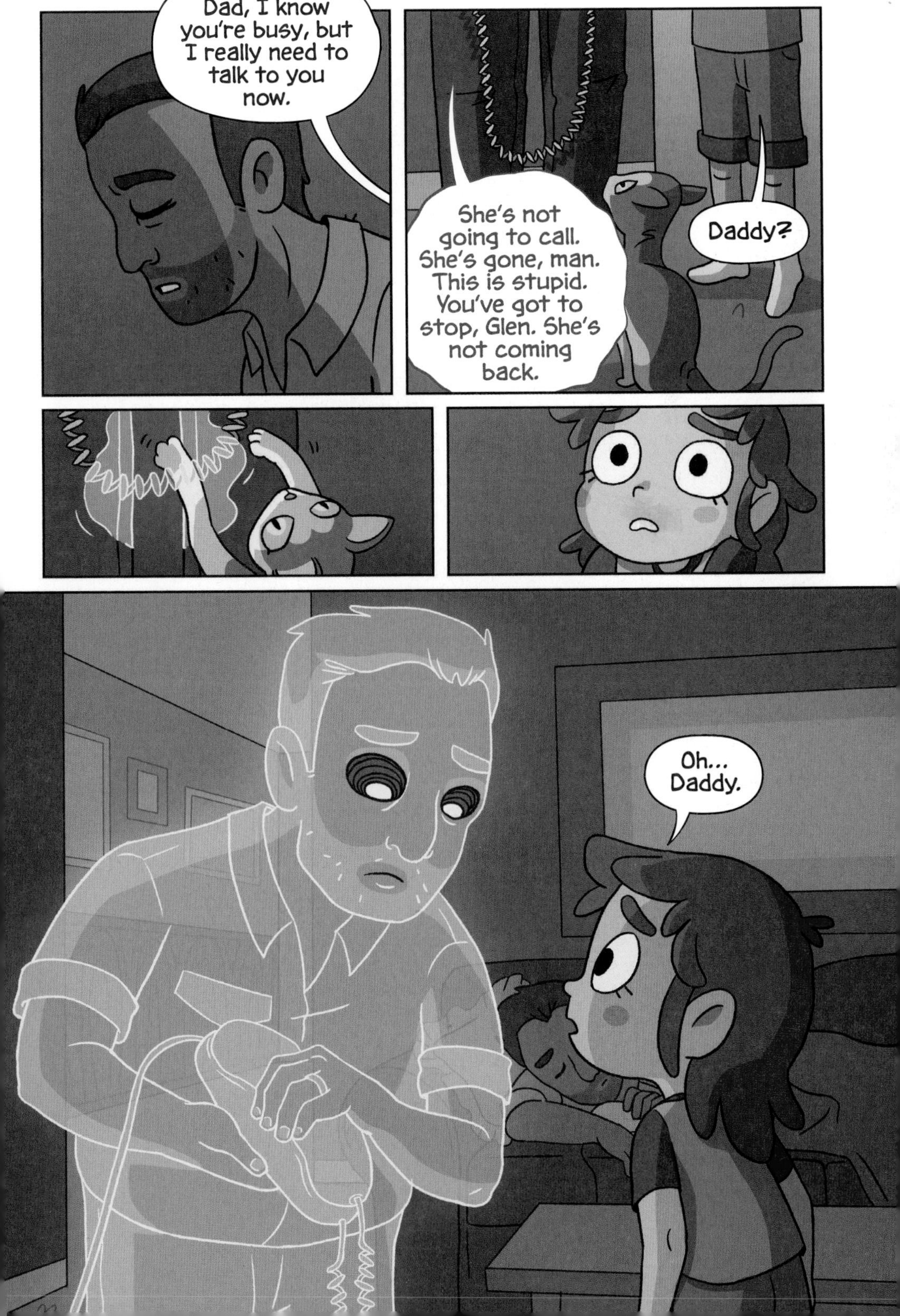
Dad, I know you're busy, but I really need to talk to you now.
She's not going to call. She's gone, man. This is stupid. You've got to stop, Glen. She's not coming back.
Daddy?
Oh... Daddy.

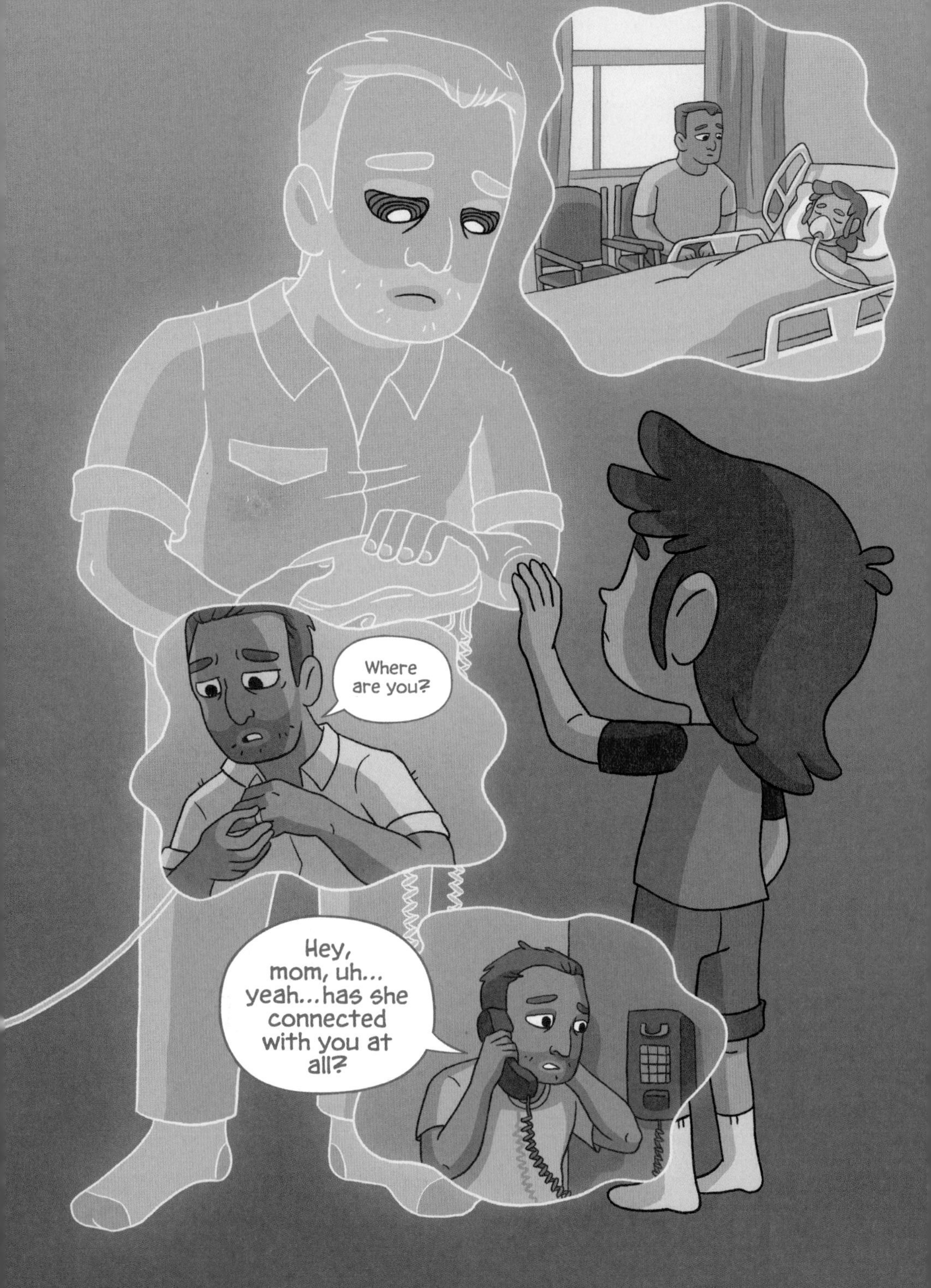
Where are you?
Hey, mom, uh... yeah...has she connected with you at all?

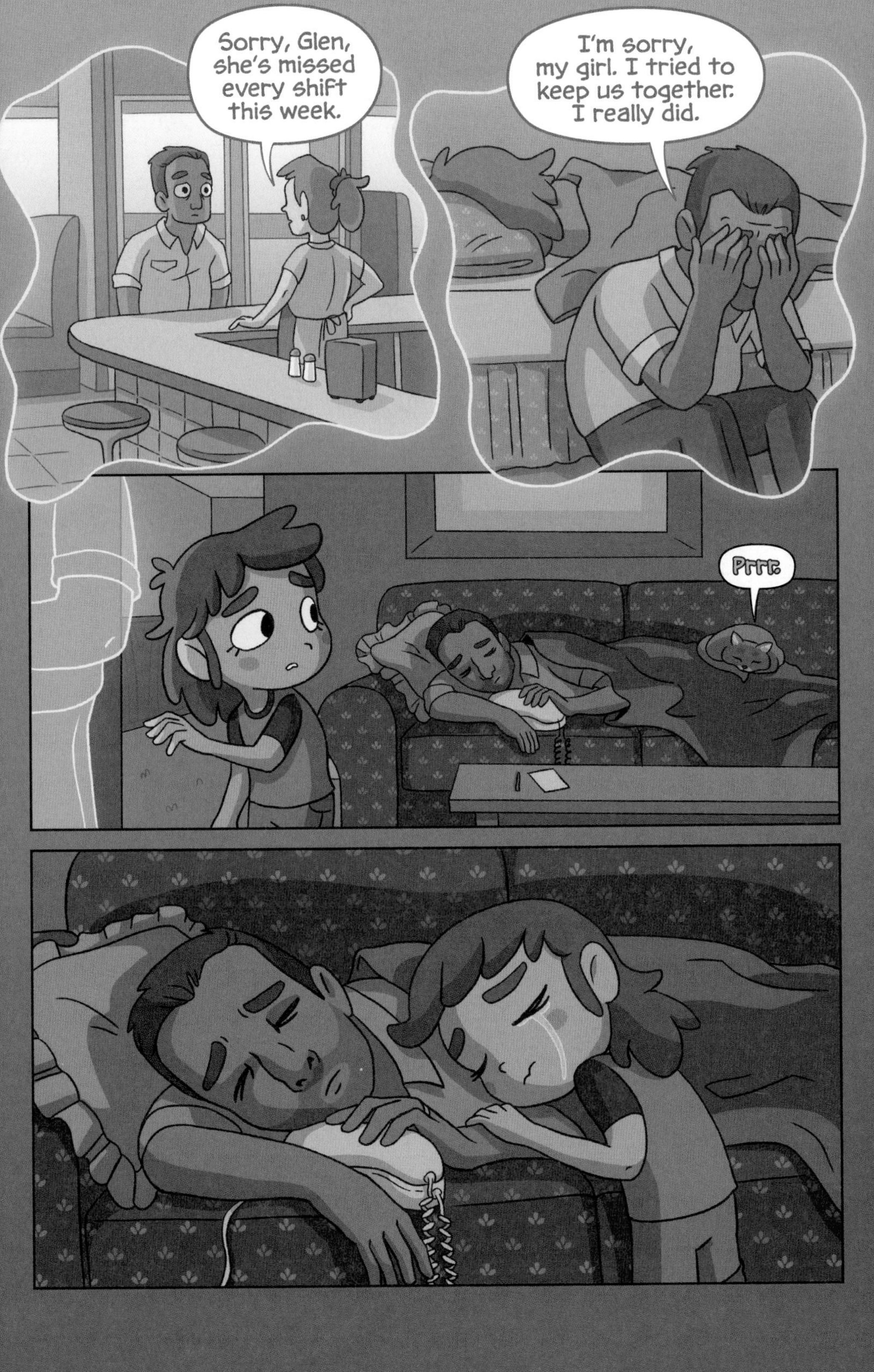
Sorry, Glen, she's missed every shift this week.
I'm sorry, my girl. I tried to keep us together. I really did.
Prrr.

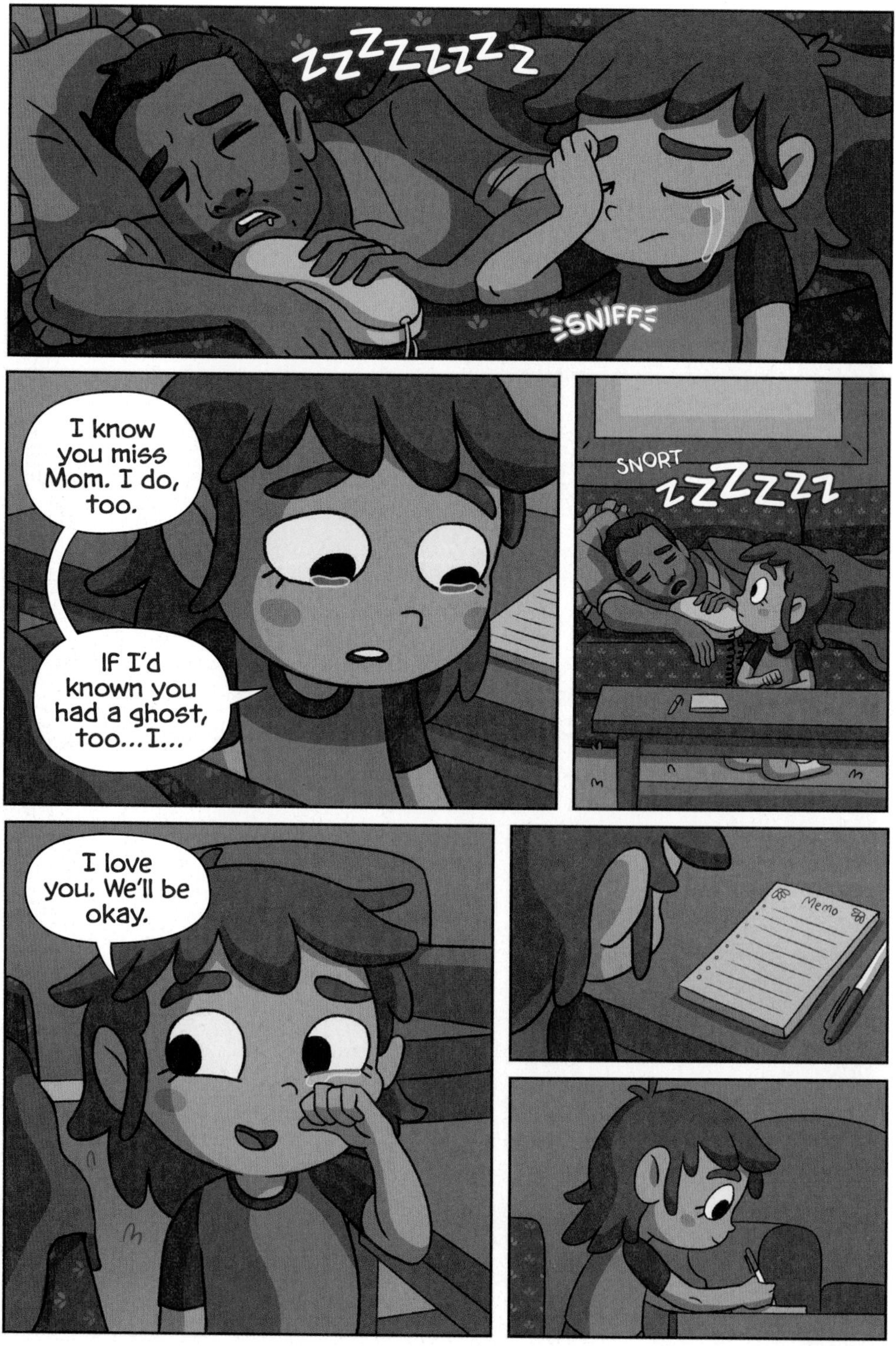
ZZZZZZZZZ
SNIFF
I know you miss Mom. I do, too.
If I'd known you had a ghost, too... I...
SNORT
ZZZZZZ
I love you. We'll be okay.
Memo

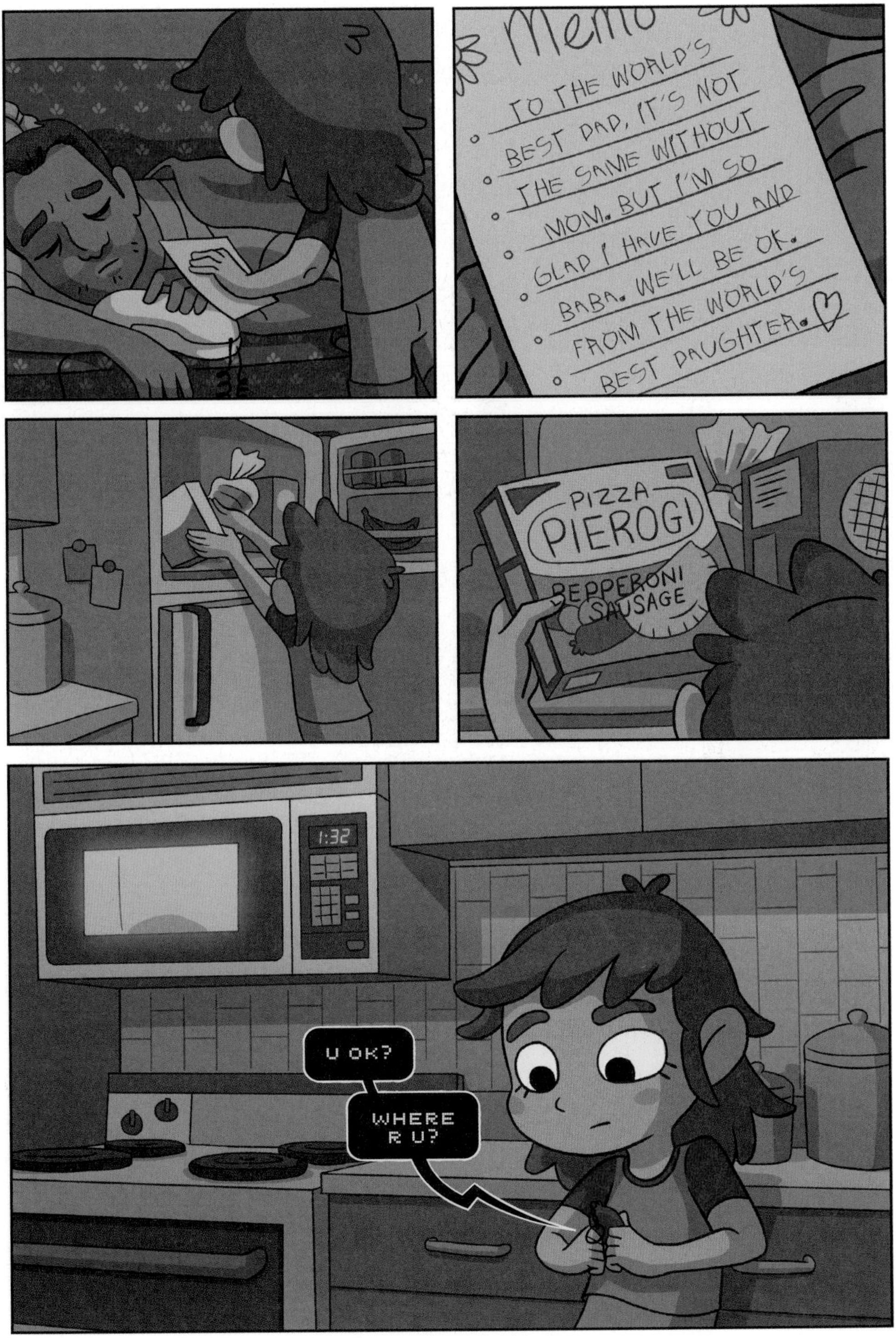
Memo
TO THE WORLD'S BEST DAD, IT'S NOT THE SAME WITHOUT MOM. BUT I'M SO GLAD I HAVE YOU AND BABA. WE'LL BE OK. FROM THE WORLD'S BEST DAUGHTER.
PIZZA PIEROGI
PEPPERONI SAUSAGE
1:32
U OK?
WHERE R U?

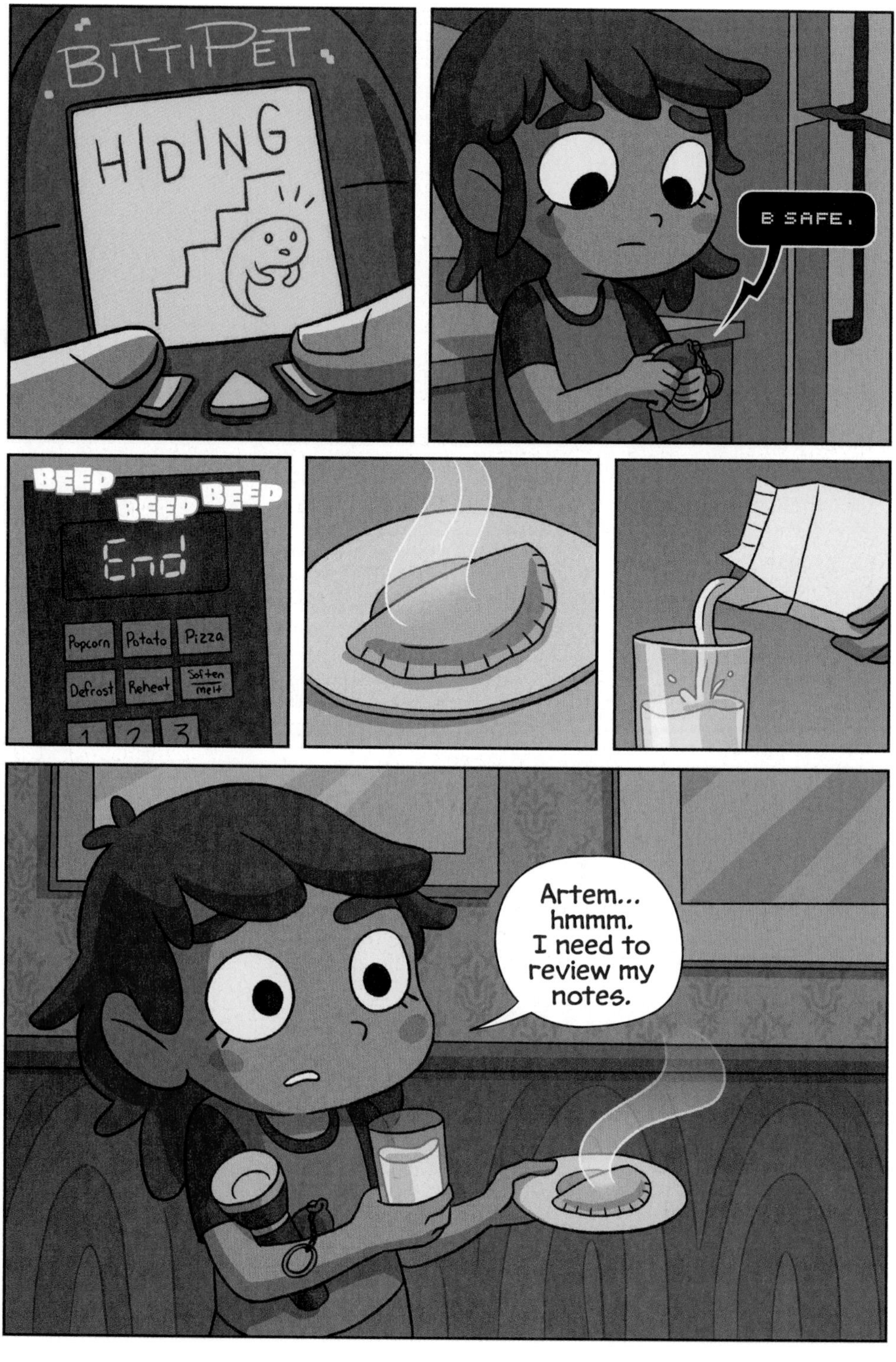
BITTIPET
HIDING
B SAFE.
BEEP BEEP BEEP
End
Popcorn Potato Pizza
Defrost Reheat Soften melt
1 2 3
Artem... hmmm. I need to review my notes.

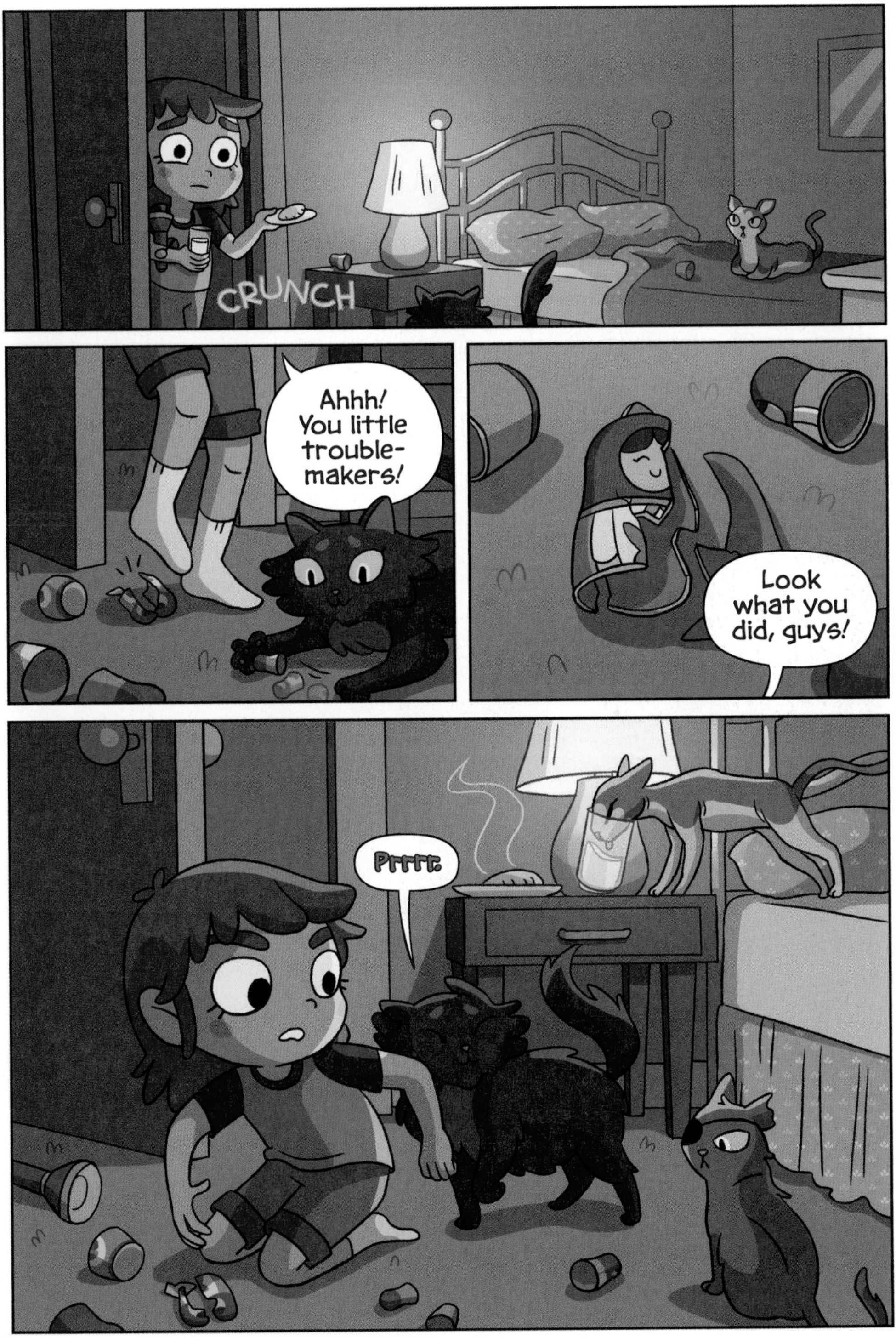
CRUNCH
Ahhh! You little trouble-makers!
Look what you did, guys!
Prrrr.

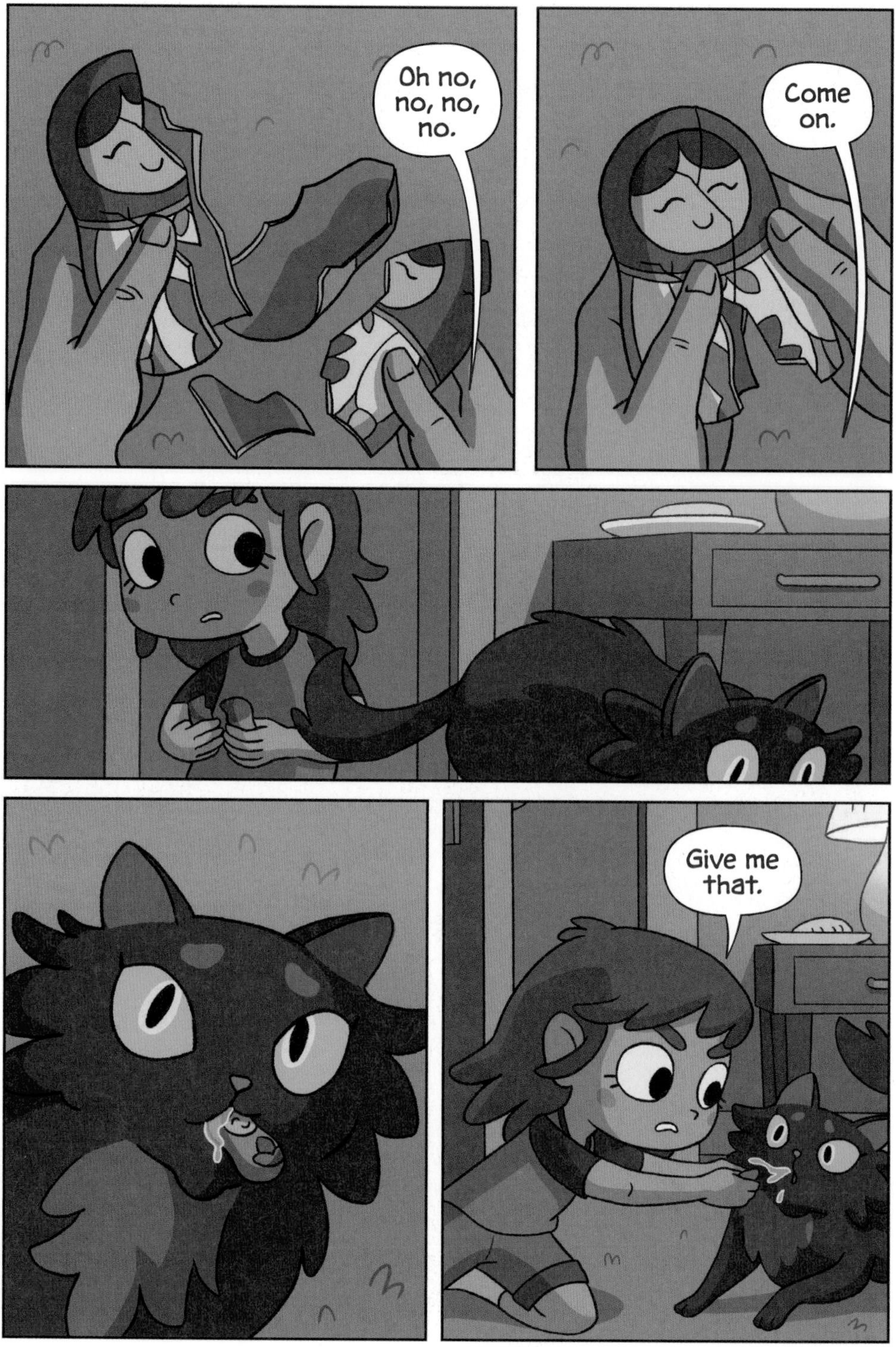
Oh no, no, no, no.
Come on.
Give me that.

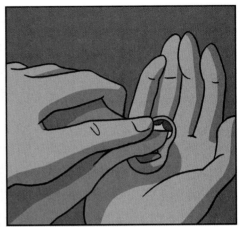

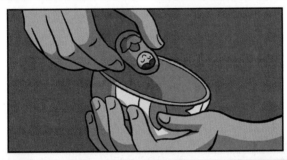

There you go, mila.

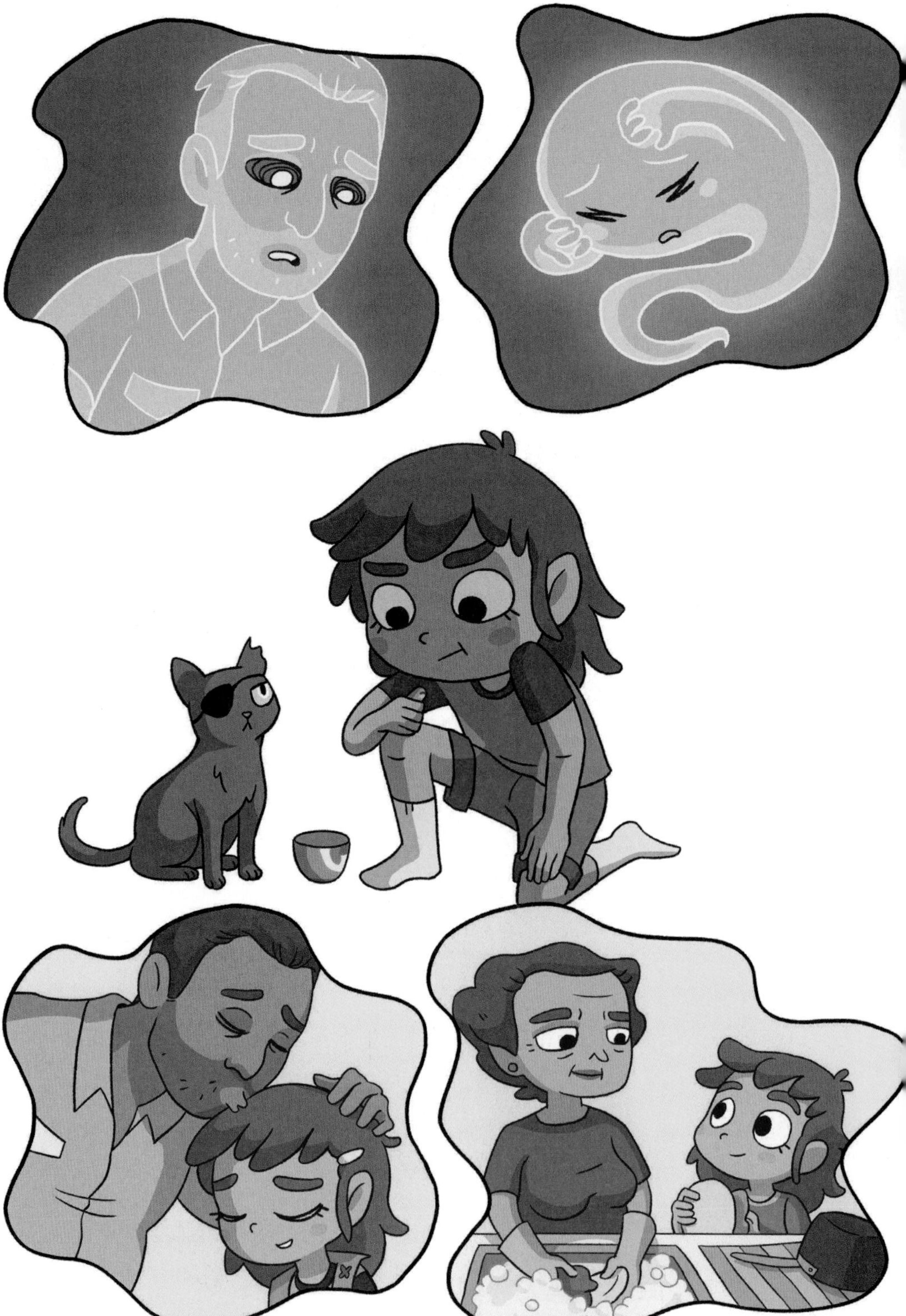

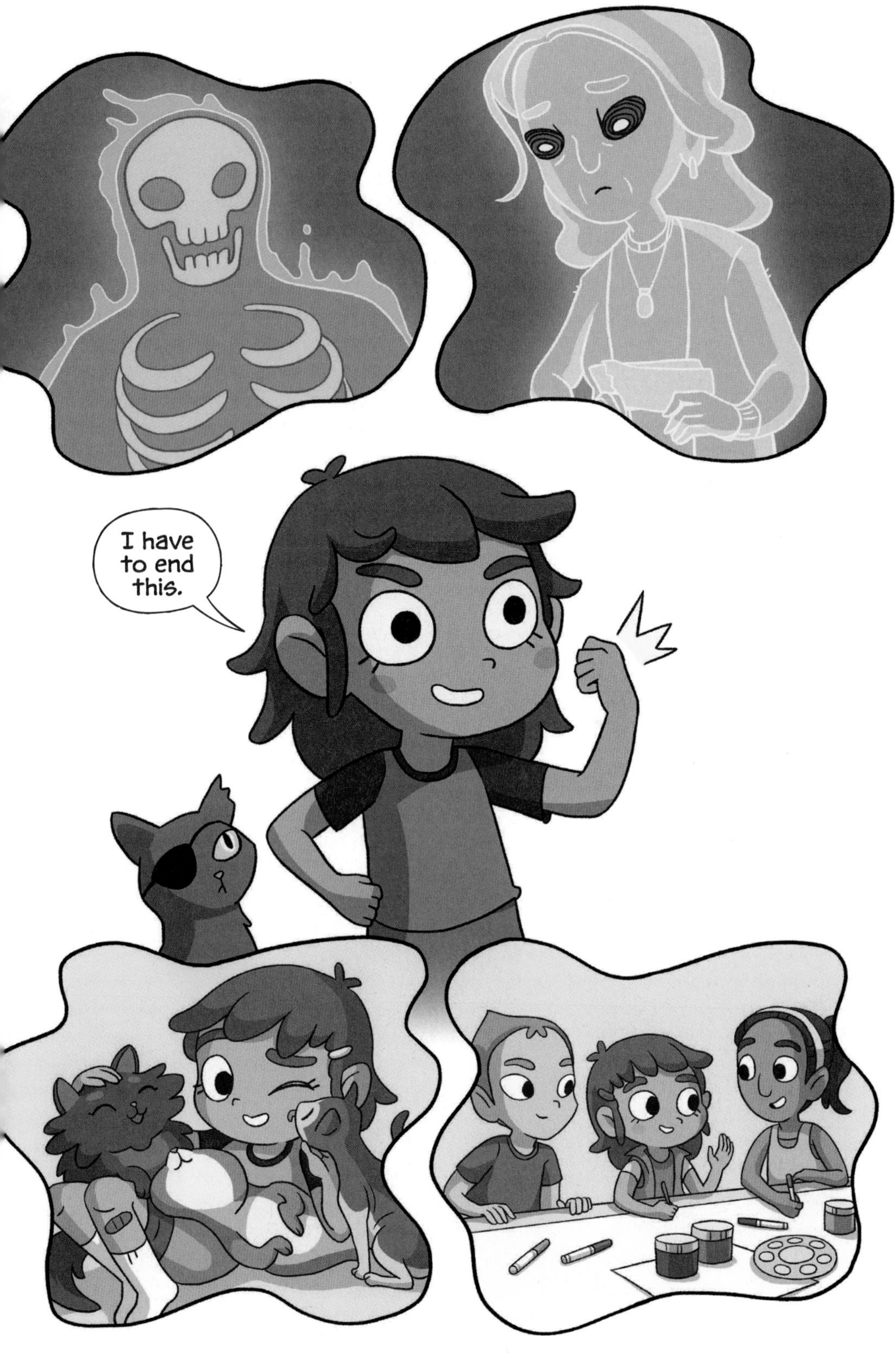
I have to end this.

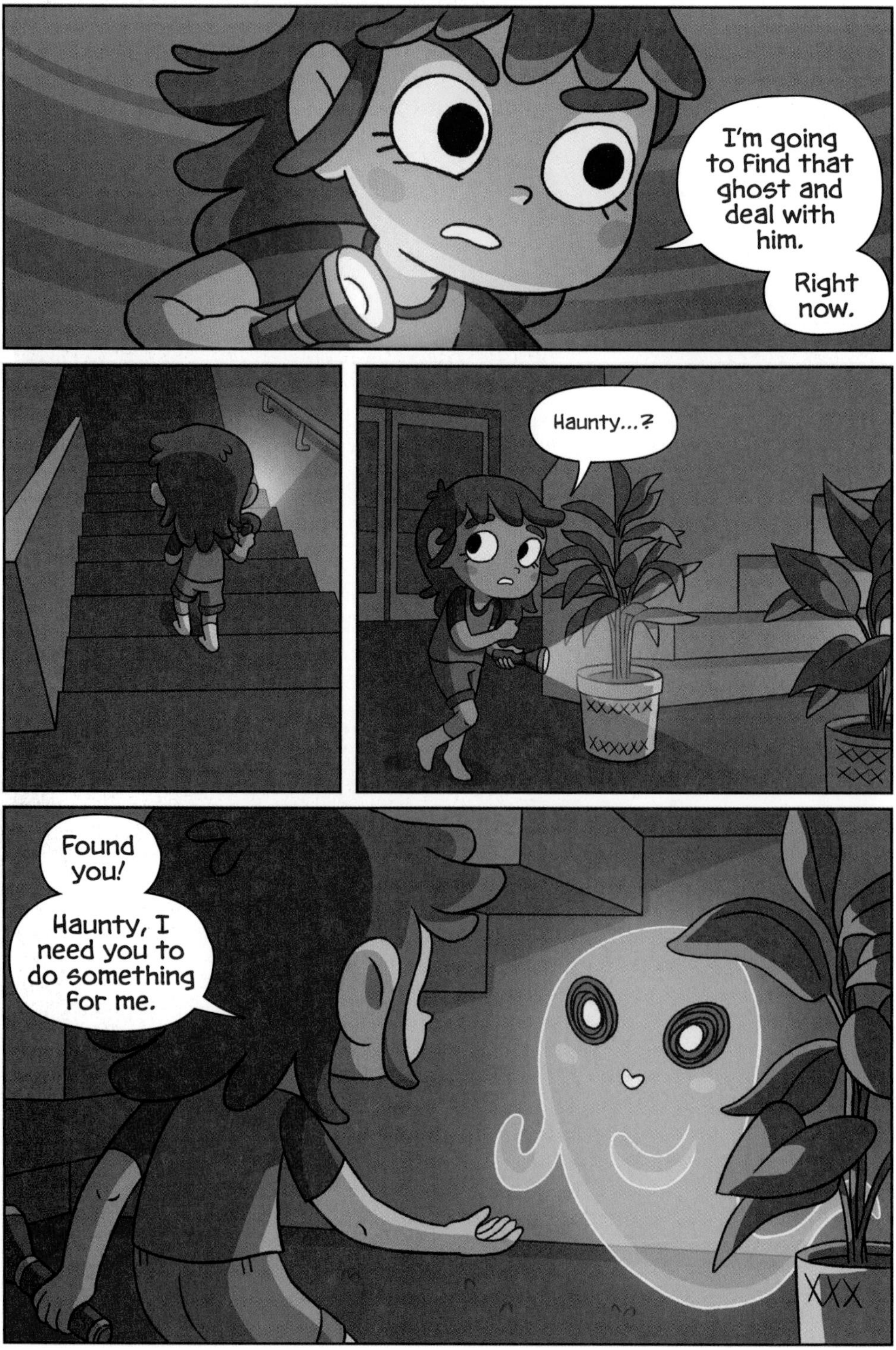
I'm going to find that ghost and deal with him.
Right now.
Haunty...?
Found you!
Haunty, I need you to do something for me.

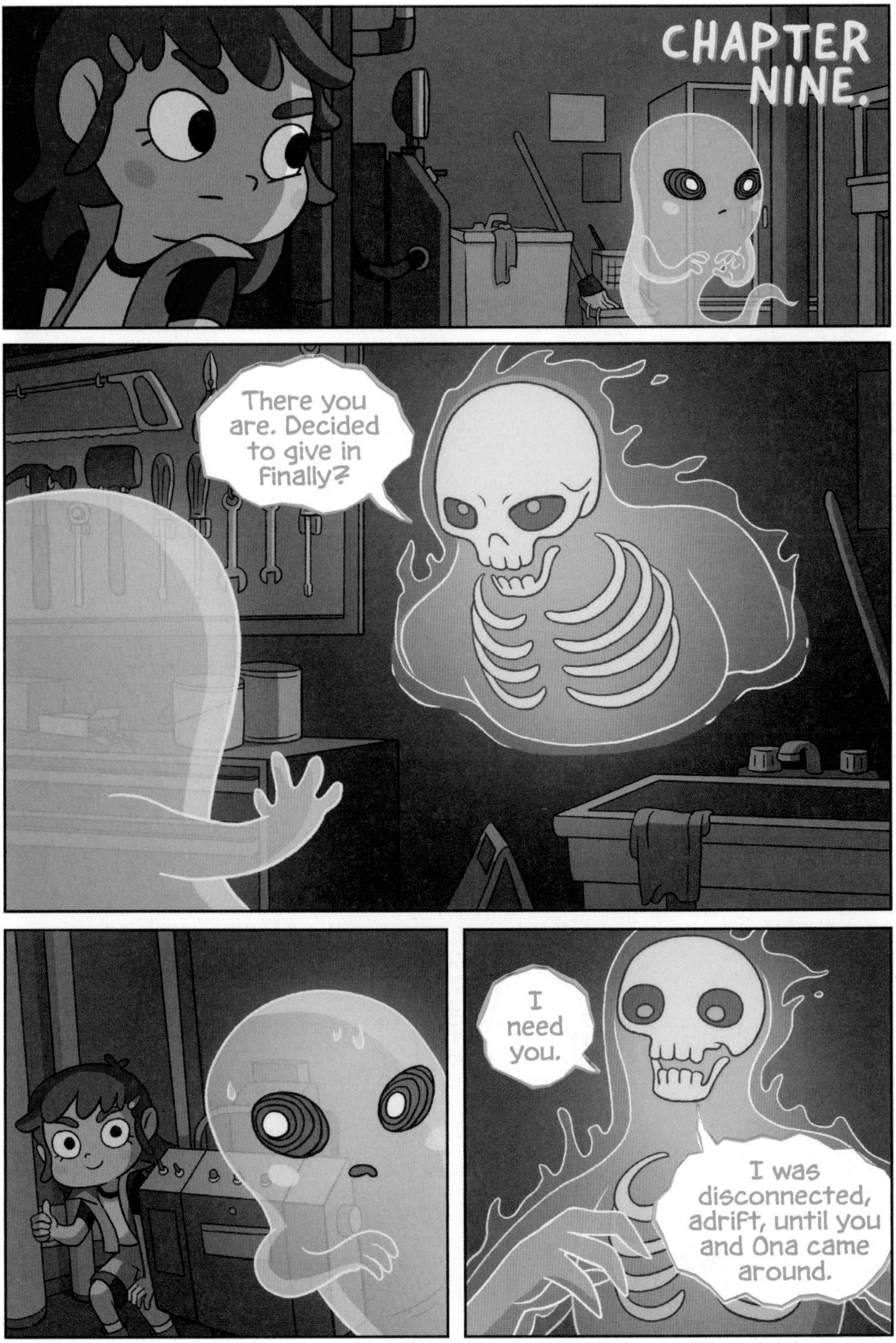
CHAPTER NINE.
There you are. Decided to give in finally?
I need you.
I was disconnected, adrift, until you and Ona came around.

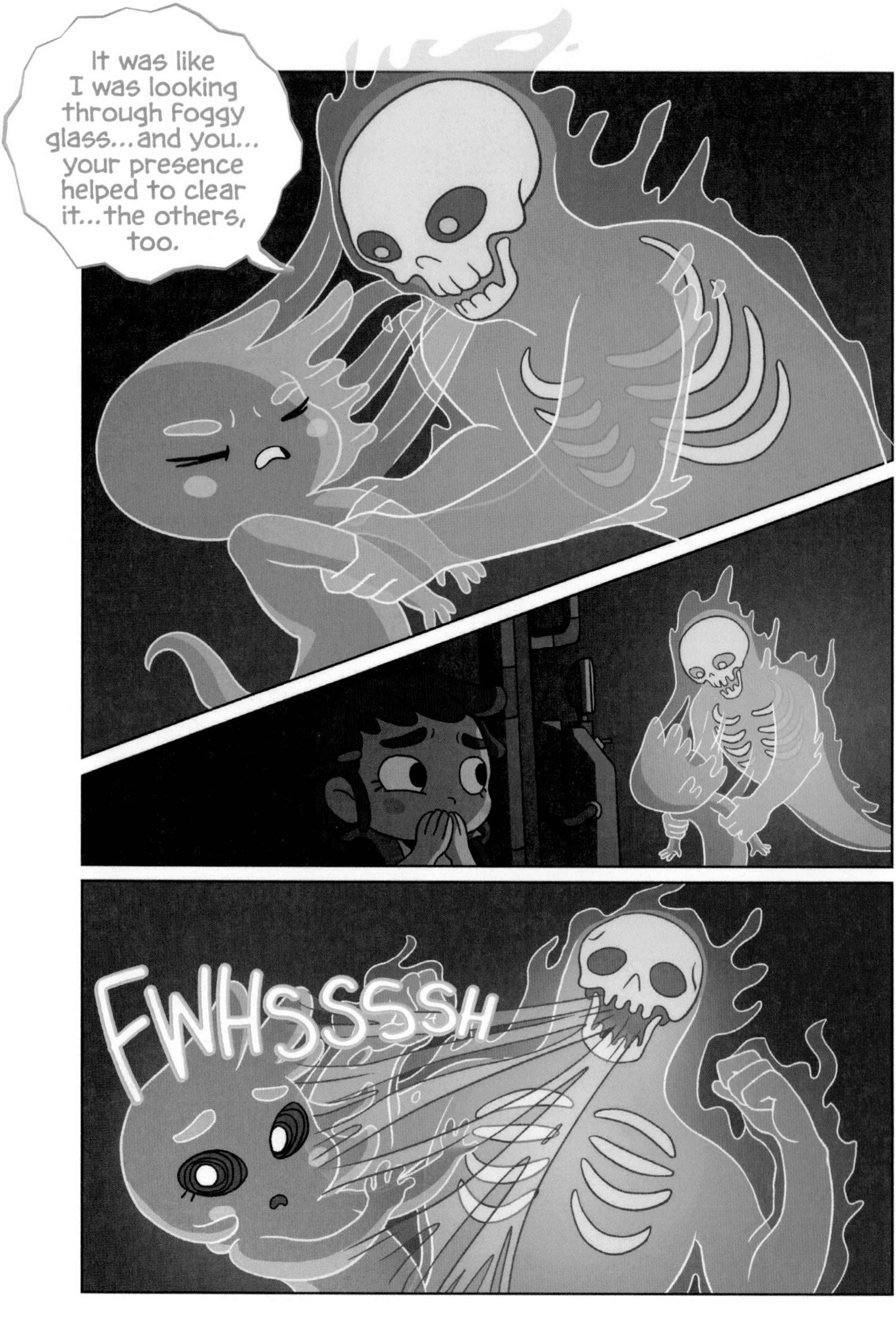
It was like I was looking through foggy glass...and you... your presence helped to clear it...the others, too.
FWHSSSSSH

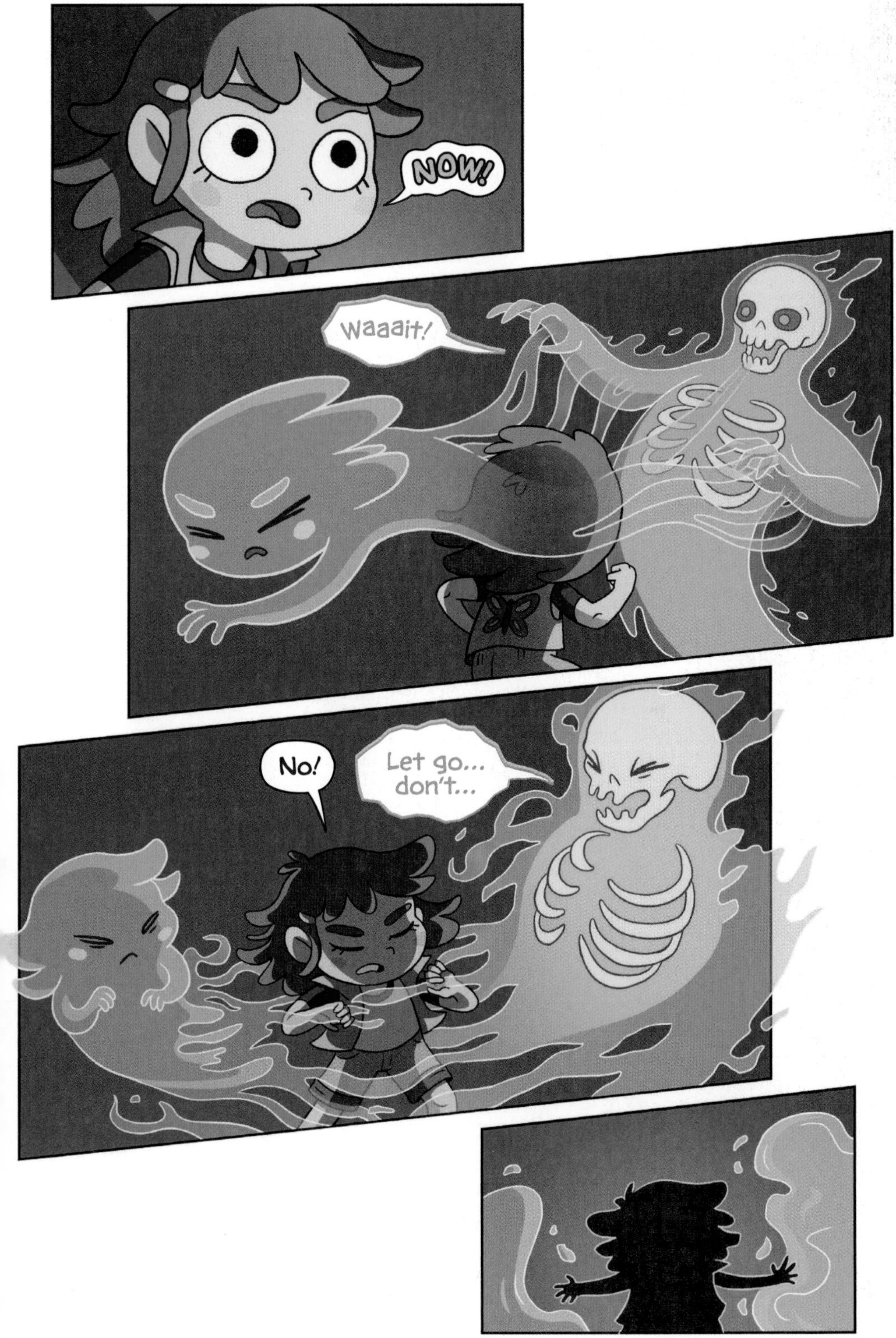
NOW!
Waaait!
No!
Let go... don't...

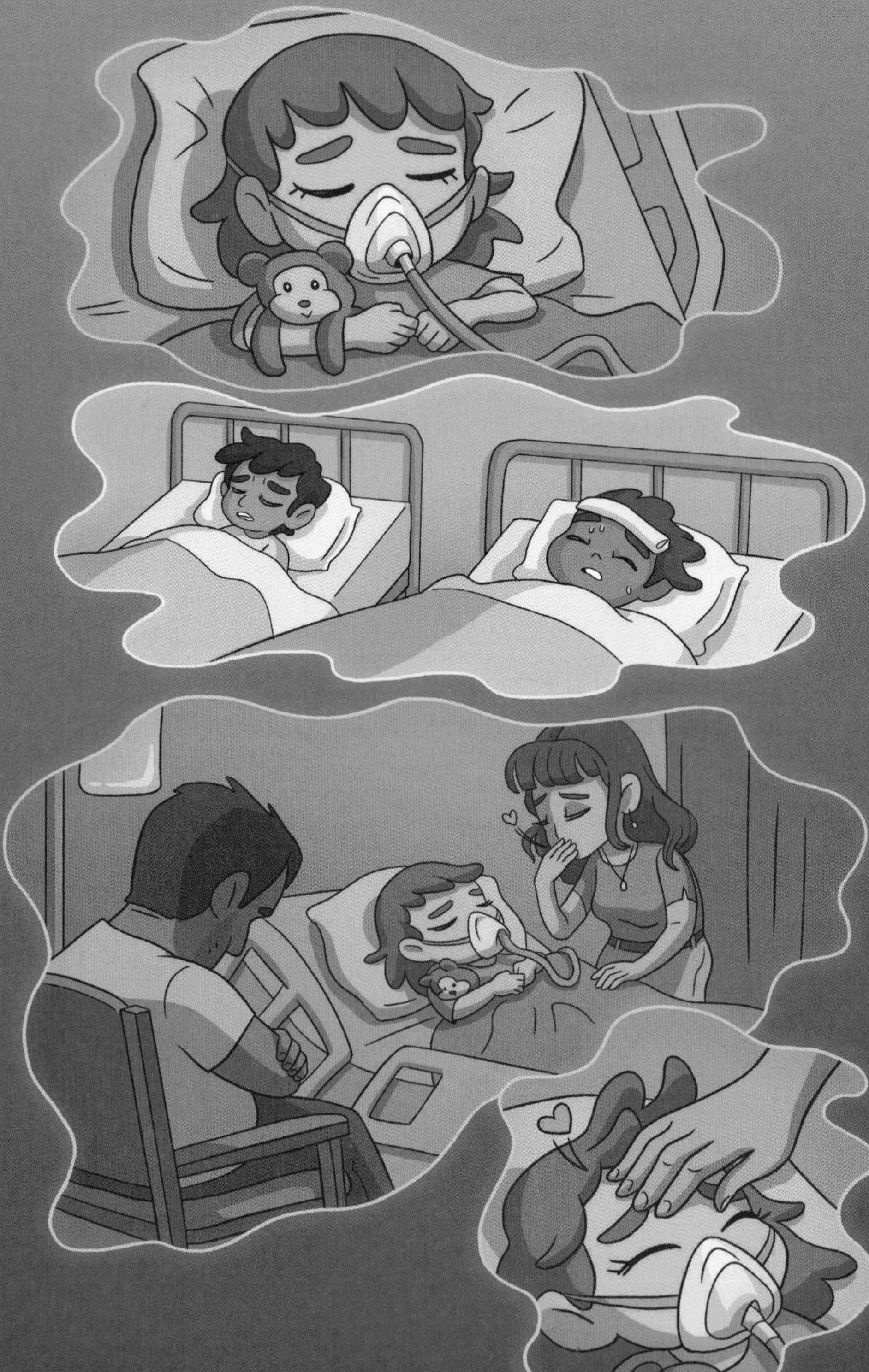

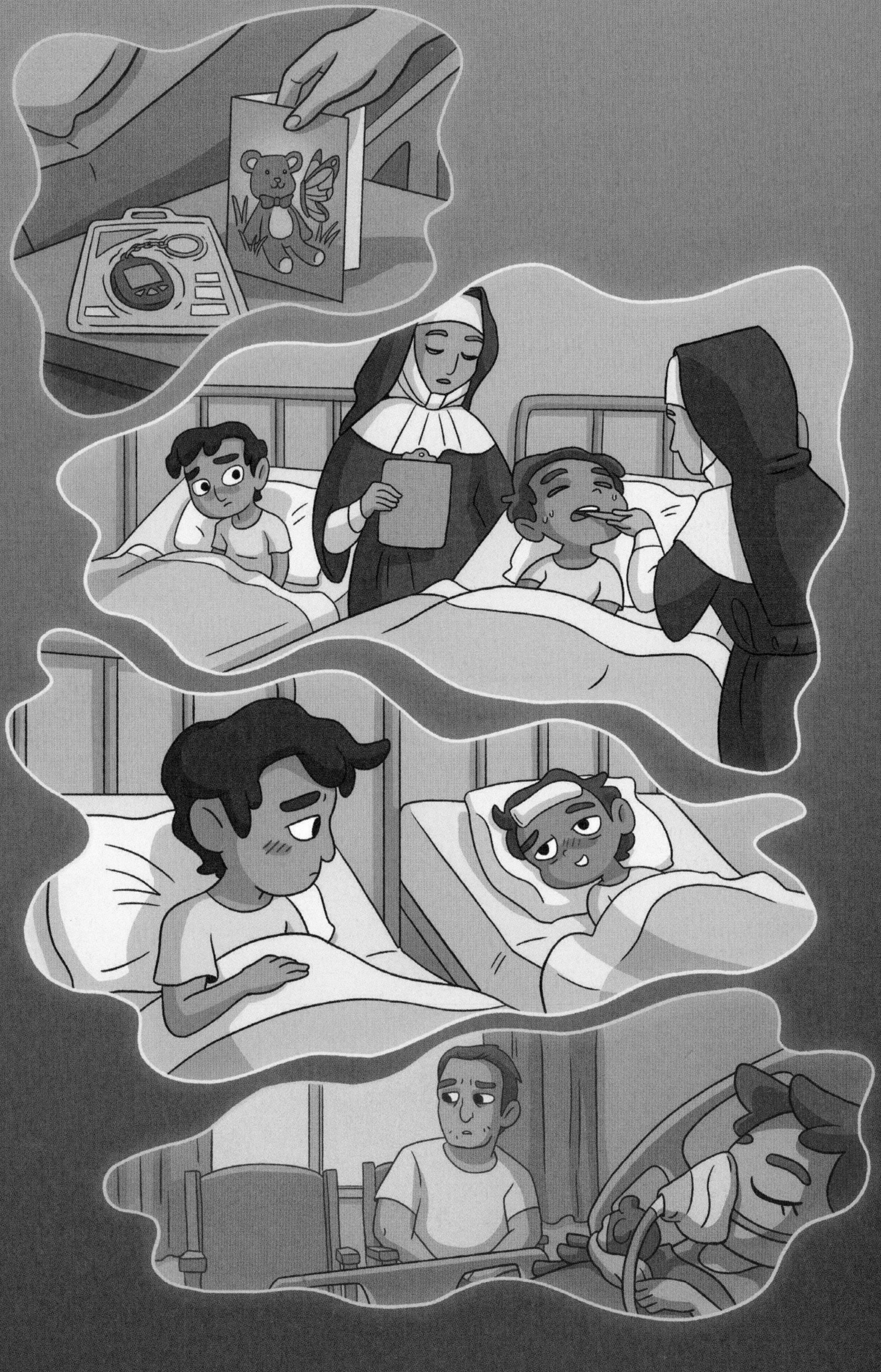

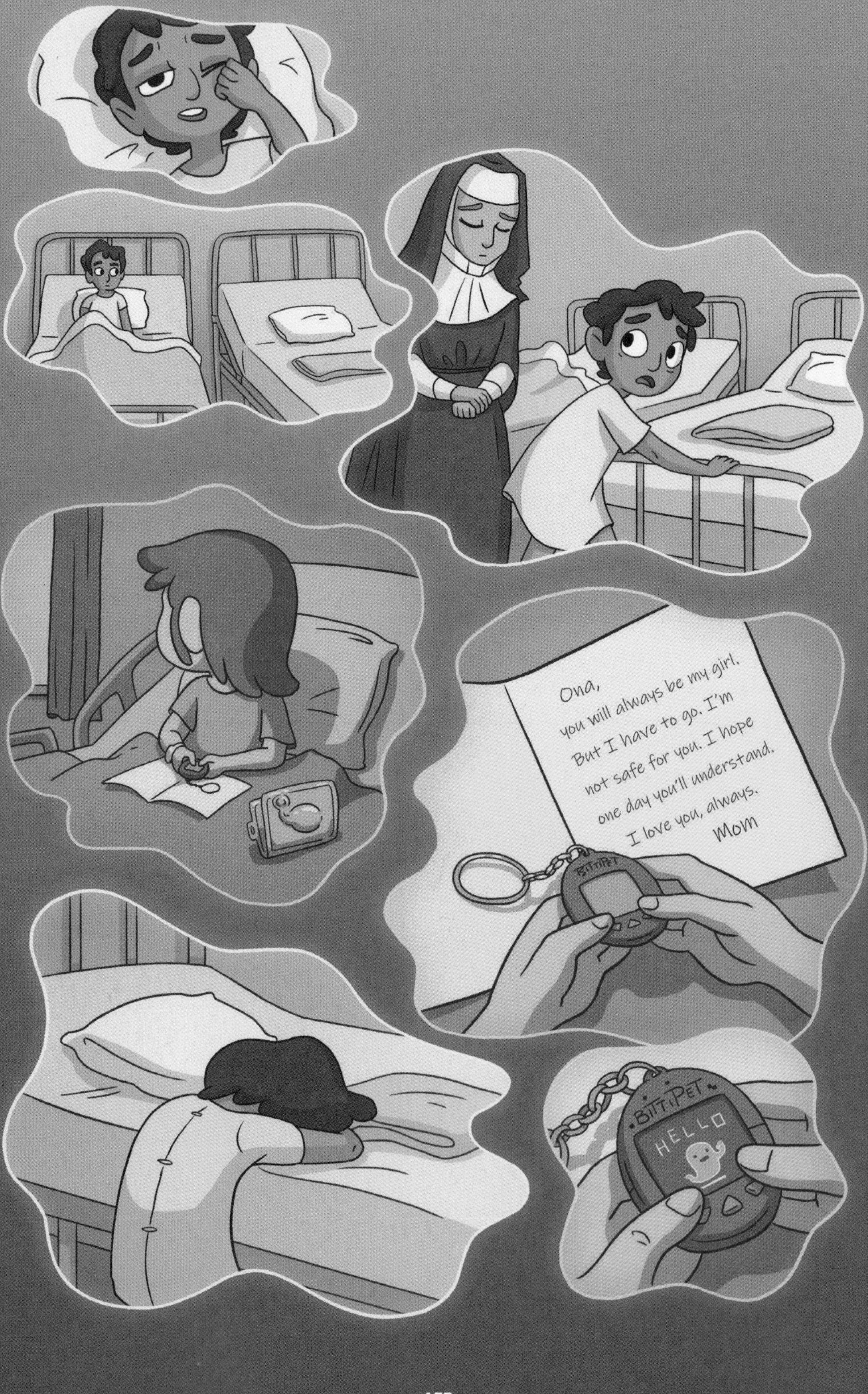
Ona,
you will always be my girl.
But I have to go. I'm
not safe for you. I hope
one day you'll understand.
I love you, always.
Mom
BITTIPET
BITTIPET
HELLO

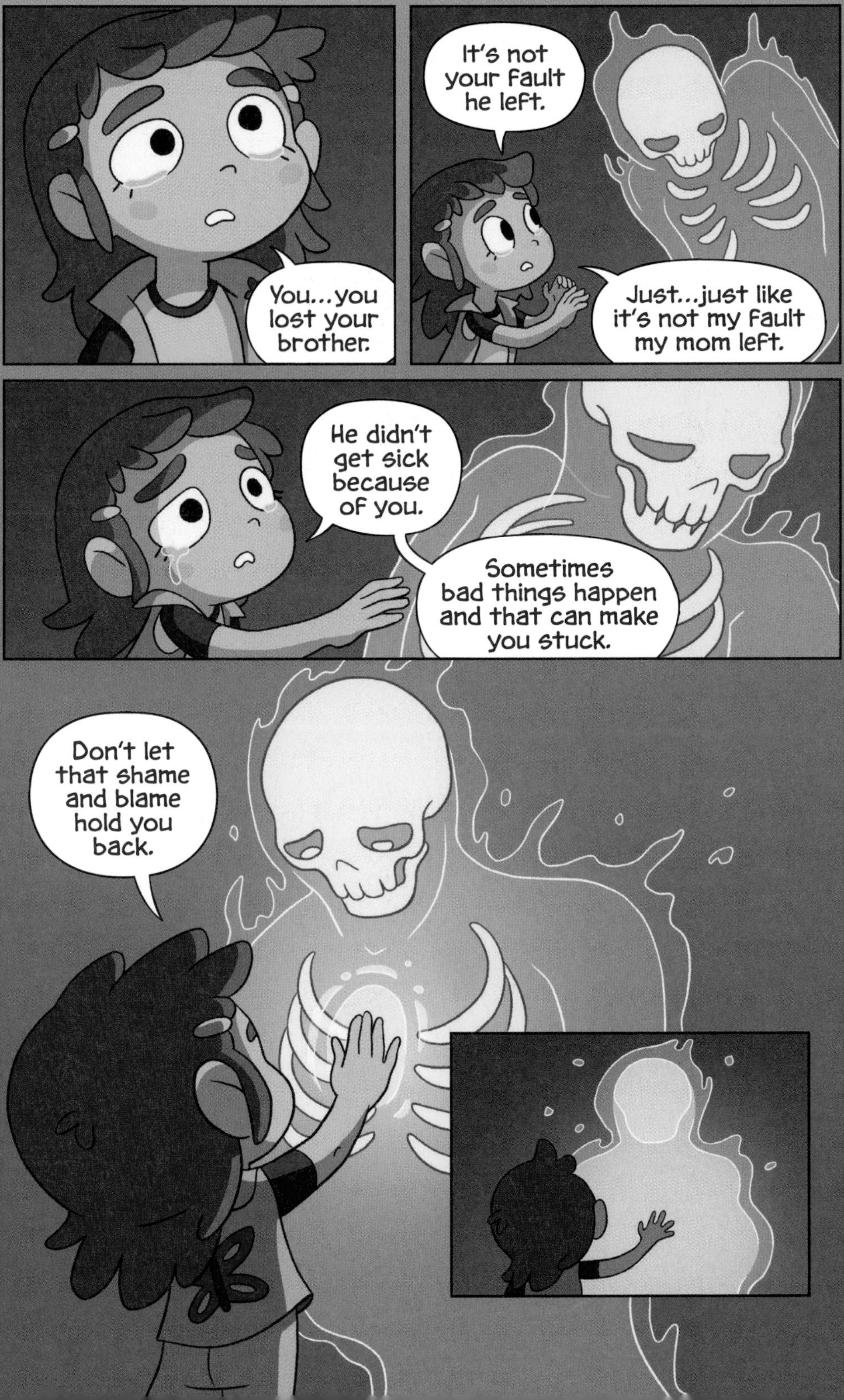
You...you lost your brother.
It's not your fault he left.
Just...just like it's not my fault my mom left.
He didn't get sick because of you.
Sometimes bad things happen and that can make you stuck.
Don't let that shame and blame hold you back.

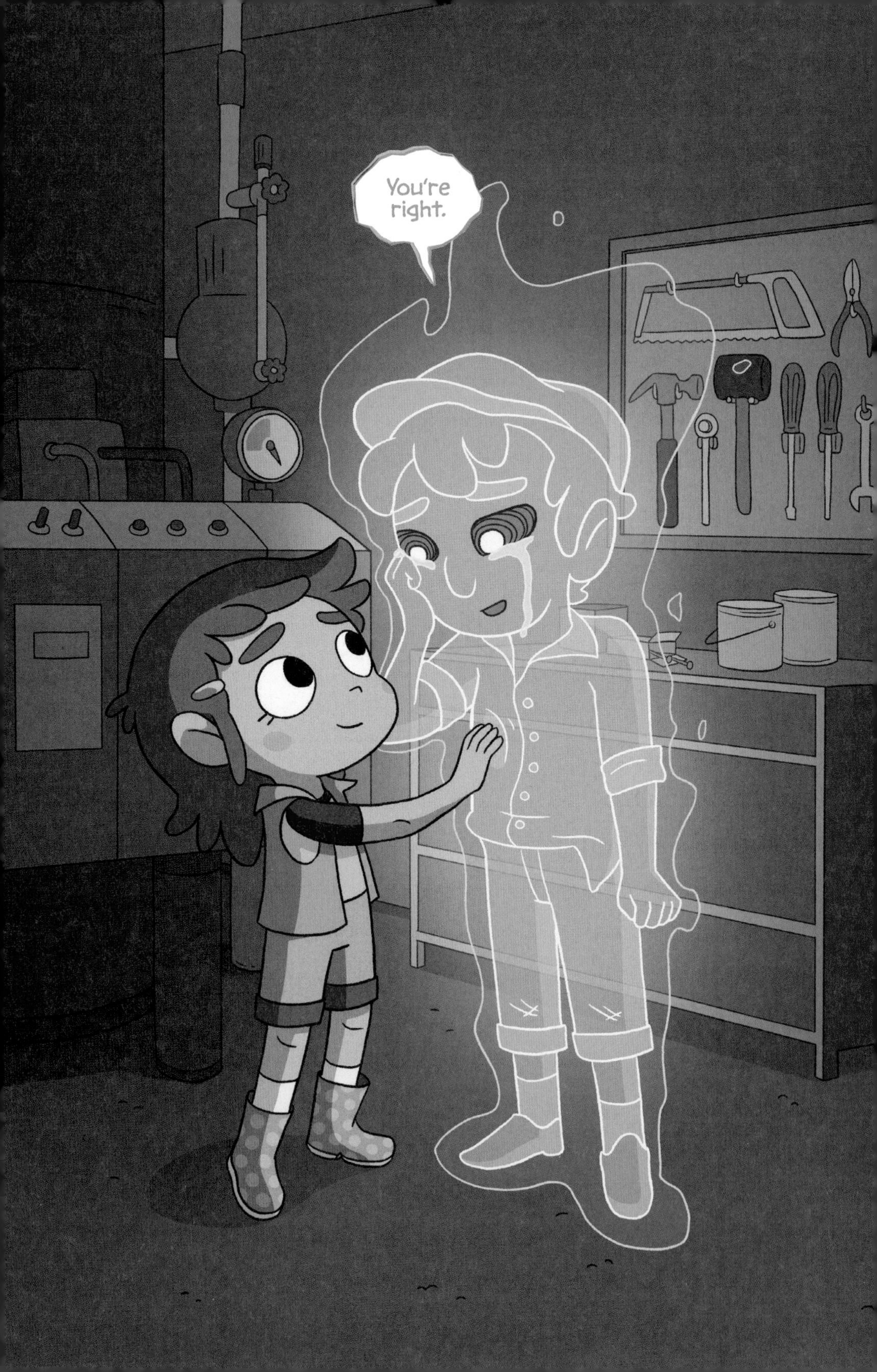
You're right.

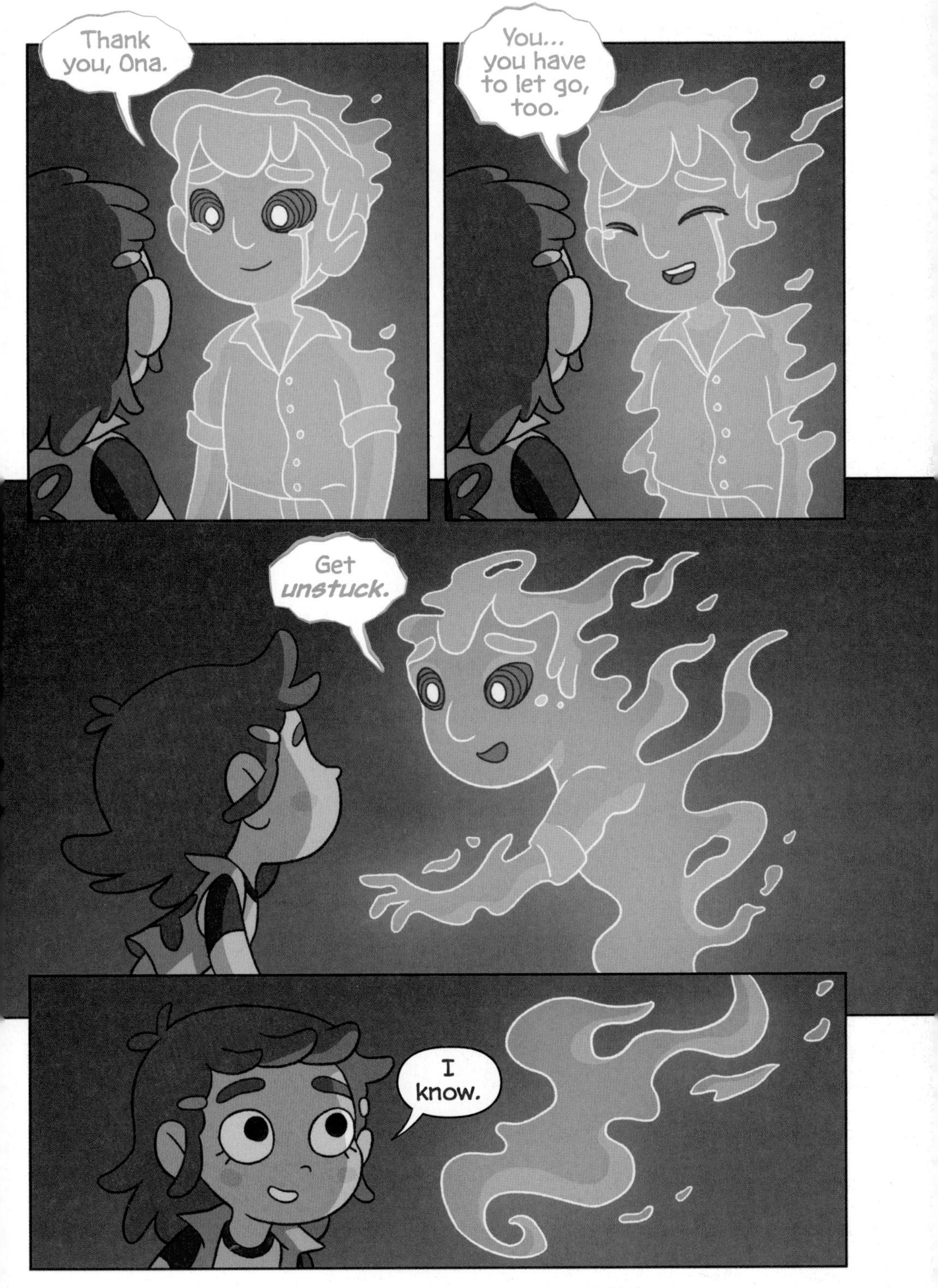
Thank you, Ona.
You... you have to let go, too.
Get *unstuck.*
I know.

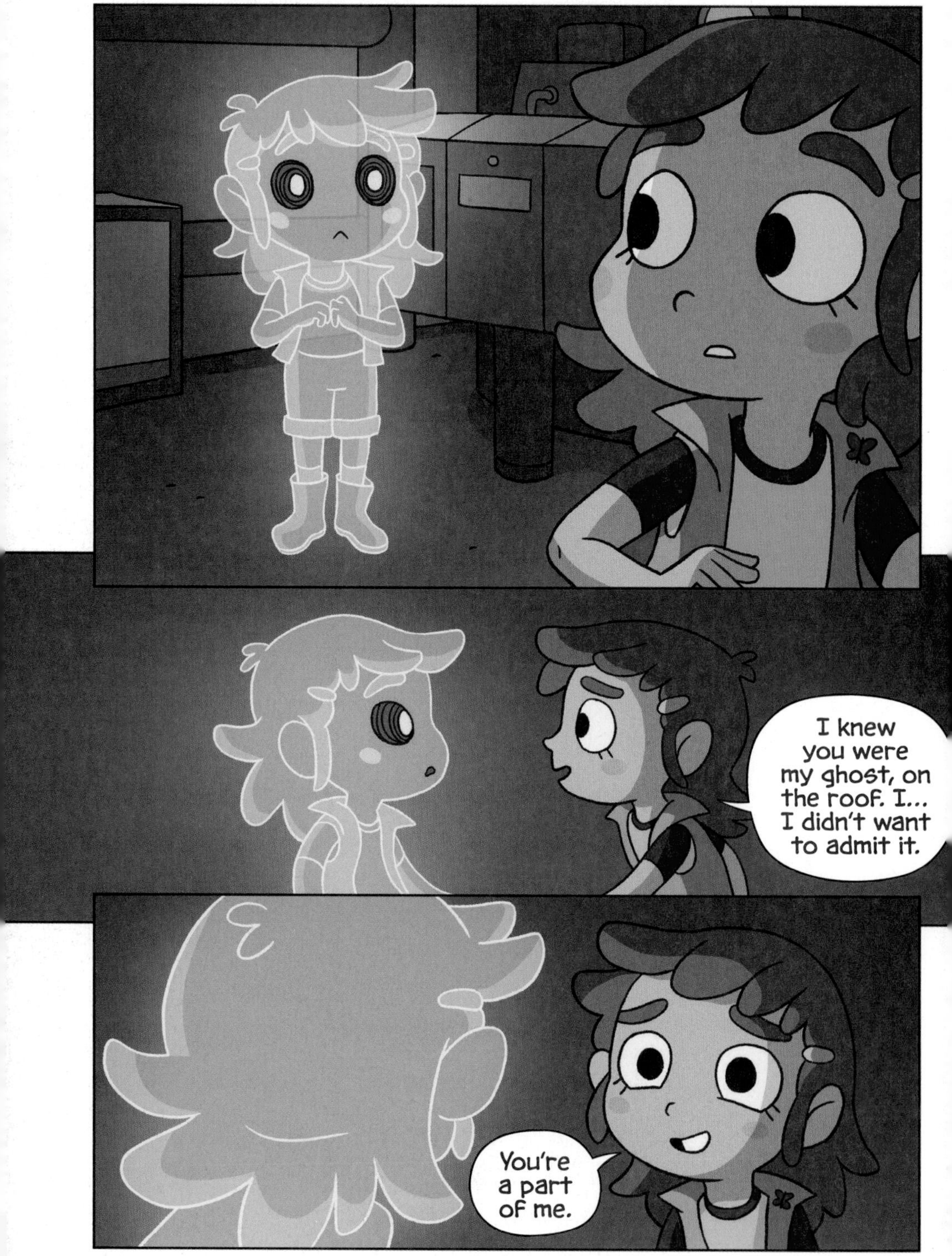
I knew you were my ghost, on the roof. I... I didn't want to admit it.
You're a part of me.

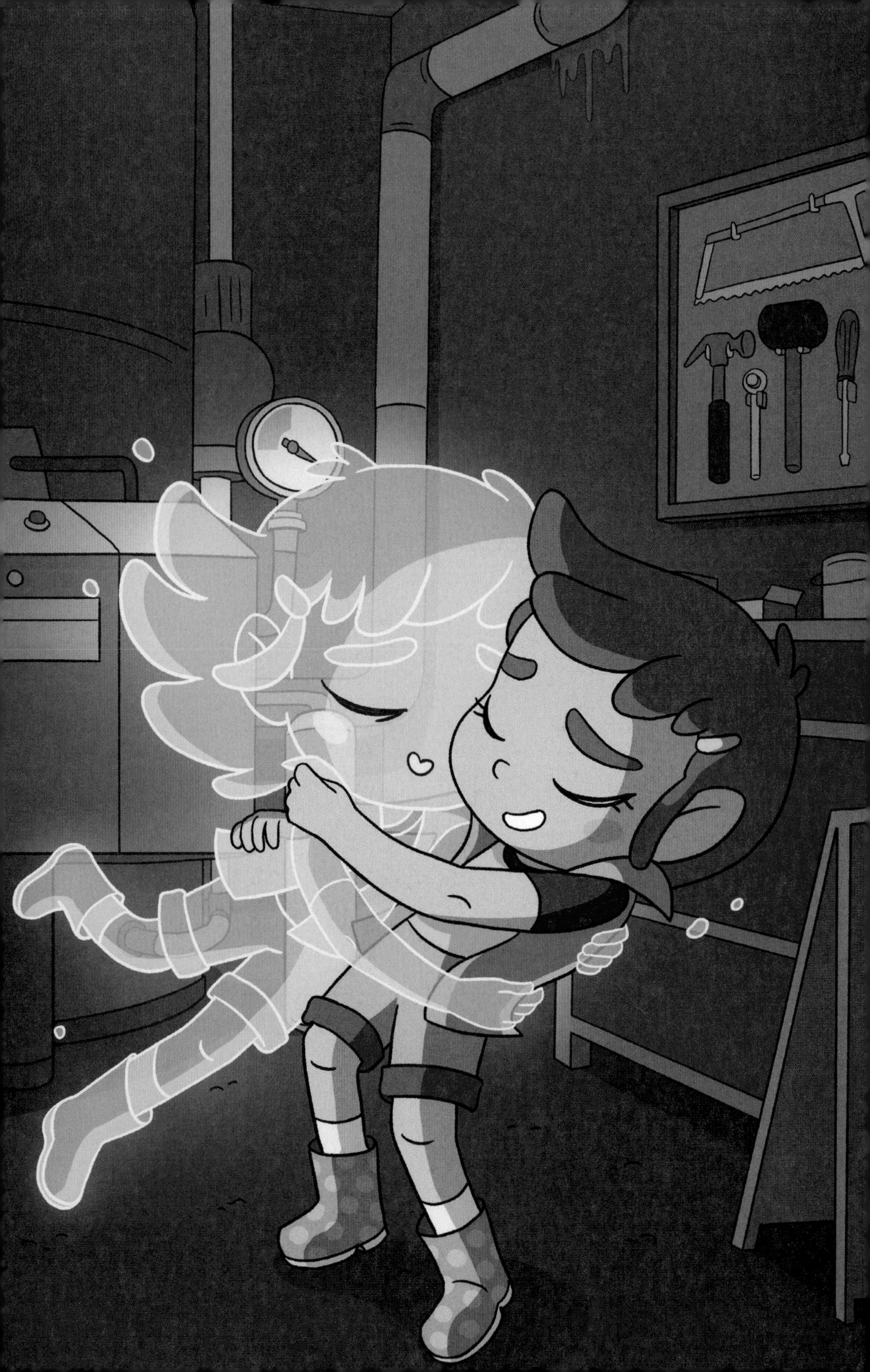

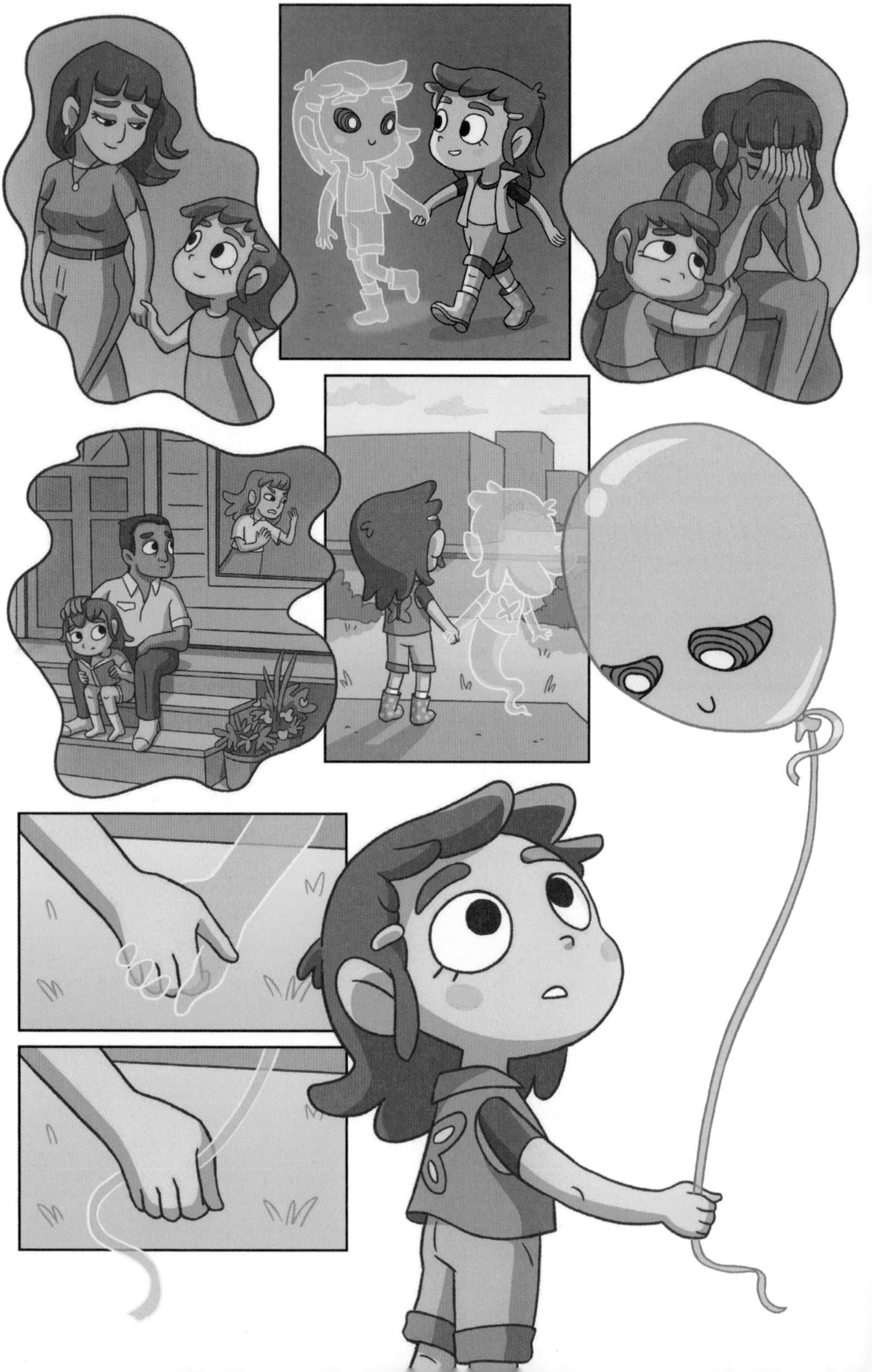

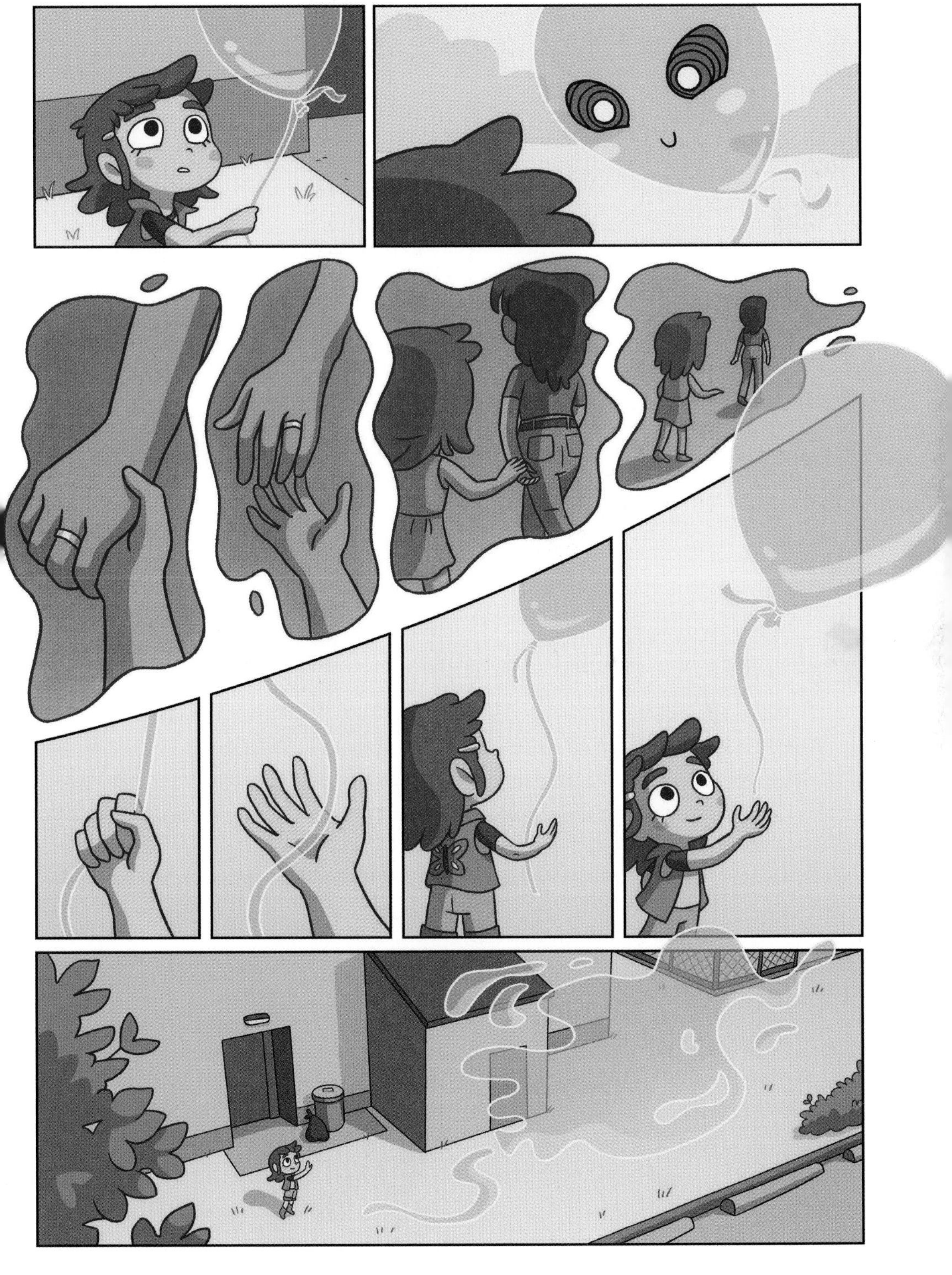

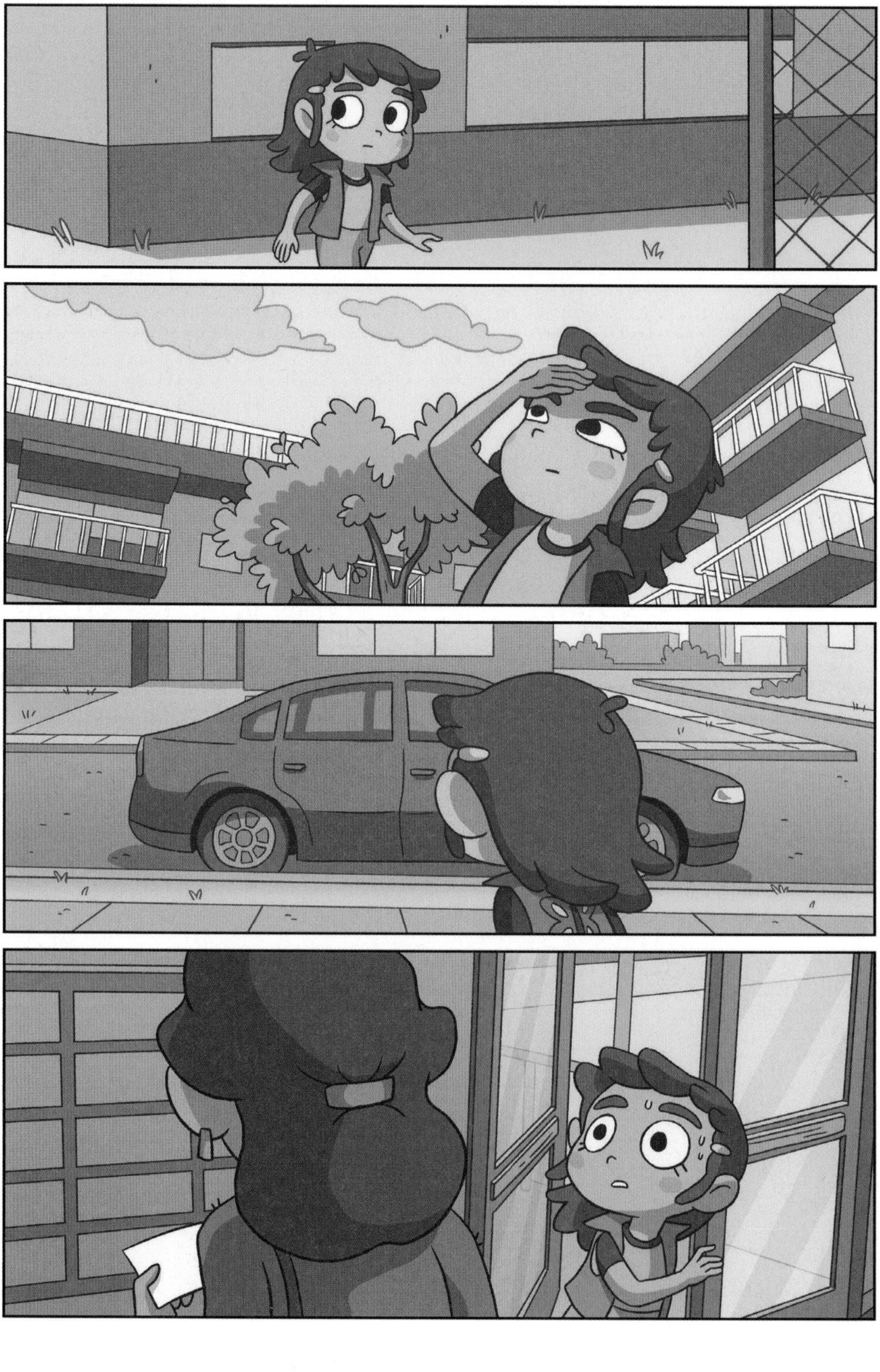

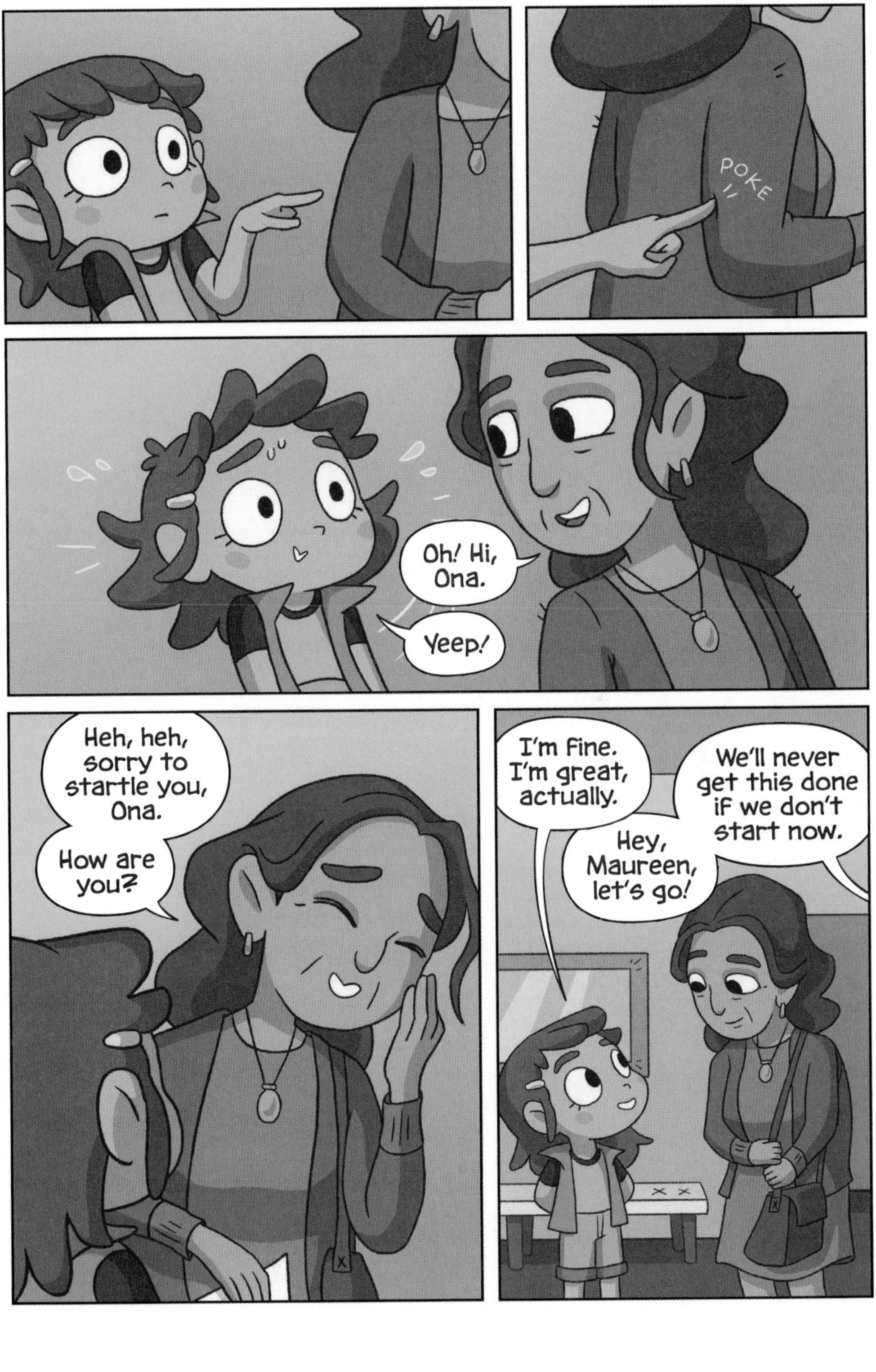
POKE
Oh! Hi, Ona.
Yeep!
Heh, heh, sorry to startle you, Ona.
How are you?
I'm fine. I'm great, actually.
We'll never get this done if we don't start now.
Hey, Maureen, let's go!

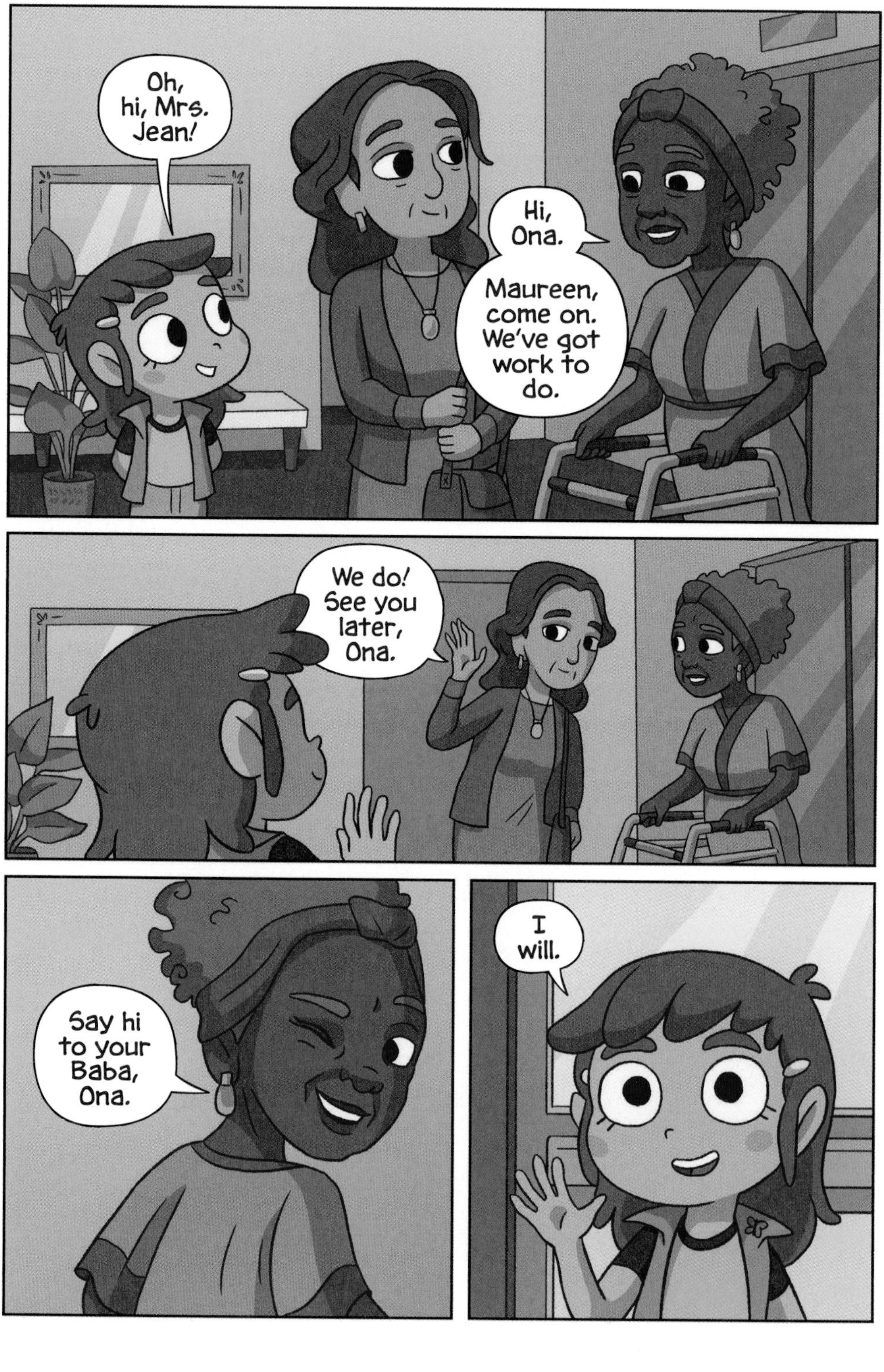
Oh, hi, Mrs. Jean!
Hi, Ona.
Maureen, come on. We've got work to do.
We do! See you later, Ona.
Say hi to your Baba, Ona.
I will.

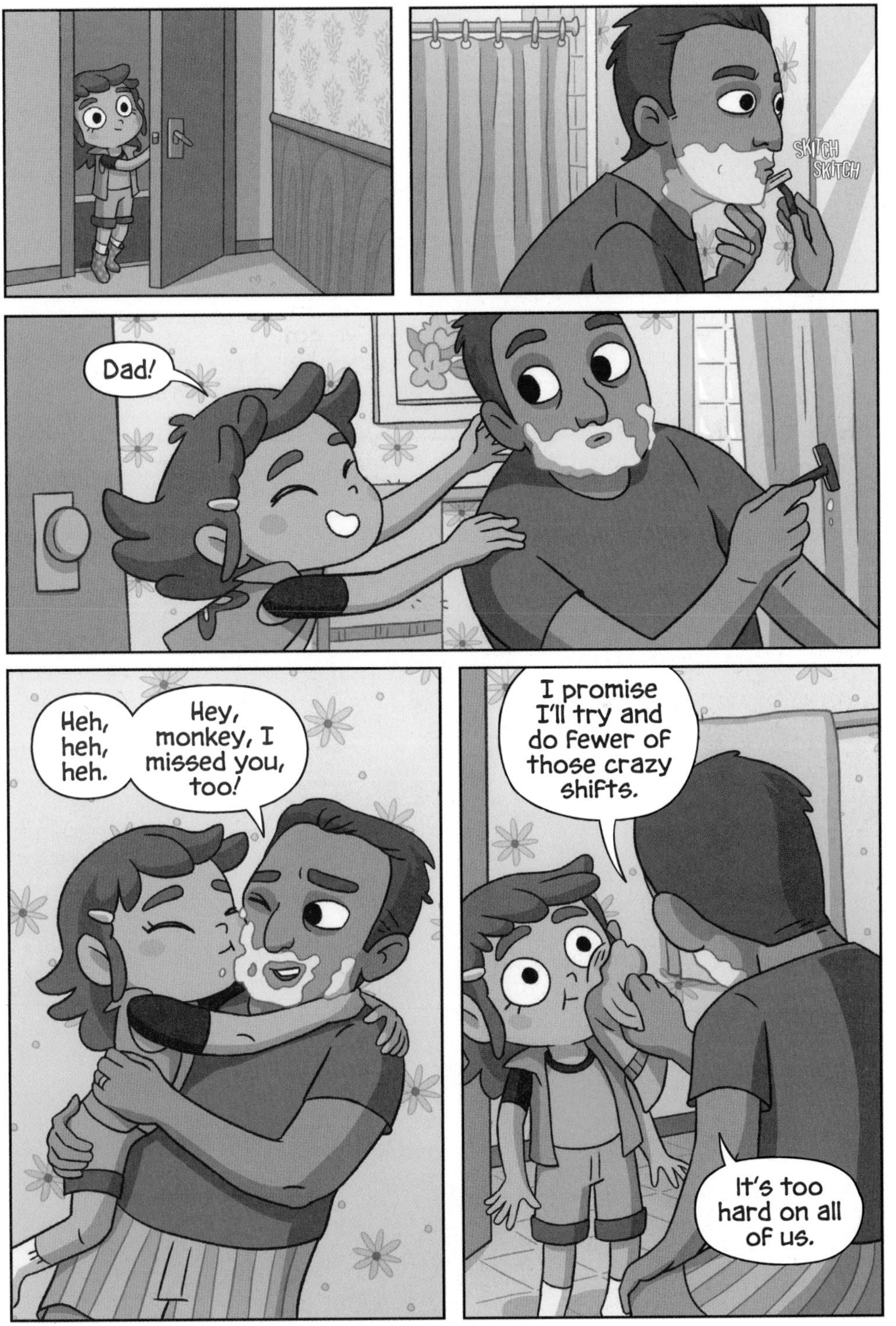

SKITCH SKITCH
Dad!
Heh, heh, heh.
Hey, monkey, I missed you, too!
I promise I'll try and do fewer of those crazy shifts.
It's too hard on all of us.

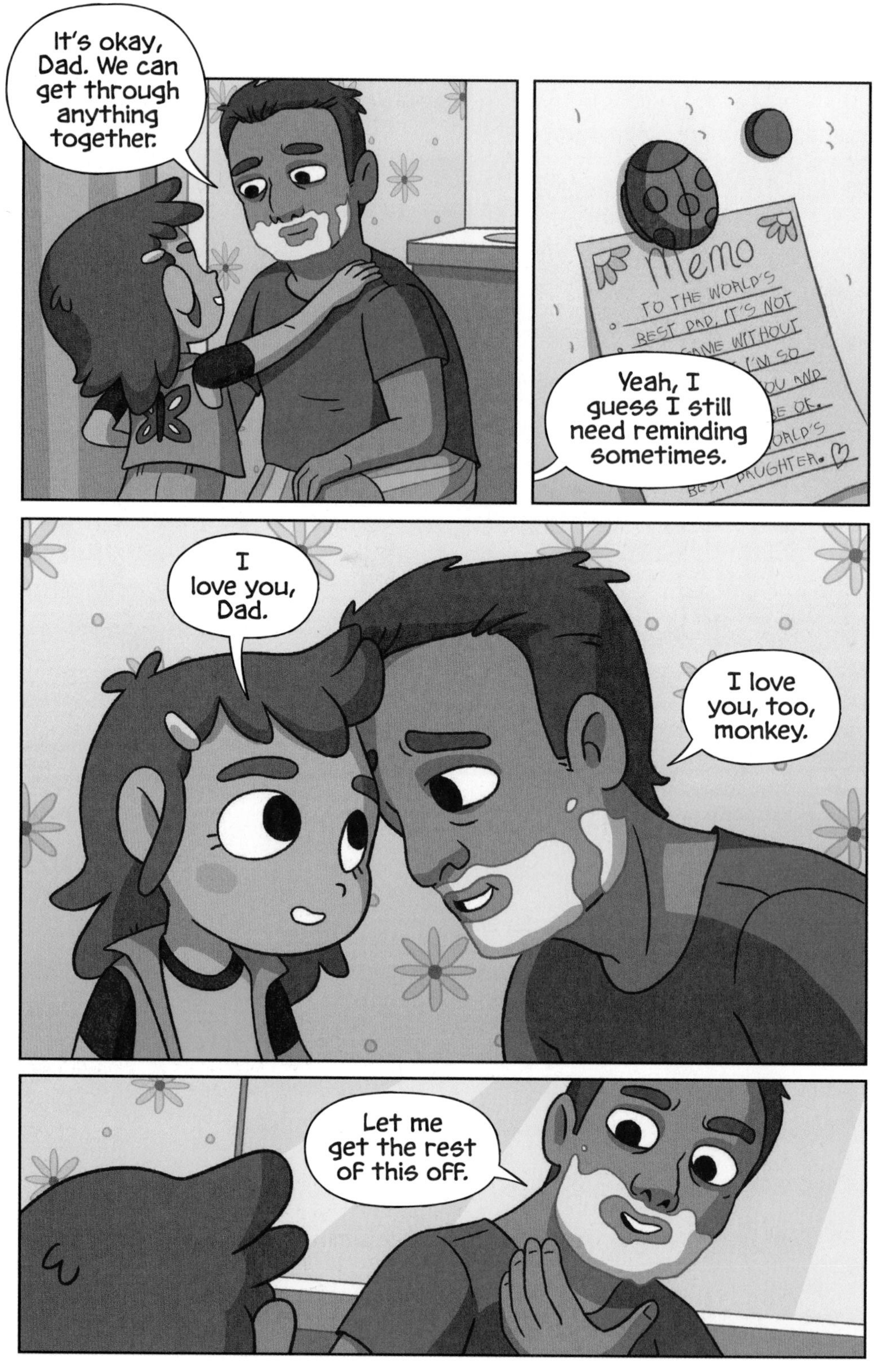
It's okay, Dad. We can get through anything together.
Memo
TO THE WORLD'S
BEST DAD, IT'S NOT
Yeah, I guess I still need reminding sometimes.
I love you, Dad.
I love you, too, monkey.
Let me get the rest of this off.

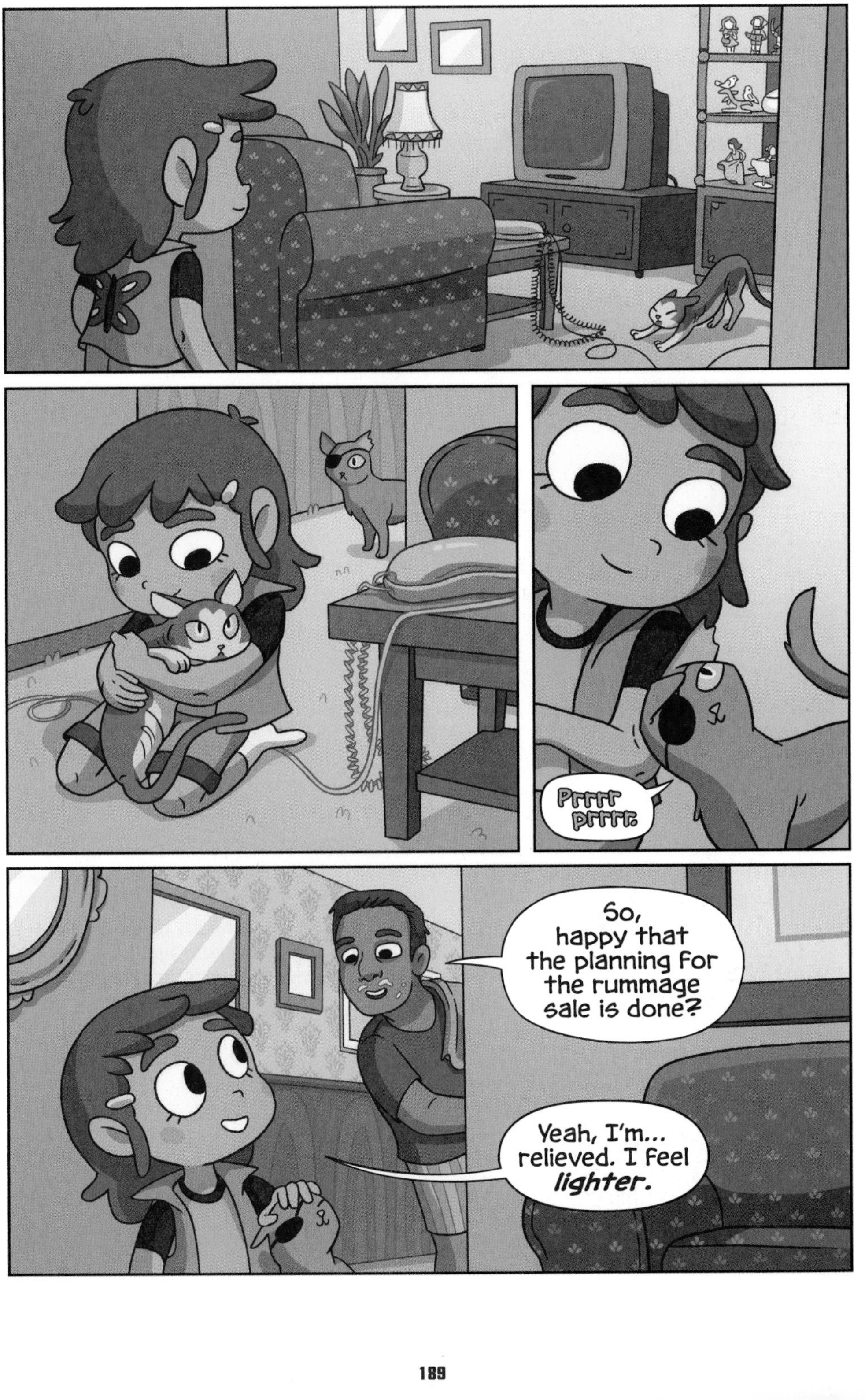
Prrrr prrrr.
So, happy that the planning for the rummage sale is done?
Yeah, I'm... relieved. I feel *lighter.*

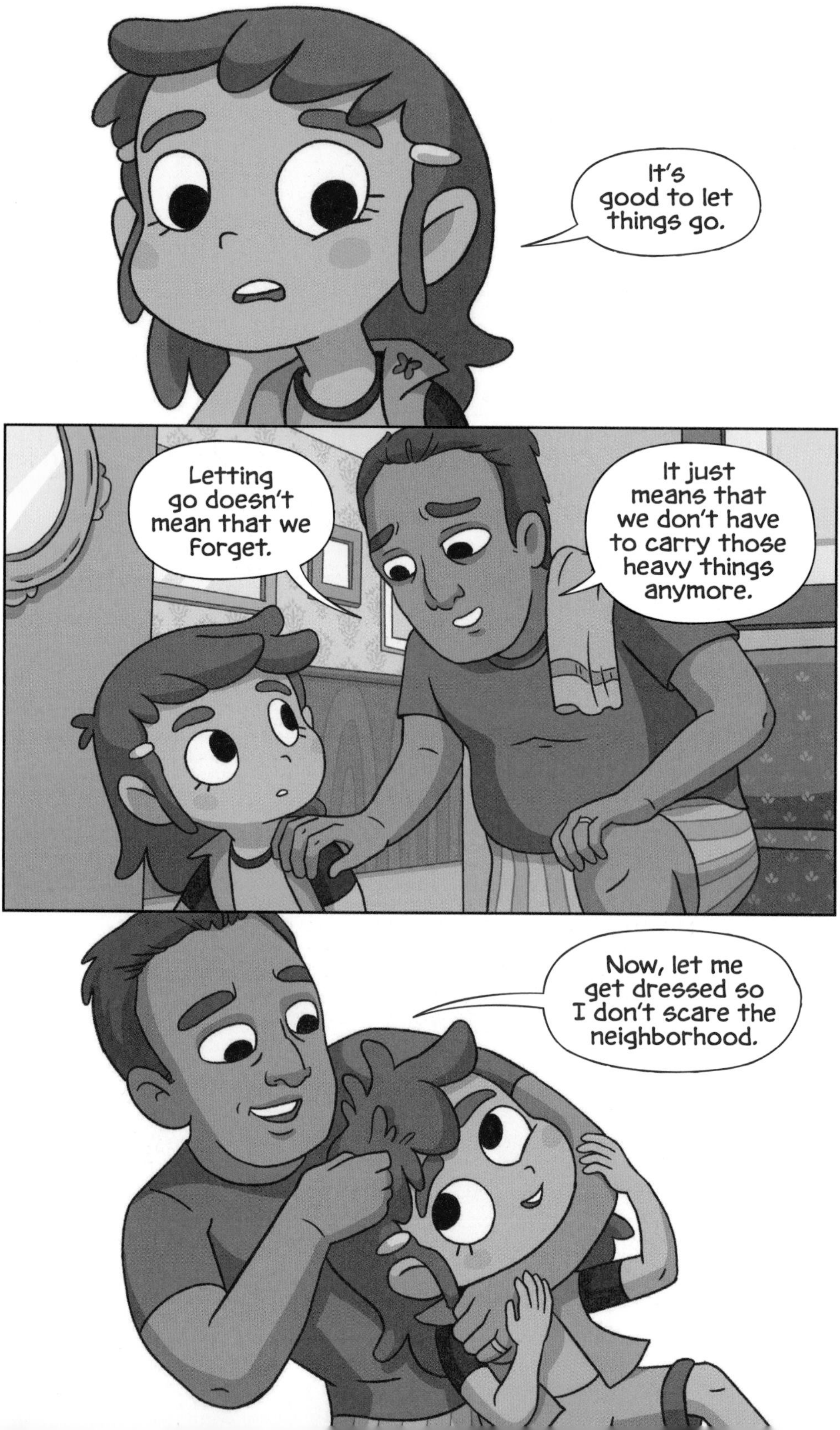
It's good to let things go.
Letting go doesn't mean that we forget.
It just means that we don't have to carry those heavy things anymore.
Now, let me get dressed so I don't scare the neighborhood.

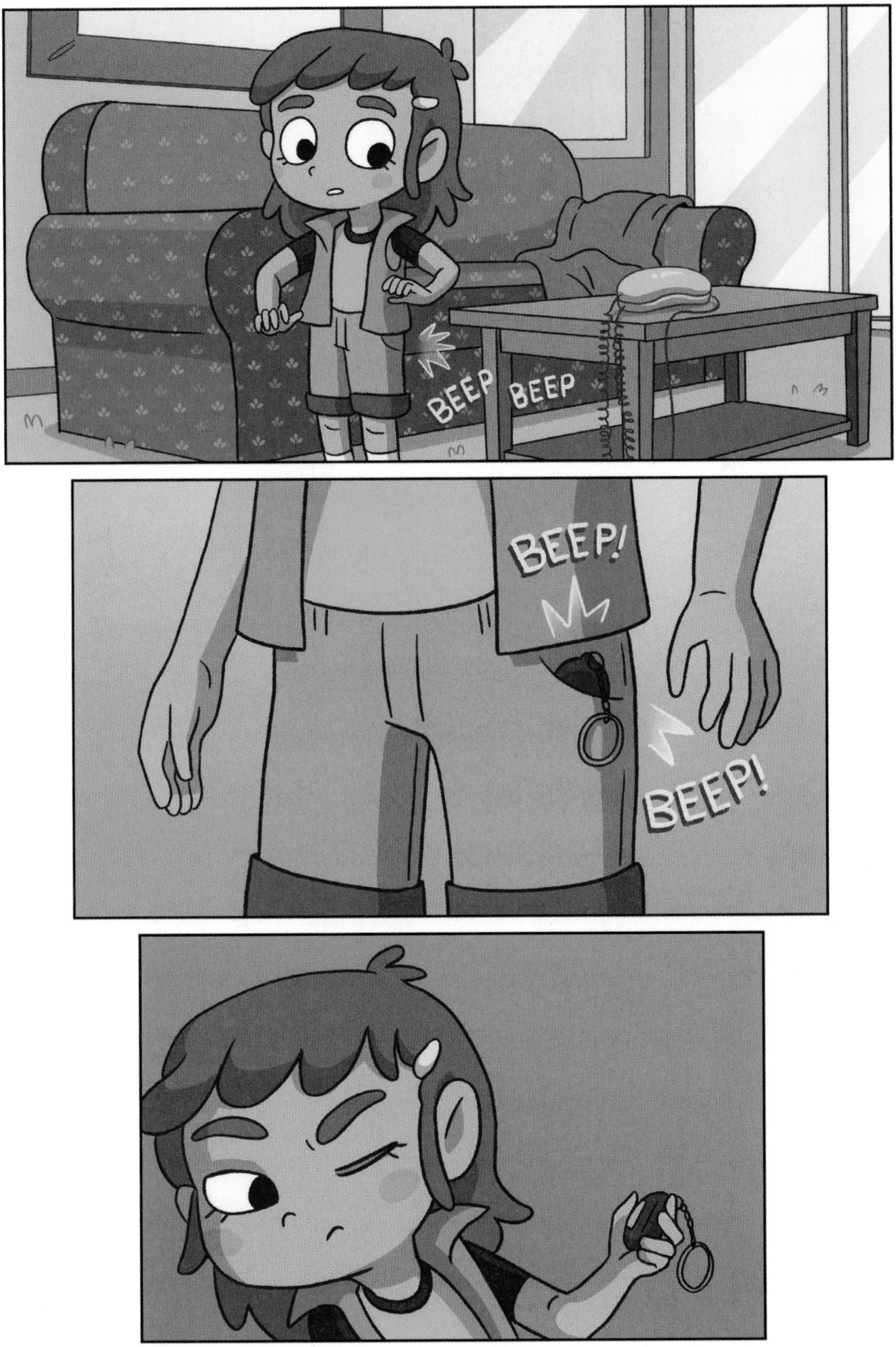
BEEP BEEP
BEEP!
BEEP!

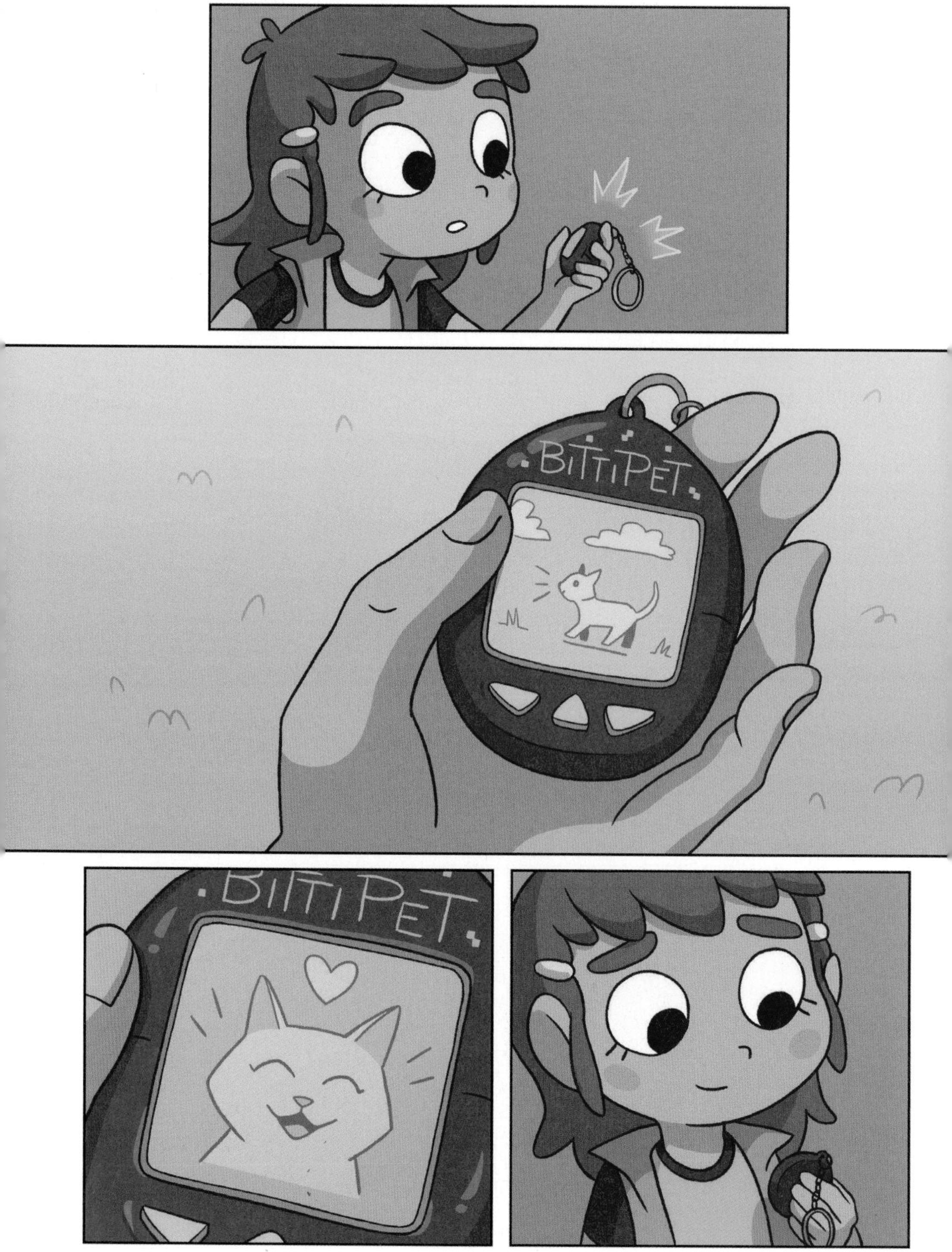
BITTIPET
BITTIPET

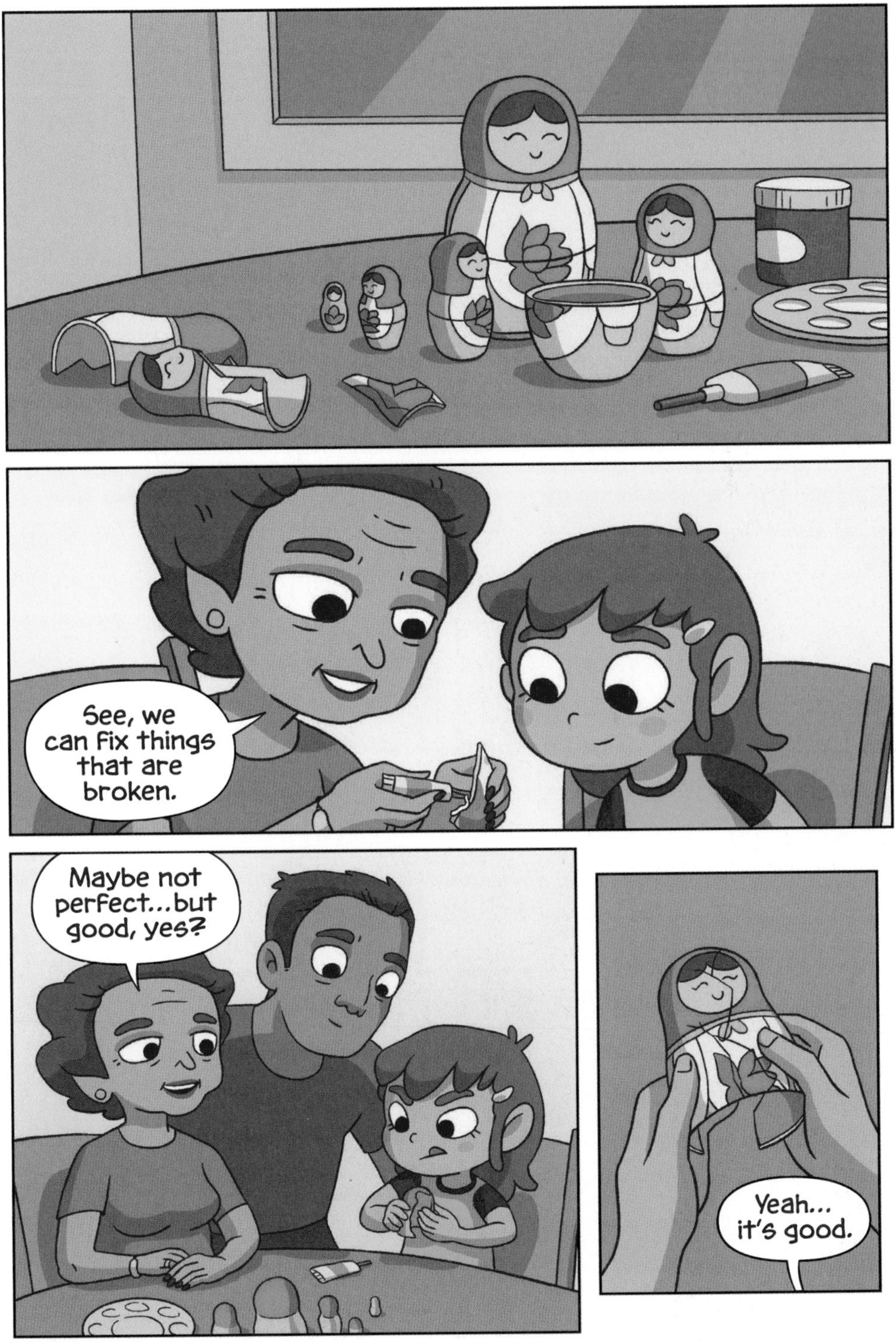
See, we can fix things that are broken.
Maybe not perfect...but good, yes?
Yeah... it's good.

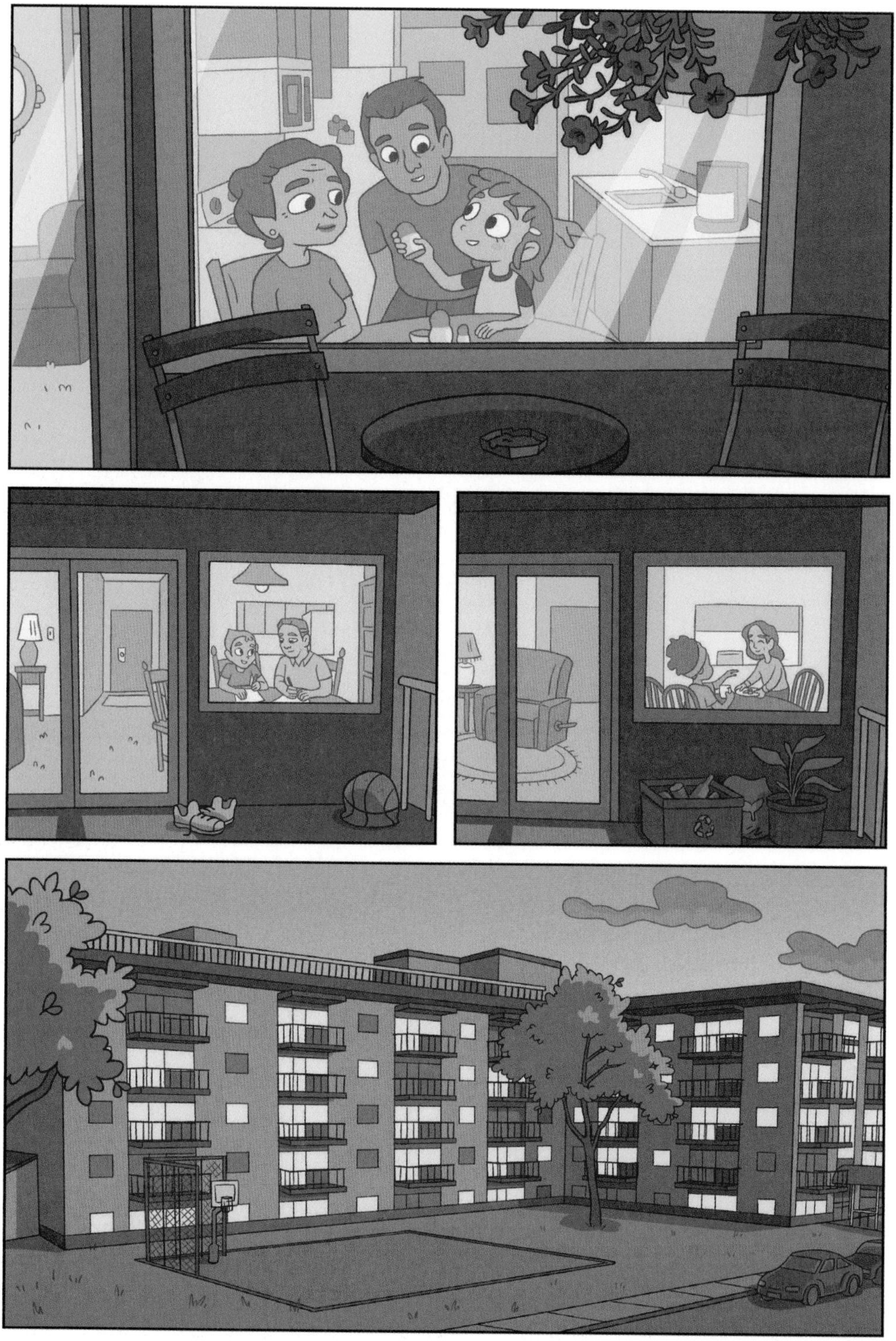

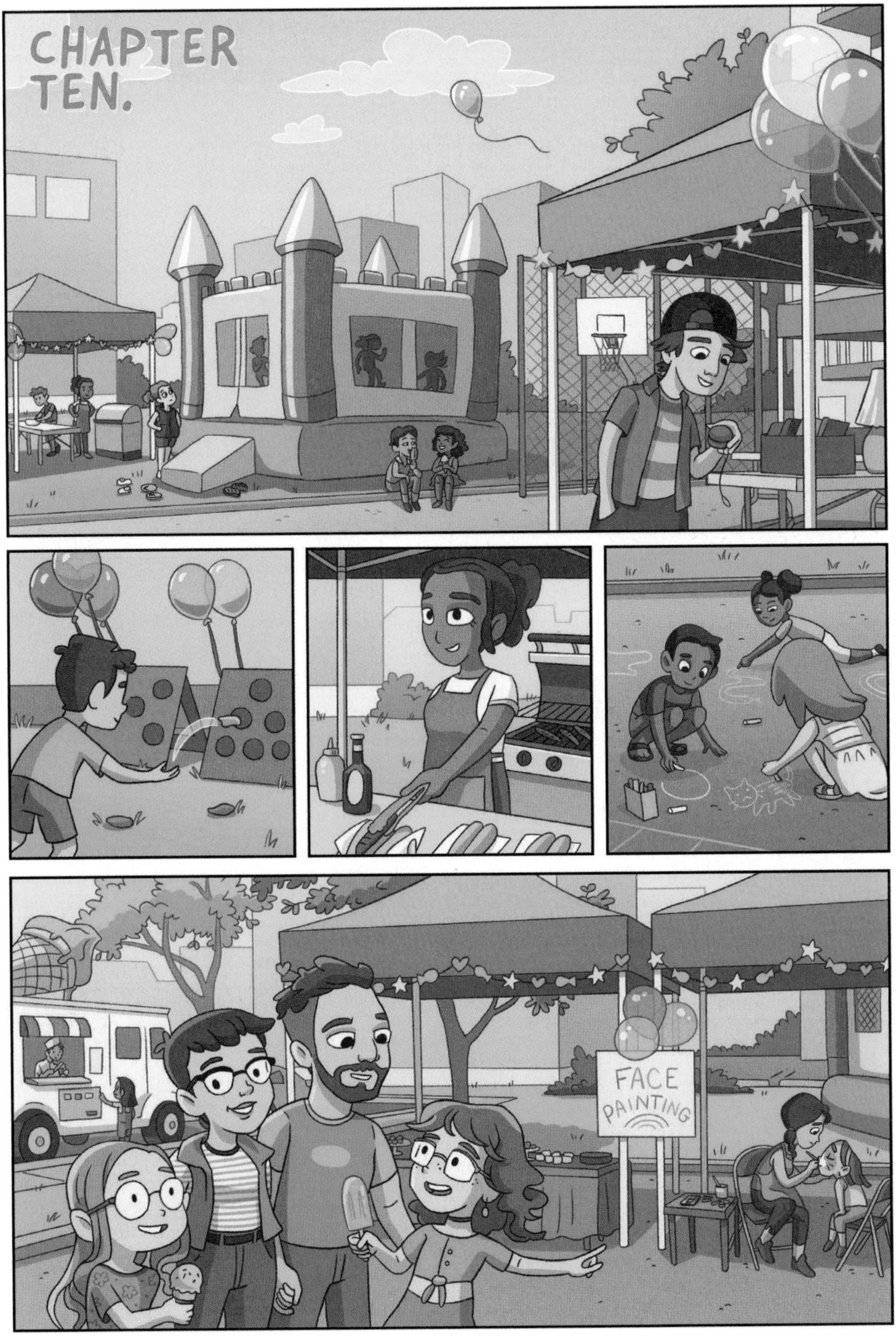
CHAPTER TEN.
FACE PAINTING

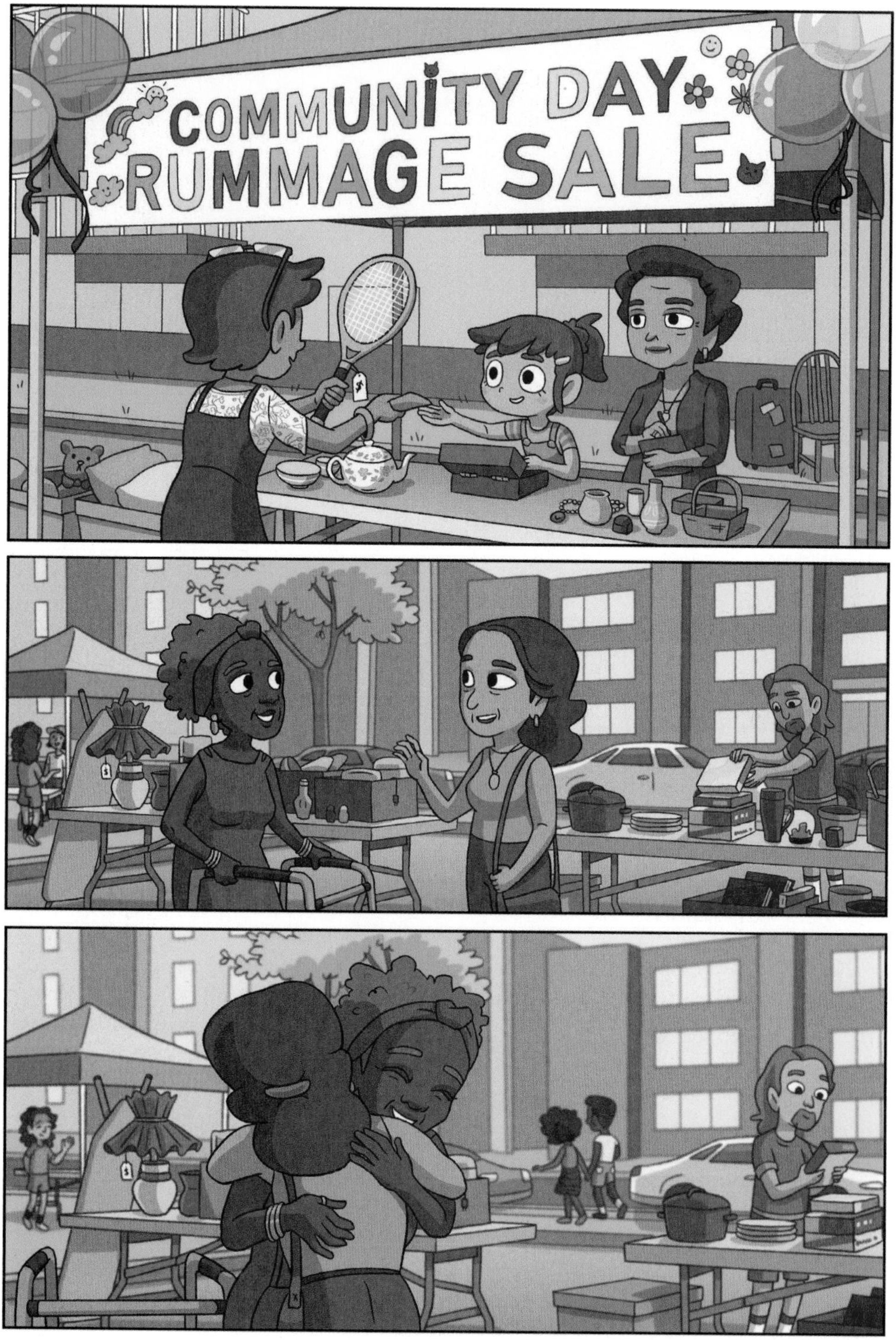
COMMUNITY DAY
RUMMAGE SALE

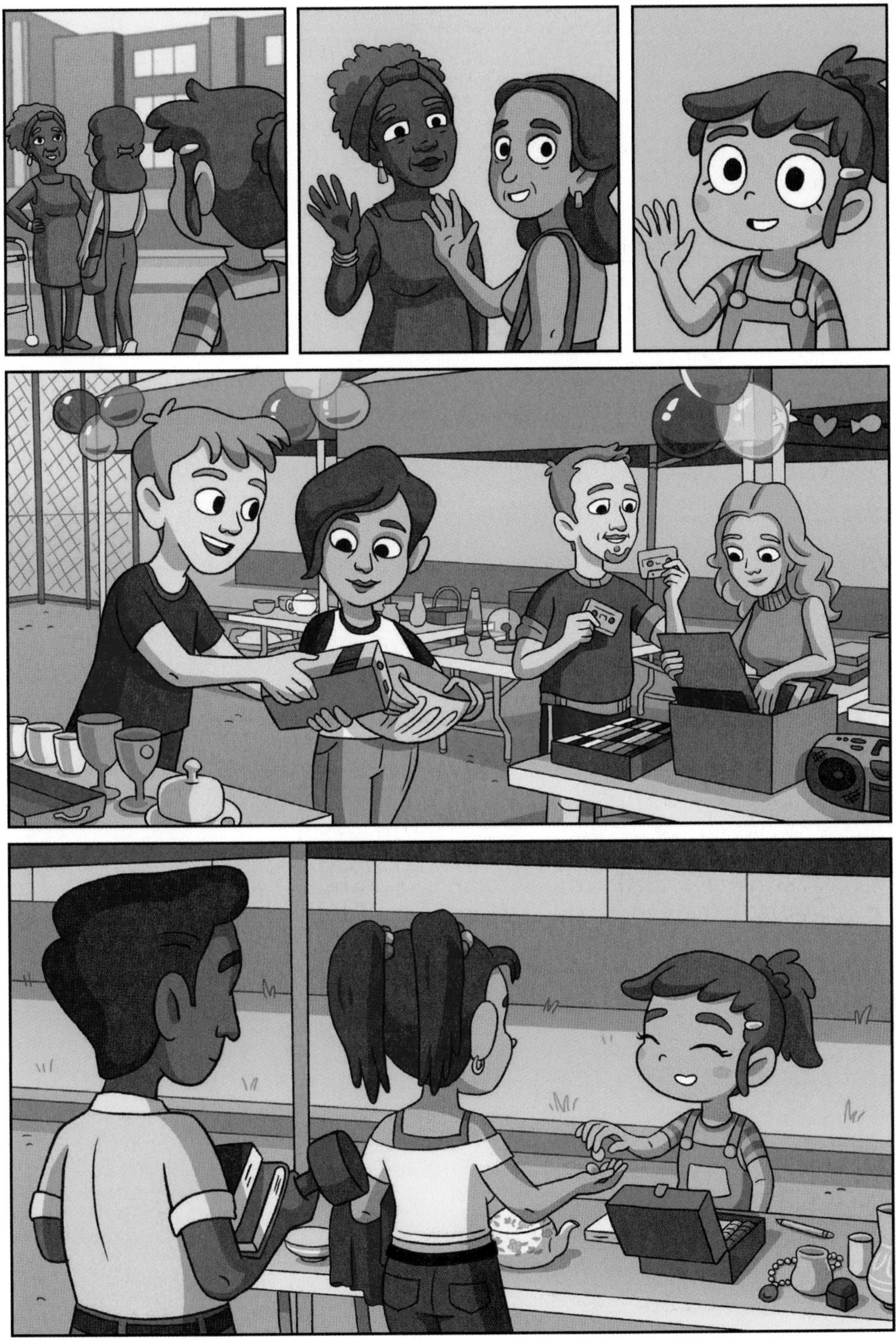

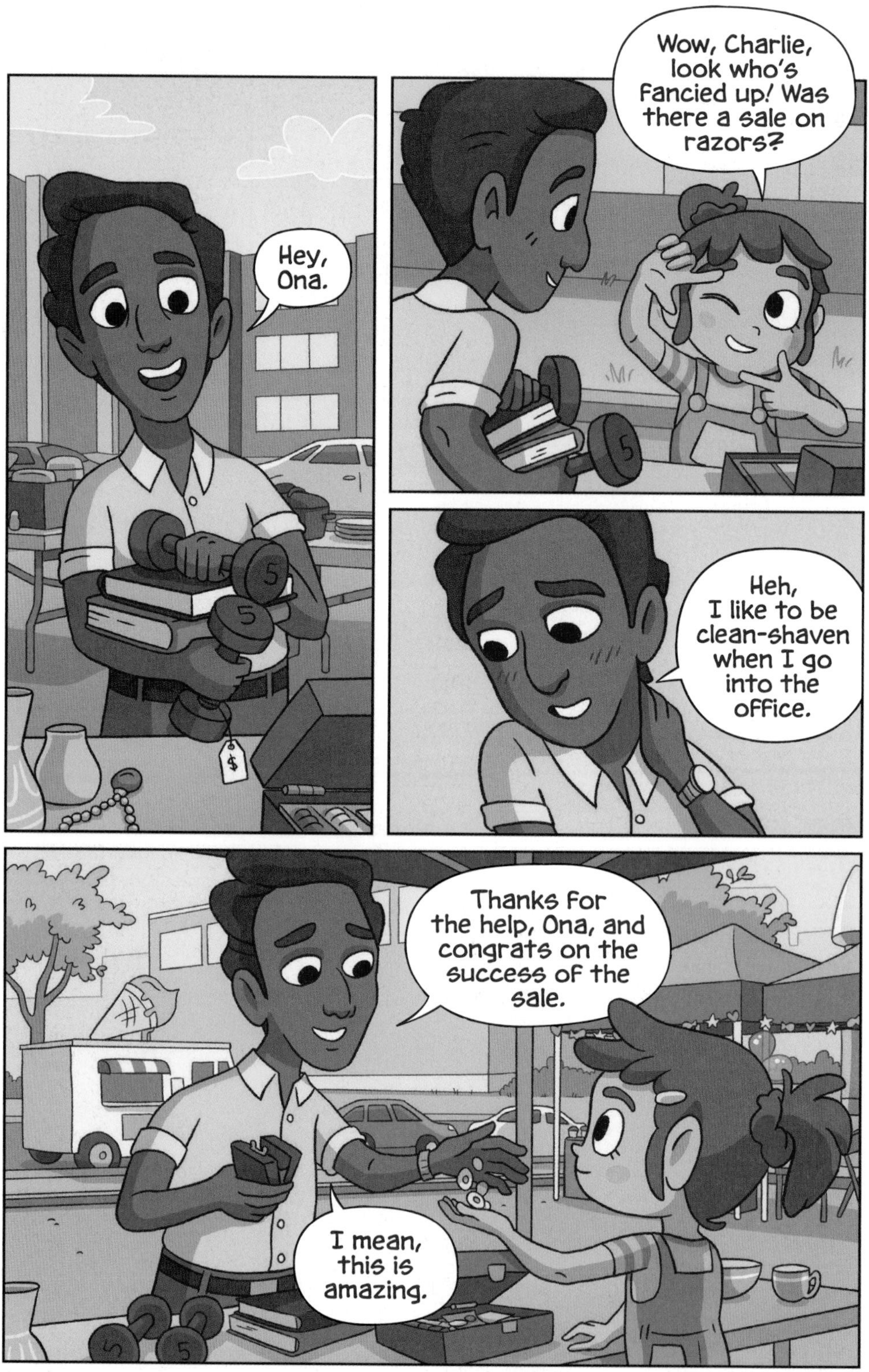
Hey, Ona.
Wow, Charlie, look who's fancied up! Was there a sale on razors?
Heh, I like to be clean-shaven when I go into the office.
Thanks for the help, Ona, and congrats on the success of the sale.
I mean, this is amazing.

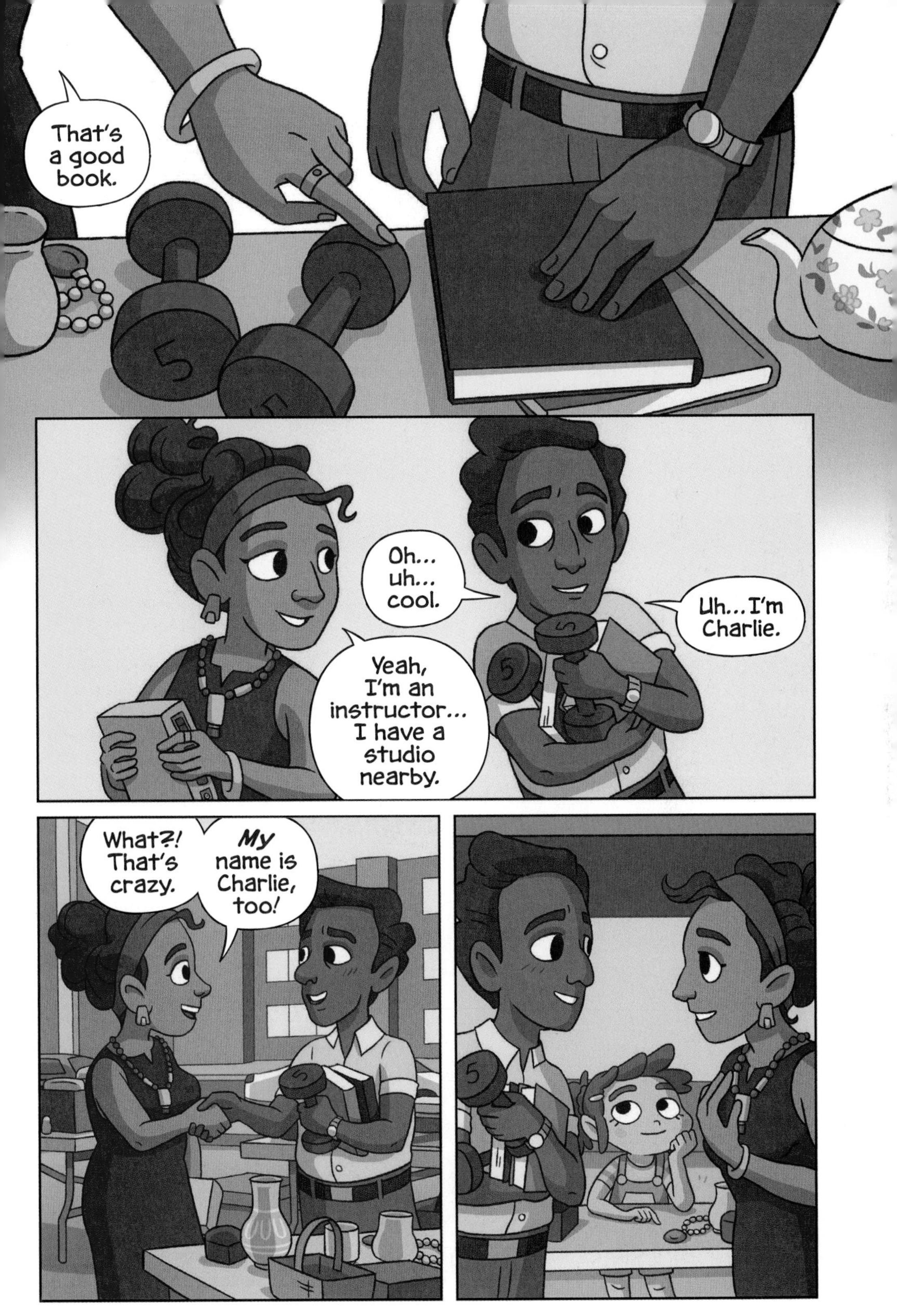

That's a good book.
Oh... uh... cool.
Yeah, I'm an instructor... I have a studio nearby.
Uh...I'm Charlie.
What?! That's crazy.
My name is Charlie, too!

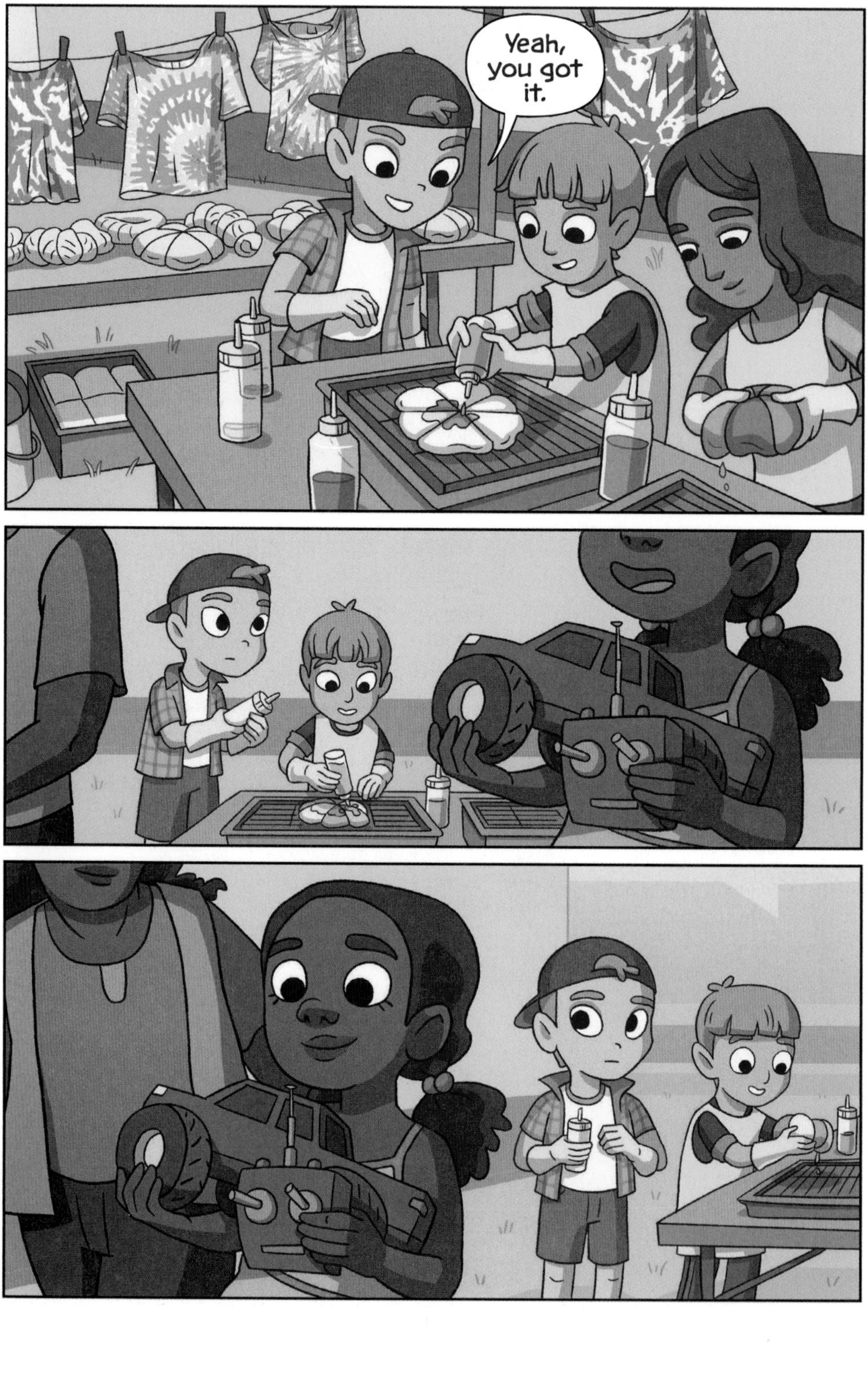
Yeah, you got it.

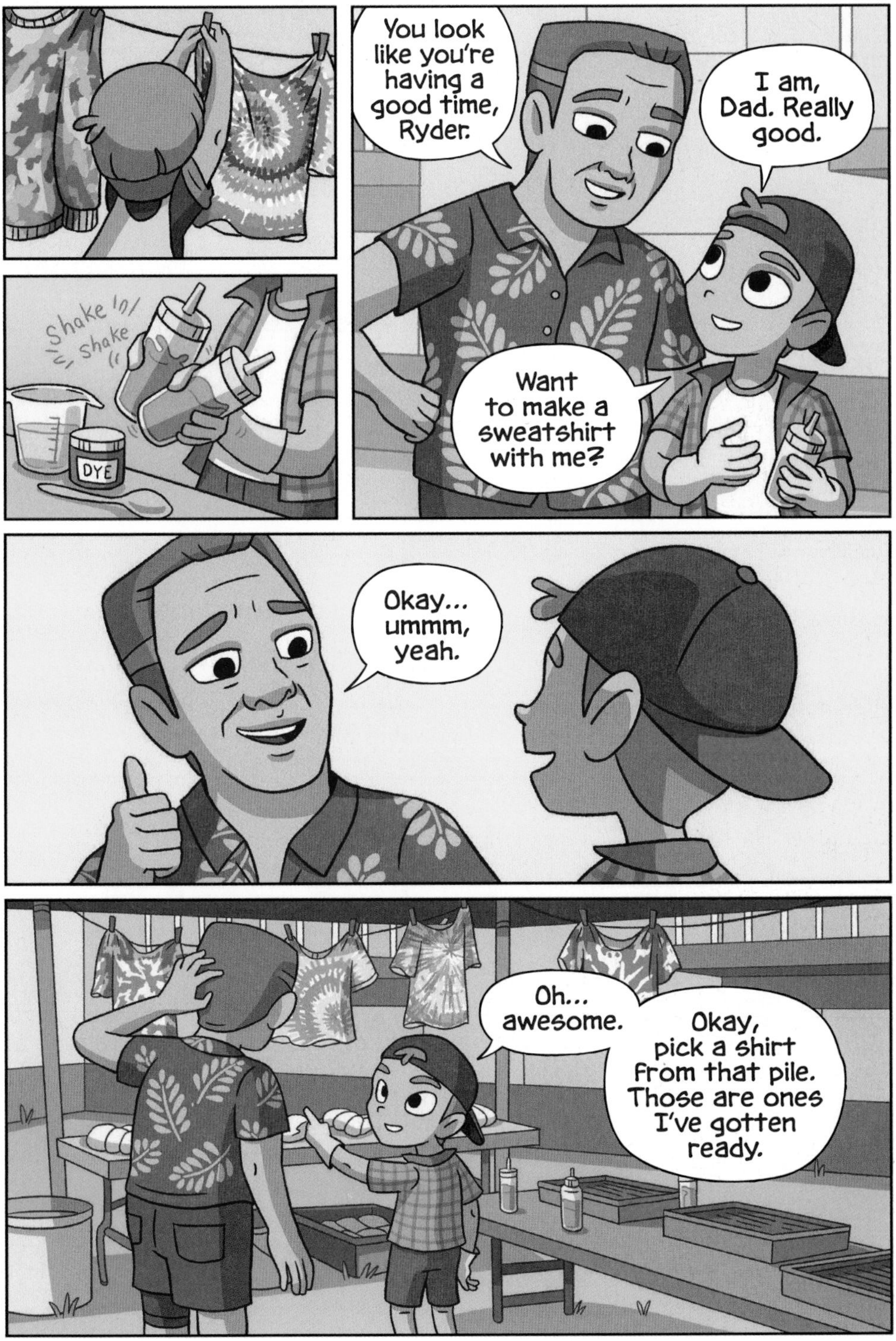

Shake
shake
DYE
You look like you're having a good time, Ryder.
I am, Dad. Really good.
Want to make a sweatshirt with me?
Okay... ummm, yeah.
Oh... awesome.
Okay, pick a shirt from that pile. Those are ones I've gotten ready.

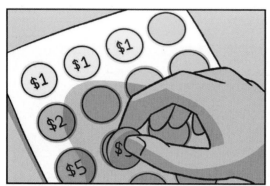

Ona! You coming to play or what?

Yeah, just a sec.

Coming!

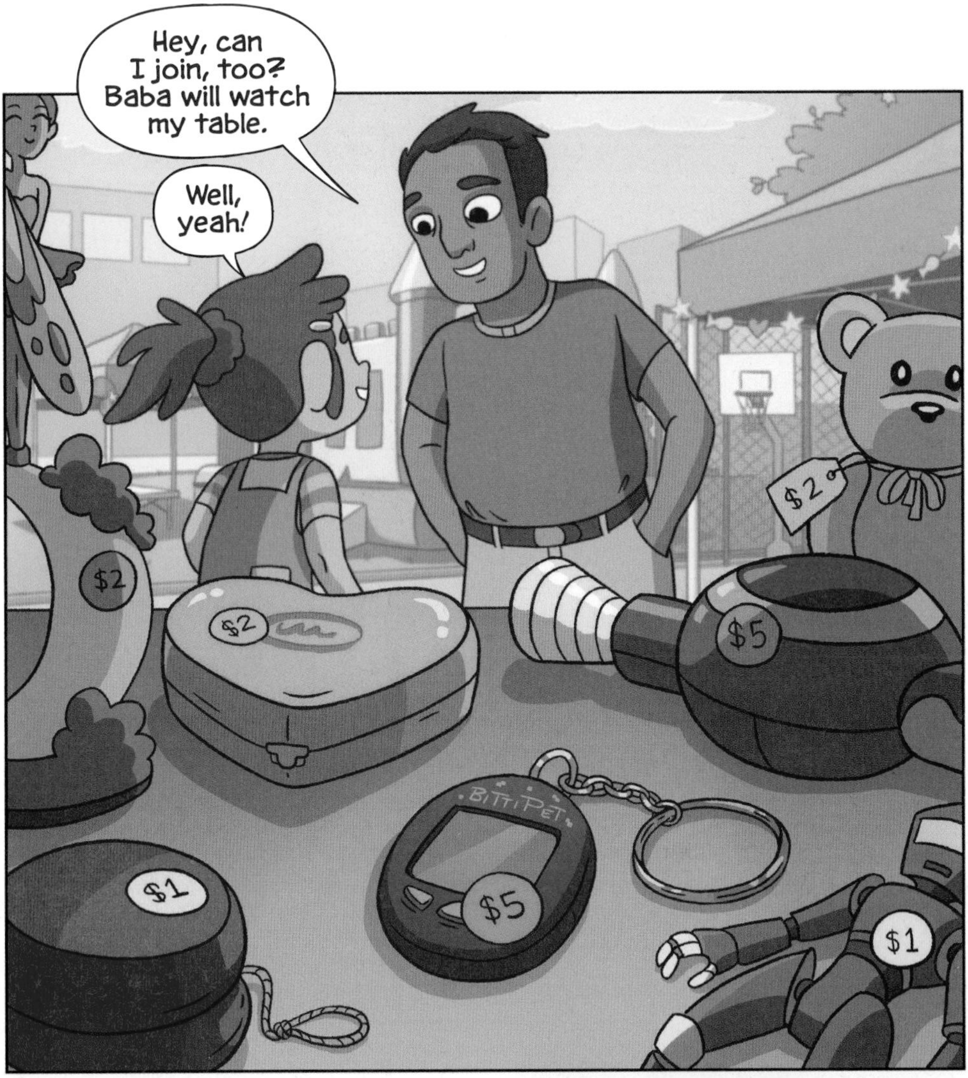
Hey, can I join, too? Baba will watch my table.
Well, yeah!
$2
$2
$5
$2
BITTIPET
$1
$5
$1

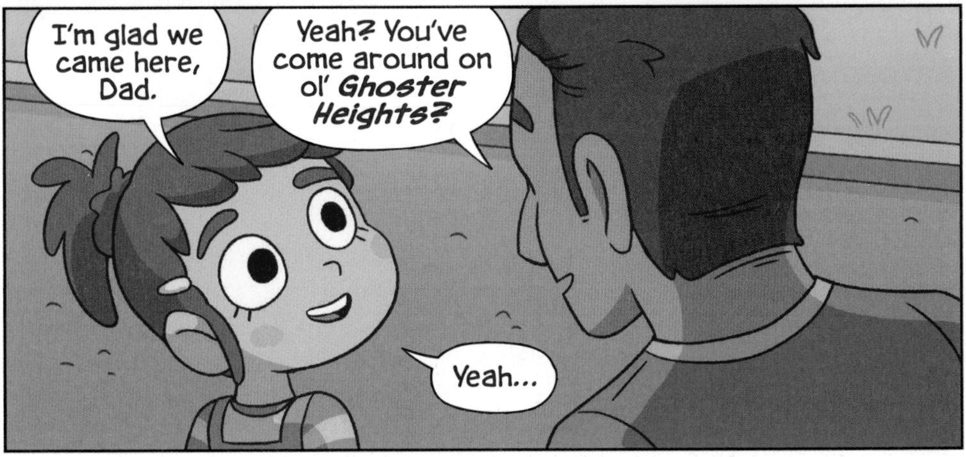
I'm glad we came here, Dad.
Yeah? You've come around on ol' *Ghoster Heights?*
Yeah...

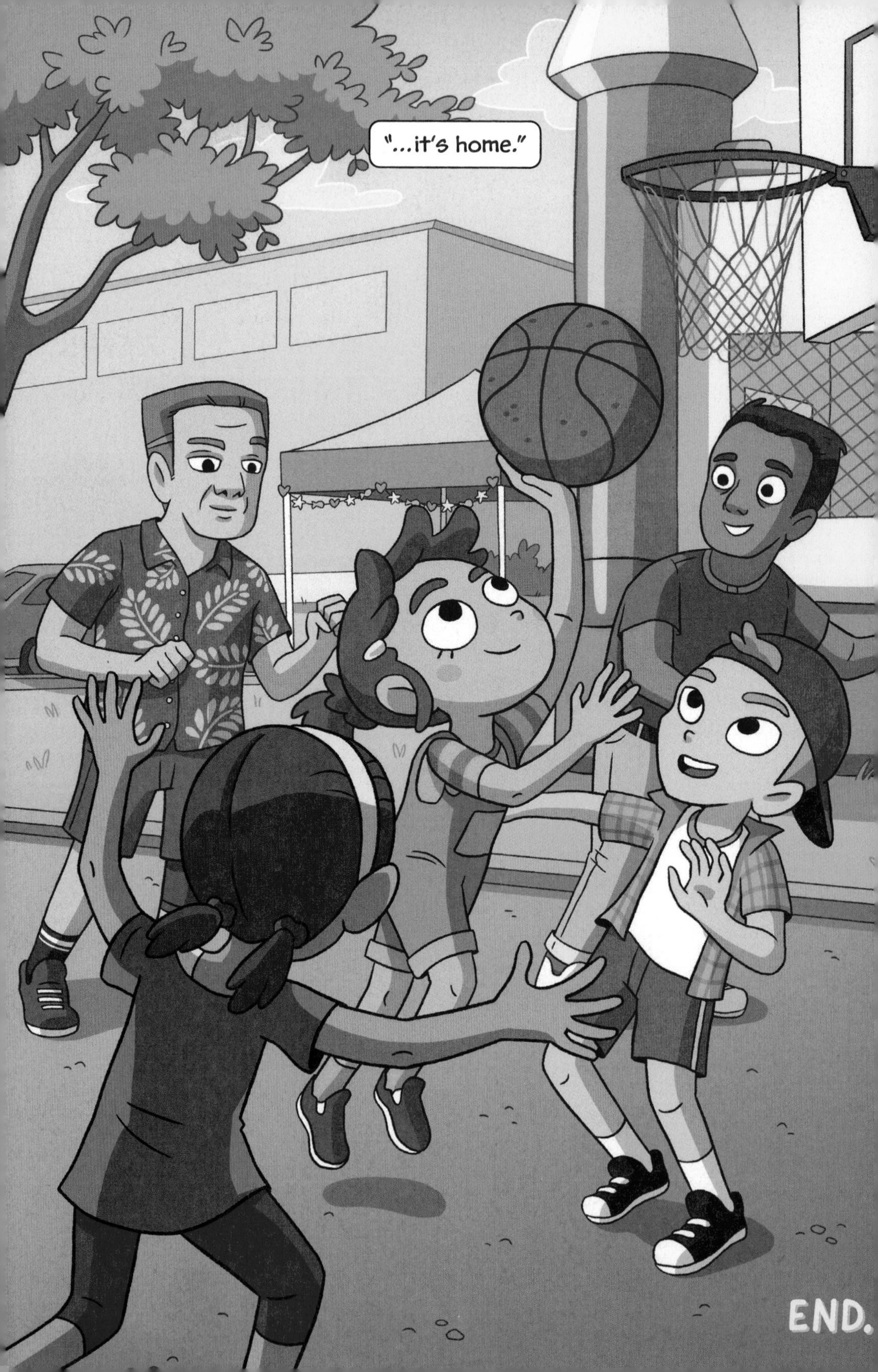
"...it's home."
END.

CREATOR BIOS

KELLY MELLINGS is an award-winning art director, illustrator, and designer. His work has appeared in comic books, TV commercials, magazines, apps, museum exhibits, and video games. He is the co-writer of *Ghoster Heights* and illustrator of the Canadian best-selling graphic novel, *The Outside Circle*. He lives in Edmonton, Alberta.

COREY LANSDELL is a Canadian born writer, illustrator, artist, animator and co-owner of the animation studio Pulp Studios Inc. He is a proud husband and father, holds a diploma in fine arts, a degree in visual communication design, and is passionate about storytelling and the fantasy genre.

LISA LAROSE is a pop surrealist painter, illustrator, and comics artist residing in Vancouver, Canada. She is best known for her paintings, Bizarre and Colourful artworks. She creates lively and exciting colour palettes and is always making something a little weird. Lisa loves middle-grade fiction (books, comics, cartoons, you name it) and so she also moonlights as a middle-grade comics artist.
lisalaroseart.com

BECCA CAREY is a graphic designer and letterer working on *Radiant Black*, *Batgirls*, *Nubia and the Amazons*, and a bunch of other super secret, super fun stuff that'll be out this year. She has the best dog in the world, named Lily.

BABA'S PEROGI RECIPE

(Be sure to cook with a supervisor! Lots of hot ingredients coming up!)

This recipe is based on Mary Ewanchuk's (Kelly's Baba!) family recipe, as made by her daughter, Paulette Macyk (Kelly's auntie!). Each family has their own way to make Perogies, and that's great...take this and make it right for YOUR family!

Baba fills her perogies most often with potatoes, bacon, and cheese. You can fill your perogies with many different things: cottage cheese and dill, potatoes and bacon, mushrooms, berries, and even prunes!

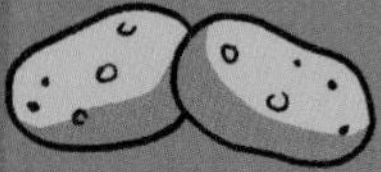

Makes about 15 dozen delicious perogies!

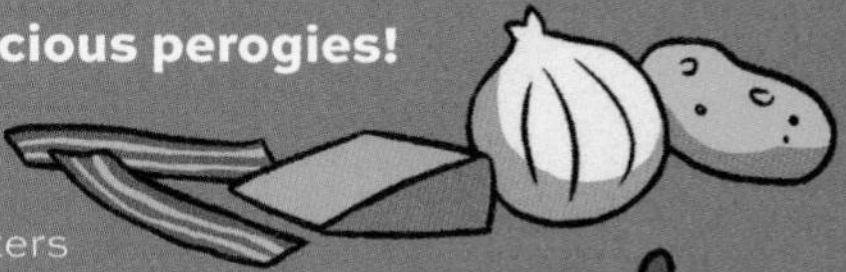

PEROGI FILLING:

6 large potatoes, peeled and cut lengthwise into quarters
2 tablespoons kosher salt
(I know it seems like a lot, but there is no salt in the dough)
½ cup margarine (less if you use the bacon fat)
1 onion
½ lb cooked bacon
1 cup Velveeta Cheese
(or 10 slices processed cheese) to your liking. More cheese is harder to blend with the potatoes.
White Pepper (Black pepper works fine, but Baba likes her filing to look creamy)

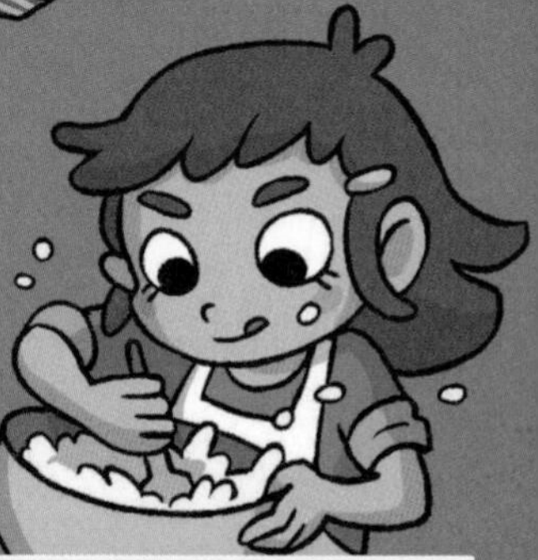

START WITH THE FILLING:

About 6 large potatoes are what Baba uses. Peel and cut potatoes, then place them into a medium pot. Add cold water until the potatoes are covered by at least an inch. Turn the heat to high, and bring the water to a boil. Reduce the heat to low to maintain a simmer, and cover. Cook for 15 to 20 minutes, or until you can easily poke through the potatoes with a fork. Chop the onion and cook with the bacon.

Drain and mash the potatoes: When the potatoes are done, drain the water and place the steaming hot potatoes into a large bowl. Save the potato water (in a hot pot on the stove), you'll need that for Baba's dough! Mix the cheese, cooked onions, bacon (broken into pieces), and bacon grease. If the potatoes are dry, use some heated margarine to achieve a better texture. If you want to make the filling vegan, use ½ cup margarine and some dried onions instead of bacon and bacon fat. Mash the potatoes with a potato masher. Then use a strong wooden spoon (a metal spoon might bend) to beat further. Don't over-beat the potatoes or the mashed potatoes will end up gluey. When the potatoes have cooled somewhat, scoop them into little balls, about a teaspoon worth. Baba uses a small ice-cream scoop or melon baller to make her little balls of filling. Add white pepper to taste.

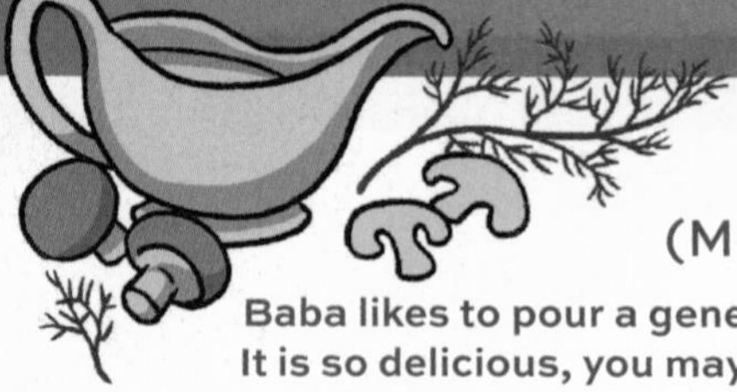

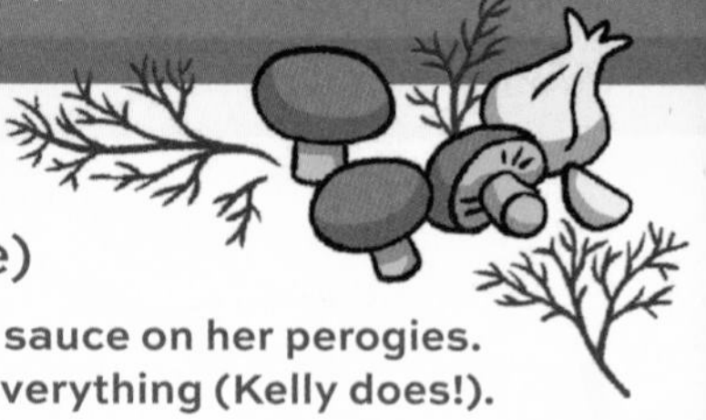

BONUS!
(Mushroom Sauce)

Baba likes to pour a generous amount of this sauce on her perogies. It is so delicious, you may want to pour it on everything (Kelly does!).

Cut and wash the mushrooms and put them in a small pot. Add ½ tablespoon butter. Cook the mushrooms at medium-high heat. Add 1 crushed fresh clove of garlic, one teaspoon of fresh dill, and one teaspoon of fresh onion. Add the whipping cream and ½ teaspoon of powdered chicken bouillon and bring to a simmering boil. Make sure you stir it because it will stick and burn. Add salt and pepper to taste. If the sauce is looking thin, add ½ teaspoon of cornstarch to thicken it. When you are done, pour generously over the perogies and add the fresh chopped dill and green onion.

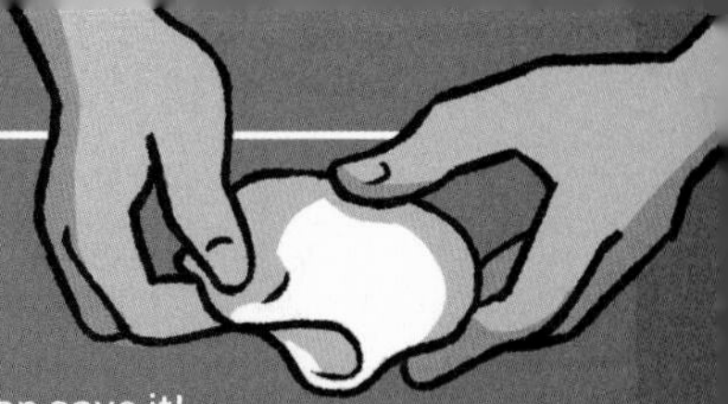

PEROGI DOUGH:

7 cups flour
½ cup oil
3 cups **hot water** — This is the secret to Baba's dough! **Get the water as hot as you can get it, it should be potato water if you can save it!**

Mix oil and water first, then flour. Use a dough hook and mix the dough until it comes away from the bowl. If you don't have a dough hook, mix by hand, but you won't be able to use boiling hot water. Knead it for about 20 minutes and let it rest.

This dough freezes well, in case you want to prepare it in advance for Perogi making. Just flatten it (if it's too thick it takes a long time to thaw), wrap it up, and freeze.

Cut a small chunk of the roll. Throw a little bit of flour on the counter and on the dough, then roll the dough very thin. If you poke the flattened dough and you see fingerprints, it is too thick! Lift the dough, flip. Using an empty tomato soup can (make sure it isn't sharp!) cut the flattened dough into circles, and place them on a tray lined with wax paper. Keep doing this until all the dough is used up. You can layer the wax paper and dough circles. Once you have the dough cut into circles, it is time to fill them up and make the perogies!

Take each ball of filling and place it in the centre of the perogi. Fold the perogi in half and pinch the top closed. Make sure that there is no potato in the seam, or the perogi will come apart when boiled. When you are done, you should have a nice half-moon shape with a small pinched edge. You want the perogies to look and feel full, like a pillow.

As you finish each perogi, place them on a wax paper-lined cooking sheet with space around them. When you are done, you can cook some immediately and put the rest in the freezer still on the tray. Once they are frozen, you can place them in a freezer bag. If you put them in a bag right away, they will stick together...not good!

If at the end there is more filling than dough, save the little balls of filling and fry them up with breakfast (they go good with eggs)!

TO COOK THE PEROGIES:

Boil water and add perogies, cook for 5-10 minutes, until they float to the top 3 times. If you are cooking the perogies from frozen and you are in doubt, do a "pillow test" and gently poke the middle to make sure that the filling is good and soft.

Once the perogies are done, you can serve with butter and sour cream or mushroom sauce. You can also fry some thinly sliced onions in a little butter or margarine and add the perogies to heat them up before you serve them.

SAUCE:

1 pint of Fresh Cremini and white mushrooms.
1 clove garlic
250 ml whipping cream
1 Tablespoon sour cream
2 teaspoons fresh dill
2 teaspoons of fresh chopped green onion
½ teaspoon Chicken bullion
Kosher salt and white pepper (to taste)
1 teaspoon Cornstarch (in case it needs a bit of thickening)

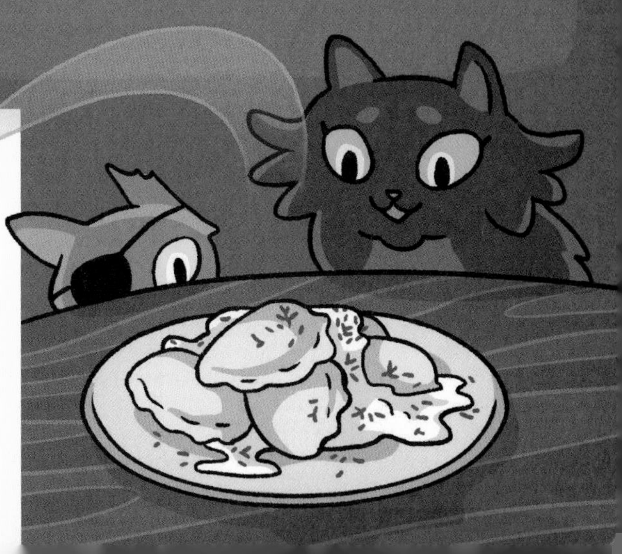

WONDERBOUND

Find these titles and more at readwonderbound.com

THE UNFINISHED CORNER

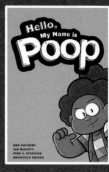

HELLO, MY NAME IS POOP

POIKO: QUESTS & STUFF

WRASSLE CASTLE BOOK 1: LEARNING THE ROPES

WRASSLE CASTLE BOOK 2: RIDERS ON THE STORM

WRASSLE CASTLE BOOK 3: PUT A LYD ON IT!

ON SALE NOW!

VERSE: BOOK 1 THE BROKEN HALF

VERSE: BOOK 2 THE SECOND GATE

KENZIE'S KINGDOM

THE BROTHERS FLICK: THE IMPOSSIBLE DOORS